and Hearts on Fire

By: Francie Burke Moritz

Dedications

To Gloria, who always believed and helped me achieve this book.

To ALL the Communications Personnel who are the true heroes and first responders

They:

Are the first to be blamed when a call goes bad.

The last to be acknowledged for the exceptional job they do every day.

Acknowledgements:

To ALL the law enforcement officers:

Your bravery and restraint in dangerous situations and everyday boredom is to be applauded not dissected by the media and citizens who have no clue what you really do.

To ALL the firefighters:

There are no words to express the respect I have for what you do.

Thank you for making me feel like I was part of the team.

To my family:

Thank you for everything. I love you.

Special thanks to:

Kendra, Ella and Carol for proof reading

My mentors:

Jimmy K.

Joe G.

Joe Riel for answering all my questions 30 years ago.

Disclaimer:

The story and characters are a work of fiction.

Certain long-standing institutions, agencies and public offices are mentioned, but the characters involved are wholly imaginary.

Any resemblance to actual persons, living or dead, or actual events is purely coincidental.

Any reference to policies and procedures for any department or agency, as well as any actions of the characters are purely fiction.

The opinions expressed are those of the characters and should not be confused with those of the author.

Enjoy the story and all its foibles.

Chapter 1

Bellamy had hit the wall. It was the hard slap of her head against eight long hours of tedium. There was the anticipation of four more hours of mind numbing boredom. She wasn't sure if it was the third twelve hour night shift that had her so exhausted she wanted to put her head down on the console and sleep or if it was the fact that her days off were fast approaching at that speed of snail. She rubbed her fists against the grit that was collecting in her eyes, yawned and turned to face her partner in crime.

Morgan sat staring intently at the CAD screen. Bellamy wasn't sure why she was staring at it. There weren't any police calls pending. There weren't any calls pending. All of her officers were silent. Bellamy continued to watch her. Morgan was sitting ramrod straight. Bellamy noticed that Morgan's hair, short and graying perfectly to blend into her light brown hair didn't have a hair out of place, at least not from the rear view. "You want to go out and have a smoke?" Bellamy asked.

Morgan visibly jumped. "Yeah, I think I will. Think you can handle all this excitement?"

"I think so." Bellamy responded confidently, even though her stomach convulsed every time an officer's voice came across the radio. As a supervisor she had to be able and competent in dispatching both fire and police. She had been promoted from call taker to dispatcher as a designated police dispatcher. Bellamy had loved the excitement. She was unflappable during the most demanding incidents. She didn't have to think about what to do her training just took over.

As the years wore on there were little things that started to gnaw at her confidence. She constantly worried that one of her officers was going to get shot while she was working and she wasn't sure she could handle that. With the escalating gang activity in the city that probability rose.

At the same time, one of the fire dispatchers she had made friends with kept urging Bellamy to come to the fire side of dispatch which at the time was located in the basement of Fire Station Number One. She liked their schedules, the location away from the call takers and the pace. It wasn't long until an opening came up at fire dispatch. Bellamy applied and was hired. She was the second female hired as a dispatcher for the city. At the time of her transfer the fire dispatcher position was called Alarm Operator.

Settling in to her position as a fire dispatcher she noticed that the firefighters accepted the dispatchers as part of their brotherhood. They didn't think of them the way police officers had as "just a dispatcher". The fire department was very inclusive. If there was a firefighter activity dispatchers were included.

On Sunday feed days the firefighters would come down to dispatch and ask them if they wanted in on it. If they did, the firefighters would tell them the cost that each participate paid so no one had to pay for the entire meal, and the dispatchers would pay up. Around lunch time a firefighter would bring the dispatcher a plate of food that they had made in their kitchen which was located directly above the dispatch area.

The firefighters, unlike the police officers, weren't dismissive of dispatchers. They didn't talk to them on the radio the way police officers did. Many of the police officers came across the air as condescending. When dispatchers were unable to read their minds they expected dispatchers to know what they wanted before they asked treated them like they were imbeciles. It made her feel like a second class citizen. But if a dispatcher returned their attitude over the radio, they were being rude and ended up being reprimanded.

The firefighters for the most part were not that way. Of course there happened to be a couple who sounded that way. There was one city firefighter in particular who sounded that way. It was Renny LaRue. He always sounded so smug. It just made her grit her teeth every time she heard him on the radio. She knew she had to respond to him in a calm controlled voice but she wanted to reach through the radio and slap that attitude out of him. And of course, he happened to be assigned to Station One. And since he was the Lieutenant for the shift he was the one who had the radio on all of the calls.

Occasionally when it was slow the entire crew, LaRue included, would come down to dispatch to shoot the breeze. It was refreshing to have them come down and hang out with her. She enjoyed their company. LaRue never said a word to her. Not one, the entire time she worked out of the basement. He would just stand at the far end of the double console leaning over the edge of the half wall. Sometimes she would look up and find him watching her intently a smile on his face. At times, she thought she saw the sadness behind that smile.

Bellamy always wondered when she saw that sadness if he was thinking about his wife who had passed away. Did he know I was the one who took the call when he had called to report his wife had died, Bellamy wondered. That call would live with her for as long as she lived. She had probably answered hundreds of death calls in her career but she had never heard a caller as distraught as LaRue. When that call was over she had to take a smoke break. She had gone outside and cried. And Bellamy didn't cry.

It snapped Bellamy back to the present when Morgan stood up and straightened her uniform. Her uniforms never had a thread out of place. Her tan slacks were always ironed. She stood for a moment facing Bellamy and took a pocket watch out of her slack's pocket. She flipped the lid open and studied it for a moment. She snapped the lid closed and put it back in her pocket. With that she sighed and strode toward the door.

Bellamy was thrilled that no one had talked in the ten minutes or so that Morgan was gone. Morgan settled back in to her office chair and swiveled back toward her computer screen. "It's close out there," she commented.

They had just settled into the boredom again when the Comm. Center door flew open and Officer Nugent came blasting through it like a rocket. In his loud boisterous voice he said to all "Boy, it sure is quiet tonight."

Four outraged female voices yelled back at him. He knew better than that. You don't say the "Q" word in a Comm. Center. It is the worst kind of swear word he could have chosen. There were swear words and then there were swear words and this was the worst of the worst. He had jinxed the shift. Soon there would be total mayhem. It was as certain as the rising sun.

He laughed out loud, lifted his gun belt to adjust it and sat down in the empty chair next to Morgan on the police side of dispatch. He offered Morgan his paper work. She attached some teletype papers to it with a paper clip. With one of her three pens, one blue, one red and one black she signed off on the entry portion of the report with the black pen.

"While you two enjoy your chat," Bellamy said, even though no one was talking, "I'm going to run outside, before the crap hits the fan."

Nugent laughed. Of course he would laugh, Bellamy thought. He'd only been a cop for a couple of years. Mass chaos was still fun for him. She knew as the years progressed it wouldn't be nearly as much fun to stir the pot but he'd have to find that out on his own.

Bellamy plodded down the two sets of stairs. Her legs felt like lead. That's what came from sitting on her derriere for eight hours and barely moving. All was silent on the first floor. There wasn't a sound coming from the report room where most of the officers sat to finish paper work. The muster room was also silent. The oncoming shift wouldn't be in there for several hours.

Bellamy went through the double doors and onto the sidewalk of the secured parking lot. A six foot chain link fence with concertina wire on the top kept the police vehicles safe. There was one police car, unoccupied and idling just outside the door. That irritated the daylights out of Bellamy. *Lazy jerk.* Nugent was the only officer still at the station so she surmised it must be his squad car. She couldn't believe he left his car running while it sat unattended in the parking lot. What a waste of gas just to make sure if he got a call he could run out, hop in it, put it in gear and go. He couldn't take the few seconds to turn the car on? And it wasn't like there had ever been an incident when someone sneaked into the parking lot through the gate when a car pulled in and the gate hadn't completely shut yet. She could just see some tweaker get in a patrol car and take off with it.

Bellamy glanced around the dim light of the parking lot as she made her way over to his car. She checked to see if he had left it unlocked in a false sense of security. Sure enough the door opened easily. Bellamy hopped inside and put the car in reverse. She backed out of the parking space and quickly put it in drive. She drove down passed the three detectives cars and parked it. She turned it off and got out of the cruiser leaving the keys in it. She picked up her cigarette that she had left smoldering in the ash tray. She took a long drag and exhaled a silent, "Serves you right" waft of smoke.

Just then her eyes caught what looked like a flash of light to the west of town. Bellamy took another drag of her cigarette and scanned the western sky. In between puffs of the cool menthol smoke she sniffed the air like her dog often did when he smelled something of interest in the air. Gritting her teeth she saw a bluish glow light up the western horizon.

Stubbing out her cigarette she hurried towards the door. She swiped her key card against the reader and grabbed the door bar. She jogged towards the stairs and started up, thinking she really needed to start working out again. Huffing, she cleared two steps at a time and met Nugent on the stair landing. Without hesitating she glared at him. He was grinning impishly, eyes twinkling. "Butt nugget," she whispered breathlessly. Laughing he slowly descended the next set of stairs.

Reaching out to swipe the card in her hand the Comm. Center door clicked. Someone inside had seen her coming and unlocked the door. As she trotted towards her desk, the phone lines started ringing as if following her. As she settled in to her ergonomically uncomfortable chair a male voice came over the mountain repeater. It was a channel that picked up radio transmissions in the mountainous area of the county. "Nile One."

"Nile One," Bellamy repeated in response.

"Nile One, we have a severe storm coming through the district. We've already lost power. I have a report of tree on a car on the Old River Road at the old wooden bridge. There are people trapped. Tone out our station and start an ambulance this way," he yelled into his microphone. Bellamy could barely understand his transmission over the wind crossing his microphone not to mention the spotty reception over the repeater.

Bellamy acknowledged him and pressed the buttons on the Zetron for their stations. The Zetron was a console with buttons for every station they dispatched for in the county. Another Zetron system set off tones for the city stations. The tones were different for every station. They were an assortment of high low tones that went out over the radio and on the firefighters cell phones letting them know they had a call. In the city it did the same but also turned off the power to appliances in the station so they wouldn't return to a station filled with smoke from a burned meal.

At the same time she quickly entered the call for service on her CAD system. CAD stood for Computer Aided Dispatch. It was a system just for dispatching police and fire calls. A call could be entered by a call taker or dispatcher. That call could be pulled up on any of the monitors in the center and other call takers or dispatchers could add information to the call. They could also be pulled up in the patrol cars' and fire units' MDTs or mobile data terminals. That was connected to a street system in the county that held every address in the county. When the address was put in the call it told the dispatcher which fire agency should be dispatched and if it was a police call which officer was the closest available unit. It would show on the screen the closest cross streets to the call. To most people that wouldn't having any bearing on where their address but to an officer it could be invaluable if he was trying to picture the closest access to the call. But at times the address given by the caller or the telephone location didn't exist in the CAD street system. So the dispatcher would have to over-ride the street system and enter the address and hope he or she was familiar with the address and who needed to be dispatched.

Of course the stupid machine didn't recognize this address and she had to force it manually. When the tones had finished, Bellamy started her dispatch, "Nile Station One, Nile Station Two respond to a tree on a car with occupants in the area of River Road and the wooden bridge." She picked up the direct line to one of the ambulance services during the brief pause, "Got a call" Bellamy told the man answering the line. That was redundant she thought, since the call also showed up on his CAD screen. Bellamy repeated the dispatch on the air and signed off "Zero four twenty five, WPAQ563." WPAQ563 was the designator for that radio channel. The FCC Federal Communications Commission required that sign be verbalized at the end of each transmission.

"Got it" the ambulance guy responded. Bellamy didn't recognize his voice. She figured it was one of the EMTs or Paramedics filling in for an ambulance dispatcher.

Multiple phone lines were ringing. The policy was to answer each call within three rings. The call takers were answering them and putting calls on hold when they determined there was no emergency. Par for the course of a severe storm, everyone in the dark was calling 911. They weren't the power company, they didn't dispatch for the power company but it didn't matter to the public. 911 was a phone number they knew and could call when their lights went out. Bellamy and Morgan grabbed a few of the calls and entered them in CAD. They weren't going to be dispatched. It was just to keep track of the calls coming in and make a list they could fax to the power company. She was sure the company already had detected the outage but this helped narrow down the scope of outages that might have damage to lines or poles.

As Bellamy, Morgan and the rest of the call takers answered phone lines Bellamy changed screens to check the calls. They were entered by priority. Calls in the category 3 were considered the highest of importance, demanding an immediate response. Category 2 calls needed attention as quickly as possible and last was Category 1 that was either for information only or to respond when they were able.

The call screen was full already in less than five minutes of her sitting down. She found a call for the tree on a car that someone had called in. She pulled it up and read the details and linked the call she had entered and this call. The caller was on scene had advised there were four people in the car. All of the occupants were injured and one appeared to be dead. "What do you mean appeared to be dead?" She yelled across to the call taker.

"As in, crushed skull and no pulse" the call taker responded.

Bellamy added the comments to her call and keyed the mic with the foot pedal while she picked up the ambulance phone again and typed in the updated information on the call.

She repeated the information to the Chief. "One confirmed, head trauma, no pulse, 3 others injured."

"Do you want me to notify YSO?" Morgan asked from behind Bellamy.

"Yes, please." Bellamy replied.

This was going to be a cluster. All of the other calls on the screen were in the Rainier district and appeared to be coming from a very narrow area. Bellamy looked up at the county map and could see the calls were coming down the narrow canyon where the Naches River snaked through the east side of the Cascade Mountain range. The river originated from run off from Mount Rainier and surrounding peaks covered with snow covered year round. There was still runoff when the weather warmed up in the mountains. It was worsened at times like this when there was a major rain storm that compounded the process. She wouldn't be surprised if they had reports come in soon of minor flash floods.

Over the blaring siren in the background, "Nile One, would you advise state that the highway going east has multiple trees on the road and some mud slides. They are going to have to close the road until the county can get out here and clear it."

Bellamy added that to the call on her screen and heard Morgan in the background, already on the line with State Patrol. It didn't surprise Bellamy that the Chief Nile One had all this information before 911 did. It was a rural setting and most of the year round occupants knew each other well and had each other's phone numbers. Many times residents would call the fire chief directly instead of bothering 911.

Bellamy pulled up each call in queue. The ones that were reporting trees or mud on the highway Morgan was already adding comments that state patrol had been advised. If the call didn't involve live power lines on the road or someone injured she just noted that state patrol had been notified. So far they had been lucky. None of those situations were showing up on her call screen. There wasn't much more the fire department could do other than maybe send a rig to stand by at the upper end of the highway to stop traffic. Bellamy was about to send out a second set of tones to divert a responding fire unit to close the highway when one of their fire units called over the radio that he would be stopping traffic. It was almost daylight but traffic was already heavy along the two lane highway. The road led to multiple lakes and camping areas as well as Mount Rainier. It was also an alternate route to the west side of the state. Bellamy hated that road and avoided it at all cost. There were deep ravines with the river snaking through the valley with steep cliffs on the other side of the road. It was a scenic route and breathtaking to most. It took Bellamy's breath alright. It terrified her.

Bellamy repeated the f word over and over under her breath as she tried to figure out how she was going to get an ambulance to the accident scene on Rainier River Road. "Nile One, I'll be out on Rainier River Road trying to clear some trees. When Nile17 responds ask them to grab a chain saw they will probably need it to make access to this location. If

YSO's unit is at the upper end, see if they have a chain saw they can use to start clearing debris. Would you also notify county and state we are going to need the road crews to start setting up barriers and cleaning up debris." Most people would think those were requests. They weren't. They were orders. Bellamy entered them into the call screen. She could hear Morgan in the background making calls for her to the appropriate agencies. Bellamy knew the area well enough that the year round residents in the area were probably already out there with head lamps and chain saws driving their 4x4's through the area looking for any downed trees on the road. As altruistic as it would sound to an outsider it was a legal excuse to cut fire wood. It was July and a dry July at that. There was a ban on cutting firewood. If it continued to be this dry the rest of the summer chances were the ban wouldn't be lifted until October. But in the meantime they were more than willing to get up in the predawn hours and clear the road of fallen trees.

As other priority 3 calls popped up on the screen, Bellamy started the tones for the various agencies. Usually there was a delay in responses from county agencies. They were mostly volunteer personnel, so it took them a while to get up, get dressed and drive to the station. They had to wait at the station until they had enough fire fighters to man the units. That was not the case this morning. The storm was rousing people from their summer slumber. It seemed to be the storm was the flame and the fire fighters the moths. They had been through this many, many times before, so they all headed to their stations to gear up and start a pot of coffee for the crews they knew would be straggling in.

Bellamy saw the power outage calls disappearing off the screen. Within a few minutes Kelly was behind her faxing a list of outages to the power company.

Most of the priority calls for service were power lines on the roads, a power pole on fire and trees down. Then the brush fires started by the lightning started filling the lines of her computer screen. So it's going to be one of those storms, Bellamy. The kind of storm that came through with wind and lightning before the rain came through. She hoped there would be rain with the storm, lots and lots of rain. Sometimes that didn't happen. Then it was not a thunder and lightning storm. It became a shit storm.

She hoped the rain would be as hard as it was in the Rainier District and put out any potential fires the lightning started. The fires sent units scrambling through their districts from one reported fire to another. Luckily the rain had come through in a major downpour. She could hear how hard it was raining by the unit's radio transmissions. It was hit or miss whether their transmission was completely received by Bellamy to begin with. There were many dead spots in the mountains. Sometimes it was so garbled she only got bits and pieces of the transmission and she either had to have them repeat it, sometimes over and over again until she got the complete transmission or she had to surmise from the portions of words what the unit was trying to communicate. She could guess at the majority but it was a dangerous game to guess.

As quickly as she could she would set off the tones for the various districts, Naches, Gleed, Cowich and Naches Heights. *I might as well wake them all up, she thought.* Somewhere in the chaos she thought she heard Nugent on the police frequency say something about his patrol car but it was drowned out by the units responding to the calls on her screen. She heard Morgan in the background, "Bellamy, you didn't?"

"I don't know what you are talking about" Bellamy responded. The mantra at the Comm. Center was when accused of something was to admit nothing, deny everything and demand proof.

Bellamy pulled the map book out of the round table that spun around like a lazy Susan between the two fire dispatch consoles. Her mind was racing to figure out if there was an alternate route that she could get the ambulances through to the accident scene on Rainier River Road. The lighted maps up in front of her were just the basic roads in the districts. The secondary or four wheel roads weren't. Sometimes to get a better idea of where a call was in the mountains, the map book was the answer. She could always pull the huge rolled up maps put out by the forest service but it was easier to grab the Delorme Atlas and Gazetteer. It had all the information and more a dispatcher could ever want on a location. She wasn't ignoring the other calls she had dispatched. They were important but she was confident that the district units would be able to access them and mitigate the situation.

The Nile District accident was a different issue. Three injured people trapped in a car with a dead body had to be horrific. It probably felt like an eternity since they reported the accident. She glanced through the call again. It was actually another party that reported the accident. Even as she noticed that she could hear one of the call takers reassuring the party that we did have people responding but due to the road conditions it was going to take some time. Nile One had advised he was on Rainier River Road but he wasn't on the scene yet. He could possibly be miles away.

Bellamy couldn't find another viable route into the area that had not reported as blocked by downed trees. Even as she was realizing this Nile One came across the air asking her to put a helicopter on standby. Bellamy gritted her teeth. They knew as well as she did that she couldn't put a helicopter on "standby". They either flew or they didn't. There was no just hanging out by the helicopter waiting to go somewhere. That was their job to "standby". They were always standing by. Bellamy called the helicopter company to give them a heads up. The following interrogation ensued. How many patients, ages, injuries, will this be a hoist or is there a landing area. What were the weather conditions? The Lat/Long of the accident and terrain of the scene were also of importance to the flight crew. If the Latitude and Longitude of the call didn't show up on that call screen, which it didn't because the system didn't recognize the location Bellamy had to find it by pulling up the map screen, which was another function of CAD. She pulled it up and zoomed in to the best guess location. She used the caller information to narrow down the location of the incident. Once she had her mouse over that location a LAT/LONG was displayed.

When she told Nile One the helicopter company had been notified, she could hear the sound of a chain saw in the background. She wasn't aware there was another firefighter with him but she assumed there must be hearing the chain saw. Nile One was now on scene but it was evident from his reply that he was out of breath. She concluded he had had to hike to the scene from wherever his command vehicle was. Again that was a dangerous assumption. But oddly dispatchers did it all the time. They visualized each scene, right or wrong. Since they rarely heard the entire story of the incident they wrote their own script in their head of what had taken place.

The pieces of the puzzle were put together, one by one. What the call taker heard added to what the dispatcher heard and maybe what the police added or the ambulance. That put the picture together in their mind. Each had a different view. Some saw the incident more traumatic than the other. If it had been a bad call they would get together at the end of shift outside the station comparing notes. Most of those pieces of the other calls littered the floor of their brain, swept out by yet another call.

At the end of the shift most inconsequential calls would be gone from their memory. Bellamy was sure of this reality. She could be asked about one of the minor calls by her supervisor and would have no idea what she was talking about. If they didn't play a tape of the call for her it was a blank. Those calls were lost to a black hole in her mind.

One by one the agencies responded to the other calls, demanding radio time. Bellamy answered as quickly as she could up-dating calls on her screen. Luckily Morgan had been answering calls for her and entering information of responding law enforcement, barricades, and road crews. Bellamy appreciated all of her help. She would have been able to do those things but it made it so much less stressful having another dispatcher help out.

Bellamy likened a night like this to playing multiple games of chess at once, moving game pieces through the maze of calls, trying to anticipate the storm's moves and put her resources where they were needed the most. The end game was to make sure all of her people went home to their families in one piece.

In a frightening moment of silence, no phones ringing, no alarms blaring and no radio traffic Elaina, one of the call takers asked quickly if they needed to call in more personnel to cover the barrage of calls. Bellamy, the shift supervisor, looked over her shoulder at Morgan. Morgan gave her a shoulder shrug and a head shake, indicating she was confident she could handle the police side of things. Bellamy looked at her board of calls and tried to weigh the costs. Could they handle it and keep their sanity or was it worth the overtime pay to call in another dispatcher or call taker.

She decided that she and Morgan could handle the dispatch side of it. But looking at the amount of calls that had already come in it appeared the call takers could use another person. She shouted back to Elaina to call in another call taker. The storm by Bellamy's estimate was only half over in their jurisdictions. It had yet to really hit the city or the eastern portions of their county response area.

The brief moment of silence dissolved and the activity broke loose again like a bolt of lightening. Bellamy was suddenly irate. She wished she could call in the big boss who had once made the comment in a meeting about hiring personnel that he couldn't understand why it was so difficult to hire good employees. *As he put it, a monkey could do this job. Well mister, she thought, let's see you do it. Come on in. I'll be out having a smoke if you need me.*

The police side of the radio remained eerily silent. It was as though the officers were bracing for the storm to roll in to the city or praying it would veer to the north as thunder storms sometimes did.

Nile One asked Bellamy to call the helicopter company and advise them that the storm was letting up in their area and conditions were improving for them to fly and do a hoist. He advised he had three trauma patients. Bellamy was gritting her teeth. "Kelly, do we have any update on patients' conditions on the Rainier Road accident?" Bellamy asked. "Never mind," Bellamy answered herself. Kelly had just updated the call and Bellamy hadn't seen it until this moment. She read through it quickly and none of the other patients appeared to have life threatening injuries but all of them were considered trauma patients which met the criteria for requesting a hoist mission. Not my circus. Not my monkeys, Bellamy whispered to herself. Nile One had made the request. He would have to answer to the Emergency Medical Director. The Emergency Medical Director was the grand pooh-bah of the Emergency Medical Umbrella for the county. He set the priorities and criteria for every person in that circle of professionals and how they responded to each and every call. This Director could be a real piece of work. He wasn't just the Medical Director. He thought he was God of all that occurred in the County. He and Bellamy had butted heads on calls several times. When she was called on the carpet once for a decision she had made that went against how he thought the call should have been handled she wrote up her report with her rebuttal and her snide comment that she didn't go into his operating room to tell him how to do an appendectomy he should be allowed to come into her Comm. Center to tell her how to handle a call. She had been afraid she was going to be demoted or fired but she never heard another word about that call. As a supervisor she had ended up working with him on numerous calls and even if they disagreed on how it should be handled they had built a mutual respect for each other. If a call wasn't done his way, right or wrong, he would hold them to the fire he lit under everyone.

A huge explosion shook the building. The storm had arrived with a vengeance. It scared the crap out of all of them. In unison was a shriek from five of the workers. "That was close." Morgan commented. The lights flickered then went out completely. "Shit!" Bellamy yelled. She fumbled around the turntable until she found a flashlight. On the other side of her console she reached for a portable radio that was in the charger. The backup generator was going to kick in any second. "Damn it" She swore. She flipped on the portable and started notifying units they had no power and were on portable radios.

Bellamy was blessed to have a crew that had been through incidents like this before. Training kicked in and so did their instincts. They all knew what their jobs were and without skipping a beat shifted into high gear. Bellamy got up and stumbled towards the computer room. The alarm went off in the center turning it into a nightmare of epic proportions. Strobe lights flashed and a klaxon alarm blared. "Fuck!" Bellamy yelled but no one could hear it except her. She was right by that alarm panel. She found the annoying alarm quickly using her flashlight and silenced it. She was just about to go in the computer room when she thought to open the door and check on the generator that was just for the computers. She looked at it and there was no doubt it had been fried. She could smell melted electrical wires. So much for surge protectors when they were needed, Bellamy thought. She was about to yell and see if someone could call the radio tech that lived in town and see if he could come in when Morgan yelled to Bellamy "Don radioed me. He just came through the gate. He had to open it manually."

Bellamy breathed a prayer of thankfulness. She went into the computer room and realized that was a futile trip. Computers are worthless without electricity. She shook her head and ran back to her desk. She grabbed the notebook she had on her desk and started dispatching the old fashioned way, pen to paper. All the times and unit up dates would have to be entered into the computer call when the computers were back up and running. She shook her head. Sometimes the old fashioned way of doing things was easier than the new more complex way. The paperless society that the city had counted on to save paper and ease the work load was out the window. In the long run it had produced more paper because everything on the computer of any significance had to be "backed up" on paper. And as with this storm they had to return to pen and paper. Bellamy could hear the chain saws in her head cutting down more trees to produce the paper they were going to be using tonight. "Would someone call James? I won't be able to bring the computers up. He's going to have to do it." Bellamy delegated.

"Do you have his number?" Sarah asked, "All of the emergency numbers are in the computer and I don't have his home number."

Bellamy yelled the f word at the top of her lungs. "Never mind," Bellamy shouted, "I have it in my cell phone." With her left hand she answered a city unit responding to a call she had given their station. With her right hand she typed in James' number on her phone. This perfect computer system did have its drawbacks. One of which was that all of their emergency contact numbers were in the computer. That was fine and dandy until the lights went out and the computers went down. If that emergency number they needed wasn't written down in a book somewhere, you were out of luck and got to sit in the dark until you could find the number or the lights came back on.

The lightning hadn't taken out the phone system and every line lit up. When the lights went out which they evidently had all over the city the easiest number to call was 911. Usually they took it in stride. But after answering a butt-load of calls, asking if we knew the power was out and asking when power would be restored Sarah told one demanding caller, "We are in the dark too, and I have no idea when your lights will be back on. I guess you should turn on a light. Yeah, I know there is no power but when the power is back on the light will come on." With that she hung up to take another call. *Or the sun will come up and you will at least have that light." Bellamy thought.* It was a good bet that the power wouldn't be restored for a couple of hours, at least.

She quickly glanced at the monitor that showed the front parking lot. She shook her head. No camera. No window to look out to see if the sun was coming up yet. She looked at the big clock on the wall, it was battery operated so it was still working. According to the time the sun should be coming up.

Bellamy thought the storm was slowly moving to the east. Over the police channel came the frantic voice of an officer. Morgan had dispatched Charlie 3 to a motion detector alarm at a furniture store on the east side of town just a block away from the Comm. Center. "Charlie 3, go ahead." Morgan answered.

"Charlie 3, my vehicle is disabled. I'm unable to respond to the alarm." He reported over the din of what sounded like a downpour of epic proportions.

"Received" Morgan answered him, "Your location for a tow?" He was in the Walnut Street underpass. It was notorious for flooding when there was a hard rain. The two of them started laughing. "Serves you right Nugent," Morgan laughed off the air. Nugent happened to be Charlie 3. Nugent, the hotdog that he was, probably forgot about the underpass. In the dark the flooding would not have been visible until he made splash down going code to the alarm. Dunking a patrol car really was a baptism by water for him. Morgan planned to take advantage of the situation. She didn't have to ask what happened. She knew. "Charlie 3 you'll need to divert traffic from your location at the top of the underpass. I'll be dispatching a tow to your location." When I get around to calling them, she mumbled off air. In the meantime Nugent was going to go wading through the filthy water to the top of the underpass and direct traffic in the rain. Not only did the underpass collect rain water but garbage that had blown down there and a good chance of urine and spit from people walking under it and using its relative seclusion at night. Jerk.

The calls continued to come rolling in, most of them involving flooding or limbs down on the road. Bellamy and Morgan were able to divide the calls to have them checked out and referred to the water department or street department or electric company. But at least their power had been restored, albeit by a back-up generator in the secure parking lot. James had done his magic from home. The computer system Bellamy thought had been fried had just tripped a breaker or something and James was able to get their computers up and running.

By the time Bellamy thought the storm was running out of steam she got a call of a car fire. It was near a building on Larue Road near a building. Bellamy dispatched the call waking yet another group of volunteer firefighters. The call taker added more information to the screen. The vehicle was a truck parked near the loading dock of the building. Bellamy tried to picture the building. It was actually on the same road she took to get home. It was a dispatcher thing. She could see the building. It always looked like a big shed to her. It was a rather dilapidated, unpainted, old wood structure. This time of year there was nothing going on there. Come August or September it would be a whole different story. It was a hop kiln if she was visualizing the correct structure where hops were dried and wrapped in burlap for delivery to various warehouses. It was a beehive of activity then, trucks loaded with hop vines coming in to the loading dock, empty trucks pulling out to return to the fields to get another load. But in July it was empty. No one should be there. "Do we know how close it is to the building?" Bellamy asked the call taker.

"No, he just said it was by the loading dock." Sarah responded. "It was just a passer by."

Bellamy was surprised. There was a ranch style house just to the west of the kiln parking lot. She assumed the owners of the kiln lived in that house. There was also a large Victorian house across the road. Bellamy was always impressed with the neatness of the yard. It had about an acre of shade covered manicured lawn and flower beds that seemed to bloom every season of the year. To the west of the house was an old wooden church with chipped white paint. It always looked lonely. But during the Christmas season there was always a light in the spire that always spoke of hope to Bellamy. It sat amid a box of lotus trees that suggested it may have been part of a homestead. She didn't know if it was now part of the property with the Victorian house but by proximity she guessed it might be. It was possible that the kiln could also belong to them.

She thought that there would be a lot of callers on that fire, especially from the house behind the large gravel parking lot of the kiln. It was a busy road. It was a country road but it was a shortcut to several businesses to the east but there was nothing. Not one more 911 call. Minutes ticked down. Finally "East Valley 2, I'll be enroute to the 1300 block of Larue for a vehicle fire" came a sleep filled voice of the deputy chief.

"Great." Bellamy moaned. *"Could this night get any worse?"* she wondered.

"There's your man." Morgan mocked.

Bellamy rolled her eyes. "East Valley 2, the R.P. was a passerby. Stated the vehicle was near the loading dock of a hop kiln," Bellamy told him. The R.P. meant the Reporting Party. It was just quicker to use R.P. Regardless of the information she gave him she knew he would have a question.

"Do we know how close to the loading dock?" he asked, adding, "I'm seeing a lot of flames for just a vehicle fire. I can see it from my location." Wherever that is, Bellamy thought. There was no AVL associated with his vehicle so she couldn't track him on her map. AVL stood for Auto Vehicle Locator system. It tracked the movement of emergency vehicles on the map screen so dispatch could see how close or far away they were from a call.

"Negative," Bellamy replied.

"Could you call him back and ask him?"

Just go. You'll figure it out when you get there Bellamy wanted to yell over the radio. He would probably be on scene before she could get the reporting party back on the line but she called anyway. Surprise, surprise there was no answer and it went to voice mail. When she looked on the call screen there was no owner information on the phone he was calling from. That meant it was a cheap phone, usually bought with cash. The minutes the caller used were bought as needed. People on TV cop shows called them burner phones. It meant they could use them for illegal purposes and they couldn't be traced. When the person was done with it they would just toss it and buy another one.

"There is no answer" Bellamy told him.

"East Valley 2 I am on the scene. We have a vehicle and hop kiln fully involved. Give me a second alarm" he said in a growl. It made Bellamy feel like it was her fault that she didn't know the building was also involved. Just the tone of his voice made her feel like a total idiot.

Bellamy grabbed the alarm book out of the lazy Susan and flipped to the page with the alarm codes. She started toning out the stations on the Zetron and adding the units to her call screen. By the time she had finished that the tones had finished cycling and she keyed the mic. Taking a breath she started verbally dispatching the stations and rigs. She had just ended the first dispatch when East Valley 2 cut in on the middle of her dispatch. It completely covered her dispatch, which resulted in a lovely squelch that garbled what she had just said.

"East Valley 2 we will also need the Sheriff's office to the scene" he yelled. *Really? Yelling doesn't help me hear you any better, jerk off, Bellamy grumbled in her head.*

"Received," Bellamy responded and continued the second round of the dispatch. She clenched her teeth. He sounded like such an ass. Bellamy picked up the direct line to the Sheriff's office. She was sure she knew what their response would be. They only had 3 deputies to cover the largest county in the state.

The direct line between fire and the Sheriff's office rang and rang. Bellamy felt horrible for even calling. The Sheriff's office was probably up to their waists in water moccasins. They only had two dispatchers and those dispatchers didn't have call takers. Those two did it all. They took the calls and dispatched them. Since they had only three road deputies and a large call load, especially in the middle of a storm the dispatchers also had to take any reports they could over the phone. The calls, like domestics, burglaries in progress or injury accidents had to be sorted and prioritized and put in queue for dispatch. And like all emergency services breaks to go to the bathroom, get a cup of coffee or something to eat was out of the question. From the waist up they were going a hundred miles an hour. From the waist down they were glued to their chairs until the oncoming shift relieved them.

When a harried dispatcher curtly answered the phone and Bellamy relayed the information requesting an officer, the female dispatcher on the other end of the line let loose with a rapid fire round of swear words, on a recorded line. Granted, it was a direct line from one agency to another but it was a foregone conclusion that every minute of every call and every dispatch during this storm would be dissected by the grand pooh-bah, the Director of the agency, Brian or his ghoul Karen. Every nuance would be scrutinized like a touchdown in a playoff football game and criticized to within an inch of its life by the Monday morning quarterbacks who ran the place but wouldn't have a clue how to dispatch a call.

The dispatcher told Bellamy exactly what she expected to hear. The upper valley deputy was enroute to the fatality up in the Nile District. The second deputy was enroute to a domestic involving a gun. He was on his way, alone, in a blackout, in an area at the far reaches of the northern most area of the county to a call with a gun. Alone. And the third deputy was in the southern most area of the county their dispatcher reported. The Sheriff's dispatcher gave Bellamy the news she expected to hear that no one was available and wanted to know exactly why a deputy was required at a fire scene. Bellamy wondered as well. She hadn't asked East Valley Two. She steeled herself to ask him over the radio. She expected him to say he needed a deputy for traffic control but his response took her by surprise. He bellowed into the radio that he had a Code 5 (a dead body) and would need a deputy for an investigation. Both Bellamy and the Sheriff's dispatcher made an audible, "Ohhhh" at the same time. "I'll call out a detective" the Sheriff's dispatcher replied. Neither of them expected a dead body at the scene of a car fire. Her tone had softened to a weary sigh. But before either of them had hung up the phone Bellamy could hear the Sheriff's office radio in the background and a familiar voice. It was Deputy Roy Morse. He was also a volunteer fire fighter with Cowich Fire Department. He and Bellamy sometimes had coffee at a café near Bellamy's house.

Even going code, with lights and siren, his response time to East Valley would be almost an hour but it wasn't. The lower valley deputy called on scene just moments later. Deputy Morse called out at the hop kiln fire. The Sheriff's office did have AVL but evidently his wasn't working. It was quite obvious he hadn't been where he said he was.

East Valley 2 acknowledged her then having to have the last word, he requested she call her city firefighter LaRue to the fire scene. *Two and two do sometimes add up to four, she thought.* East Valley Two was a LaRue. And now he needed one of her Battalion Chiefs with the same last name. She had never made the connection that they might be related. She was still confused exactly why her B.C. or Battalion Chief would be needed at an East Valley fire scene but she pulled up his information in the computer.

LaRue was a very familiar name in this area. They owned a lot of property in the East Valley and Black Rock further to the east. And there happened to be at a fire on Larue Road. Even though the 'R' wasn't capitalized in the road name it was still the same family. Her Battalion Chief owned all the hop yards around her house. When her parents passed away she did not want to be an apple orchard owner. She had sold the property, minus the half acre her house occupied to the LaRue family. She refused to sell that half acre and her house as it was a little piece of her history.

It wasn't the same last name that connected the two firefighters in her head though. It was their command of the radio that made her think they had to be related. They both had the same obnoxious tone of voice when they responded to calls. She found her B.C.'s number in the book and started to dial it, when East Valley Two advised her she could disregard. He would call him. She shrugged. It was one less thing she had to do.

Chapter 2

In the final hour of her shift she managed to get the helicopter up and to the fatality in the Nile area to transport the critical survivors. She sent a funeral home to the call, although she wasn't sure how they would get to the scene. At the moment that wasn't her problem. One of the fire units would have to direct them from the road closure.

Bellamy got the coroner enroute to the fire scene in East Valley.

She thanked the weather Gods that the storm had veered a bit to the north as it continued east, taking it onto a huge chunk of federal land called the Training Center. Aptly named it was a training center for military agencies from around the world. The area was a good twenty miles from Bellamy's house but there were times when the atmosphere was just right that she could hear the ordinance as though a war was right across the road. At night she could see the paratroopers as they glided through the sky to the ground. Sometimes there would be flares. She wondered what people traveling through the area thought when they saw these things or heard the bombs going off but was not aware that the Training Center was there.

To the right of Bellamy was another computer system that monitored hundreds of fire alarms in Yakima. When the power went out then came back on all of the fire alarms they monitored in the power outage area rang up on that computer terminal. While dispatching she still managed to put one finger on the silence button for the alarms and silence them all until she could look at each one and make sure they just showed a power outage and not an actual fire. Now she cycled through the alarms she had silenced to see if there were any that had not cleared. She couldn't see many because power was still out in many of the areas where the alarms had been tripped. She made sure none of them were actual fire alarms, water flow or smoke alarms. There were none. The oncoming shift could clear the rest of them when the power was restored to those areas.

By the time her relief sauntered through the door, the mayhem had been roped in to just a small riot of cleanup with the exception of the fatality in the Nile District to the far west in the mountains and the fatality in East Valley. Like the rest of her shift mates she couldn't wait to get out the door and into the freedom of three days off.

After briefing her relief of the stormy shift she grabbed her purse and slowly stretched into an upright position and left the building. Morgan was right behind her. The three call takers were gone. They had hit the exit like a bullet train.

Once outside, both Morgan and Bellamy stopped and leaned against the wall, first inhaling the freshly washed air and enjoying the last flashes of lightning as the storm disappeared behind the foothills to the north. In unison they both lit cigarettes and took long drags off of them. All of employees had some kind of addiction. Bellamy and Morgan were addicted to cigarettes. Others had eating disorders that cycled through the newest fad diet. Some of the employees used their faith to cope. Many used alcohol to numb the sting of the career they had chosen.

"I am going home and breaking out the bottle of Pendleton. Tonight calls for a drink," Bellamy told Morgan. "Want to join me?" She asked Morgan. That was an invitation she had never extended to Morgan, or any co-worker for that matter. In all the years she had been there she could count on her right hand how many times she had socialized with them outside of work. It wasn't that she didn't like them she did. They were like family. She spent more time with them than she did with her family. But she was also their supervisor and it felt wrong to hang out with them one day and have to counsel them for some infraction of policy the next. She thought it better just to keep them at arm's length.

Morgan stubbed out her cigarette and pushed away from the wall they had been leaning against. "Another time, I have to get up early and go help Kathy clean out her mom's house," she mused, groaning. Kathy was Morgan's partner. Kathy's mom had gone in to an assisted living facility so her family was getting together today to tackle the difficult task of cleaning out a lifetime accumulation of belonging. Morgan and Bellamy exchanged knowing glances. They had to do it too, Bellamy when her parents had died, Morgan when her mom had to go to a nursing home. It somehow felt like an invasion of privacy to go through a loved one's personal belongings while they were still living. It just felt wrong.

"Oh," was all Bellamy could say. "Another time then." The two of them went to their cars without another word.

As was Bellamy's habit she couldn't help but replay every moment of the storm in her mind. She hated it and wished her brain had an on/off switch she could flip but it wasn't so. She was hoping a couple of fingers of Pendleton would at least temporarily mute the tape running through her head.

Mindlessly she navigated out of town and down the highway to the exit leading to her house. She had already taken it before she realized what she had done. Crap, she growled at herself. She would have to go right by the car fire she had dispatched. She had meant to avoid it and take the next exit and come in the back way. As she turned the corner onto Larue road, she could already see the rotating colors of lights of the emergency vehicles. Most of the units had cleared and returned to their stations but there were a couple remaining. One was still putting a stream of water on the collapsing old wooden structure. A command vehicle sat unoccupied away from the charred vehicle. As she slowly passed, she could see the coroner's van and the Sheriff's detective's Chevy Impala with the wig-wags still on as if to announce to the world that the occupant of that car was really, really important.

Half a mile away from the fire scene Bellamy pulled down the dirt road that took her the rest of the way to her house. A covey of quail scurried across the road. Moms and dads as well as a group of their babies, fuzz balls on twigs rushed back and forth in front of her. They never seemed to know exactly where they were going. They zigzagged in front of her. She stopped to let them pass. She waited. There were always a couple stragglers that would run out in an attempt to catch up to the rest of the covey. Bellamy's Silver German Sheppard was at the edge of the driveway, his entire body wiggling in anticipation of

Bellamy's arrival. Bellamy grinned. Seeing Jax made everything all right.

Jax greeted her with his hearty barks and growls as she got out of the car. He bounced up and down in the air like an old fashioned pogo stick. Bellamy leaned down to hug his neck. No matter how long she was gone, whether it was five minutes or five hours his greeting was the same. He was elated to have her back home. His barking was replaced with whines and cries as though he was telling her exactly how traumatic his night had been. In comforting tones, Bellamy apologized to him for her absence and went in to her sanctuary. A hundred pounds seemed to slough off her shoulders as she kicked off her shoes and stripped off her uniform sweat shirt. Yes, it was the middle of July but if she didn't want to freeze to death all night at work she had to wear a sweatshirt. The Comm. Center had to be kept cool to appease all of the computer equipment. She left the dark blue shirt dangling on a kitchen chair next to her shoes. She un-tucked her uniform t-shirt stripped it off and it fell to the dining room floor. By the time she reached her bedroom she had unfastened her bra and flung it onto her bed with a heap of clothes occupying one side of her expansive bed.

She had replaced all that was work related and pulled on a soft cotton night shirt and shorts. Sighing, she slipped in to a pair of flip-flops and scuffed her way back to the kitchen. Jax was still complaining about her absence. He made it sound as though he had been tied outside on a short chain and left to suffer the worst of the storm, without food or water, when in fact he had most likely been snoozing on his comfy bed beside her bed or in the living room on the couch. She glanced at his food dish. It was obvious he had noshed some of his kibble throughout the night and counter surfed a piece of left over pepperoni pizza. The drool marks that snaked across the tile floor told her he had drunk some water. Another bowl she had filled with ice cubes drizzled with Pepsi before she left had also been consumed. She wasn't too concerned about his complaints. She opened the freezer where a fifth of Pendleton whiskey sat staring at her at eye level. She took it out and held it for a moment before setting it on the counter. The seal hadn't even been broken.

When she reached in the cupboard for a glass Jax went nuts dancing and barking for a treat. Bellamy took one out of the jar next to her glassware and made the excited dog sit before giving it to him. He gobbled it down like he hadn't had anything to eat in days and sat begging for another.

After Bellamy washed the slobber off of her hands she filled her glass with ice from the dispenser. Jax did his silly prancing dance, hoping Bellamy wouldn't forget him. She poured the contents of her glass in his empty Pepsi dish and refilled her glass with ice. She broke the seal on her whisky and poured a few fingers into the glass, and another finger of the golden liquor, the middle one, to sweep the remains of the shift into the trash bin in her head.

She shuffled out the back door with her drink in one hand and a dish towel in the other. In her damp back yard she sat her drink down on the dripping side table and wiped off the remains of the rain from her favorite lawn chair. She sank into it and let it comfort her. In a moment of pure ecstasy she took a swallow of the ice cold whisky. She sighed. Frigid, electric heat began to do its magical soothing trip down her throat, plummeting into an empty stomach. The knotted muscles in her shoulders began to untie.

Leaning back in the chair she gazed at the morning sky. Soft billowing clouds in hues of white and gray slowly glided across the light blue blanket above her. Try as she might she couldn't turn any of them into something other than clouds. Maybe she had no imagination. Maybe her brain was overloaded.

Lying silently by her side, Jax's head suddenly perked and his large radar ears stood erect and scanned the area for a sound he thought he heard. Bellamy didn't notice at first. Her mind was still running through each of her calls of the night at warp speed. She scrutinized every detail, every word, over and over again. Her weary mind kept hitting speed bumps of uncertainty. Had she missed anything on her two fatalities? She took another swallow of whiskey and caught sight of movement beside her. Jax was doing his low crawl as he scooted forward on the lawn. Watching him as he silently stood up, head down, eyes darting to the left of her, her eyes followed his intent stare. He had zeroed in on something in the dense green field of hops. Momentarily she closed her eyes and prayed it wasn't a skunk. Opening them again she saw a man emerging from the darkness of the dense hop canopy. *Well crap, she thought, a perfect end to her week.* The raised hackles on Jax's back lowered into place and his tail began a slow wag. How he could like this man she had no idea. He was such a pain. It was only the most annoying city firefighter she knew, B.C. LaRue not to be confused with the equally annoying East Valley Deputy Chief LaRue.

Renny regarded Bellamy seriously. He knew she would be there, lounging in her purple deck chair. Had he waited a bit longer he would have found her passed out, head tilted to the side, her long blond hair brushing against her face. When he had found her like that in the past, he had wanted to sit beside her until she awoke. But he never had the courage to do that. But if she fell asleep like that today chances are when she awoke she would find him sitting next to her. It was going to be extremely hot today with temperatures predicted to be above 100 degrees. If Bellamy fell asleep outside today she would probably find herself looking like a boiled lobster when she awoke.

But Bellamy's expression right now could have frozen the Sahara Desert. Bellamy was giving him an inconvenienced look that she had so often shown him at work when his crew came to visit the center. He wasn't sure why she didn't like him. Maybe it was because he loved messing with her on the radio. He would mimic the tone and cadence of her voice. As the call would progress her voice would become more strident and low as if his mere existence was more than she could bear. He caught her as she started to roll her eyes then quickly stopped. After all she didn't want to get caught rolling her eyes at her superior of sorts. They were both Fire Department employees and even though she wasn't under his immediate command, he still outranked her.

"I was hoping I'd catch you out here," he began. He rubbed the velvet of Jax's ears. Jax leaned against LaRue's leg. Bellamy's blue eyes regarded LaRue coolly. She took a sip of her drink to steel herself.

She felt obligated to be hospitable. "You want one? It's Pendleton." She offered.

Without hesitation Renny accepted her invitation. After all, in their jobs, it was Thursday night. It wasn't Friday morning. Bellamy gritted her teeth having to oblige getting him a drink. It was Friday morning. What kind of a farmer drank this early in the morning? She rose from her chair and headed toward the house, "Whiskey? No beer?" Renny asked in jest. They really should be drinking beer considering they were in the middle of his hop yard. He felt like it was being unfaithful to the beer it would eventually become. But the truth was he didn't care much for beer. But he wouldn't admit that to Bellamy. He and Jax followed her into the house obediently.

Over her tensing shoulders she responded curtly, 'No. No beer."

In all the years they had known each other, Renny had never been in her house. If they had to talk to one another it was always outside on her porch or on the road in passing. Even then, Bellamy always looked irritated. Maybe he needed to let up on mocking her on the radio. He really would like to see what she looked like when she smiled at him. He knew she would be even more stunning than she was right now.

Her kitchen was small but cozy. It was a little messy around the edges. Dirty dishes were soaking in cold slimy water. Clean dishes were stacked in a drainer. Fast food cartons and takeout cups littered the small amount of counter space she had. It looked like she had started stripping off her uniform as she came through the back door and left it where it fell. Renny watched as Bellamy took a glass from the cupboard. What little light there was in the dim morning light of the kitchen he could see the outline of her body through the thin material of her night shirt. She had lovely breasts of medium size that cupped perfectly then tapered to a taunt belly. Suddenly he thought better of his decision to accept a drink but it was in his hand before he could think of a way out. Bellamy was staring at him when he realized his gaze had been lost in the curve of her breast. "Let's' go outside where there's a bit of a breeze. It's going to be a hot one today," Renny suggested. He turned, his scarred cowboy boots slipping on the tile floor. Stepping outside, Bellamy motioned to an old wrought iron rocker. She wiped it off with the dish towel on the wrought iron table and Renny lowered himself into the chair. It was surprisingly comfortable. "I was hoping I'd find you here," Renny said.

"You said that," Bellamy replied.

"Yeah," Renny said taking a long draw from his drink. "We are going to be spraying today." He lit a Marlboro red when he finished. "Just thought I'd let you know so you can keep your windows closed and Jax inside."

Bellamy rolled her eyes, this time making no attempt to hide it. "Thanks. I appreciate that." She was so tired and the alcohol had suddenly taken possession of her. She really needed to sleep and Pedro would be out there on a spray rig going up and down the rows of hops spewing chemicals which no doubt would leak through the filter on her central air. She knew ear plugs couldn't drown out that sound. "What time is Pedro going to start?" She asked.

"What?" Renny asked absently.

"What time is Pedro going to be spraying" she asked her voice a little more irritated.

"Oh, ah, around ten but it will be the crop duster," he replied.

"Great," she mumbled, lighting her own cigarette. She definitely wouldn't be getting any sleep this morning, "Maybe I'll go fishing" she mused out loud.

"Drive?" Renny asked her considering the slight slur in her voice.

"That's how we get to the lake these days, cowboy. We drive" she said, digging at his age and his cowboy boots. He wasn't all that much older than she was but enough that she could twist a dagger in his ego.

"Not a good idea after being awake all night and sipping this brew," he cautioned. She knew he meant well but it still made her feel like a foolish child. 'Where do you like to fish?" He asked trying to undo whatever he had just done because he could see she was pissed off again. He hoped this girl didn't play poker because her face would give away her hand every time. His voice had softened though as he spoke.

"Clear Lake," Bellamy revealed.

"The west side," Renny asked? She nodded. "How about you take a little nap and I'll pick you up in an hour or so. I'll drive, you can sleep," he offered. "I need a getaway too. Last night was a nightmare." He rubbed his dark blue eyes. His deep voice was gravelly and resonated in Bellamy's chest. Her head snapped to attention.

'I didn't hear you on the radio. You weren't on duty, were you?" Bellamy asked. Renny's voice was very unique. There was never any question if he was working. She believed she could identify his voice in a crowd of hundreds. His voice was deep and intense.

Renny looked at her incredulously. He was making a statement without verbalizing it. "No, I wasn't working. I got called to the scene because the kiln is mine." He informed her.

"What?" Bellamy asked, genuinely surprised.

"It's my kiln. You really didn't know? How long have you lived here?" he asked, knowing perfectly well she had grown up here. She was living in the house she had lived in since birth in the hop yards that had once been her parents' apple orchards. When Bellamy had sold the orchards the LaRue Corporation they had pulled all the trees out within a year. Then they had planted the acreage in hops. With the exception of a few ancient apple trees on Bellamy's property all the trees had been removed. Even though the kiln was on Larue

Road it just didn't occur to her that the kiln belonged to the LaRue family as well. The kiln actually sat behind a house owned by another grower. She had just always assumed it belonged to them, not the LaRues.

"I, ah, I don't know why but I thought that it was someone else's kiln," she said.

He lowered his head and shook it. "No. It was mine. And I'm pretty sure that the truck was Pedro's." His voice was sorrowful. It was a tone she had only heard in his voice once before. But then she had never spent more than a few minutes exchanging un-pleasantries with him. Most of their transactions had been over a radio or messages typed on a data terminal.

"What? Pedro? Was that him in the truck?" Her voice soft for the first time he could ever remember. "What happened? Why was he there?" She asked. Tears welled in her eyes.

Renny shrugged his shoulders, his head slightly bowed. "No idea, there was absolutely no reason for him to be there. The kiln is empty this time of year. No one should have been there unless Pedro was checking on something. Maybe he saw someone messing around or a door open. I don't know. We won't even start harvest until the end of next month or September."

"Wow. I, uh, are you sure it was Pedro?" She had no idea what to say. In one of the rare moments in her life she was speechless. She knew Pedro. He was a nice guy. She would see him out in the fields, slogging through the irrigation ditches or checking to make sure the vines were growing as they should. Some days he would be in what looked like a hazmat suit on a tractor getting ready to spray God knows what on the plants. He always made a point to find Bellamy to make sure Jax was in the house and out of harms way.

There were days when she would see his beat up white Ford pickup going down the dirt road. When she wasn't working she would keep an eye out for him. If the weather was extremely hot like today she would make sure she had a large glass of iced water or cola for him. If it was cold she would meet him at the edge of her yard with something hot to drink, coffee or cocoa. If she had baked cookies or made a batch of fudge and she knew he was working she would find him and give him a container full of goodies. Even though her Spanish was limited to mostly swear words and his command of the English language seemed to be about the same, they managed to communicate their friendship. They had an unspoken affection for each other.

Often she would go out to work in her yard and find that her garden trimmings had been picked up and hauled off. She assumed it was Pedro who had so graciously done it since she didn't have a pickup. If it snowed she would often find a path shoveled to her car and her car windows scraped. To Bellamy he was kind of like Santa Claus you knew he was responsible for the kindness but you actually never saw him do it. And even though she had a great security system with good cameras she could never figure out exactly who it was doing it. Somehow they always managed to be just outside the perimeter of her cameras.

"Does Pedro have a family? I mean a family here?" Her question sounded inane even as it escaped her lips.

"They are back in Mexico I think. Right now they are trying to make a positive I.D. on the victim so they can locate his family for a death notification." Renny told her solemnly as he again closed his eyes and massaged them with a fist. In telling her that he realized just how much he didn't know about Pedro. He felt like he should know these things. But he had never asked Pedro and Pedro had never offered the information. They rarely talked about anything other than business.

"Any idea what happened to start a fire? Where did it start, his truck or the kiln?" she asked. These were questions dispatchers and call takers rarely got an answer to. They always knew the beginning and middle of a call but never the outcome. For a normal person it would be like reading a book all the way through and find the last chapter had been removed. For Bellamy it was an accepted way of life. Unfortunately that allowed her to make up her own endings. And that was usually grimmer than the actual conclusion.

Renny shook his head, his short, sandy hair waving. It looks so soft, Bellamy thought. It never looked that way when she saw him at work. He always wore it slicked back like an old man or a gangster from the 40's.

Taking a gulp of his drink, his eyes caught her light blue eyes. They were no longer blue but a rich green color. Maybe he had imagined it. He continued to stare. "They don't know yet Amie," He said quietly, pronouncing her name with a throaty French accent. No one called her Amie. It caught in her chest for a moment as it reverberated there. Amie was a word used to mean the person was a friend. But when Renny said it, it sounded like a deeply personal nickname that someone would use to indicate an intimate, loving relationship. "They are doing a death investigation. Hopefully they will know something soon." He paused for a moment before saying 'I can't believe he's gone. He wasn't just an employee. I considered him a close friend, family really which was strange because he hadn't been with me that long. A year."

"I know. He was a really good guy. I liked him. I'm going to miss him." Bellamy added with a catch in her throat. "I know it sounds really cliché but if there is anything I can do, let me know."

The two of them sat silently then, lost in their own thoughts as a warm breeze washed over them. They stayed that way for some time until Bellamy broke the silence. "Renny, I think I'll pass on fishing today. I am way too tired. Maybe I'll go tomorrow morning, when I'm conscious." She ruminated, chuckling a little. If she sat there much longer she was either going to fall asleep or kiss him, she didn't know which. Kiss him? Where did that come from? She couldn't stand this man. He always sounded like a condescending jerk on the radio. His tone made her feel like an imbecile. A light flipped on in her head making a connection. Renny and East Valley 2 had the same last name, LaRue. And they both had that obnoxious tone that sounded superior to anyone they were talking to. They had to be related. Maybe that tone of voice was a family thing, genetic.

"Tomorrow huh? I'll pick you up around five." Renny told her with that deep, commanding voice.

Bellamy's mouth went slack. She felt her head nodding even though she was relatively certain she hadn't invited him. "Um, okay." She caught herself accepting his invitation or command or whatever that was, when every fiber of her being cringed at the thought of spending time alone with him. She unsteadily rose to her feet as if she were walking in her sleep and added, "I need to go to sleep." He offered her his empty glass.

"Sleep well Amie" he replied matter-of-factly. He strode off towards the way he had come in to her yard and disappeared through the maze of hop vines.

She turned and went in the house with Jax on her heels. She locked both her door and Jax's doggy door. She didn't want him out while they were spraying the field.

She sat the glasses on the kitchen counter and made her way to her bedroom. Without ado she flopped face down in the middle of the bed crosswise, her feet dangling off one side of the bed. Some garment she had tossed on her bed was wadded up uncomfortably under her ribs. She made no attempt to move it. That was the last thing she remembered until Jax licked her foot and she jerked awake. She glanced at her bedside clock. It was early afternoon and hotter than an oven in her bedroom. She must have forgotten to turn on the air conditioning. Her nightshirt and shorts were stuck to her body and her hair was dripping with perspiration. They must have sprayed but she hadn't heard a thing. She stumbled out of bed and fumbled with the thermostat to turn on the air conditioner. Summer had arrived, finally. Two weeks ago she had been wearing her winter coat when she was outside working in her garden. Today she wondered how much clothing she could remove and still be legal in public.

Bellamy stumbled through her weekend routine of housework. With twelve hour shifts she was lucky if she managed to take off her uniform and fall into bed. There were times she had awoken on the couch, fully clothed in her uniform, shoes included, with an afghan over the top of her. Doing mundane everyday tasks like cooking, cleaning and laundry had to wait until her weekend. She didn't have the energy or desire to do anything more than eat, sleep and work. And eating usually consisted of fast food that she picked up on her way to work. Cook was another four letter word that dispatchers tended to spew. She didn't know how her co-workers with families managed to survive the schedule. Maybe she was selfish but she couldn't imagine taking care of anyone but herself and Jax. And some days she wasn't sure about taking care of Jax. She wasn't sure her schedule was fair to him.

Doing chores and drinking coffee didn't distract her from going through all the calls from the night before. She questioned every decision she had made throughout the night.

She critiqued every word she had said on the air, just as she knew her supervisors would. She wasn't usually that compulsive about a shift but last night had rattled her for some reason.

Each critical call would be scrutinized. They would have a vague idea of the activity going on in the center but it wouldn't matter to them that they had been inundated with calls. They wouldn't care that there had been pages of calls pending for service. Or that the power went out in the center and the computers crashed. They would pick and choose what calls they would review and Bellamy knew for sure that the fatality accident up in the Nile District would be on their hit list to tear apart. The other call would be the car fire that turned in to a structure fire that turned in to a fatality. They wouldn't take into account any of the circumstances that they were working under in the center that night. No, none of that would be taken into consideration if there had been mistakes made, no matter how small. She knew she would be called up on the tone of her voice as she dispatched the two fatalities. One of the command officers from either Nile or East Valley was sure to complain that she was being rude. And she would give the same explanation for the tone of her voice. She enunciated the words of her dispatch because in the Nile District radio traffic was so sketchy in some areas that she tried to be very clear, hoping beyond hope that they would be able to hear her. And it was always strident when she had to repeat information for a second time, sometimes a third time. She was trying to enunciate but it never failed, those two ass-bites always complained that she was being rude, never mind how their voices sounded on the radio. And it did irritate the crap out of her when East Valley Two didn't listen to her and asked for the same information again, or that he would request something and before she had a chance to respond he would talk over the top of her wondering why it was taking her so long to get what he needed. The supervisors wouldn't take into consideration the ringing phones, alarms blaring, people talking over them on other channels and they were complaining that she wasn't answering them. She sighed. She was ranting again in her head. Great way to spend her days off, getting in trouble before she knew for sure that she was in trouble. She took a deep breath and strode out into the back yard. Enough, she told herself, drop it. And she did for about five minutes before she started playing that tape in her head again. She pulled some weeds and left them in a pile on the grass, realizing that Pedro wouldn't be picking them up anymore. Her eyes started watering again.

Early evening Bellamy began to focus on the next day of fishing. She needed to get ready. To her fishing was just as much about noshing as it was about throwing a line in the water. She opened her fridge and stared inside. She was looking for inspiration. That didn't work. She looked through her cupboards. She scowled. Jax followed her around the kitchen hoping something would fall out of a cupboard that he could consume. He seemed to scowl. It didn't happen for him either.It wasn't inspired by any stretch of the imagination but she had the ingredients for peanut butter cookies. She mixed everything together, covered the bowl with plastic wrap and put it in the fridge to chill. While she waited she changed out the laundry and actually put some of the folded clothes where they belonged in her empty dresser drawers and closet.

When she had the first batch of cookies in the oven, she once again looked in the refrigerator and took stock of what she had to make something edible for the two of them. An assortment of packages of half consumed cold cuts from the previous week was about all there was to eat. She had a couple of relatively fresh brioche buns. That would have to do. She stacked the buns with smoked turkey, ham and sliced Swiss cheese. She wrapped them and put them back in the fridge. In the door of the fridge was a plastic container that had long lost its lid. It was full of a collection of fast food packets of mustard, mayo and ketchup. She tossed a handful into a plastic baggy. Viola! Lunch was made.

Chapter 3

Renny spent his day in his shop. He had a small office in the back behind the equipment waiting to start harvest. He kept thinking Pedro would come wandering into the shop to tinker with this or that, making sure all the vehicles were in fine working order. In his head he knew Pedro wouldn't be coming in but he couldn't accept that right now. Maybe it wasn't his charred pickup sitting next to the kiln. Maybe the toasty corpse in the driver's seat wasn't his friend. A sad emptiness gripped him.

He knew this emotion. He had felt it before, when he had come home after a 24 hour shift to find his wife, asleep in their bed. Her long dark hair was obscuring her face. Quietly he had stripped off his clothing and climbed into bed beside her. The bed felt oddly heavy. He had turned to pull her body close to him but it was ice cold. He had scrambled out of bed, his heart racing at a maddening pace. There was an alarm in his ears drowning out the sound of his own cry. She was dead. He knew a dead body when he touched one. Melanie was dead.

Renny remembered his body trembling uncontrollably and the room closing in on him. Darkness was enveloping him. He wanted to be swallowed up by that darkness and never wake up. If Melanie was gone he wanted to leave this world too. But he didn't leave. He gasped for breath and the muted light of the bedroom returned. Stunned he just stood there staring at his wonderful wife in an everlasting peaceful slumber.

He didn't know how long he stood there but his legs felt like they were about to buckle. He crumpled to the floor beside the bed. Fumbling on the nightstand he found his cell phone and tried to call 911 but his fingers wouldn't work. It was just 3 numbers but he couldn't hit the right ones. It took him several tries. When that voice answered on the other end of the line his emotions emptied into the phone. There was another person with him. He wasn't alone. He muttered through the call, trying to answer the questions the call taker had asked. It had been Bellamy on the other end of the line. She had been a call taker at the time. Her voice had been controlled and compassionate. She had talked to him until a rescue unit had arrived and started talking him. "Ok Mr. LaRue, you can hang up now." She told him but he didn't want to hang up. He wanted to have her there on the phone as his comforter. She could hear the phone being passed to someone else and another voice telling her they were on scene and she could hang up.

She was gone. Melanie was gone. His whole world was lost to an aneurism the coroner had told him. That didn't matter. What mattered was she wasn't there anymore. He would never touch her or kiss her. He would never see her dark eyes watching him as he talked on the phone when he got called in for an extra shift. He would never hear her laugh again. He would never hear the sound of her feet on the floor as she walked quietly down the hallway to come to bed. Gone.

Now Pedro was gone.

His phone buzzed in his shirt pocket. He answered it absently.

It was the Sheriff's office asking if he had a key to Pedro's house. He did. He owned the house. Of course he had a key to the small house that Pedro lived in. The house was a few roads away at the edge of another large section of hops that stretched up the side of a hill to the south.

He climbed into his cherry red Ford pickup and headed down the dirt road toward Larue Road. That was a good idea, he thought to himself to go to Pedro's house. Maybe when he got there Pedro's truck would be in the driveway and they would find him having a cup of coffee at his kitchen table. The Sheriff's office hadn't positively identified the vehicle or the body. Renny wasn't certain that charred pickup had been Pedro's and there was no way in the world he could identify the corpse. It was charred beyond recognition. He cringed. Did that person burn to death? Did he have a medical emergency that caused him to die? He had so many questions.

He had planned to park in the driveway when he arrived but bright yellow police tape completely encompassed the property. He shivered. He drove passed the property and pulled off on to the shoulder of the road. He slid out of the truck and started towards the officer standing at the edge of the yard with a clipboard. After identifying himself the deputy raised the tape and ushered Renny under. He started to tell him where he need to go, but the detective came over to lead him up to the house.

He introduced himself as Detective Osborne. He wasn't familiar to Renny. He knew a lot of the deputies but this was not one of them. "So, you really think that was Pedro?" he asked pausing before they walked up the steps to the door.

"We are relatively certain. We won't know until after the autopsy. He was pretty badly burned." Detective Osborne advised arrogantly.

No shit! Renny said to himself. He had seen the body. Sadly it looked like most bodies found in structure fires or vehicle fires. They were images that lived in a box in his head. He left them there, locked in the dark and refused to let the images out to haunt him. Unfortunately sometimes the demons escaped the box and tormented him until he was able to push them back in the box.

Renny gave the key to the detective and stood aside as he opened the door. "You'll need to stay out here while we clear the house" the detective instructed. He called for another man in plain clothes to come assist. *Clear the house of what,* Renny wondered, *mice?*

It was getting hot. The midmorning sun was beating down on his head and he started to sweat. He hoped the air conditioning was working in Pedro's house. It was a small, one bedroom house so he figured it wouldn't take much time to go through it.

In a few minutes the two detectives came back to the door, both holstering their guns. "Okay, can you come in with us? Don't touch anything. This is a crime scene now. See if you see anything missing or out of place." Detective Osborne instructed.

"What do you mean a crime scene?" Renny asked. The heat was starting to irritate him. It was already scorching hot and it wasn't even noon.

"I should have said we are treating it as a crime scene because of the probability that it was Pedro in that vehicle," Detective Osborne said.

Hesitantly Renny stepped through the door trying to gather his wits for what he might see inside. Then he looked back at the detective, "Isn't that a bit presumptive?" He wasn't sure he liked this guy. Even though it was cooler inside the house the heat was still suffocating him. The atmosphere was heavy. Renny quickly looked around the living room. He wondered how he was supposed to know if anything was out of place or missing. He had never been in the house since Pedro moved in. But it appeared there was nothing out of place. The kitchen and laundry room were the same. In fact it was so tidy Renny would have thought it was vacant had it not been for a pair of muck boots by the back door and a worn out work jacket on a hook above them. He also noticed a Spanish newspaper open on the kitchen table. For some reason he leaned over and looked at it. He didn't know Spanish. But he saw columns of boxes that looked like want ads to him. One of them, mid page was circled. Next to the paper was a note pad with East Valley perfectly printed in English. A pencil was lying on top of the paper. On the kitchen counter was a dish rack with one coffee cup.

The detective led him through the living room. There was what looked like a second hand love seat and a recliner with a small end table next to it holding a TV remote. There was a nice flat screen TV affixed to the far wall. Renny stopped for a moment considering the room. There was nothing on the walls, except the television. There were no personal touches of any kind. Missing in Renny's mind were family photos, some kind of memento from home. It was oddly empty. Granted he had never been inside the house but it just didn't fit the man he knew. Then again he realized that in the year he had known Pedro he had never spoken of family or his home in Mexico.

Down a short hall there was a bedroom on the right side and a bathroom on the left. Renny glanced into the dark, windowless bathroom. The only thing out of place was a hand towel crumpled on the counter next to the sink. A bar of soap looked moist, like it had been used recently. But he didn't see a razor of any kind. He thought that was a little strange. Most men left them on the counter by the sink unless there was a woman in the house that made a place for the razor or shaver to live. The shower and tub appeared to be dry. A bath towel was neatly folded across the side of the tub. In one corner of the tub rim was a bar of soap and a generic brand of shampoo.

In the bedroom there was a queen sized bed with a single pillow on it. There was no pillow case on the pillow. A single ragged blanket was tossed over the mattress. There were no sheets on the bed. A small chest of drawers was pushed against the wall on one side of the bed, a small nightstand with a lamp on the other side. There was a lamp, just a lamp, no photos, no books, absolutely nothing personal.

The closet door was open and there was one shirt hanging on a hanger. Renny was confused. This man had to have owned more than one shirt. There were no shoes or slacks that he could see. Most of his clothes might be in the dresser drawers but still, people usually put stuff in the closet to store it. Not one box or random soccer ball was in there. As he thought about it he didn't even see any dirty clothes lying around. He hadn't remembered seeing a laundry hamper anywhere. Where would he put dirty clothes? Heaven knew he had to have some somewhere. He had to have come home filthy after trudging down rows of dusty hops. As he walked back to the front of the house he glanced in the bathroom again and there was no hamper there either. No laundry basket on or in front of the washer either.

"It doesn't look like he lived here," Renny commented. "It doesn't look like anyone lived here."

"You sure you don't see anything missing?" the detective asked again.

"How would I know, I've haven't been in here since Pedro moved in." Renny responded, his own irritation simmering. "I need to get out of here. Can I go now?"

"Let us show you out" the detective said. "We need you to be available to come in to the station to give us a statement." Renny nodded absently. "Did you notice anything out of place or missing?" He asked one more time.

Renny looked squarely in the detectives eyes. "Did you not hear me a minute ago? I have no idea. I haven't been in here." There was nothing personal in the entire house. It looked like an empty hotel room, not a place where a man like Pedro would have lived for over a year.

The detective said nothing as Renny walked out of the house. He paused for a moment on the steps. He looked around at the buzz of activity. It was surreal. It had to be a nightmare. One of those demon images must have gotten out of that box in his head and was creating this whole thing.

When he got to his truck, it became real again. A ping pong game was playing in his head, real, unreal. Pedro was dead, no it was a nightmare. He would wake up again and Pedro would be alive out in the fields checking the soil acidity or alkalinity. At the end of his day Pedro would come up to Renny's office and report on any issues while he sat with Renny sipping a beverage. He could see Pedro's dark skin glistening with sweat his bright smile meeting Renny's face. Renny tried to shake the image from his mind as he drove back home.

His house sat just above Pedro's house at the end of a long private road to the top of the hill. His brother said he had built a house up there so he could survey his kingdom. No, he had told Jon, he had built it to put some distance between him and the house he had shared with Melanie. He wasn't trying to cast out her memory. He never would be able to do that and he didn't want to remove her memory. Now years later she was a sweet memory that he held in his heart. He needed to allow her to be just that. He needed to start living again and he knew he couldn't do that living in a house they had once shared.

Renny sat at his kitchen table staring at a sweating glass of iced tea. He had a pad of paper too close to the glass and the pages were soaking up the condensation from the glass buckling the pages. He was tapping his pen against the pages of the paper, his mind racing. From the looks of Pedro's house his family probably didn't have the funds to transport his body home for burial if they were still in Mexico. Pedro must have been like many of the field workers he knew who sent the bulk of his earnings back home to Mexico to support his family. Renny paid him a good wage and provided housing for him. But Pedro certainly didn't spend any of his earnings on any frivolous items for himself if his house and truck were any indication. His money had to have been spent on something. If the Sheriff's office found his family Renny would gladly pay for the transportation of his body back to his home town or wherever his family wanted him buried.

He squirmed in the rigid oak chair. They were extremely uncomfortable to sit in for more time than it took to eat a meal. Melanie had picked them out to go with the rest of the farmhouse style she loved but even she had referred to them as Mormon torture chairs. He wasn't sure what that meant but he had to agree on the torture part. The table and chairs were the only furnishings he brought with him when he moved into this house. The tone of the oak complimented the rest of the wood in the room.

He got up to refill his glass of tea and stopped in his barefooted tracks. He hadn't even thought of his kiln. What the hell was he going to do without that kiln? He and Jon had another one at the opposite end of valley. It was newer and dried the majority of his hops but this kiln was just as important. It dried some of the specialty hops he produced for local micro breweries. He knew it wasn't needed but he tried to keep those hops completely separate from the specialty hops. The hops he and Jon grew for commercial use were referred to as bitter hops. That is what was used to give beer its bitterness. The few acres he had dedicated for micro-breweries were called aromatic hops. They gave the IPAs their unique flavors. Renny was trying to see where it was going. There had been a shift in the hop market in the last ten years. Local micro-breweries had popped up across the state and were spreading across the nation as quickly as Starbucks had when the country discovered lattes. It seemed there were just as many varieties of hops desired by these new industries as there were IPAs. IPA stands for India pale ale. Why micro-breweries used this name was a mystery to him. He had tried to follow the trend, putting in a few acres here and there of these special varieties most sought after. It meant more acreage, more work and in a few years hopefully more income if the trend continued. But any relatively new rage was a gamble. The bottom could fall out of the micro-breweries leaving hop producers with a huge quantity of hops they couldn't sell. Even a small amount of acreage could impact their corporation. That is why he only committed to a few acres until the micro-breweries proved themselves as a stable market. In the meantime he wanted to dry them in a separate kiln just to keep the flavor of the cones as individual as he could.

It was a business balancing act that Renny juggled carefully. He tried to weigh the current trend against what seemed to be the new brews on the horizon. He didn't even really care for beer but it was his business to keep up on the subject. He spent most of his downtime at the fire station reading current publications on the commodity. It was a very complex situation that was constantly growing and changing. Trying to gauge the market was difficult when it came to negotiating his contracts with the large hop buyers that would produce a viable income for the three to five years length of the contracts. The contracts he and Jon had were iron clad. It didn't matter if a wind storm or a new pest or fungus or disease took out their fields. If the fields yielded a bumper crop they would make more money. If his crop was a total loss due to some unforeseen reason and they couldn't deliver the agreed upon tonnage their company lost money. The contract was supposed to protect both the buyer and grower from the ups and downs of the market. In a way it did. As much as the growers tried to balance the possibility of damages and repair and replacement of equipment, not everything could be foreseen. This was one of those instances. Of course they had insurance. The insurance could cover the cost of the kiln but it would never cover the loss of Pedro.

His bare feet lightly slapped on the glossy wood plank floor. He poured another glass of iced tea, padded back to the table and looked at his phone. It was still early in the afternoon, so he looked up the number for his insurance broker, to start the process. When he had finished the call he called Jon to let him know he had filed a claim. They spent several more minutes discussing the fire and business in general.

As soon as he had finished the call his mind went back to Pedro. What would he do without Pedro? He counted on him to get everything done every step of the life of hops. He knew everything there was to know about Renny's business. He knew more than Renny knew about his own business when it came right down to it. Because of his schedule, he was able to spend a great deal of time on the ranch but there were still days when he was working as a firefighter and couldn't be on the ranch. With Pedro he never worried that something wouldn't get done. He managed all of the employees. He had to depend on Pedro since Renny spoke only minimal Spanish and most of his employees only spoke Spanish. It was imperative to have a second in command who could communicate clearly with them. How would he ever find someone to take his place? Pedro had only been with him a short time after his previous field manager had retired but he stepped into the position like he had done it all of his life. It was a rare commodity to have someone step into a position like that and be able to pick up where the prior manager left off without a hitch.

Chapter 4

Bellamy had her long weekend routine down to an art. Drink coffee. Check. Do chores during TV commercial breaks. Check. Sometimes she got involved in what she was watching and missed a commercial break or two. But for the most part it worked. She could get a lot done during one movie.

Break one, gather laundry, sort it and start a load in the laundry room. Next commercial break, she threw out all the takeout containers in the kitchen. Another break she stacked the dishes, ran the dish water and put the first batch of dishes in to soak. And so it continued until the dishes were done. When she got into the rhythm of things it didn't take long to get the house cleaned up and still manage to lie around and scratch Jax's ears.

As the afternoon turned into evening she started thinking about going fishing again. Her stomach tightened. She loved fishing but wasn't sure how much she would enjoy spending a day with Renny. She shook her head. It was a long drive to the lake. It took a good hour to get there. *What in the world would they talk about?* She wondered.

This morning had been the longest conversation they had ever had in all the time they had known each other, except maybe the time she took his call when his wife had died. She closed her eyes remembering the call word for agonizing word. Probably ninety percent or more of the calls she had ever taken were lost and forgotten by the end of shift. Only ten percent would live on in infamy in her mind. That call was one of that ten percent. Maybe only because she knew who he was or maybe because of the pure sorrow she had heard in his voice.

Renny's house was in the East Valley fire district. Calls outside of the city of Yakima could mean a long response time. It took time to dispatch the call and wait for a crew from that fire district to assemble at their station and get going. An ambulance would take about the same amount of time, ten or fifteen minutes to arrive on the scene. Call takers would try to stay on the line with the caller until help arrived. Sometimes because of call load it was impossible to do but that day she was able to stay on the line with him. He had been so distraught his raw emotions poured out over the line. She had a hard time remembering many calls when she had heard a man sob on the phone but Renny did. His voice had been so sad. Bellamy found tears dropping on her notepad as she sat listening to this man, trying to interject comforting words every now and then, asking if she could call someone for him, a family member, friend, clergyman to be with him. After he answered no to the first two, he paused quietly and requested we call Father Berger from the small, rural church in East Valley. Bellamy had put Renny's call on hold and asked the other call taker to call Father Berger. She got back on the line with Renny and told him the other call taker was making that call for him. He choked out a thank you.

There wasn't much she could do for him on that call other than listen to him as wave after wave of grief seemed to wash over him. She kept checking the time lapse on her screen. Only five minutes had passed and there was at least another five minutes until a crew was finally on their way to his house. Finally in a gesture that was far out of the confines of department policy she asked Renny if he wanted her to pray with him. Without hesitation he said yes. Bellamy closed her eyes and began to pray. She wasn't Catholic so she didn't know their rituals but she knew the "Our Father" prayer. Slowly she recited the prayer. When she had finished she just prayed what was on her heart, that God would comfort and strengthen him. She prayed for peace to fill his heart. And then she heard the scrabble of a phone being moved and a different male voice on the other end telling her East Valley fire was on scene and she could hang up.

She knew she would be admonished for praying with a caller but somehow this had felt important to do. She had never done it before and couldn't remember doing it again but Renny was different. He was one of their firefighters. One of their family and it was the least she could do for him if she thought it would be a comfort to him.

When she hung up the phone line, she removed her headset and took a very long cigarette break. She needed a moment to collect herself.

In the following years there were times he and his crew would visit the center but not a word of the call ever passed between them. Maybe he hadn't known it was her that had taken his call. It didn't matter, really, but it was a call that would live in her memory for life.

She sighed then, her thoughts coming back to the present. Fishing. She got her fishing gear together and made sure she had everything she needed. After she had cleaned some bits and pieces of petrified worms out of her tackle box she took inventory of all the odds and ends of lures, bobbers, knife, hemostat, etc. The sun had gone down in the west and she had completely missed it. But her body had felt it and had begun to shut down for the night. It was still fairly early. The big houses on the hills to the south that she could see from her house reflected the last fleeting gold of the sunset while the rest of the hills had turned purple. The landscape melted into a soft pastel purple/blue. Her mother had called that time of day the gloaming. It made her melancholy. She was rarely lonely. She was alone but not lonely. However there were nights, like tonight, when it would be nice to just have a man standing next to her, or hearing his breath as he slept. Those feelings were usually fleeting. Tonight they lingered a little longer than they usually did.

Chapter 5

In that blink of sleep her phone alarm started squawking from under her head. Bellamy had fallen asleep with it plastered to her face. How or why it was there she had no idea. Her hands struggled through the heaviness of sleep to grapple with her phone to silence it. She automatically hit the snooze button. Just a couple more minutes was all she needed to gain control of her faculties to face the day. She closed her eyes. It was only a moment.

Bellamy jumped at the impatient blare of a car horn outside her bedroom window. Disoriented, her heart pounding hard against her chest, she struggled to sit up. Her addled brain tried to connect the shiny little dots floating around in front of her eyes. As the synapses started firing, she leapt out of bed, tripping over Jax. Her brave, alert, silver shepherd yawned loudly, stretching out his best downward facing dog. He hadn't even barked at Renny who for all he knew could have been an axe murderer.

Bellamy struggled again with her phone in an attempt to call Renny, who she guessed was the one impatiently and rudely honking his horn to get her attention. After a few seconds of fumbling she threw her phone on her bed. She didn't have his number. Why would she? She couldn't stand the guy.

She ran, stumbling towards the back door where the annoying sound was coming from. Throwing it open she ran outside, her bare feet slapping against the cold pavement. She got to the end of the walk and yelled his name. "I overslept" she added as if he hadn't figured that out himself. "Come grab a cup of coffee" she yelled in her gravelly morning voice. She wondered why the hell he hadn't gotten out of the truck and come to the door and knocked. "I'll just be a minute."

Bellamy hurried back into the house. Jax had run out of the house and after relieving himself on one of the two old Rome apple trees, he trotted after her with Renny following him into the house.

Renny fumbled around the dark, quiet kitchen trying to find a light switch. Yesterday her kitchen had been dark. Today it was darker still. She had all of the drapes and curtains pulled to block out any sliver of sunlight. Until he found a light switch he wouldn't be able to get a cup of coffee. He couldn't even figure out where the coffee pot was on the counter. When he finally found one he saw that there was freshly brewed coffee in the coffee maker and a thermos sitting next to it. He found a cup in the cupboard above the coffee pot and filled it with the hot nectar of firefighters everywhere. Except, he thought, those generation X, Y or Z firefighters who brought their Chi whatever it was to work every shift or the green slimy milkshakes that looked more like something a person would throw up after a night of drinking than something a person would want to voluntarily drink.

He leaned against the counter and sipped the coffee. As irritated as he was that she wasn't ready to go, the rich, smooth coffee softened his mood. It gave him a moment alone to take in the interior of her house. He was going to snoop with his eyes. It had been transformed from the mess he had witnessed yesterday. The kitchen counters were clean, with no dishes in the sink or drainer. The clothes that had been draped over chairs and strewn in piles on the floor had mysteriously disappeared, leaving a shiny tile floor. Her kitchen table that appeared to have been a recycling bin for assorted paperwork had been cleared and replaced by a vase of roses apparently clipped from her garden.

The living room looked like it had been staged for an open house. The beige couch looked inviting, with just two orange printed pillows. His head tilted a little. Orange? Bellamy didn't seem the type of young lady to have orange pillows. They gave off an edgy modern look that didn't seem to fit with the down-to-earth kind woman he had spoken to yesterday. A large, square coffee table that looked like it was made out of galvanized steel pipes and fittings, with a barn-wood top sat center stage with three glass obelisks, one red, one yellow and the other orange. They seemed to fight the table for attention.

On the opposite wall were two uncomfortable looking club chairs in retro orange vinyl. Above them on the wall was a large painting of what appeared to be rocks in a stream or puddle of water, with autumn leaves in bright hues of red, orange and yellow. Even with the bright colors it was soothing to look at.

The far wall between the couch and chairs was taken up by a huge rock fireplace. The mantle appeared to be a long plank of barn-wood inset between some of the river rocks. There were the obligatory candles every mantle he had ever seen had adorning it. Another large painting on the mantle leaned against the rock face. It was a painting of a wheat field, ripe for harvest. There seemed to be movement in the wheat stalks as though a breeze was rustling them. It too had a sense of tranquility to it.

On each side of the fireplace were built in book cases. They held a collection of books and treasures. He wanted to examine it more closely but he heard rustling around in what he assumed was Bellamy's bedroom.

She came out of her room like a dirt devil on a hot summer day. Her long blond hair was tousled and fell loosely around her shoulders. A union fire fighter ball cap covered the top of her head. She had on a dark green hoodie sweatshirt over something loose sticking out from under it. It appeared she was wearing a pair of camo printed, baggy sweat pants. She plodded heavily across the tile in a clunky pair of hiking shoes. A small backpack of some sort was flung over one shoulder flopping back and forth against her side as she walked.

Renny took another sip of his coffee. He grinned to himself as she bustled into the kitchen. She opened the fridge and grabbed the bag of food and beverages for them. "Do you have a cooler" she asked with her back to him as she filled the awaiting thermos with coffee. Before he had a chance to answer Bellamy started towards the door. "Ready?"

He put his cup in the sink and followed her towards the door. 'You have to stay Jax. You have food and water. Be a good boy and I'll bring you a treat," She promised. Jax slid from sitting to a dejected down position. Renny glanced at him. Jax looked up at him with soulful, pleading eyes. He felt guilty for taking Bellamy away from him. Renny didn't feel guilty enough to take him along.

Bellamy tried to grab her pole and tackle box as she started out the door. Renny quickly took them from her. She closed the door behind them and set the alarm. Bellamy rushed to the truck. Renny chuckled. "Slow down. We have all day." Immediately he saw her shoulders relax and her gait slow as she neared his truck. She visibly sighed as the tension of being late left her body.

As irritated as he had been when she wasn't ready when he arrived, he gave her props. She had donned her fishing attire as quickly as some firefighters donned their fire fighting turnouts. He wasn't sure if she had looked in the mirror though. Her hair was just all over the place. It was long and flying like a palomino's mane in a wind storm.

He gave her some additional points for having all of her fishing gear ready and even had food for the two of them, or maybe it was just for her but it looked like a lot of food for just one skinny woman.

Renny stowed Bellamy's gear and put the food in a cooler already filled with ice. That wasn't lost on Bellamy. Men in her past rarely had the forethought to fill a cooler with ice unless it also contained a twelve pack of beer. There was no beer. She did notice a small Styrofoam container in the ice chest. She could see night-crawlers squirming around under the lid. A man after her own heart, she thought. Yeah, she had seen a "River Runs through It" probably a hundred times. But they wouldn't be fishing in a stream or river. And they definitely wouldn't be fly fishing if his rod and reel were any indication. She had tried fly fishing but she never could get the hang of it. She had even hired an instructor to teach her how to fly fish and she just didn't get it. Where that sport was concerned she had no natural abilities. She had no learned abilities either. All of the three large rivers that converged in Yakima were deemed blue ribbon fishing, so fly fishing was a must. To Bellamy fly fishing was a must not.

Renny opened the passenger side door for her. She stood dumbfounded at the gesture. She couldn't remember the last time a man had opened a car door for her. "Are you getting in or do you plan on driving?" His voice was jesting and even in the early morning hour she could see a glint in his dark blue eyes.

"Not unless you plan on speeding, tailgating, not using your turn signals or passing other cars on the pass." She shot back. She handed him her coffee and climbed up in his truck. After she was buckled in she took her cup back. "Or messing with your cell phone," she added. Closing her door he walked around to his side of the truck trying not to laugh. She wasn't afraid to goad him in to driving safely not that he had any plans to drive like an idiot especially on that pass.

Neither one of them spoke until they had made it passed the remains of the kiln, still taped off with crime scene tape. *Like that would keep anyone out,* Bellamy said to herself. Only it wasn't to herself. She had said it out loud. Renny glanced at her and shrugged. She was right. He did notice that the pickup was gone, probably towed for storage at the Sheriff's office.

"Something isn't right with all this" he said to Bellamy, resting his left elbow on the window sill.

"What?" She asked confused by what he meant.

"For one, his house," he began. "The detective had me go to his house and see if anything was missing." He paused, going over it again in his head. He started to light a cigarette. Bellamy took it from him, lit it and handed it back. He smiled and took a drag.

"And?" she prompted.

"I'd never been in his house before. There seemed to be a lot of things missing. There were no personal things. He's been there for over a year. There weren't any family pictures. No mail, nothing. I've seen more stuff in the back seat of a car than he had in the house." He shook his head while he focused on the road ahead.

"That is weird." Bellamy agreed, studying his profile in the early morning sunlight that had just crept over the distant hills to the east. His tanned face was golden in the light. It was tanned from hours spent in the sun. He had deeply etched smile lines that belied the serious set of his jaw and lips. His nose graced his face as though it was sculpted by an artist to the perfect proportions of his other features.

It was at that moment that Renny felt her eyes on him. He took his eyes off the road and turned to catch her studying him. She straightened a little in the truck seat and tried to look away, but his grin caught her off guard. She smiled back then and tried to turn innocently away, regarding the road ahead with interest. 'It's really dry this summer isn't it?" she asked rhetorically.

"Very." He was still smiling at catching her studying him. "I'm surprised we haven't had more wildland fires yet. By this time last year, half of the state was charred."

She nodded in agreement. Their conversation about fire conditions diverted her from the embarrassment of getting caught staring at him like a schoolgirl looking at her first crush. "Why do you always talk to me like I'm an absolute idiot on the radio?" Bellamy asked like a shot across the bow of a ship. It just bubbled to the surface and out her mouth before she could filter it.

Renny stiffened at the question being caught completely off guard. "What?" he asked stalling for a moment to think how to respond.

"You always make it sound like I'm a child you are scolding when you talk to me on the radio." She said again mimicking the cadence of how he sounded when he spoke to her on the radio.

"I don't know what you are talking about. You, on the other hand, always sound like you are pissed at having to do your job. When I request something you make it sound like I am taking you away from reading a gossip magazine or doing your nails."

"And you make it sound like I'm not smart enough to know how to do my job. Like, like, asking me to dispatch an ambulance to every fricken' medical call. Of course I am going to dispatch an ambulance. Ya think? That's a given, it's a medical call for heaven's sake. You think I'm going to send you an ice cream truck?" She snarled.

"It's policy." He responded, his voice getting that edge that she always heard over the airwaves.

"There. There. That's the sound!" She accused. "Of course it is policy. And if you took a moment to look at your MDT (Mobile Data Terminal) you would see an ambulance was dispatched. Or notifying the power company for a structure fire, really? Of course I send the power company. Really LaRue, I do know my job." She was fuming.

"I know you know your job. You are the best. But if I don't ask it on the air, even though it is on the MDT other apparatus responding or the brass may not know I asked for it. Then it falls on me if the run goes to shit." He told her in that tone that said that should be a given. That she should know he had to ask. "I'm not saying you don't know how to do your job." He reiterated. Trying to derail her tirade he asked, "Do you need anything at the store?" He asked in an attempt to avert more jabs. "Last chance before we get to the lake." He told her.

I know it is the last chance, Bellamy screamed at him in her head. *It isn't the first time I've been to the lake. What a condescending asshole.* Instead she folded her arms over her chest and shook her head, uttering a quiet "No." This was going to be a long day. She had made a mistake, a big mistake. "And for your information big shot, I read the firefighter manual the city has for studying for the test to become a firefighter. Or I read 'Chiefs' magazine when I can get a hold of it. I was just reading about different roof types and how each one burns and how you have to fight it to put it out. Or how much water pressure you lose per foot of hose length you have to use, depending of course, the diameter of the hose and the rise of elevation." She blustered.

"Why in the world would you do that? Do you want to become a firefighter?" He asked. *I hope not. I couldn't stand working with you.* He thought to himself. *I'd be living in a cold shower trying to keep my hose in my turnouts.*

"No. I am doing it so I know what the hell you guys are doing out there. So I can anticipate what you are going to need. So I know why you are doing an exterior attack and not an interior attack. Stuff like that." Then she thrust her hand in front of his face. "Do these look like manicured nails to you?" Her nails weren't stubs but they were short and neat.

"Boy howdy! It doesn't take much to get your dander up." He chuckled. He realized in that moment how she misunderstood his jesting with her on the radio. "I am yanking your chain on the radio. You didn't get that? I'm sorry. I'm just playing with you over the air." He admitted then.

"You are an asshole Chief LaRue!" She snapped in jest. She didn't know he was doing it to get a rise out of her. Now she did. Things would change on the radio. He laughed heartily.

"Truce?" he suggested laughing out loud.

At the Y in the road several miles ahead they veered to the left. It would take them up the White Pass. A large area of mountains separated White Pass from Chinook Pass but eventually both roads led to Mt. Rainier. Each pass had a river that ran down beside the road. Both converged just below the Y and ran another twenty miles before they both joined the Yakima River. The rivers running through each pass had been designated as Blue Ribbon water. A stupid name that meant you were restricted to the type of lures and hooks you could use. It also meant that both rivers were catch and release only. To Bellamy it sounded like the rivers were for bragging rights only. The fishermen could hold up their catch for a photo opportunity then gently release it back into the water. That seemed like a total waste of time to her. If she was going to work that hard to catch a fish, by golly, she was going to keep it and eat it. Yes, she understood the conservation side of it but still it seemed like a waste of a good trout. But maybe she was just being a spoil sport since she had invested in all that money in fly fishing equipment and went out in high hopes of catching something. She caught some things alright, mostly tree branches, exposed boulders in the river and a few snags along the far side of the river. She lost all of her flies within an hour. She had been tempted to throw her rod into the river too but instead took it back home and propped it up in her bedroom as a reminder that she was never going to try that again.

Her mind switched gears as they climbed into the oak scrub along the road. "There weren't any bills lying around or check stubs?" she asked out of the blue. It was a dispatcher thing. They were so used to having conversations interrupted by phone or radio traffic that sometimes it was hours before they could pick up on something they had been talking about. It was nothing for them to jump back in to the conversation exactly where they had left off.

"What?" Renny asked, truly confused by the question.

"Pedro's house, you would think that there would be utility bills or sales fliers lying around" she clarified.

"No nothing that I saw but as neat as the place was he may have put them in a drawer or something. Obviously the detective didn't allow me to touch anything, so I don't know" he told her, still baffled at how she flip/flopped topics like that.

"Cancelled checks?"

"Not that I saw."

"No deposit slips for checks? Don't you get them back from the bank when they are cashed?"

Was she part pit bull? Renny wondered. She wasn't going to let this go.

"Not anymore. It's all on line."

"Wouldn't that tell you where they were cashed or deposited?"

"Probably, I never looked. We have a secretary and an accountant who take care of that part of the business." He slowed the truck and turned on his blinker. Bellamy looked at him wondering what was wrong. Why was he going to pull off the road?

He pulled into the parking lot at Tim's Pond. There wasn't a sign that said that was the name of it. It was one of those places that locals assumed everyone knew the name. Akin to giving directions to turn at old man Amos' red barn or at the big oak tree at the end of Gentry Road. Those were common directions locals gave call takers when reporting an incident. Each district had those landmarks. The firefighter's tended to know where the caller was talking about but not always the dispatcher. Tim's Pond was one of those locations that Bellamy learned of the hard way. It was a drowning call. All the caller could tell her was that it was at Tim's pond on White Pass. When she dispatched the Naches Fire District they knew exactly where they were going. Bellamy on the other hand didn't. She still struggled with that call, wondering if she had known the location she could have got the district going quicker. In the end it really hadn't mattered. The guy had been underwater for over twenty minutes before someone decided to call 911. The victim in his intoxicated wisdom had decided to dive into the lake fully clothed, including cowboy boots. Since the pond wasn't that deep the firefighters figured he had hit his head on the bottom. Instead of floating to the top of the pond, his boots had filled with mud and water and weighted him to the bottom. She stared out across the small pond and shook her head. How sad that something as stupid as diving into the water with cowboy boots would have such a tragic end.

Renny put the pickup in park and pulled his cell phone out of his Carhart jacket pocket. He tapped numbers onto the keypad and after a few rounds of soft swear words he finally seemed to have found what he was searching for.

Bellamy watched him curiously. He scrolled through some pages and finally expanded what he was looking at with a widening pinch of his fingers. He tilted his head, trying to read something. "It looks like he never cashed a check or deposited it. What the heck?" He regarded her with his bright blue eyes. "Want to get out and have a smoke, stretch our legs?"

She nodded the affirmative and climbed down out of the pickup. It was still quite chilly. She lit her cigarette, took a much needed drag and went around to the front of the truck to stare across the lake and up at the pinnacle cliffs. They were columns of basalt extruded from long ago volcanoes. She was awed every time she looked at them. She wondered if she would take them for granted were she to look at them every day. She doubted it. She always saw something new each time she saw them. Rock climbers often dangled from them during the warm months. Sometimes they fell. It never failed, the reporting party had no idea where they were and it was a game of twenty questions trying to figure out where they were and how responders were going to get to them. She swore outdoor enthusiast needed to be banned from the outdoors if they couldn't give an identifiable location of where they were at any given time. There were columns like that on each side of the road and they stretched for miles. The rock structures were broken up by sections of grass and sage brush so it was a crap shoot trying to figure out which ones they were referring to.

"What are you thinking about so hard?" he asked, studying her serious expression.

"Oh, uh, the pinnacles or columns whatever you want to call them. I am always so awed by them. I mean, I know, scientifically, how they are formed but still, that took some amazing planning on the part of our maker to figure out exactly how He was going to do it and where." She said, turning to face him.

"Yep," He agreed, taking in the vista. In unison they snuffed their cigarettes out in the gravel, returning them in their hands. "Here," Renny said offering his hand. Bellamy gave him her cigarette butt. "I have an ashtray in the truck. You ready?" Bellamy nodded. Again he followed her to the passenger side door, opening and holding it while she got in. He closed it once she was settled.

The rest of their drive to the lake was relatively quiet. Each pointed out deer and squirrels to the other as though it was a nerdy game of 'I spy'. The terrain changed as they climbed, from oak trees to pines. The air coming in the truck was sweet and brisk. Bellamy sighed. She didn't mind the smell of hops but inhaling the forest air was intoxicating.

After going through a snow tunnel the lower lake appeared. It was large and glassy with fishing boats already littering the surface from one end to the other. As the day warmed up the water crafts would change from fishing boats to speed boats towing skiers, water boards and inner tubes. The screams of excitement from the people playing in the lake would echo off the mountains on each side.

The above the upper spillway from Clear Lake there was less boat traffic on it. An occasional kayaker would slice silently through the water. On the far side of the lake kids from a summer camp would be out at times in inner tubes or canoes splashing about, squealing and shouting. But for the most part, Clear Lake was serene.

He pulled into a parking space and she hopped out of the truck and walked over to the pay station to pay the five dollars to spend the day fishing or picnicking. It was a "day use" park only. Renny was on her heels trying to beat her to the little kiosk. "Here, I'll get it."

She furrowed her brows at him. "It was my idea, and your gas. I got it." Bellamy informed him. He relented and put his hands in the air like she was threatening to hurt him if he did not back away.

He went back to the truck, loaded up his arms with their gear and headed down to one of the two large wooden docks. He staked his claim on their fishing site even though he knew they would probably have to share their space with other people fishing but for now it was just them and he spread out their chairs.

Bellamy took another load of their stuff to the dock. It was amazing how much one little fishing trip required. Well, maybe required wasn't the right word for all their stuff but it sure made fishing more enjoyable if her stomach wasn't growling and she knew hers would be rumbling soon enough.

She made herself comfortable in one of the camp chairs and put her rod and reel together. She checked her line, set her bobber at about five feet, made sure the lead weight was positioned correctly and that she had the right hooks on her line. She opened the container of night crawlers, then as an afterthought, looked over at Renny, "May I?"

He laughed out loud again. It made her smile. "That's what I brought them for."

"Well, I was going to get some out in the yard last night but I just lost track of time." She explained as she pinched one of the fat worms in half and put the squirming, slimy worm on her hook, making sure it was skewered by the treble hook.

She didn't notice Renny smiling at her. He had never met a woman who was willing to go out at night with a flashlight and yank the big worms out of the dirt between the blades of grass. He watched with admiration as she jumped right in and got all of her gear ready to cast. And cast she did. A very nice cast he admitted to himself. When she had mentioned fishing Renny actually doubted she was serious. She just didn't look like the kind of lady who fished. She seemed a little too dainty like she would squeal at the thought of ripping a worm in half and he would spend half of his time baiting her hook or casting her line for her. He was pleasantly surprised he was wrong.

"What?" She asked when she noticed him staring at her. She leaned her pole against the railing around the dock. She took a big packet of baby wipes out of her tackle box and wiped the worm guts off of her fingers. She wadded it up and put the soiled wipe in a small trash bag she shook out.

He shrugged his shoulders and returned to the task of setting up his cast. She sat the wipes on the ice chest between them. Once he had cast out his line, he too took a wipe and cleaned his hands. Now the wipes he had expected. He guessed she would have some kind of wet wipes to clean her hands with.

They sighed in unison and relaxed against the backs of the chairs like an old couple nestling down in a couch together to read the Sunday paper. Renny recalled out loud, "There was a paper on Pedro's kitchen table, a Spanish paper. I think it was open to the want ads. I remember seeing phone numbers. There was one ad circled but I couldn't tell you what it was. I don't read Spanish."

She tilted her head to one side, wondering what he would be looking for in the want ads. A car maybe, or a new job, maybe a personal add. It would be hard to tell. She read Spanish as well as she spoke it, possibly a little better but not much. She was able to get more of a gist of the contents by dissecting the words. The root words were sometimes similar to English words or Greek words. "As far as I know there is only one Spanish paper in the valley. Maybe we could pick one up on the way home."

He couldn't figure out for the life of him how that would possibly help him figure out what happened to Pedro but he would try anything. He knew it wasn't his incident to investigate. He wasn't a cop. But the fact that Pedro was his friend compelled him to want to find out what had happened to him and why.

"Oooh, ooh, got a bite." Bellamy announced excitedly. She gave her line a jerk and started reeling her line in. As quickly as her excitement escaped her lips, it abated. "Nope, must have ripped his lips off." She continued to reel her line in to check her bait. Renny sat quietly laughing at her. Sure enough, her worm had been gnawed to pieces with just a few stringy worm guts dangling from her hook. She pulled it off and went about replacing it with another half of worm.

Renny's quick movement made her look up. He had a fish on. She watched as he reeled in a nice rainbow trout about ten inches long. Bellamy reached for a net to bring it in but Renny had already brought it over the railing and onto the wood planking of the deck. Thank God, Renny thought. He wasn't sure his ego could handle it if she got the first fish. He knew it was chauvinistic but he couldn't help it. That hunter/gatherer part of him had been ingrained from a young age. Man/provider, Woman/nurturer.

Bellamy hadn't been this relaxed in a long time. The sun in her eyes and against her chest was making her sleepy. She yawned widely. It made her eyes tear up and her nose run. She took a tissue out of her pocket and dabbed at her eyes and gently blew her nose.

Try as she might she couldn't keep her eyes open. She pulled her baseball cap down a little lower over her eyes and slouched a little farther down in her chair. Within minutes she had drifted into a hazy mirage of sleep.

Renny smiled as she watched her falling asleep. He knew she would be absolutely horrified if she knew she had a little bit of drool dribbling out of the side of her mouth. He thought it was cute, hilarious. He stifled a laugh. He had a chance to really look at her without feeling like some kind of a letch. He wanted a picture to commemorate the moment. He pulled his cell phone out and snapped a couple of pictures. Her hair was still mussed as though she had just got out of bed. It probably was, he thought. She had rushed to get dressed. He doubted if she had taken the time to brush it. It didn't matter. Her hair was down past her shoulders and golden yellow. It looked like it might be her real coloring, although now days it was hard to tell. Her perfectly shaped brows were a bit darker than her hair but still light. Her long eyelashes were dark and curled slightly. She had a luscious peach blush from the sunlight on her cheeks. Her lips were wine colored and he had a desire to trace them with his fingertip.

That thought had just snuck into his mind when her rod bounced against the railing and had he not jumped and grabbed it, her rod and reel would have ended up at the bottom of the lake. Bellamy jerked awake.

She caught herself slurping as she struggled to sit up. Dang it, she thought. She had fallen asleep and slobbered. She wondered if she had done the shoe strings like Jax did when he anticipated a treat. *Way to impress a man!* She caught herself at that and wondered why it mattered to her if she impressed him or not. She didn't really like him all that much. He wasn't her type, not that she would admit she had a type, but she did and he really wasn't the poster boy. She had all those thoughts in a nano-second while trying to reach for her pole. Her hands felt spastic as she tried to wrestle the pole from Renny. "I've got it," she assured him. She reeled in her own trout, not quite as long as Renny's but plumper.

She had stripped down to her tank top and capris. Renny had shucked his jacket and was down to a white t-shirt and jeans. She sat there watching the chipmunks as they scampered around on the deck begging for food. She had opened a package of sunflower seeds and set them on the deck next to her chair while she checked the bait on her line. When she had cast out again, she reached for a few seeds and instead her fingers started to close around something furry. She and the chipmunk both jumped and Bellamy let out a little shriek of surprise. The chipmunk scampered away. He had been stealing sunflower seeds from her package. "Hey," she said to his retreating tail "Didn't you see the sign? We aren't supposed to feed you. You will forget how to forage for yourself." Then her politically incorrect voice slipped out. "Could you tell that to some of our humans? They seem to have forgotten. They are so used to the government giving them free food and money they don't want to work for it."

Renny laughed out loud at that.

"Sorry. I didn't mean to go all political on you." The chipmunk slowly approached Bellamy again. It kept staring at her as she picked up the bag. She sat it in her lap, although now that it had chipmunk spit on it. She wasn't going to eat any more seeds. The chipmunk jumped up on her lap unabashed started stashing the seeds in his cheek. Laughing she watched the little guy. It wasn't every day she got to have a chipmunk in her lap and she was enjoying seeing one up that close. Satisfied with his good fortune of seeds he hopped down and scurried off but evidently not before he spread the word to his little buddies. When Bellamy turned to see where he went there were about twenty of the chipmunks scurrying here and there on the deck. "We've been invaded." She scattered the rest of the seeds on the deck behind their chairs.

After they finished their lunch, Renny limited out. Bellamy had caught more than enough fish to satisfy her. They looked at each other knowingly. It was time to leave. She could see a nice pink coloring on her skin. By the time they got back to her house that pink would probably be as red as Renny's truck.

She was right. She was bright red when they got to her house. Renny on the other hand had just turned a deeper shade of tan.

She immediately cleaned their bounty at the kitchen sink putting the guts in a separate garbage bag to take out of the house. That would start stinking in very short time. And what stank to her Jax would find irresistible. Renny grabbed the bag without saying a word and took it out to the large garbage can by her storage shed.

It was as though there had been a conversation between the two of them without words that dictated their evening. Maybe their careers caused them work like a team. Without an invitation or suggestion he went out, found her charcoal and started a fire in her grill. It was as though they had done this together many times before.

She took a couple of potatoes out of her crisper to bake and a bag of coleslaw. She was great about buying vegetables with the intent of eating healthier then ended up throwing said vegetables away with her good intentions. She even had a couple of ears of corn she had bought at a fruit stand one morning on her way home from work. Jax followed her around the kitchen waiting for something to be dropped. Bellamy finally got him a treat. He sat pretty for it and as directed took it gently from her fingers.

She filled a couple of glasses with iced tea and carried them out to the backyard. Renny had taken a chair in the shade filled yard and was smoking a cigarette. He looked up over his shoulder when he heard the slap of the screen door. When her eyes met his she could see sadness had returned to his eyes. It may have been from all of the bright sun of the day but his eyes were tinged with red. She handed him a glass and sat down in a metal chair across the small garden table from him. For a few moments there were no words. She felt the joy of the day had been replaced by the responsibilities of his life at the moment.

He sighed as he took a drink of the tea. The cold, bitterness of the tea froze the lump growing in his throat. "I should be feeling the loss of Pedro and I am but I still have to keep my eye on the season. There is so much I need to do before harvest that Pedro would have taken care of for me. He would have started recruiting people for harvest. He seemed to find the best people. His crews were always trusted employees who knew what they were doing. I have no idea how he contacted them." He stopped then and took another drink, his thoughts tripping over each other in his head a jumbled list of things to do.

"Maybe he used the unemployment office. Is that even around anymore or is everything on line now?" he asked rhetorically. "Or maybe he had a list of people he recruited from other jobs he had done. I never asked. I never had to. He would just come in and tell me he had a crew hired and hand me a bunch of names scrawled on a piece of notebook paper. A week later he would come in with the employment paperwork on the crew. I never had to question that the papers were filled out right. Pedro always had everything completed with copies of needed documentation attached. I would just give it a cursory going over and turn it over to our business office to take care of from there."

"The paperwork was all filled out?" From what little interactions she had had with Pedro something didn't quite fit.

"Yeah, absolutely, he had great handwriting. I was kind of jealous. He block printed everything. My reports at work look like a teenager filled them out. I scrawl, I misspell words. Not Pedro." His voice trailed off. He scratched his chin thoughtfully. He stood up, stretched and went over to check the coals. They were getting close to being ready but he wanted to give them a little more time. "I'm a real idiot. What an astute businessman

I am that I didn't catch that." He berated himself, returning to his chair. "He couldn't have filled out those forms. He could barely speak the language, let alone complete that paperwork. Who was doing it?" He asked, again the question was more for his own benefit than for Bellamy's.

She shrugged her shoulders. "If it were me, I'd have a friend or maybe girlfriend filling them out for me. Was there someone he had working with him here that may have been doing it?"

Renny shook his head. "Not that I know of, once the hops were up and trained he was the only one working most of the time. There really isn't a lot that has to be done that one person can't handle even with the large amount of acreage I have. He had to make sure the water was working. Spray occasionally. But it was something the two of us could manage."

She went back in to get the fish, Renny behind her and Jax following the two of them.

Renny made himself at home in her kitchen, looking through the herbs and spices collecting dust in spice rack resting on the back of her stove. He found what he was looking for and took some of the lemon slices she had left after garnishing their tea. He went out to put the fish on the grill.

She made the dressing for the coleslaw and dumped the contents of the plastic bag in a large bowl. She put it in the refrigerator to cool and went about setting the table. She couldn't remember the last time she had set the table. She never set if for herself. She always ate in front of the TV or standing next to the sink. It wasn't so much laziness as it was the aloneness of her existence.

Her parents had passed away years ago. Being an only child she didn't have any other immediate family. Occasionally she saw one of her cousins, usually in a grocery store or a funeral but that was about it. There was no one she was close to that she invited to dinner. She had a small circle of friends and when they were able to get together it was at a restaurant not one another's homes. She and Roy Morse had coffee together if he was at the café they haunted. There were also a couple of retired cops she had coffee with on occasion but that was about the extent of her social life. Bellamy had long since passed the partying age and even when she was that age she wasn't on the "A" list of invitees to police or fire clique get-togethers. Those gatherings were closed to single people and specifically dispatchers and call takers. They were considered badge bunnies and were shunned by the badge bunnies that had already snared their cop or firefighter prey. If the dispatcher or call taker was already dating or married to a cop or firefighter when they started at 911 then they moved up to the invited group. It was a secret society she didn't miss being included in.

She started to light a lone candle on the table but had to wipe the dust off of the rim first. It seemed to be a sad statement of her life. She chuckled to herself. Funny, she thought, she didn't realize how isolated she had become until she had someone having dinner with her. As odd as it felt having dinner with Renny it also felt as comfortable as wearing her winter sweat pants when it was cold outside.

She had a couple of wine glasses out on the counter. She waited until Renny came back in the house with the grilled fish before she decided what to put in them. "Would you like wine with dinner?"

He made a face of indecision "Sure, if you are having some."

She opened a bottle of Airport Ranches "The Mark" Reisling. She had bought it solely because of the label. It had a fingerprint on the label with the name "The Mark" on it. Since she worked with cops it seemed appropriate and it had a very high rating on wine blogs. That was always a safe choice if you had no clue what you were doing. She hated warm wine. She knew it probably was supposed to be served at room temperature but tonight it was being served cold. The only reason she had any wine at all was in case someone stopped by. She chuckled at what a joke that was. No one except Lauren ever stopped by. Bellamy still kept a red, white and rose in her refrigerator.

She carried the glasses and bottle to the table and made a few more trips for the rest of the dinner. "Please," she said inviting him to take a seat. "I think we have everything."

She lifted her glass in a toast to the sky. Her eyes caught and held his gaze, "Thank you Lord for this day and spending it with a very special person and for the food you have blessed us with."

Renny smiled then "Amen."

When they had finished eating Bellamy felt as though she had just enjoyed a five star meal. She hadn't enjoyed a meal like this in what seemed like…ever. Renny made her laugh. The two of them kept swapping war stories. It was just a natural instinct to recount the incredulous things that had happened to them at work over the years. He would recount a story, which would remind Bellamy of a story, which would remind Renny of one, and on and on it went until the bottle of wine was empty and Bellamy was feeling just a bit tipsy. Carefully she cleared the table and apologized for not having any dessert.

Renny laughed. "This whole day has been dessert." He told her, his blue eyes fixed on hers as he stood next to her placing the empty wine glasses on the counter. Renny's calloused fingers brushed her arm as he gently turned her to face him. His other hand brushed the hair out of her sunburned face that seemed to glow in the dim light of the solitary candle. Taking her face gently in his hands he lifted her lips to his and breathlessly touched them, first lightly then more intently when he felt her responding. He hadn't meant to kiss her. He really hadn't. But he had been thinking about it from the moment she confronted him about his tone on the radio. It had been the fire in her eyes that had challenged him and he had been excited by her boldness especially knowing they were going to be spending the day together in close proximity. That whole incident could have turned the day into a shit storm but instead it had been one of the best days he had spent with a woman in a very long time.

"Thank you," his voice throaty when he had slowly pulled away "For everything today."

"You too," she stammered, "I mean, thank you too. It was wonderful."

"I need to go," He said. "Uh, yeah, I need to go," he repeated as if trying to convince himself that he needed to go. The kiss was embarking on what could be a very dangerous adventure for them.

She sensed there was something else he was going to say but he didn't. "Good night," he said. Renny turned and she watched him as he slowly walked out the back door.

"Good night," she responded as an afterthought. She wasn't sure if he had even heard her.

He had heard her but he knew if he had turned around he wouldn't go. He couldn't do that. He knew himself well enough that he had a propensity to just have superficial encounters with ladies. There was something about Bellamy that stopped him. Workplace gossip traveled fast and he didn't want her to be the topic of speculation by his crew or the rest of the department where that was concerned. His brief dating habits had already gained him the nickname of "hound dog" because he liked the chase. He loved the chase but once he caught his prey he immediately dropped it. Just like the ladies. He had always laughed it off but he didn't want Bellamy to be one of his "birds".

After Melanie had passed away it took him a couple of years before he came out of the shadow of her death. When he did, he still felt broken. He wanted that physical connection and that was what he looked for. He didn't care what kind of personality his "prey" had. He never stayed around long enough to experience their personality. He wasn't proud of his reputation since Melanie had passed away and he didn't brag about his conquests but firefighters tended to associate only with other firefighters so the social pool remained small. The ladies he met were usually introduced to him by a firefighter's wife or girlfriend who felt sorry for the sad widower and felt the need to tell him they had "Just the right gal" for him. None of those gals were the right one but they were a distraction from the loneliness he fought each time he walked through the door of his house.

Tonight that loneliness gripped his chest. The salty sweet of her lips lingered on his. He savored it. *What was I thinking kissing Bellamy?* He should have shook her hand or given her a hug or something but kissing her? He shut his eyes and berated himself for being such a dope.

Bellamy stood silently in her kitchen until she heard the sound of Renny's truck fade as he drove away. Her heart was still thundering in her chest. She took Jax out for one last potty break for the night. Her legs were weak. Wow! She thought as she stared up at the night sky and wondered what on earth had just happened. She replayed the kiss over and over again in her head. It was her heart that fluttered, not her head. She felt her face burn even more than it did with the sunburn. Maybe it was just a consolation kiss for a day well spent. Maybe he just wanted to see what it was like to kiss her. Maybe it was new bragging rights to take back to his station like the amount of fish he had caught. Or maybe he kind of liked her.

She could still feel his lips against hers. It was a very pleasant kiss. It set off a flurry of butterflies in her stomach. She remembered the caress of his hand as it stroked her face. It was unexpected but very nice. She had to admit she was just a little infatuated with him. She jumped when Jax let out a low growl. He had crawled unnoticed under her chair and pushed through her feet. He worked his way into a guard stance in front of her. He was staring at her shed at the back of the yard. She reached out to touch the back of his neck and could feel his hackles. Again he growled, low and menacing. She slowly stood up with Jax still between her legs.

She knew Jax and how he reacted to threats. She could tell the difference between his response to a skunk or coyote. It wasn't either one of those. This was his reaction to a person encroaching on his territory and threatening his human. "Guard. Guard," Bellamy whispered to him. His ears, like radar antennas, were pricked and twisting slightly as if to get a better idea of where the predator was. "Here," she commanded softly. Jax came out from between her legs and turned with Bellamy close to her side, his back to the threat. He walked by her side as she went in the house. Once in the house, Jax sat staring at the door, until Bellamy had locked it and his doggy door. He sniffed at the door jamb, checking for whatever he had detected.

Bellamy went in to the kitchen and got Jax a treat. "Treat," she offered. Jax took the bite from her hand as she praised him for being such a good dog. She took her phone off the counter and activated her security cameras and the perimeter fence. The electronic fence was mostly to deter Jax from straying from the yard but it could also be set to detect anything over five pounds that came into her yard. She wasn't a paranoid scaredy cat but she was a single woman living in the country. There were no street lights. The nearest lights were a quarter of a mile away at Renny's equipment shop, so it was dark at night, very dark. Bear, cougar, coyotes and bobcats had been known to wander into the ranches. And the canal bank that ran behind her house was a popular locale for kids to make out or party. It was also a perfect haunt for thieves. It was a rather desolate location and easy pickin's for burglars.

Renny's shop was a good target for thieves. Large security lights weren't a deterrent if a thief wanted to steal something. Bellamy was sure the shop was alarmed but even then it didn't protect it from being burglarized. By the time law enforcement could get there chances were pretty good that the burglar would be long gone.

The road that led to the shop and past Bellamy's house was a dead end of sorts. It ended in the parking lot of the shop. However, the road that snaked through the hop yard along the Roza Canal was easy to gain access to. A criminal could traverse the entire county along that dirt road. There were hundreds of places they could exit along the canal bank. It ran from the dam up near Kittitas County to Benton County providing irrigation to farms and ranches making a perfect getaway for bad guys. It was a great place to dump stolen cars and dead bodies.

Bellamy went around the house checking to make sure the windows were locked and pulling the drapes. It was just a prudent caution, like the loaded 12 gauge shotgun behind her bedroom door and the .9mm handgun in her nightstand.

She showered and got ready for bed. She was exhausted. Renny's kiss lingered on her lips and in her head. She was obsessing over the kiss and its meaning. What was his intent? Did he like her? Nah. He was just being nice. He didn't mean anything by it. She warned herself not to read too much into it. It was just a friendly good night gesture.

She tossed and turned, the sheets twisting around her. She could hear Jax. He was pacing the perimeter of the house. His nails clicked across the tile floor in the kitchen. They transitions to the hardwood floor in the dining room and living room. He came down the hallway. She heard him pause at the spare bedroom then continue on down the hall towards the bathroom. He lingered there for a moment before coming in to Bellamy's bedroom. Jax came up to Bellamy and sighed, as if to say all was well and it was safe for her to go to sleep. She reached out and stroked his neck and ears. She told him he was a "good boy" and he could lie down now and go to sleep. Jax stood on his bed for a moment, decided he wasn't close enough to Bellamy and jumped up to snuggle against her. Bellamy draped an arm across him and finally fell asleep.

Chapter 6

Bellamy awoke late Sunday morning. The house felt heavy. It often did in the summer heat with the humidity from the irrigation in the hop yard. As she stretched to get out of bed her skin was tight and hot. Her sunburn really did burn. Waiting for her coffee to brew, she let Jax outside. She ran through a grocery list for the coming week. She added items to the note page of her phone. If she didn't, by the time she backed out of her driveway she would have forgotten half of the items she needed.

Sunday was her day to finish up any last minute details for the upcoming week. She needed to get groceries and pick up her mail, get gas, make sure her uniforms were laid out. She had to water the lawn and her garden, pull a weed or two and fill up the bird feeder and bird bath. In a nutshell that was her life.

On the way out of the grocery store she picked up a Sunday paper. Next to it was the Spanish paper. She bought one of those too, not that she could read it, but maybe she could get some kind of idea of what Pedro had been looking for. Their intention of getting one of those papers and going through it had been lost to the relaxing day she and Renny had shared.

As she started down the dirt road to her house, she was met by a County Sheriff's patrol vehicle. She raised her hand in a friendly country wave and was met by a loud blast of a siren and dust billowing up as the 4X4 came to an abrupt stop as her car started to pass him. She stopped then too and lowered her window when the dust had settled. "Hey, Roy," she greeted once she recognized the face behind the sunglasses. He and Bellamy had known each other for years, shared a cup of coffee now and then and even a lunch at the local cop eatery in town.

"Bellamy, what are you doing out here?"

"I live out here. The only house on the road, Roy," she said. She knew darned good and well he knew who lived in that house. He would have checked the location in his MDT if he was out here looking for someone or something work related. She doubted he had any interest of how the hop crop was growing. She could tell by his expression he had been caught. "What's going on?"

"Can we pull over and talk about it?" he asked, although it wasn't really a suggestion.

"Come up to the house, Roy, I'll get you some tea or something cold to drink."

"Okay."

She pulled away and drove the short distance to her driveway. She took the grocery bags and her purse and started towards the house, as Roy pulled in behind her car. He was about to get out of his 4X4 when Jax came out of the house at a dead run barking. "Knock it off Jax. Friend." He stopped barking immediately, his rear end in a wiggle. "It's okay Roy," she reassured the lanky deputy.

Roy got out of his rig and started toward Bellamy. Jax sidled up to the deputy, sniffing his leg. Roy offered his hand for Jax to smell. Jax still wasn't quite sure if his human was telling him the truth about this guy and backed away from him with his hackles up. Jax followed them up to the back door and stood between them waiting while Bellamy unlocked it.

Inside she put her grocery bags on the counter, got Jax a treat, washed her hands then asked Roy, who was still standing by the back door what he would like to drink. "Whatever you are having," he responded.

"Make yourself at home, please." She gestured for him to pick where he would feel most comfortable sitting.

As she got a couple of glasses, filled them with ice and tea, Roy took a seat at the table facing her. "Do you take anything in your tea?" She took the glasses to the table. He shook his head and silently mouthed no.

She took a seat across from him. His dark brown eyes, regarded her coolly. "What's going on?" She was suddenly nervous, like he had caught her stealing candy from a store.

"I just need to ask you a few questions," he said. Roy took a notebook out of his chest pocket and opened it to an empty page and scribbled something at the top of the page.

She narrowed her eyes at him. "Okay," she responded cautiously. She could feel her arms tensing and her hands starting to shake. "If you will tell me what this is all about," she continued. She hadn't done anything wrong but her dispatcher senses told her Roy thought she had.

He laid his pen down on the table and took a drink of his ice tea. "The burglary down the road, at Mr. LaRue's shop?"

"What?" She blurted incredulously. "When?"

"Sometime yesterday or overnight, I'm just hoping maybe you saw something, possibly an unfamiliar car or person in the area.'"

Bellamy shook her head slowly, trying to think if she had heard anything. "I don't think so. I went fishing yesterday, so I was gone all day. I didn't get home until early evening. I was home all night and just went out a couple of hours ago to get groceries."

"Can anyone verify that?" Roy asked, his voice a cop tone that Bellamy hated. It was accusatory and it irritated her. She furrowed her brow and pulled her head back defensively.

"Why would you even ask me that? Why would I have to 'verify' my whereabouts?" She could feel her face transforming into her serious, pissed off expression that was not at all pleasant. 'Yeah, I can. Renny, Mr. LaRue and I went up to Clear Lake. We didn't get back until 4:30 or 5. We bar-b-qued some of the fish we caught, had dinner, sat around swapping war stories and he-" Bellamy paused for a split second before she added, "He left around one."

Roy looked at her, this time like the guy she had coffee with, not the cop in that stupid polyester uniform that had to be hotter than hell. "So…you and Mr. LaRue…" A bit of a sneer turned up the edges of his lips.

"No. Not like that." Her voice was harsh, "That was the most time we have ever spent together, on or off duty." *Shut up Bellamy*, she yelled in her head. Don't even qualify that. It was too late. That dang cat had scampered out of the proverbial bag and was doing a happy dance in her mind. She got up from the table then went to the freezer, taking two storage bags out. She walked back to the table and slammed the bags of frozen fish on the table. "Trout. Sunburn. Proof enough?"

She was angry and there was no doubt in Roy's mind that she was telling the truth. If a woman got that angry being questioned like this, generally they were telling the truth. He learned this from years of experience asking hard questions of questionable women. He nodded.

She took the fish and tossed them back in the freezer. She came back to the table but did not sit down,

"Nothing after he left?" Roy was not at all intimidated by her posture.

"No." She answered quickly. Roy saw her look up and to the side like she was remembering something. "Wait," she said, "I took Jax out to go potty. He came back and started growling and guarding me like someone was out there. We came back inside. I locked up, turned the alarm and security cameras on and went to bed."

"You have security cameras?" Roy asked. That got his attention. "Do any of them point at the road?"

"Yeah, they do. Do you know how to use the app? I know you can send the video to another person but, I mean, I can pull up the app but I've never sent anything before." She took her phone out of her purse on the table, tapped in her security code and opened the app. She handed her phone to Roy. He put on a pair of reading glasses and held the phone at arms length. He worked for a few minutes with the keyboard on her phone. After a short while she heard the phone in his chest pocket ding that he had received an email. Still holding Bellamy's phone he pulled the Velcro pocket flap open and took his phone out of his pocket. Now he held his phone at arms length and studied the screen.

"Got it" He fiddled with her phone a little longer then handed it back to her. "Thanks. That might really help." He stood up from the table, returning his phone to his pocket and his notebook to the other.

"I hope so."

"Thanks for the tea." He walked towards the door.

"You are welcome." She told him then asked to his back, "Is Renny ok?"

'Yeah," Roy said as he walked out the door leaving it ajar. Jax followed behind Roy. He was going to make sure this guy left. He made his human angry.

For some reason she didn't believe him. In a few minutes she heard Roy's SUV idling in her driveway. She assumed he was typing up the rest of his report while he sat in the shade of the big Sycamore tree on that side of her house. When she heard him leave she started putting her groceries away. Her mind was running rampant. Her thoughts were like a hamster caught on a wheel that she couldn't stop or couldn't get off. She found herself slamming cupboard doors when she wasn't able to stop her thoughts from running from one topic to another even for a moment. "What did they do to you?" a voice asked loudly.

Bellamy jumped and shrieked. Jax started barking excitedly.

"You scared the crap out of me!"

"I can see that. Sorry. Can I come in?" Renny asked through the door still standing open.

"Yeah, come on in."

He wrestled his muck boots off, tossed them aside then entered her house in his stocking feet.

Her heart did a little dance in her chest. She would have to have her doctor check her heart. That wasn't normal. It might be a medical problem. "Would you like something to drink?" She seemed to be asking that question a lot.

"Do you have some water?" He asked.

Really? He must be kidding. "I have sweet, pure well water, bottled water, on the rocks, or neat? Now if you want sparkling water, I am all out. I am always out. I hate sparkling anything, except wine. Now that is a different story. Especially Moscato. Sparkling Moscato is the exception. Oh my goodness! Have you ever had sparkling Moscato?" She was babbling. *For heaven's sake Bellamy what is wrong with you?*

"Well water on the rocks." Renny cut in. "And yes, I've had sparkling Moscato. It was Melanie's favorite."

"I just always heard about people ordering pink champagne cocktails. I thought it sounded so sophisticated. That's what the sparkling Moscato reminded me of. And I didn't know Melanie, but I can tell she had good taste." She filled a tall glass with ice and tap water. The well her father had drilled so many years ago had been deeper than needed to reach water. He had drilled passed the shallow water table that tasted like sulfur and turned your clothing yellow. He had drilled down until he hit an aquifer that ran through the deep valley floor. That water was entirely different. It was water that satisfied your thirst but still made you want more. It was so refreshing that most of the time Bellamy drank only that when she was home.

Bellamy suggested they go in the living room but Renny sat down at the kitchen table. "I'm filthy. I was out checking the irrigation to make sure the timers were working. I wanted to stop by and make sure you were okay. I saw that Roy had stopped in to talk to you."

"And see if I knew anything about your burglary." Bellamy told him.

"Yeah," Ren knew Roy from working different fires together. Roy was also a volunteer firefighter with Cowiche Fire. It wasn't unusual in this rural area that there were several firefighters who volunteered as reserve police officers and law enforcement officers who volunteered as firefighters in the district they lived. Roy was one of them.

"He was checking my alibi!"

"Mine too. You have to admit that it is a little too coincidental to have an arson fire, dead body and now a burglary." Renny took a long drink of water, almost emptying his glass.

"Yeah, I guess so. But still." It was a pretty lame response but she couldn't think of anything else. "What did they take?" Bellamy asked, her head thinking tools, maybe a generator, something small that was easy to take and sell.

"Nothing that I could tell. They just rummaged through the drawers in my office.

Papers were scattered around like they might have been looking for something specific. What I can't imagine though."

"What kind of papers do you keep in your office?"

"Business related papers." He didn't mean to sound condescending or sarcastic but he saw Bellamy bristle. "I didn't mean it to come out that way. Receipts, contracts, tax information, bills, employee records. Just standard stuff," He explained. "I'll have to sit down and go through everything to see if I can figure out what they may have been looking for. But all the important business papers, like the originals are at the main office I share with Jon. What I keep at the shop are just new receipts or invoices I haven't taken in for our secretary to take care of. I always keep a copy of employee records there too. Nothing earth shattering." He sighed heavily mentally exhausted.

They were silent for a moment, when Bellamy remembered the paper. "Hey, I bought one of those Spanish papers. Do you think this is the one Pedro had?" She asked and slid the newspaper in front of him.

"Could be. I don't know. The paper was open. I didn't see the front page." He looked weary. His shoulders were hunched and his hands were cupped around his glass like it was full of alcohol instead of water and he was hoping it would take the weight off of his back.

"Have you eaten today?" When she couldn't figure out what to say, food was always her answer. She could see he was trying to remember. He shook his head.

"How about you go relax on the couch or recliner and let me fix you something?"

"No. I am filthy. I have mud all over me and I'm sweaty." He declined, pulling out his t-shirt that was plastered to his chest. He sniffed it. "Ehh, no."

"Go home and get cleaned up and I'll fix something. Or if you are too tired, go take a shower here. I have some men's sport shorts and a few t-shirts that will probably fit you."

Renny looked at her oddly trying to picture wearing her clothing. Thankfully her stature was considerably different than his. She rolled her eyes completely misunderstanding his expression as he studied her figure. "Really, I won't peek. Come on."

He was too tired to argue the point that this probably wasn't a good idea. Like Jax he got up and followed her obediently down the hall. She went into her bedroom while Renny stood respectfully at the door. He looked around her room. The walls were a shade of gray on the verge of blue. Her bed was a chipped white painted wrought iron headboard that looked original to early the last century. It had a patchwork quilt as a bedspread that also looked old and loved. Her walls were cluttered with framed art that looked like it might have been from the 30's or 40's. They appeared to be prints from one specific artist. They all shared the same blued hued ethereal color scheme and style.

Bellamy stood up as he was studying the prints on her wall. "I like them because they all look like a dream." She handed him a pair of shorts and an extra large sized soft t-shirt. He held it up and saw the Seattle Skyline with a fire logo. "My workout clothes. I know they are huge. Don't judge me. They are just more comfortable than tight leggings and a cute little sports bra."

He wasn't judging her but he thought he'd like to see her in leggings and a cute little sports bra. He thought she would look rather fetching. "*Fetching?*" He thought to himself, "*Really? Am I becoming my father? I can't come up with a better word? Like hot? Really hot! Not appropriate.*" He cautioned himself.

She pointed towards the bathroom. "There's a lock on the door, you know if you feel the need to lock it." She was teasing him. He shook his head at her and traipsed into the spacious pale green room.

She left him to his own devises and went to the kitchen. Even though the house was cool, outside the temperature had crept into the 90's. It was just too hot to have anything heavy to eat. Her stomach growled. She was starving. She had forgotten to eat too. Not something she often did. She enjoyed food. It was comforting. That's what she needed. She decided on the quickest thing she could think of to fix. She settled on Kielbasa with barbeque sauce, macaroni and cheese and some cornbread. It wasn't exactly summer fare and it was 'heavy' but it just sounded good and it was fast.

Renny emerged from the bathroom as she was putting the cornbread muffins in the oven. She turned to regard him wearing her workout clothes. There was no doubt he looked better in them than she ever did. The t-shirt was snug against his well defined pecs.

And the shorts although they came to just above his knees showed a nice set of legs. She caught herself staring at his physique. "Feel better?" She asked. *I'm sure you do feel good,"* she thought *"You look like you would feel lovely to touch.* Internally she shook her head, admonishing herself for even thinking that. She barely knew this man and she was thinking very intimate thoughts of how his body would feel to caress. She turned back to finish making the macaroni and cheese. She put the mixture in a casserole dish, added some bread crumbs to the top and slid it in to the oven with the muffins. She stirred the Kielbasa even though it didn't need it and turned back to see him sit down in a kitchen chair.

"Yes, thank you. It smells really good in here."

"Nothing fancy."

"Hey, a home cooked meal? I really try to cook but I have no incentive to do it. It's just easier to make a sandwich or something."

"I know the feeling. I always thought it would be a cool idea to get the single people we work with together and create a traveling dinner party. You know, one week you might be in charge of dessert for however many people are in the group. I might be in charge of making the main dish. Someone else a side dish and so on. And we have it at your house one time, someone else's another time. Just a fun fellowship. I guess today it would be called networking. But a way to have a home cooked meal at your house or someone else's. Even if we only did it once a month it would still be something to look forward to doing."

She had her back to Renny, turning slightly to check his expression.

She couldn't read his face. She was usually pretty good at knowing what a person was thinking but his poker face revealed nothing. He was smiling now as he looked at her backside. It was well rounded and snug against her capris. He tried to convince himself he was just appreciating the female anatomy in front of him. It wasn't working. He had to admit it was more desire than appreciations. *Man, this is not a good situation to get into.* Were she anyone other than a woman he worked with he would not hesitate to initiate an intimate relationship with Bellamy and see where it could go. But if for some reason the relationship didn't work out it could make working with her, even if they were separated by her on one side of the radio and him on the other side it could really be dicey. It already was. He didn't want to exacerbate it.

Coming back to his senses he tried to focus on what she had been saying. "Fellowship? Fellowship? Interesting word choice but I get the idea. It would be nice to hang out with other single people and have a meal together."

"Fellowship," she laughed as she checked the casserole in the oven. Her past was sneaking into her present. "Yeah, it was a church thing my parents did when they were alive. They had a group of friends they had known for years and maybe once a month or so they would do that. They would have dinner together then plan the next time they would get together. I always thought it was kind of cool. Not really a church function just a group of people function, kind of like the shift 'feeds'."

Usually on a Sunday, each fire station in the city would decided on a meal, go to a grocery store, get their groceries and hope they didn't get a call while they were there. Once they got back to the station they would start preparing a communal dinner. They would divide the cost of the meal per firefighter and ante up whoever paid for the groceries at the store. When the Comm. Center had been located in the basement of Station One, the firefighters would always include the dispatchers and call takers in the feed. They had always included them. It made Bellamy feel like one of the "guys'.

Once the Comm. Center was moved into a new building with the police dispatchers, that comradery was no longer part of her life. Her crew sometimes got together if they were working a Sunday day shift and put a meal together but other than that they brought or bought their own food. Having their own "feeds" was nice but the city had annexed more property into the city extending the boundary and ramping up their work load. Most times their meal was cold before they had a chance to enjoy it. Depending on the day each one of them would run to the kitchen, microwave their plate of food and run back to their desk in hopes they might get a few bites of warm food before they got busy again. The food would go cold and they would go through the microwaving over and over again. Their union contract with the city assured them that each employee would get two 40 minute meal periods and an hour of workout time each twelve hour shift. They laughed and laughed and laughed. The contract might guarantee those breaks but Bellamy could count on her hands how many times that she had even got one 40 minute break away from the radio in all the years she had worked there. So Bellamy and Morgan took those eighty minutes in smoke breaks that they tried to sneak in once an hour. Running back in to the office felt like it should be considered workout time. It was a fair trade. The call takers did the same thing.

"Bellamy? Hello?" Renny asked from right behind her. She had gotten lost in her thoughts and totally zoned out. She jumped.

"Gosh! You startled me!" She clutched her chest. It must be a heart problem. It couldn't be the fact that he was standing within inches of her. She could smell the scent of her bath soap on his skin. His chest was at eye level. His pectoral muscles were so big. His biceps were firm and tanned. His abdomen was lean and chiseled against the shirt she had loaned him. Her heart was flopping around inside her chest like the trout she had landed on the deck yesterday. Her breath caught in her throat and she was having trouble breathing. She tried to control her breathing but it wasn't happening. She couldn't catch her breath. She really was going to have to see her doctor about this problem.

"Are you okay?" Renny could see her breathing had changed. It was shallow and rapid, like she was having a panic attack. She tried to tell him she was alright but she would feel much better if he would step back a few inches. Unfortunately for her he didn't. "Sit down." He took her wrist with one hand and the other reached around her waist guiding her to a chair. "*Not helping,*" she thought as she melted against his chest. She just wanted to stand there with his arm holding her against him but that was exactly the problem. It had been so long since she had been with a man that her senses were overloaded with pure physical joy. The synapses in her brain were shorting out. She was trembling. *Really Bellamy? Get a grip! This isn't the first man who has ever touched you! What the heck!* It didn't help.

Renny morphed from the guy having dinner with a friend to paramedic mode. He was firing questions at her in his "all business" tone. That tone just made the situation worse. She hated that tone. It made her feel like a little girl being sent on a time-out for being naughty. But she hadn't even begun to be naughty and she doubted he would send her for a time-out if she was naughty.

"Dinner," she said as she struggled to breathe. "Burning," Bellamy added.

Renny quickly turned off the oven and burner. He took the mac and cheese and muffins out of the oven and sat them on the top of the stove. He dropped the hot pads and going back to Bellamy.

He instantly resumed his medical assistance. "Slowly, in through the nose. Deep breath. Out through the mouth." He inhaled deeply and exhaled slowly demonstrating what he wanted her to do.

She tried to follow his instructions. Finally when she looked up into his eyes she started to relax. Her breathing slowed and her thundering heart resumed its normal pace. His deep blue eyes held her stare. "There ya go. You stay here, I'll get dinner on the table," he added as tried to stand up. His hands were hot as he gently pushed against her shoulders. She gave in and leaned back in the chair.

He found a pitcher of what appeared to be lemonade in the fridge. He filled a glass with ice from the ice machine in the fridge and poured a glass. He sat it on the table in front of her. She started to object but changed her mind. It might help. He would figure it out once he took a sip from his own glass. She had made hard lemonade with what was left of her whiskey. She took a drink and felt the cold, smooth lemonade slide down her throat. She was finally able to take a deep breath.

He put dinner on the table and waited for her to fill her plate. He watched as she took her first bite before he began to dish up his own plate. He took a drink of lemonade before he started to eat. "What, what is in this?" He asked trying to catch his breath after he had taken a long pull of the lemonade.

"Pendleton. I made hard lemonade. It just sounded refreshing. I don't drink very often but it just seemed like on a hot day like today it would be a nice addition."

"Very," he agreed.

About halfway through their meal he caught her gaze. "So what brought on your panic attack? I am pretty sure that is what it was." He asked her gently, not wanting to bring on another one.

She averted her eyes. She wasn't sure she wanted to be honest with him. But lying didn't seem like a great option either. It was a few moments and another gulp of lemonade before she admitted, "You." Her heart was drumming away in her chest.

Renny regarded her seriously. He was surprised, shocked. *"What now? How am I going to handle this?"* He hadn't thought it through. He had thought about it, a lot, but he hadn't made it to a conclusion. In his mind he hadn't let it go any further than it already had. He had fallen on his sword and like a gentleman stopped at the kiss. He had tried to convince himself it wasn't going to go any further. Now his heart was trying to jump out of his chest. He looked down at the shirt he was wearing because he was afraid she would see his heart pounding through the tight fabric.

When he didn't respond to her comment right away, Bellamy started babbling. "I know, I know. It's stupid. I've never done that before. I don't know what happened. I am so embarrassed. It seems I'm a little conflicted."

"Me too," he admitted. "We can, I don't know, take it slow. See what happens. Or we can forget I ever kissed you. But I don't see that happening so I'm at a loss. You have to know this isn't a good idea. Once the gossip gets to the brass, and you know it will, they could make life miserable for us. Or if we, ah, get more involved, serious, and you dump me or something, yeah, I don't even want to go there." Now Renny was word vomiting.

"So, you, um, you, like me too?" She asked. She felt like she was a teenager again in that uncertain time when she liked a boy but she wasn't sure he liked her and they were passing notes in math class to see if they liked each other. They were fumbling their way into a boyfriend/girlfriend status. This was uncharted territory for both of them. She hadn't been known for her longevity in relationships either and the idea of something beyond the friends with benefits status freaked her out. She wasn't good at that and tended to hurt the men she became involved with especially if they showed any interest in taking it into the realm of seriousness. She just disappeared. No warning. Like a ghost vanishing into a wall. She heard Renny responding to her question.

He shook his head, chuckling. "A little."

She smiled, her heart fluttering. He liked her. He really liked her too.

"You know, we kind of are the brass. I mean you are a B.C. I'm a supervisor. Not that that makes any difference. I'm just saying."

He chuckled his warm, reassuring chuckle.

When dinner was done and the dishes cleared, she put the leftovers in the fridge and the two of them sat down with the Spanish paper opened to where Renny thought Pedro's paper had been opened. It wasn't a big paper, as newspapers went. Because of the columns and boxes he surmised it was opened to the want ads. He made an educated guess as to what page and box Pedro had circled.

Bellamy sat watching him as he looked intently at the page. "Can I look?" He slid the paper over to her. "Can we look together?" She pushed the paper to the middle of the table and pulled her chair to the long side of the table. Renny scooted his chair close to hers. She thought it would be uncomfortable having him sit so near to her but it wasn't. The two of them sat studying the ads. "Do you see any phone numbers that look familiar to you?"

He cocked his head towards her. "I'd have to look at every contact in my phone. I wouldn't know my own brother's phone number if it wasn't in my phone. I don't know anyone's phone number anymore. Do you?"

"True," she conceded, laughing.

She looked at the ads, having the internet translate headings then common words in the categories. "Any idea if he was looking to buy a car or take a side job doing hauling for people? Maybe looking for a girlfriend or something? A goat?"

All Renny could do was shake his head. "A goat?" Renny asked laughing.

"I don't know. I'm not being prejudice. In the town I grew the kids always played with the hoof. I don't remember why. But I remember the adults butchered them for parties and stuff. The neighbors would get all freaked out. We get calls on that quite a bit." She said matter-of-factly. She turned the page and scanned down the page. That page appeared to be the personal ads. "What was Pedro's phone number?"

He pulled out his phone and looked it up. He read it off to her. She wrote it at the top of the page. She quickly scanned the ads for his phone number. Nothing. She flipped to the last page. Near the bottom of the page, she saw it. 'Renny, look." She circled an ad in red, using a pen she had inadvertently purloined from the Comm. Center.

There in bold type was Pedro's phone number. She copied the information to her phone and had the internet translate the ad. When it couldn't translate it she knew that they had a problem. Renny looked at her quizzically. "It says he has some burlap to sell on the spot, make an offer," she said. "That's as close as I can figure it says. Burlap?"

He sat considering the ad and what it meant. It didn't make any sense. "Is the ad saying on the spot meaning selling something right now? Or does it mean a location?"

"I don't know. We'd have to find someone who really speaks fluent Spanish to tell us. Especially if it was like a code or slang."

"The hop growers and buyers sometimes list some of their harvest in a virtual place we call 'the spot'. It is usually small amounts of specialty hops that we aren't contracted to grow but feel we can make money from. It also gives us an idea of what the independent brewers are looking for, a way to get an idea where the market is headed." He explained. "But we wouldn't be selling burlap. We would be selling hop bales in burlap, not just burlap by itself."

He paused for a moment then added, "It sure would be nice if we could get a hold of his phone records and see who called him."

"I somehow doubt the Sheriff's office is going to give up that information," she said sarcastically though not directed at him. She continued scanning the ads. She wasn't sure what she was expecting to find but none the less she thumbed back to the beginning of the want ads section. She had started down the middle column of the paper when her gaze stopped. A phone number jumped out at her. She turned the page and found the number she had written at the top of the page in red. She flipped back to the previous page and found it was Pedro's phone number again. "Look," she pointed out. He glanced at the number and then at her. She started translating the ad. It turned out to be a want ad for hiring upcoming hop harvest crews. That was a let down.

Bellamy closed the paper and swirled the ice in her empty glass. Renny's glass was also empty. "Would you like some more?" She asked as she stood up. "I think I'll have an iced coffee," she told him.

"That sounds good," he agreed.

She put the coffee she had brewed that morning over ice then turned to ask if he took anything in it. He shook his head. "Want to have it outside?" She suggested. He stood and followed her.

The sun had dropped behind the mountains to the west. The heat of the day was going down with it. The valley really was a pleasant place to be in the summer. As soon as the sun went down the temperature began to go down too and the humidity rise. A heady aroma of night jasmine, roses and hops floated on the cool moist air. She breathed deeply and sighed as she sat in her lawn chair. Renny took the chair next to her and his hand inadvertently brushed hers. She shivered at his touch but did not move her hand away. She couldn't remember if she had agreed to the take it slow or the stop now suggestion. At the moment she didn't care. In fact the speed up option sounded good to her. The weight of his hand on hers was strong and electrifying. It felt like a scene from a sci-fi movie where you could see the electricity streaking between them like little lightning sparks. Her breath was catching in her throat again. She was about to pull her hand from his when he slowly turned to face her and began to kiss her cheek. His lips were tender and warm against her cool skin. She fumbled to sit her glass of coffee on the table beside her. She responded in kind, her fingers stroking his face, tracing his jaw and ear. He shuddered.

His eyes closed to take in the full thrill of her touch. His mouth met her lips and a whispered moan formed in his throat. He wanted to enjoy every second of this kiss. It wasn't like the other kisses he had experienced since Melanie had passed. It wasn't like Melanie's kiss either. This was more than physical contact. There was an emotional component as well. This was consuming. It was reaching a depth of him he had forgotten existed. It was intoxicating. He wanted to linger in the softness of her lips.

A fight or flight response was battling inside Bellamy. She was terrified of this mysterious energy passing between them. She had felt the fluttering of infatuation before. This was not that feeling. Although it had been quite a while she also remembered the flush of lust. It wasn't that either. She wasn't sure what it was that was taking her breath away and making her light headed. She felt like she should push away from him but as his lips lingered and became a bit more urgent. She could feel herself surrendering her fight. She wanted to be closer to him to feel the weight of him against her but the lawn chairs set up a barrier between them.

Renny slowly pulled away from her, brushing her hair out of her face. Her light blond hair tumbled over her shoulders. "Would you give me a ride back to my truck?" He asked hoarsely.

Bellamy nodded her head. Words were lost at the moment. She didn't think she could form the word yes, let alone string together a sentence. The blood that fed that part of her brain was gone. She didn't know where it had gone but it was definitely not in her head. Awkwardly she got out of the lawn chair and went back into the house to get her keys. She flicked on the overhead light. It stung her eyes and brought her back to reality. She glanced at the clock on the range. It was late. It was way passed her bedtime for a morning shift. It was a short shift, only four hours, but still it came very early.

Silently she started out the back door. Shutting it behind her, it locked automatically. Renny was waiting, with his muddy muck boots and clothes draped over his arm. He smiled and followed her to her SUV. It was a bright red, almost the same shade as his truck. Barefooted he navigated the way across her gravel driveway and got in the passenger side. Jax followed. "Jax, here," Bellamy commanded. Jax rounded the car and jumped into the back seat of the car.

The two were silent on the short drive to his truck with the exception of Jax in the back seat, his head stuck through the seats between them, panting. Bellamy pulled up so Renny could get out and climb into the driver's side of his truck without having to walk in the gravel around her car or his truck. The two of them sat in the still illumination of the dashboard and the pale light coming from the light on a pole by his shop. *What should I say? Do I just say good night and lightly punch him in the arm like he was just a pal? Should I just say good night? Do I kiss his cheek, like he is a good little boy? Or should I...*

Renny answered all of her questions when he leaned across the console and gently tugged her by the hair at the nape of her neck to him. He kissed her hard and deep. She felt like a flounder flailing in a net trying to move her arms around the steering wheel to wrap them around his neck. When she did get her hands behind his neck she had just about wiggled her way across the console and onto his lap. She didn't but it wasn't for lack of trying. Whatever was going on she wanted more. She didn't want the stop or slow down option. She wanted every part of him.

He forced himself to stop kissing her, "I really need to go. I don't want to but I have to go."

"Yeah, you do," she told him breathlessly kissing him again cupping his face in her hands. A stubble of beard brushed against her palms. Even that sent shivers of excitement down her back. She liked his lips. She liked them a lot. She felt like a teenager making out on that ditch bank lit up in her headlights. There was a fleeting feeling of doing something that she wasn't supposed to be doing and the wonderful thrill that being just a little bad was really, really good.

She finally pulled away from him and straightened her shirt that had twisted in their good night embrace. She looked straight ahead in the line of her headlights. "Go" she told him sternly, a big grin on her face.

'I'm going," he replied jokingly. "I'm going."

"Wait," she said suddenly reaching for his arm. "On the canal bank. I thought I saw someone." Without waiting for him to respond she put her SUV in drive and hit the gas. Her car had a habit of rabbiting when she hit the gas peddle just right. Renny was jerked back in his seat, his car door still open. His hand still on the handle he pulled it shut. She shot up the bank, maneuvering like a back woods hillbilly up the embankment of about eight feet above the parking area of the shop.

"Shit!" Renny exclaimed. "Wha-- what are you doing?"

"Going after him." Her voice shaking from the hill climb she had just done. She thought she caught air at the top, jerking the steering wheel to the right. Her rear wheels came dangerously close to the edge of the canal bank. Her heart was pounding and she prayed her front wheels would land soundly on the road. Luckily for her the car did as she had hoped and she accelerated again along the top of the canal bank with a cloud of dust following her. Renny had a death grip on the "oh shit" bar above the passenger door.

Bellamy didn't see the figure any more. Whoever it was had probably disappeared into the hop field. She slammed the car in park and opened the back door. "Seek!" she ordered Jax. He ran to the front of the car, sniffed a few moments then took off at a dead run. About ten feet beyond her car he disappeared over the edge of the ditch bank into the dark abyss of hops. She stood by her open door listening for him. When she heard him begin to bark and then growl, it sounded as though he was about a hundred yards into the field. Then she heard a man yelling. Renny was out of the car now his bare feet sinking in a few inches of dust that held the heat of the day. "You want me to call him back or hold him for the sheriff's office?" Bellamy asked Renny.

"Call him off. You know how long it will take S.O. to get here," Renny said after he had thought about it for a second "I don't want Jax to get hurt."

"Release" Bellamy yelled! Within just a few seconds they heard a loud report of a gun shot. "Son of a bitch!" She screamed going cold. It never for an instant entered her mind that whoever was out there might have a gun. Fear that someone had injured Jax sent a freezing shock wave through her. "Jax!" Bellamy screamed.

Within a minute Jax came barreling up the bank of the canal. Bellamy fell to her knees and hugged him. She ran her hands over him, making sure he hadn't been hurt. He dropped something slobbery on her arm. She looked at it in the car lights. It looked like a denim pocket. She offered it to Renny. "Let's get back in the car" Renny urged.

Jax pranced circles around Bellamy proud of what he had done. She praised him exuberantly. He jumped into the back seat and sat panting after his sprint. She opened the console and took out a treat. Praising him again she gave him a large piece of turkey jerky. Reaching back into the console she took out a .38 revolver and handed it to Renny. Renny laid it in his lap and felt through his now dried mud caked pants for his cell phone. He called the sheriff's office and asked them to come out and look around. Bellamy drove a little further up the canal bank until she could find a place to safely turn her car around and drove back to the shop parking lot. She pulled up next to the shop door and put her car in park. Her head swiveled surveying her surroundings.

"We might be safer inside the shop than out here if whoever that was decides to use us for target practice," Renny suggested. Without hesitation she turned off the car, let Jax out and came around her car to where Renny was opening the door.

Once inside, Renny shut the door. The immense metal building reverberated with the rattle of metal on metal. He locked the door behind them and they stood in the huge metal shop. In the back of the building there was a dim florescent light that made the large farm vehicles look like an army of hulking monsters ready to attack. He took her hand and led her to the back of the building into a small office area that was sectioned off by a half wall. There were two desks and three office chairs. Renny offered her a chair. 'I am sorry to keep you here but I don't want to let you go back home if there is someone out there prowling around with a gun," he told her. She took the leather paddle holstered .38 he had been holding and tucked in into the back of her pants.

"I don't want to go home with someone wandering around out there again either," she told him.

"Again?" Renny asked.

"I don't know. Last night. I was outside with Jax and all of a sudden he started growling and guarding me. I wasn't sure what was out there but he had never done that before."

"Why didn't you tell me? Did you call YSO?"

"I forgot about it. And no I didn't call them. Come on, even if someone had been out there, by the time they got there, whoever it was would have been long gone or I'd be going to jail for shooting someone."

Renny cocked his head at her. He thought that was ballsy for a single woman living alone out in the boone-toolies. "Anyway, I just turned on the alarm and security cameras and went to bed with my personal bodyguard," she said scratching Jax behind the ears. "Hey, you know where I work, right? I'm a single woman, living in a rural area," was all she needed as explanation. She was quiet for a moment until her mind had changed track, "Renny, what is going on here?"

He rubbed his temples. "I don't know." He had no idea who or why someone was roaming around the property. He was also clueless as to where she learned to drive like that and why in the world she would chase after someone like a bounty hunter. It was exciting but also a frightening. He wondered what other talents she had that he didn't know about.

"This is bizarre. I can't imagine what someone would want in here or why they burned down the kiln or why someone would want to kill Pedro." He mulled as he walked back to Bellamy. He wrapped a protective arm around her waist and guided her back to her chair.

It was approximately fifteen minutes later when a Sheriff's car came slowly down the dirt road and blacked out as he pulled into the parking lot. They could hear the deputy's radio traffic from inside the shop. He pounded on the door like he was trying to wake the dead. *Subtle.* This guy was a major failure if he thought he was sneaking up on a bad guy. He unlocked the door and opened it to the deputy. Bellamy and Jax stood behind Renny's wide shoulders. "Are you Mr. LaRue," the deputy asked. Renny answered the affirmative. "Could you step outside please," the deputy asked although it was quite apparent it wasn't a friendly request but a demand. Renny and Bellamy stepped out of the shop onto the parking lot illuminated by vapor lights. Jax followed and sat next to Bellamy quietly. He began to take information from Renny rapidly writing in his notebook. Renny explained the situation to the deputy in as much detail as he could. "So you didn't actually see the person," the deputy asked, sounding a little exasperated to be called out here just to look for an unseen prowler. They both told him they hadn't.

Bellamy spoke up then "I saw movement on the canal bank. I knew it was a person because of the size but I couldn't give you any details, except for this." She handed the deputy the soggy denim pocket that Jax had retrieved. “He yelled, so I’m sure it was a man. And he probably has some pretty good bite marks on him somewhere, probably on his butt. Jax likes to go for the butt.”

The deputy gingerly held the piece of damp fabric between his fingers and his notebook.

“And who are you?” The deputy asked, nodding his head to Bellamy. She gave him her information and stood with her arms crossed. She explained she owned the only house on this road. “And the two of you were at your house before you came down here,” he questioned. They both nodded. He paused for a moment, “And you didn’t hear anyone pass by the house?” They looked at each other and both shook their heads. Jax shook his head at the same time as though he understood the question too. Bellamy figured he was just shaking off the buzzing of a mosquito near his ear.

“I’ll check around, just in case someone is still in the area,” the deputy assured them. Bellamy closed her eyes for a moment, lowered her head and shook it softly. She almost laughed at his effort. The suspect was long gone. They all knew it but she knew the deputy had to sound diligent in his job. Renny thanked him for coming out. As the deputy went out to his 4X4, Renny locked the shop then followed Bellamy to her car gingerly walking across the gravel. The deputy, who hadn’t noticed he was barefoot before rolled down his window and asked above the sound of his engine, “Where are your shoes?”

“Boots and they are in her car,” Renny offered holding up the mud caked boots for the deputy to inspect. He turned his attention to Bellamy. "I'll follow you home."

After closing the door behind Jax she climbed into her dust covered car and turned it around and drove the short distance to her house. Her head lights swept the side of her property as she pulled into her driveway. All appeared fine. She hadn't turned on her alarm when she took Renny back to his car. She hadn't even thought about it. She didn't think she would be gone more than a few minutes. The clock on her dash told her it had been much longer than a few minutes.

Renny's truck pulled in behind her. He got out of his truck, pulling on a pair of old athletic shoes. He opened Bellamy's car door. She thought better of putting her gun in the console. Instead she tucked it into her purse, climbed out and opened the door for Jax. He jumped out and nose to the ground checked the perimeter of her property for any interlopers. When he was satisfied that nothing had encroached on his territory he trotted up to Renny and Bellamy as they started in her back door. Jax wove through their legs and into the house, again, nose to the floor. He did his routine of checking every nook and cranny for anything that didn't belong. He returned to Bellamy's side as she put her keys on the counter. Her cell phone was next to the keys. Out of habit she hit the home key and a banner lit up. There was a phone call and voice mail from David, the fire dispatcher who had the remainder of the 12 hour day shift they shared the next day. Bellamy cringed. He had probably called to ask if she would cover his 8 hour shift that followed her four hour shift. She shook her head. "It's work," she grumbled. She was going to ignore it for now.

"Go ahead, take it," Renny urged.

Reluctantly Bellamy took her phone and pulled up the awaiting voice mail. Before even greeting Bellamy she heard him clear his throat. It was an involuntary habit David had before starting most of his sentences. The same way his voice dropped an octave before dispatching a call. "Hi Bellamy, if it is ok, I'll pick up your four hour shift in the morning. After looking at the trades, I need those four hours to get in my 40 hours this week. Let me know, ok. Just leave a message, I'm heading to bed."

Bellamy hit redial and left a message telling David the shift was all his. "Woohoo. I don't have to work tomorrow," she told Renny. "Oh, that's not nice of me. Isn't tomorrow your first shift?"

He shook his head, keeping his eyes down so she couldn't see the excitement in his eyes that he might get to spend more time with her. "I've taken a few shifts off and then I start vacation. I figured I was going to need the time to get all of this mess straightened out before harvest starts. Poor choice of words but I don't know what else to call it."

"I understand," Bellamy leaned against the kitchen counter. "Yeah, Tuesday is my last day shift before vacation. Yay! I need it." She told him, then switching tracks mid conversation she began, "You know, I have consumed more alcohol in the last couple of days than I have in the last year but I feel like I really could use a nightcap, as they used to say. Would you like one?" She offered Renny.

"Have any Pendleton left?" Renny asked. She did now. She had picked up a fifth at the grocery store. She had put the remainder of the other bottle in the lemonade, so she had needed to replace her stock.

"You want to put on some music? Just turn on the TV and click on music and choose your genre." Bellamy inclined her head toward the remote on the coffee table.

She poured a shot for each of them over ice and took their drinks into the living room. She had just set them on the coffee table when a George Strait song called "I Just Want to Dance with You" started playing in the back ground. She started to sit down but Renny stood and gathered her lightly against his chest, one hand resting against her lower back, the other cupping her hand in his. Her throat went dry and she felt a herd of butterflies break dancing in her belly. He slowly led her onto the wood floor in the center of the living room. She felt herself melting into his arms until he twirled her around as the song suggested. She giggled standing on her bare tip toes as he guided her where he wanted her. He was smiling, oh so handsomely at her as he swung her back against his chest.

She felt like a feather floating in his arms. If there was a magic dance partner, Bellamy was it. She seemed to anticipate his every move and complete each step as though they had danced together for years. It was an art that he and Melanie had never perfected, no matter how much they danced together. It had never really mattered to either of them and they had always enjoyed their time on the dance floor. This was different. Everything meshed. When the song ended and the music trailed off a Trace Adkins' song came on and the two of them sat down on the couch in unison. He took a sip of his drink savoring the cold refreshment. "I'm staying here tonight," he informed her.

There was no hesitation, no argument. She nodded her head and took a sip of her drink. She welcomed a man in the house tonight after someone had taken a pot shot at her dog and could still be hanging around in the maze of hops. She had never been afraid in this house. It was her sanctuary. She never felt the need to have a man protect her. She felt she was capable of protecting herself if she needed. She had taken enough self defense classes that she thought she could hold her own against an assailant if she had to. But there was something about having Renny here tonight that just felt right.

Renny kicked off his shoes and slid them under the table. "I'll sleep on the couch. I have no ulterior motives. Well, maybe a few," he teased, "but we'll save them for another time."

"Promise?"

"I promise Amie" he said, his voice throaty as he put a protective arm around her. Renny studied her eyes. He had never seen eyes like hers. They were a pale blue, ringed in a dark blue halo. He enjoyed looking into them. He enjoyed looking at her face. She looked more Swiss than French, even though her last name of Boisseau belied her linage.

She was fair, her hair the color of ripe wheat in the noon day sun. It fell loosely, silky and fine.

There was no doubt about his heritage Rene Pierre LaRue. He was only six foot. Not as tall as most of his coworkers. He had a good physique, he thought. Firefighters couldn't get away with gaining those extra pounds like the police officers sometimes did. If firefighters slowed down too much and couldn't pass their fitness test, they could be put on probation until they conformed to the benchmarks set for them. If they couldn't do it or refused to do it in the allotted time set for them they could be demoted or fired. Renny was getting too close to retirement and had finally achieved his career goal of Battalion Chief. He had worked too hard to screw that up now. He wasn't at retirement age set for most professions, but because he had been working in the fire service in one capacity or another since he was in high school, he could time out at any age.

"Renny? Where are you? I lost you."

"I got lost in your eyes," he recovered nicely.

Another slow country song started playing and he stood and offered his hand to he like a boy at his first dance at the local Grange.

Bellamy took his hand and stood. He gently drew her against his chest, holding her as he waltzed her out onto the floor. His eyes were again lost in hers. Her breathing was ragged and her head buzzed. She was trembling in his arms. She rested her head against his chest, his heart beating calmly. He stroked her hair as they moved against each other, step for step. "I won't hurt you Amie," he told her as though he knew she was panicking again. She sighed heavily then and melted into his arms.

He had a reputation. "Hound Dog" his crew had dubbed him, since Melanie had passed away. He had lived up to it. He bounced around from one relationship to another. He couldn't really call them relationships. He never stayed with one woman long enough to consider it a relationship. He was always up front with the women he dated, or as the probies called it, hooked up with. He wasn't in it for the long haul. He was only in it for a distraction from the loneliness. He missed that physical contact with Melanie. With the women he had dated since her death it was just the physical act of sex and gratification that brought. What he was searching for was the intimacy that came from loving the woman you are with. That kind of touch was different.

Renny pulled off the t-shirt she had given him to wear. It was tight and he really didn't want to wear it all night long. He would have loved to remove the shorts too but since he was wearing nothing under them he thought twice about that. He settled down at the far end of the couch, leaning against the pillow, one leg on the couch the other on half hanging over the side. He pulled Bellamy up against his chest positioning her between his legs. She was afraid to move. She was in a rather interesting position. He pulled a quilt off the back of the couch and loosely covered the two of them. She slowly rolled onto her side her hair brushing against his chest. Now it was Renny who drew a ragged breath. Bellamy, her hot breath against his chest whispered, "Breathe deeply. In through your nose, out through your mouth," She exhaled against his neck as she slid up against him. He gripped her arms tightly and held her. 'I promise I won't hurt you." He moaned and she could feel his desire growing against her. She bit her lip. She wasn't sure who was going to give in to these feelings first. She wasn't sure she cared, as long as one of them did.

"Amie," he whispered, covering her lips with his. She was driving him to the edge of madness. This very reserved young woman he thought he knew was seducing him. He wanted to stop her but he found he couldn't. He was paralyzed under the magic of her touch. He tried shifting his position under her but her pelvis was slowly rocking with him, making the situation harder to ignore. "Amie, stop. You have to believe me. I want you so much but not tonight. We have time." He begged her.

"Renny," she whimpered. And she didn't whine. "I don't want to wait. Please, make love to me." Now she was begging. She had never begged or whined to get a man to make love to her. This was completely foreign to her.

Again, he covered her mouth with his for a moment. When he stopped kissing her he sat her up and unwrapped his legs from around her. "Bellamy, my Amie, please, try to trust me on this. I want to be with you more than I have anyone in a very long time, maybe ever. But it is just too soon. We've only been together a very short time. I don't want you to regret anything. I want it to be perfect for you. I want you to know there is nothing, no one else, more important than when I make love to you. And right now, that can't be."

She believed him. She knew he was right, sort of. He didn't want her caught up in this fire, dead body and burglary. And she knew when they made love, and she knew they would, that it would be perfect. But she certainly wished it could be now.

"I'll wait," she told him at last. She leaned her head against his shoulder and they both settled down against each other and fell asleep.

When Bellamy stirred in the middle of the night she was spooned against Renny. She listened to his steady breathing and she felt herself drifting off to sleep again when Jax sat up from where he was lying next to the couch and nudged Bellamy's foot with his cold wet nose. "Listen," she whispered to Jax. Jax sat silently, his ears pricked. A low rumble started in his chest and made its way out, growing louder as he slowly moved toward the front of the house that faced the dirt road. She shook Renny's arm that was draped over her. He roused quickly, sitting up. "Someone or something is out there," she whispered. "I need my phone." She extricated herself from him and found her phone on the kitchen table.

She unlocked the phone and pulled up the security cameras on her screen. She touched the screen for the front yard and road. She just barely caught a glimpse of someone at the far side of the road. The person was in the shadow of the hops behind him. She watched as he walked off towards Larue Road. It was just a shadow. She couldn't make out anything other than a person. She held the phone up for Renny and rewound the image. Jax was at the door whining and growling. Bellamy told Jax to whisper. As ridiculous as the command sounded he stared at the door but did not bark. He continued his deep growl.

He started to put on his shoes. "Call YSO."

"Whoever it is will just disappear into the fields again. I'll call them but it is fruitless," she said. "We don't need to be out there again. He's walking away from here. Let him go for now. If he comes back Jax will let us know. And if he comes in the yard, the alarm will go off."

"I want to know who it is and what they want. This is nuts. You wouldn't have another gun in the house would you?" He asked.

"Yeah, you call YSO, I'll get the gun." She responded. If he was going to go out there at least he could level the playing field. He had a handgun but it was in a lockbox in his closet. It wasn't going to do him much good tonight.

She heard him talking on the phone while she took the .9 mm out of her purse. It was holstered. He had hung up by the time she returned and handed him the gun. "There is one in the chamber and ready to fire."

Renny took it and grabbed his keys. "You are staying here. YSO is actually in the area. So I won't be alone for long."

She watched as he trotted to his pickup. Once she heard the engine turn over she closed and locked the door. She pulled up the camera again on her phone and watched as he backed up and disappeared down the road in a cloud of fine dust. When he was out of sight, she picked up the remote and turned the music off. It was eerily silent. Jax slid down on his belly by the front door and sniffed for any stranger on his turf. Satisfied that no one was close by he got up and walked to Bellamy. She told him he was a very good boy and ruffled his fur.

Renny had only been gone a few minutes when her phone rang in her hand. She was so jumpy she dropped the phone on the couch. She scrambled to pick it up and saw that there was no number. She answered it anyway. "Bellamy, don't say anything," A mans voice said in perfect French. "I'm sorry I'm calling so early in the morning but I have to be at work shortly. Thank you for taking care of my old hound dog. Keep an eye on him. My neighbor thinks he's the one that's been killing his chickens but I'm sure it's some weasels. I'm trying to catch them but until then they are going to be coming after my hound dog. Just keep feeding and watering him, he's a very good boy. He's warming up to you. I gotta go now." The man said. He didn't say good bye and Bellamy didn't have a chance to say anything. His voice was vaguely familiar but he had been speaking quietly like he was trying not to be heard by anyone. She didn't think about recording the call. Then again she couldn't. She didn't know how to do that. Who in the world was that and what did he mean to keep feeding his hound dog? She wasn't caring for anyone's dog. She didn't even know anyone who had any kind of hound dog, basset hound, blood hound, coon hound or keeshond. She sat down on her couch and stared at the phone.

She looked at the clock on her phone. It was zero 430 hours. The sun would be coming up soon, so she put on a pot of coffee. She doubted she was going to go back to sleep at this point. She jumped again when there was a knock at the back door. Jax went nuts barking like he was going to go through the door to get whoever was on the other side. She peeked out the window blinds and saw Renny on the other side. "Enough," she ordered Jax. He stopped barking and sat next to Bellamy as she opened the door. Renny came inside shivering. "It's a little chilly out there."

The air that followed him into the house was quite brisk. "I have coffee on, you want a cup?" *Dumb question.* There was never an hour in the day that a full fledged, hose dragging, axe toting firefighter would turn down a cup of coffee.

"Please," he said trying to shake off the chill. "We didn't find anyone."

"Ren," Bellamy said, shortening his name even more. He grinned at her. "What?"

"Ren. My mom is the only one who ever calls me that."

"Oh, uh, I hope I didn't offend you. It just seems to fit you more than Renny. Renny sounds like something you'd be called when you were a kid. Rene? I don't know, just doesn't seem to fit either. Sounds like you are about to be taken to the woodshed."

He laughed. "It sounds good coming from you. Ren, I mean."

She handed him a cup of coffee and the two of them sat down at the table. "Is the deputy gone?"

As he took a sip of coffee, lifted his head and nodded.

"Um, while you were gone, I had a weird phone call. I don't know who it was. His voice sounded familiar, sort of." She said and proceeded to tell him about the phone call. Renny's mouth opened wide when she mentioned feeding and watering his hound dog.

She stopped when she saw his reaction. "He's talking about me, Bellamy. The guys at work call me a hound dog, or bird dog." Bellamy cocked her head to one side.

"Maybe it was one of the guys. I just can't place the voice." She shook it off and continued with the caller's message. "Ren, whoever it was spoke fluent French."

"Killing chickens? Weasels? What the hell does that mean?" Ren asked.

"No idea. He just told me to take care of you." she reiterated.

Ren rolled his head and neck trying to work the kinks out of it from sleeping on the couch. He couldn't complain about it. It was well worth it to wake up with Bellamy next to him. "I'll have to tell the detective when I go in this morning. I have to be there by ten to give a statement."

"Ren don't do that. He told me not to say anything. I'm not sure if he meant during the phone call or whatever but let's just keep it between us for now," she urged. "I don't know. I just don't feel right about all of this. Roy was acting like an ass today, yesterday, whatever day it was. It just didn't seem to be the way I would have expected him to handle all of this. There was just something uncharacteristic about the way he talked to me."

"Well something isn't right. You have no idea who it was on the phone?"

Bellamy cringed. "I know it's just wishful thinking, or being half asleep, but playing it over and over in my head, it sort of sounded like Pedro." As the words passed her lips she felt more confident about her words.

Ren however didn't appear to share her certainty. He shook his head dismissively. "I saw the truck, Bellamy and his body."

Bellamy heard that condescending note in his voice again. She tensed. "You saw *a* truck and you saw *a* body. Can you tell me with absolute certainty that it was Pedro and his truck? I'm sure one crispy critter looks pretty much like another." Immediately she regretted saying that but it was already out of her mouth.

Ren's face grew irritated and he wanted to fire angry words back at her. It was his friend who was dead not hers.

Before he could Bellamy was on the offensive. "Ren, I said it sounded like it might be him, his tone and cadence. I listen to voices all day long. I'm pretty good at picking up on the subtleties. But no, I'm not positive it was his voice. This man spoke flawless French and perfect English. Even in our rare encounters, it was pretty clear Pedro didn't, so don't get all pissy."

Ren chuckled softly, "Our first fight." An innocent smile turned up the edges of his lips. "Can we kiss and make up now?"

She couldn't help but smile back at him. He was quick with his comebacks. She slowly stood up and walked toward him. She went behind his chair and stood there. For a moment Ren wasn't sure if she was going to strangle him. He felt her warm hands on the back of his neck. Her thumbs started kneading circles on either side of his spine in the hollow below his skull. It hurt but felt amazing too. Firmly her hands moved down his neck to find knots along his shoulder blades. He moaned. She pressed against the muscles that had knitted themselves together and made agonizing little bumps under his skin. Her thumbs felt like magic as they first caressed then intensified the pressure against them. She could feel him tense up under the pain she was inflicting. She leaned over and whispered against his ear her warm breath sending a shiver down his spine. "Relax."

Relax? You expect me to relax when you are doing that? His body was reacting like any man's body would react at having a woman whispering in his ear. Her breasts were resting oh so lightly against his head. Her hands were making him crazy. Relax? That was not happening. He reached back and his strong hands guided her around him and lifted her up and seated her on the table. She flipped one leg over the top of his head and slid down into his lap facing him. He closed his eyes and moaned. He cupped her face in his hands. His lips found the base of her neck. He worked his way up until his lips reached hers and kissed her deeply. He wanted to make love to her so badly that it really did hurt. "You need to stop." He said seriously. He forced himself to push away from her and stand up. He held her waist as he stood her up in front of him. He turned away from her as quickly as he could. He didn't want her to see the desire she had created in him. He leaned back and pecked her on the cheek.

Her advances rejected by him, she turned away and bit the inside of her cheek. Tears were threatening to spill out of her eyes. Was she really that undesirable that this proclaimed "hound dog" didn't want her? Was he just playing with her like some dogs did when they retrieved their prey? It felt that way. He would hold her and kiss her and take her to the heights of exhilaration, then he would stop and she would land hard on the reality of not having him.

When he turned back, her shoulders were hunched and her eyes closed. Ren rubbed her shoulders softly and kissed her moist eyes. His lips brushed her lips and cheeks and quietly he whispered, "Ma cherie amour, I want you more than you can imagine. But I just can't right now. You mean more to me than you know and I don't want to mess this up. I want to take it slow. You have no idea how hard it is for me to do that. I don't want to hurt you. Please trust me," He felt her nod against his lips.

Damn it, she swore in her head, *he was good. He was saying all the right words.* He had definitely awoken something exciting in her. The sensation was also alarmingly frightening. As cliché as it sounded in her head she had never felt like this before. Bellamy wasn't quite sure how to handle the emotions that were swirling around inside her. She had only known him, really even talked to him for a few days and she was falling in love with him. Crazy. It had to be the relentless heat outside that was making her crazy. None of these feelings she was having towards him made any sense to her so she had to blame it on something. The weather was causing it.

"I have to go Amie. I probably won't see you again today. I have got to figure out what to do with the kiln. And I'm going to have to talk to that detective…what's his name, Osborne. That's it, Osborne. Hopefully that won't take too long. Can I call you later?" He asked as he walked to the sink and rinsed his coffee cup and sat it in the sink.

'Yeah, of course." The view of his back was as nice as the view from the front. He had wide sculptured shoulders that slimmed down to his waist. His butt was marvelous. His thighs were strong and heavily muscled. It was probably from the many stairs he had climbed with all that gear. For a structure fire they packed around seventy extra pounds with their turnout gear and SCBA tanks. He turned around and caught her studying his legs.

"Amie I need your phone number," he told her. He took his phone off the counter next to his truck keys and found his contacts page. He added her name and lifted his eyes to wait for her to give him her phone number.

She rattled it off and asked him for his. He looked at her curiously as though he wasn't sure if he wanted to give it to her or not. As if reading his mind Bellamy added, "For Pete's sake Ren, I am not going to stalk you. That's not me. If you don't call me don't expect me to call you. If you see my number on your phone you can be sure it's an emergency. It'd be a little embarrassing if I had to call the office to get your number to tell you the road was flooding again because of another great squirrel invasion," she reminded him. It happened one summer day when the ground squirrels had breached the wall of a small ditch that fed his irrigation system. It had made a huge mess before she could get a hold of him to let him know. That took a couple of days to clean up, she remembered, but the stupid squirrels weren't deterred one bit and just moved to a different area, closer to her property to begin their burrowing. Her target practice at the range paid off in the great squirrel blitz. As sure as Ground Hog's Day was on the second of February, on the third day of February the little hamster looking critters would pop their heads out of their channels and start destroying everything in their path. She had always thought they were cute until she realized the amount of damage these miniature prairie dogs could do. After the road debacle, she and a couple of her cop friends got together for the great squirrel shootout. The most effective ammo was .17 bullets. The squirrels just disintegrated when hit. It had become an annual outing on February the third of each year. It included snacks and beer for the guys. They would get together, lay down their astroturf rugs, set up tripods for their rifles and start their assault.

"Are you ready?"

Her mind snapped back to the present and she added his number to her contact list.

He kissed her sweetly at the door. She sighed and closed the door behind him. She sat back in her recliner and turned on the TV to keep her company. She missed him already. She wondered where this sort of relationship was going to go. She stared at the news channel not hearing anything they were reporting. She wasn't even aware of her eyes closing but she awoke three hours later, drool sliding down the side of her chin. She slurped then quickly wiped the rest of it off on the shoulder of her shirt. She seemed to drool more than Jax did. How attractive, she thought like farting in front of a guy for the first time. She cringed.

Chapter 7

Ren's drive home seemed very short, although it was several miles from Bellamy's house. It sat on a hill not far away, above the some of his hop yards just above the house Pedro occupied. He got out of his truck and opened the door. A silence hit him that he hadn't noticed for a long time. It was emptiness, loneliness. It gripped him tightly. He kicked off his sneakers and walked across the wooden floor to the staircase that would take him up to his bedroom.

He opened the shades with the remote and stared out at the morning. The sun was painting Mt. Adams and Mt. Rainier pastel hues of pink and blue. There were no clouds at all but there was a haze to the west over the mountains. He wondered if they were going to have another thunder storm tonight. The haze was sometimes the harbinger of a storm coming in later. Either that or there was a wildland fire somewhere. The only thing he knew for sure was it was going to be very hot today. Listening to the radio on the way back to his house the weatherman predicted temperatures in the triple digits. It wasn't rare for the valley to get temperatures that hot in July and August but it usually only sizzled for a few days at a time, followed by wind and sometimes rain, in the form of thunderstorms. He liked thunderstorms when he could be home and enjoy their power and majesty. They cleared the air and dropped the temperature. At work it was a different story. Like all the other firefighters he hated thunderstorms because it meant they would be running all over the city putting out small fires and sometimes big fires, checking on down power lines, trees down and alarms going off. Unlike storms in other areas of the country the storms here were generally quick moving. They didn't sit over an area for a prolonged period of time. For that, they were grateful.

Ren took a long shower, shaved and put on some cologne. He chose a pale turquoise polo shirt and a pair of gray slacks. He stepped in to a real pair of shoes, a pair of dark gray Wolf & Shepherd"s leather loafers. He actually put on a wrist watch that Melanie had given him on his last birthday with her. He was a businessman after all and sometimes he had to wear something that would pass as casual business attire. The rest of his off duty time he was gentleman farmer, well worn Wrangler jeans, his country cut shirts and a straw cowboy hat or ball cap with the name of a hop related company logo and a pair of Durango leather cowboy boots. If he was going out to a function at the Grange or a barn dance he would still have on the same attire, just classed up a bit with his Stetson and his favorite pair of black Ferrini French Calf cowboy boots. Fashion wasn't important to him but he had a pair of cowboy boots for every occasion. At home he would either be wearing a pair of swim shorts and a t-shirt in the summer and sweats in the winter.

He made a cup of coffee and sat at the bar making notes in his phone of things he needed to take care of today. He had a feeling it was going to be a very trying day.

When he was ready to leave for his interview he took some money out of his wallet and left it in an envelope on the entry table for his maid. If he hadn't hired a maid, his house would look like the county dump. He hadn't adjusted well to Melanie's passing where domestic duties were concerned. He wasn't a slob exactly but he just had no desire to clean toilets or mop the floors. Why bother? No one was there to see it. So he gave up and hired a maid. She came in once a month to do those things. She was used to coming in when he was gone. His schedule didn't allow him to be there all the time. She worked for several of the other firefighters so he felt safe having her in his house when he wasn't there. It did feel tacky leaving money for her in an envelope but it was the most convenient way to make sure she got paid. He thought about it as he locked the door and realized she was the only woman, not related to him, who had ever been in his house. He was a private man so he hadn't invited many of his peers to his house. Just a couple of his crew had come up after he had finished building it. But women, or even a woman, no. He didn't want a woman to come to his house. Part of it was a feeling that she may see dollar signs instead of him. The other part was a feeling that he hadn't met anyone he wished to share it with.

He realized some people would look at him and probably consider him rich. He had a beautiful home, a swimming pool, a nicely landscaped yard and several large parcels of hops. He had a maid, a landscaper and even a pool guy. It all cost money. He was comfortable by local standards but he was far from rich. One bad year of hops and he could be scraping the proverbial barrel to cover his contracts and costs to keep his crops growing.

One good year and he'd be sitting pretty, until a machine broke or, like now, he had to rebuild a hop kiln. He rubbed his forehead. For everything he had there was something he gave up.

Growing and selling hops was a unique business. The company that bought their hops had a cost analysis produced by one of the universities in the state that they used to determine what they would pay for the hops. Since the amount of hops produced each year varied they had to project how much money they would make. The contracts they had were from three to five years in duration. If they had a bad year and didn't produce enough to cover the contract they lost money. If they were lucky and had a good year and produced more hops than expected Mid-Valley Hops had to pay the LaRues more.

The valley produced approximately 75% of hops in the United States although some accounts said they produced 90% of the hops in the U.S. and 46% of the hops in the world. To think it all started in the valley with Alexander Graham Bell seemed like a bizarre connection. Bell saw a market and started investing in it along with his father-in-law Gardiner Greene Hubbard. They recruited farmers with the lure of money, acreage and irrigation to move to the valley and start producing crops. Numerous crops were tried, some failed, some thrived. It was the hop industry that flourished in the area thanks to the recruitment of French-Canadian farmers. The farmers continued growing hops and passed the legacy to their children, such as Ren and Jon. A few of those families, like Ren's, had come to own the majority of the hops grown in the valley. The competition was increasing as more and more hops were being planted in Oregon, even in Wisconsin due to the micro-brewers demand for different varieties of hops to produce their specific types of beer.

Germany bought the majority of the hops produced in the valley. The company, Mid-Valley Hops that the LaRue's contracted with had international sales people who made the sales around the world for beer production. Depending on the international demand the prices of hops being sold could skyrocket or plummet. If the price went too high because there were less hops to buy then Mid-Valley Hops made bank. If they had a glut of too many hops world wide and not enough sales, the price of hops hit the skids and the company made less, a lot less money, some years because they had to pay their growers for the over abundance of hops even if they couldn't sell them. It was a simplified analogy of how the market worked. There were other factors too, the extract and the pellets that were becoming more popular with brewers. Some of those products could be stored for several years if not sold immediately. Baled hops were a different story. Even in a cold storage unit they had a very short shelf life compared to other commodities. Selling them quickly was paramount if the company was to make money.

Ren shook his head. He had been in the hop business his entire adult life. He and his brother Jon held a huge amount of cultivated acres. Between the two of them they held close to a fourth of all the hops produced in the valley. It was a huge undertaking. Without Pedro it was going to be an even bigger undertaking. When he got through with this interview at the sheriff's office he would have to reach out to Jon and some of the other growers and see if they knew a field man that he could hire so late in the season.

Ren waited for the detective in the room adjacent to their dispatch center. It was completely foreign to him. It was nothing like the 911 center in the city. He could see three women behind a four foot counter. One was busy typing on a computer. Another behind her was filing papers when she wasn't answering the phone. The third, head down was writing on papers in front of her when she wasn't answering the radio. It appeared to be a busy but efficient office.

Detective Osborne opened a door, just beyond the communications center and held it open for Ren. He was carrying a large file folder full of papers in his hand. "Thanks for coming in," he said ushering Ren down the hallway and into a small cubicle with a table and three chairs. It was windowless. One wall had a large mirror which he guessed was for another detective behind the mirror to view the interview undetected. He glanced up while he was sitting down and saw a camera up in the corner, its black lens staring down at him. Detective Osborne sat across from him and placed a digital recorder on the table between them. "You don't mind if I tape this interview do you? It just helps me so I don't leave anything out in your statement when I have you come back in to sign it."

Bullshit, Ren thought but agreed to it anyway. He had nothing to hide.

Detective Osborne turned the recorder on and spoke into it giving his name and Ren's name, the date and time of the interview. Just like on TV, Ren observed.

"We are investigating the fire of a kiln you own and the death of an unknown person in a burned pickup," the detective told him. "It would be a great help if you could tell us anything you might know about this incident." He looked Ren square in the eyes and asked him "Where were you when you found out about the fire?"

"I was at home, asleep." Ren answered.

"Was anyone with you?" The detective asked.

Shocked by the question Ren sat up a little straighter and shifted in his chair. "No," he answered hesitantly. He wasn't going to elaborate on anything this guy asked him. This question alone set him on edge.

"How did you find out about the fire?"

"Jon called me and told me to come to the scene, as you can see by my phone log."

"Who is Jon?"

"My brother but that night he was also the East Valley Deputy Fire Chief." Ren responded. This guy was obtuse. He knew who Jon was.

"And what exactly did he tell you when he called?"

"He said there was a fire at the old kiln and I needed to come to the scene."

"He didn't tell you about the pickup or the body inside it?" The detective probed.

"I don't recall him telling me about that. Ask him."

"What is your relationship with Jon LaRue?" He asked.

Ren shook his head in disbelief. "He's my brother." *Did you not hear me the first time?*

"What time did he call you?"

"I don't know I'd have to look at my phone," Ren took his cell phone out of his pocket and punched in some numbers and brought up his call log. He slid it across the table to Detective Osborne.

"How long did it take you to get to the fire scene?" Detective Osborne asked.

"I don't know. I had to get dressed and drive down there. Ten, fifteen minutes," Ren guessed.

"Are you sure it wasn't longer than that, a half an hour or so,"

"I don't think so. Check the remarks in the call screen from dispatch. I'm sure they logged it when I arrived on scene."

"Do you know whose vehicle that was in the fire?"

"I don't know. I thought it was Pedro's."

"Pedro?"

"Pedro Ramirez, my field man."

"Do you know his date of birth?"

"Not off hand. I'm sure it is on his employment record at the shop or with our office manager at our corporate office."

"If you could look through your records and give us a call I'd really appreciate it."

"I'll give you the office number. You can call them. I'm sure they will be glad to look it up for you." Ren snapped back. *Do your own job!* He yelled in his head. *Don't ask me to do it for you!*

Then with a quick follow-up question the detective asked, "Do you happen to know if he had any family around here?" He sounded a bit exasperated that he wasn't getting any answers he needed.

"I don't know. He was my employee not my drinking buddy. Didn't you find anything in his house?" Ren asked, wanting some answers himself but knowing after he had walked through the house they most likely had found nothing.

"I can't release any of that information." The detective returned with a tone of superiority leaking out. That in itself was a telling answer. They didn't have squat.

"Oh quit, detective. Don't try to play me. I'm not some gang banger punk. Tell me what you think I might know that you don't and let's get on with it. Don't waste my time."

"Did you kill Pedro Ramirez and set the fire to cover it up?"

"Kill Pedro? Are you out of your fucking mind? I didn't kill Pedro or anyone else." Ren snarled. "I don't know who it was in the truck. The body I saw was burned beyond recognition. I certainly didn't burn down my own kiln. Do you have any idea how much money it is going to cost to replace that, or how much it is going to impact the harvest? If that was Pedro in that vehicle do you have any idea how important he was to my business? If it was him I can't replace him," Ren voice remained even but dangerously on edge. "He was in charge of the whole operation. He hired all the workers, coordinated the work, made sure they were harvesting the hops properly, made sure the propane was full for the burners that dried the hops in my kiln. He was my right hand man. I have no one I can depend on to do that. When I couldn't be there, Pedro was." His voice was now severe.

"Are you sure it was Pedro and that was his truck?" Detective Osborne persisted.

"Do you have a hearing problem? I just told you I couldn't tell you if it was his truck, or if it was Pedro. For all I know it could have been your mother." Ren sniped. "Once you identify the body, if it is Pedro please let me know. If his next of kin need any kind of help I'd like to know. But right now if you don't have any other relevant questions for me, I'm going to go. I have other business to take care of." He stood up and started to leave. "If you think of anything, feel free to call me, but don't waste my time with bullshit like this. Make sure you record this detective. You need to take a few classes in interview techniques because you aren't very good at it." Ren thought he could hear laughter from the other side of the mirror.

Ren left the detective sitting in his chair. He could feel eyes following him out of the room. When Ren got to the end of the short hallway, Sheriff Paul Hastings came out of his office to catch. "Hey, sorry, it's routine. We have to ask. Truth is we don't know who was in that truck. The body was so badly burned the coroner wasn't sure if we would be able to get any DNA. Pretty much all we have are skeletal remains. Dr. Thana is going to do his best to get some from his teeth or femur but he couldn't promise anything. And the pickup? Yeah, we don't know. No VIN. Gone. Even the hidden VIN was gone. It could be a Ford but we are just going on what is left of it. It is our assumption that it belongs to Pedro because of the proximity to the kiln and what we found in his house. Did that seem a strange to you," the Sheriff was talking to Ren like he was a long lost friend. Ren knew him from different EMS drills they had to attend as well as public education events but to think of him as a friend was a stretch. He hadn't even voted for him. Talk about skeletons. He had a big one in his bathroom closet. Ren almost laughed at the memory.

It had been a long time ago, back when Hastings was just a lowly deputy. He had been tempted by a badge bunny and taken to thumping her on a regular basis, unbeknownst to his wife. Cop gossip was he had been doing it on duty, back before AVL (Auto Vehicle Locator) was available and his location was known at all times. He would go to his bunny's hutch, park as close as he could to her bedroom window, toss his radio mic through her window, just in case he got a call and didn't want to answer on his portable. It was easy to tell the difference between a response on a car radio and that of a portable radio. Anyway they would do the bunny hump and he would leave. Well gossip being what it is the gossip got back to his wife. Cops can't keep their mouths shut any more than the bad guys can and their dirty deeds always catch up with them just as it did for the fair haired Deputy

Hastings. His wife at the time didn't take kindly to his deeds.

Since he was an upper valley deputy, he often took his lunch breaks at home. He also took his bathroom breaks at home. One infamous day he was sitting on his throne at home with his uniform drawers down around his ankles when his sprite of a wife opened the door and fired at him with a hunting rifle. Not being a hunter the recoil knocked her on her ass. Deputy Hastings, scared out of his wits, not knowing whether he had been shot or not, and deafened from the rifle fire wasn't sure what to do first.

Some long lost training came back to him. He lunged at his wife from the toilet, tangled in his pants. He fell on top of her and was able to subdue her and cuff her. He pushed the rifle into the other room. Out of breath he realized dispatch was calling him frantically on the radio. He hadn't heard it. The ringing in his ears had completely deafened him. He grabbed the portable and screamed that shots were fired and he needed assistance at his residence. Dispatch advised him law enforcement was on scene. The small town of Tieton had one patrol officer and he had arrived at Deputy Hastings home and was coming in, clearing the rooms as he entered. As he rounded the corner of the hallway that led to the bathroom, he found Deputy Hastings sitting on his wife's back, buck ass naked from the waist down. She was screaming profanities at both men at the top of her lungs. The officer holstered his gun and went to the aid of Deputy Hastings who, quite literally was stuck on the back of his wife by his twisted pants and gun belt. Even before he had a chance to yank his polyester uniform pants around so he could pull them up, another deputy and a detective came around the corner of the hall. They stood gawking at him trying to stifle their laughter. Deputy Hastings still near deaf asked how they had known he needed help and they started laughing hysterically. "Dude! The whole county knew you needed help. You were laying on your portable mic. Everyone heard it."

The Sheriff is now divorced and his ex-wife is out on parole. At least that is the way Ren heard it. And he preferred to remember it that way.

Renny almost laughed again. *Too bad they didn't have body cams back then. That would have been one for the books.* It suddenly occurred to him he hadn't answered the question. He tried to regain a serious expression as though he had to ponder his answer.

"Of course it sounds strange to me. That was my kiln that burned down and possibly my employee in that truck. I want to know what happened as much as you do. I am just curious how you made the leap from a dead person in a truck to my employee. A little presumptuous don't you think? You must have had some kind of probable cause to get a judge to sign off on that warrant to search his/my house. What was it?"

Sheriff Hastings leaned on the half wall of the dispatch center. He didn't answer Ren and he didn't skip a beat, "Do you think it has anything to do with the burglary at your shop or the prowler?"

Ren shrugged his shoulders. "I have no idea but just an uneducated guess I would say they might be related. How I don't know. That's your job, right? To find out if they are related." It wasn't a sarcastic response but it wasn't exactly friendly either. He was just stating the obvious. Ren didn't wait for the conversation to continue. He turned on his heels and walked out to the parking lot feeling like the temperature had increased about ten degrees since he went into the office. He climbed into his truck and pulled out into traffic to head to Mid-Valley Hops that was only a few blocks from the Sheriff's office. He pulled into their paved parking lot and took a parking spot near the door. Since he was in the area he thought he might stop in and see if they might know of another person looking for employment as a field man this late in the season.

He sat in the cold interior of his truck thinking. He wanted to talk to Bellamy. She had worked with the police long enough to know if any of this made sense to her. He trusted her. Even when she sounded like a snot nosed teenager on the radio he knew she had his back. She anticipated his needs and sometimes took care of them before he asked. He could tell that the welfare of her firefighters was her utmost priority. He pulled out his cell phone and dialed her number. It rang several times before she answered.

"Hello Ren," she answered, "How did the interview go?"

He held the phone away from his ear and stared at it. She was doing it again. She was anticipating this call and his welfare.

"That was the biggest waste of time. They asked me how I knew that was Pedro in that truck. I didn't. Don't. They were the ones who suggested it was him. And they wanted to know what kind of information I had on him. He was my employee. Very little. Well that isn't completely true. I knew him a lot better than I told them but it wasn't the kind of information they wanted or needed. Anyway, when I asked them what made them think it was Pedro they didn't answer me. And then I asked them how they got a warrant for his house. They didn't answer me. Wouldn't they need probable cause?" He was running off at the mouth. There was a long pause before she responded.

"I hadn't thought about it. They had to have some kind of probable cause. Who owns that house?" Bellamy asked.

"I do. I just use it for employee housing. Since Pedro was my field man, or orchard manager or whatever you want to call his position, he was like my number one employee. It was his to use as long as he worked for me," Ren explained.

"Did they give you a copy of the search warrant?" Bellamy asked.

"Yeah," Ren answered. "Right here. I never took it out of the truck." It was lying on the seat next to him.

"Look at it," she told him, "Who is named on the warrant?"

It was several moments before he answered. "Son of a bitch! It has my name on it. Why is my name on it?" He was incensed.

"You are the home owner. They have no right to enter the house without that warrant or the owners consent."

"Son of a bitch!" He shouted again. He rambled off a litany of swear words. They had no particular meaning the way he had strung them together but Bellamy knew what he was saying and had to agree. "Why didn't they just ask me if they could go in, instead of getting a warrant?"

"I am guessing they thought you would say no, so they got a warrant. They have to have some kind of probable cause. Read on. What did they list as the reason they were trying to secure entry into the house and what evidence they had to convince the judge to grant it."

"It says because they suspected Pedro or me of starting the fire and were looking for any kind of evidence that might be in his residence. That since I was the property owner I was the one who needed to be served. "What the…They don't even know who owns the truck or who was in the truck and a judge gave them a warrant to search his house. How would they make that assumption that Pedro or I had something to do with it?" His voice was still loud but not as loud as it had been. "Never mind. I connected the dots and see the picture now. But they haven't searched my house. Why?"

Bellamy assured him they must have something that pointed towards he and Pedro as suspects. From what Ren had read to her off of the warrant, it sure didn't sound like it. But it also intimated that Ren had killed Pedro.

"This is crazy Bellamy. It was my kiln. Why didn't they have a search warrant for my house? Or my shop?"

"I don't know. I really don't. But what you are telling me is that Pedro might not be dead. That means he could have been him that called me."

Ren snapped to, he had been so irritated at the interview and reading the warrant he hadn't had time to process it to make that connection. "I uh, yeah, I guess it could mean that. And that they somehow think I might be involved in this."

"Just relax. I'm sure that isn't what they meant. They were just fishing. Listen, I'm on my way out the door. I have some shopping I need to do but if you want to come over, I'll make dinner for us.

"You don't need to go shopping for that, I'll bring something over." He offered.

Bellamy felt herself blush. "Uh, that's not what I was going shopping for."

"Ummm," Ren hummed suggestively, smiling then for the first time since he had left her house. "Why don't you come to my house for dinner? We can do Door Dash or something. But while you are shopping you might want to pick up a bikini to wear in the pool."

"A pool?"

"No. A bikini. I'll provide the pool." Ren said jokingly. He was sure he could hear her face getting red over the phone.

"Yeah, um, ok. What time? Where do you live?" Ren told her then ended their conversation. All of a sudden everything felt better as if the stars had suddenly aligned somewhere.

Chapter 8

He got out of his truck into the oppressive heat and went in to the office area of Mid-Valley Hops. Generally it would be rather subdued this time of year. The office staff would be getting ready for the upcoming harvest but the majority of the contracts had been set so now it was just a waiting game for the office.

Today the room was a beehive of activity. Susan and Madeline were on the phones. Amy was looking for something in the appointment book. Donald, the big boss, owner, was leaning over Amy's desk trying to read the information over her shoulder. Ren was taken aback from all of the serious expressions and the feverish activity.

Ren usually knew how to work this crowd. Make the girls smile. He would offer to run and get them food or coffee, on him of course. He'd pay a few compliments, make good eye contact and he could pretty much get whatever he needed in quick order. This was obviously not going to be one of those days.

Amy looked up from her paper work, caught his eye and held up an index finger indicating it would be a minute until she could get to him. "He was supposed to be on a plane this morning for Japan. It left on time but the airline confirmed he was not on it." Susan said over her shoulder to Donald when she had ended her call.

"Where the hell is he?" Donald asked, more to himself than anyone else in the office. Donald didn't swear. His brow and upper lip were both moist from perspiration. To Ren he looked a little blue around the lips. Donald was in his late 60's and over weight. Prime time for a stroke or heart attack, Ren thought watching him. "What the hell is going on around here?" Donald asked again to whoever was listening. He looked up and caught Ren watching him. "Jason. He's missing. No one has heard from him since Wednesday. His wife is hysterical," Donald told Ren.

Jason was one of the two international sales people Mid-Valley Hops employed. He was overseas more than he was in the states. He was late thirties, married but no children. No wonder he didn't have any kids, Ren thought to himself, the guy was never home. It was pretty hard to propagate babies if you were in Germany and your wife was here in Yakima.

"Ren, come on back to my office, I need to sit down for a minute. My back is killing me today," Donald told him. Ren followed him back to his office where Donald took a seat behind his huge walnut desk, scattered with papers. It looked messy but Ren knew the man well enough to know that Donald knew exactly what was where. He suddenly leaned over and vomited in a garbage can next to his desk. He spat in the can a couple of times and sat up, apologizing to Ren. "Sorry you had to see that. I got sick just after I came in this morning and it just seems to be getting worse." Donald sighed heavily and took a bottle of aspirin sitting on his desk, took out several pills, popped them into his mouth and washed them down with what looked like the wedges of an entire lemon floating in a glass of lemonade.

"Has he been reported missing?" Ren asked.

Donald huffed, "His wife is trying to. But she keeps getting the run-around. He's an adult so they say he has the right to be missing if he wants to be so they weren't going to take the report. Once she finally convinced them that something wasn't right, that he wouldn't do that, they started to take the report. But they got to the part about where he was missing from and it turned in to a cluster. Evidently a report has to be filed with the jurisdiction he is missing from. All well and good but we don't know where he was. He had been in Germany but was supposed to be home on Wednesday before heading out for Japan today. He never showed up at home. Cindy just thought he got held over somewhere, you know, with all the trouble with the airlines right now, but she was sure he would have called and let her know. She didn't call us until this morning because she was finally able to find out he was on the plane that landed in Yakima. But what happened to him after that, no one knows. I don't know why she waited but she did. So, we are trying to help but we are at a loss of what to do." He told Ren while he rubbed his left shoulder. Donald looked like he couldn't hold still and his words were machine gun fast.

"Donald you aren't looking too good right now. Let me check your pulse," Ren suggested. He had heard the story about Jason but Donald seemed to be struggling with his breathing.

'No, no, I'm fine. Really, I'm just feeling a little anxious about all of this, your situation included."

News seemed to travel fast in the hop industry. He ignored Donald's objection, got up, went around his desk and took his wrist. The man was in a cold sweat. Ren found his pulse and he was immediately worried. It was bounding and as erratic as a drunk driver. It was about 140 beats a minute. He dropped Donald's wrist. Donald looked up at Ren, "See I told you I was fine."

"Buddy, you are far from fine." Ren punched 911 into his phone and reported an MI, possible Mio-cardio Infarction. Donald was going to object but he was now holding his chest. "Do you want to lie down Donald? Would that be better?" Donald shook his head at Ren.

"Hey, ladies, can one of you come here a minute?" Ren shouted.

Amy was at the door in an instant. The blood drained from her face when she saw

Donald. "Move my truck, would you, honey? Make room for the ambulance." Ren tossed her his keys. She wasn't expecting the toss and the keys hit her in the belly then landed at her feet. She snatched them from the floor and hurried out. Ren kept the call taker updated on Donald's status while they waited for the ambulance. The two other women showed up in the doorway. Ren felt like he needed to keep them busy and keep them from crowding the room. "How about one of you call his wife, let her know Donald is a little under the weather and he's going by ambulance to the hospital to get checked out." Madeline was left standing in the doorway. "Could you get a cold wet towel?" He directed to her. A wet towel wasn't going to help Donald any but it would get her out of the doorway. Before she could return with the towel Mark, Donald's younger brother and a third owner in the business came rushing down the hallway to Donald's office. Ren shook his head. "Hey Mark can you help Amy direct the ambulance crew in? Donald is good. He just needs to go in and get checked out." Ren assured him and he disappeared to the front of the office. Madeline returned with a paper towel, dripping wet. He put it across Donald's wrist.

He could hear the ambulance coming from the west. It gave a final whoop of the siren when it pulled into the parking lot. Another siren followed the ambulance in to the parking lot. That would be Engine 94. It was routine for an engine to assist on a cardiac run. If the call went to crap there were enough hands to work on the patient and get him to the hospital. There were frantic voices in the front office, as the crews started down the hallway. In a few moments there was barely room to move. Ren stepped out of the room and stood out of the way while the crews attended to Donald.

Captain Davis nodded at him, "Work just follows you wherever you go, doesn't it LaRue?" Ren half chuckled and nodded his head back at the Captain.

Once Donald was loaded up in the ambulance, Ren stood at the counter again. He waited until the excitement of the incident started to lull then asked Mark if he had a minute. Mark cocked his head in the direction of his office.

Mark sat down in his office chair. The chair squeaked loudly. Ren sat across from him. Compared to Donald's desk Mark's was completely the opposite. It had no clutter. Everything seemed to have a place to be and it was. He leaned back in his chair.

Ren went on to explain his situation. Mark thought about it for a minute, as if trying to pick a name out of the air that might be able to help Ren get ready for the harvest. "Not off hand Ren, but let me work on it. I'll give you a call later this evening when everything has calmed down here." Mark was sitting, with his arms crossed behind his head his fingers laced in a relaxed pose. Ren thought it looked strange considering the things going on in the office right now. His brother and the major stake holder of this multi-million dollar, international business had just been transported to the hospital with a possible heart attack. One of his most important sales people in the international market, Jason, was missing. Ren thought he would frantically be making phone calls to the other office to let the third partner in this business, Daniel the third Jeffers brother know his oldest brother had just gone to the hospital. Instead Mark looked like he was trying to figure out if he could sneak out for a couple of rounds of golf. Ren just expected him to be showing more concern. But he was calm. It just struck Ren as odd but then everything seemed odd to him right now. He was contemplating all of that when he realized he was staring at Mark.

"Is there anything else I can do for you Renny?" Mark asked. Now his voice sounded like he was hoping Ren would leave so he could get on with his daydream or whatever he was planning on doing.

"No, that's it. Thanks Mark," Ren said standing to leave his office.

"Thank you Ren, if you hadn't been here Donald might be dead." Mark said. Then he added, "I sure hope losing your kiln and Pedro doesn't affect your harvest." Ren turned to look at his expression. He was rather surprised that Mark didn't walk out with him. That was something he had always done in the past but not today. He stayed in his chair.

"Me too. Hey, keep me updated on Donald and Jason. And if his wife continues to have a problem getting an agency to take the missing report, let me know, would you? I might know someone who can help," Ren said.

"Will do." Mark assured him. *Will not, you weasel. Snake in the grass.* Ren thought as he left the office.

Mark waited until he heard Ren leave the building which wasn't difficult in this old cave. He could hear Donald pass gas in his office. If he wanted any privacy at all he had to make sure his office door was closed and even that was no guarantee no one would hear him if he was on the phone. He usually had music playing quietly in the background in his office. He did it not because he liked music that much but because it muffled any sound coming from his office that he didn't want everyone in the building to hear.

Sometimes Mark would go out onto the warehouse floor where there was always a forklift running somewhere. That usually made enough noise that if he didn't want Donald or the office staff to overhear his conversations. More and more of his phone calls were made on this cheap pre-paid phone than on his personal cell phone or office phone.

He was so tired of this place he couldn't wait until he could move into his new office in the new building. Right now it was just sitting empty waiting for him to occupy it but that could be years from now if Donald had anything to say about it. Mark hoped today might be the day that Donald gave up the building, gave up everything.

Donald was determined they weren't going to move in to those offices until all of the products he was storing in this warehouse was sold. And that all depended on Jason and his sales prowess. Mark couldn't wait to go through the contracts he was able to secure in Germany to get rid of some of this overstock. The contracts were on his desk waiting for his signature but he hadn't been able to go through them because of all the other crap going on in the office. And Donald, damn him, had started pulling out hop bales they had in cold storage that they hadn't been able to sell and bringing them here to turn them into extract before they turned into a worthless stack of burlap bags.

At least the extract took up less space and stored longer than the hops did. It was just an expensive process and using the Hexane was becoming a thing of the past. It was such a dangerous process because of the flammability of Hexane, but Donald was determined to use it to make room for this year's hop harvest in the new building. But doing that just added one more day until they could close this piece of crap building that was now archaic. It had been the whole point of building the new warehouse facility on the west side of the city.

Mark hit speed dial on his phone and waited for an answer. When the man on the other end of the line answered he briefly told him that Donald was in the hospital but he had no idea what his status was. Yes, he would keep him posted. Yes, they were still on for tonight and wanted to make sure everything of his surprise was ready to go. The man on the other end told him his wife's birthday present was ready and waiting. Mark ended the call and went back to his office.

Renny told the ladies good bye and thanked them for their help. After retrieving his keys from Amy, got in his truck, turned it on then called Mid-Valley Hops. Amy answered on the second ring. "Amy don't say my name. It's Ren. I asked Mark to keep me posted on Donald but I got the feeling he won't. Would you? I'm really worried about him. And if Jason's wife can't get law enforcement to take a missing persons report, would you call me. I know someone who can help." Ren told her. He didn't know for sure but he figured if anyone would know how this worked Bellamy would.

"No sir." Amy said abruptly in the phone, "We don't sell hops in anything smaller than a bale in size and we sell in bulk, not individual bales." She said then, "You are welcome. You might try 'the spot'. 'The spot' sir. It's on the internet. You might find something there. Have a good day." The call was disconnected. He thought maybe someone else had picked up the call or were standing too close to her. She would definitely call him and update him. He felt certain of that.

He sat for a minute trying to collect his wits. That entire experience in there was unreal. He was having a hard time wrapping his head around it. He tried to shake it off. Even his call to Amy was odd. She definitely jumped right in with some crazy scenario so that no one would figure out it was Ren. He was quite impressed.

He took a deep breath and put his truck in gear to head out to the next best place to find a trustworthy replacement for Pedro, the coffee shop. The hop growers gravitated towards a mom and pop place just over the Yakima River, close to the freeway. When he pulled into the parking lot, sure enough there were several farm trucks, caked with dried mud parked in the lot. It was a sure sign some of the growers were there.

Ren went in, headed to the back of the restaurant and heard the familiar sound of dice clicking around a leather cylinder. The boys were playing dice. It was usually a game to see who was going to pick up the check. "Don't leave on my account." Ren started.

"I knew we should have left earlier. We can't hide from you Renny no matter how hard we try." One of the men jeered. Ren pulled up an empty chair at the table and filled a cup with coffee from a thermal carafe the waitress brought to their table to reduce the amount of times she had to return to fill their cups. That table was where the majority of real business took place. To the untrained eye it appeared to be a group of unwashed farmers swapping jokes and fish tales but for the hop growers it was Wall Street. Not to say a fair amount of fish tales and dirty jokes took place across the Formica top but vital industry information was also slid across the surface.

There was a cool breeze that seemed to swirl in the undercurrent in the room around Ren. It was as if the fire and dead body at his kiln had been thrashed and boiled into a story that left him feeling as though he really was interloping on the group gathered there. Ren was not one to just let an uneasy moment pass by without confronting it. "Okay you guys what is going on? I feel like you know something about this that I don't or that you think I had something to do with it. So which is it?" Ren asked,

Pierre, sitting mid table across from Ren, was avoiding eye contact and the other men were glancing at Pierre. "You have something to say Pierre?" The men seated around the table were all French-Canadian, second or third generation hop farmers. They were the major stakeholders in the market.

"Roy from the Sheriff's office stopped by earlier for a cup of coffee and was asking us questions about you and the fire. He didn't say it outright but he suggested you might have had something to do with it." Pierre told him.

Steam rose up inside Ren as he looked around the table at each man. He could see that there was a bit of suspicion in all of them. In French Ren let out a litany of swear words in a quiet but angry tone. All the men at the table were still fluent in French and Ren fired off at each one of them. It roughly translated to, "And you believed him? You idiots! How long have we known each other? And you don't trust me? You really think I could have done anything so despicable?" Ren stood and threw a five dollar bill on the table and strode towards the door. Apologetically they tried to call him back but he waved them off with a hand and kept walking. He was incensed. It was the ultimate betrayal to Ren. These men, most of whom he had grown up with, gone to school and mass with believed this deputy who didn't have the brains of a piss ant. He couldn't believe it. He would do anything for any one of the men at the table if they asked. When Pierre's cutter broke Ren had loaned him a backup cutter he wasn't using. They had loaned them trucks when theirs broke down. In fact he had loaned the use of the kiln that burned down one year when one of the farmer's specialized conveyer broke. He had been unable to dry his hops to fulfill his contract. Without hesitation Ren had let him use the kiln and even paid for the propane they used to dry their hops. And now they thought he had burned that kiln down and possibly kill Pedro? That hurt. What a devastating blow!

Until all of this happened he really did like Roy. They had enjoyed coffee together at the café many times. He trusted his abilities not only as a law enforcement officer but a firefighter he had worked with on many fires. Now he wanted to rip his head off. How dare he try to sully Ren's reputation with these men he worked so closely with in the hop industry?

He started his truck and headed for home. He really needed to check his other hop acreage but right now he was just done with it all. He called Jon. He answered on the first ring. For a moment he was silent. He wasn't even sure what to say, that he was about to lose it? That he felt like his world had turned upside down in less than a week and he had absolutely no idea what to do about it? "Jon, I could use your help. Would you check on my acreage for a few days until I can find someone to take over? Or would you have someone you think might fit in to Pedro's position? I need a little time to get a grip on this whole thing. Do you realize they think I had something to do with that fire? I can't believe it."

Without hesitation Jon told him he would take care of it and that he might have just the man for the job. He would get back to Ren in a day or so. "Renny, I'm here if you need to talk it out. I know you didn't have anything to do with this. I'm glad you called me. I'll handle this end of it." A weight lifted off of Ren's shoulders. He still had a mountain of things to take care of but just having someone care for his hops for a few days would be a huge relief. They weren't 'his' hops. They were just the hops he and Jon had divided the responsibility for. His brother's belief in him was such a blessing. He said a silent prayer, thanking God for the blessing of his brother who really was acting like he thought a brother should and not like Mark.

Chapter 9

Bellamy walked in to Macy's department store in search of some pretty underwear that weren't granny panties. There weren't many places that carried lingerie anymore in Yakima or so it seemed to Bellamy but then again she couldn't remember the last time she had bought some panties and bras that were not utilitarian. When she was the only one that saw them cotton granny panties and boring white bras were fine. Now that there was actually a man who might someday see them it was suddenly important to her that they were pretty. She felt totally out of her element going in to the intimate wear section of the store. The last intimate wear she bought was a pair of thermal underwear she could wear when she was out hunting. They soon started doing double duty at work under her uniform during the winter months.

She wandered through a section of panties that were pretty but seemed outrageously expensive to her, considering the small amount of skin they would really cover. She finally found some matching sets. That was more like it. She picked a set of pale pink and another in black. She wasn't sure about the black but she got them anyway. Strolling on she saw a table piled with single pairs of panties. She tried her best to find pairs in her size to mix and match with the bras she found.

By the time she got to the actual lingerie she was a bit overwhelmed. Anything would be an improvement over the night shirts she had that were three sizes too big. There were some nighties that looked like something her grandmother would have worn. She passed those without a cursory glance to find a rack of short silky night gowns with spaghetti straps. It took her quite some time to find a rack that actually had something she liked. She wanted her selection to say 'Hi, come hither' not suggest she wanted to be spanked. She found a set with a camisole and tap pants that she thought might fit that sentiment. A little further in to the section Bellamy found some choices that were a little more provocative, a red bustier with high cut panties. She found a short night gown that was actually form fitting showing off the assets a woman had to offer. Bellamy chose a gown in pale sea foam that had a tiny floral print that was very subtle. Suggestive but subtle seemed to be a good combination of sentiment.

Bellamy paid for her purchases and strolled towards the swimwear. This was as intimidating as buying unmentionables. She made a note to herself that she sounded like a spinster prude from the 1800's. Part of her wished she was then she could travel by steamer to Europe and get her clothing made in Paris by a famous designer. Instead she was pawing through swimsuits with designer monikers on them but something millions of women were probably wearing around the world. She started laughing quietly to herself when she found a tiny white bikini with yellow poke-a-dots. Bellamy remembered a retro song about a teeny-weenie-yellow-poke-a-dot-bikini. It was a really cute bikini but she doubted Ren would get the reference. He was probably too young to get the joke. She knew the song from listening to the radio in her house when she was growing up. Her mom would turn it on sometimes and dance around the living room with her. Her heart hurt for a moment remembering that sweet time in life.

She finally chose one that she liked and it fit perfectly. It was black with splashes of purple and blue. It covered her butt but showed off her curves. She had no desire to have one that was a string tied together under the guise of being a swim suit. She wanted to leave a little bit of mystery for Ren to discover if and when he was ever ready to do so.

She thought about that as she strolled towards the fragrance section of the store. Most men she knew would have been in bed with her the first night of their meeting. It was just the reality of the times it seemed. Everyone, her included, seemed to want that instant physical gratification. If she felt an attraction to a man and he seemed to be reciprocating there were no bounds to stop two consenting adults from enjoying a night together. Sometimes it led to more nights together, sometimes it didn't. It just wasn't a big deal. Ren, however felt like a big deal. He felt like he was the real deal. Bellamy knew deep inside her that this was going to be something worth waiting for. In fact it felt as if this is what she had been waiting to experience her entire life.

She made her way around the counter giving this perfume and that perfume a cursory sniff based solely on the design of the bottle. There was one she had just got a brief whiff of when she came in to the area that smelled good enough to eat. She proceeded to sniff a bunch of pieces of paper sprayed with fragrance. Some made her sneeze and some that only old ladies would have found attractive and a few that honestly smelled like they could kill flies. She finally found the one that smelled intoxicating. She couldn't get enough of it. She carried the little paper around with her for a while to see if she still liked it after the initial spritz had worn off. She walked over to some dresses she noticed on her way to the swim suits. She couldn't remember the last dress she had bought. The color of one immediately caught her attention. It was a pale aqua colored dress. It was a halter type dress, with an open back. It was short but not uncomfortably short. Bellamy took it in to the dressing room and tried it on, facing the dreaded three mirror torture chamber. It was form fitting with built in cups. She shimmied into it like a belly dancer. She checked herself in the mirrors. She cringed at the farmers tan she had been rocking until they went fishing and now it was tan up to the top of where her t-shirts came and sunburn from there up. She looked like she had a skin condition. But when she looked at the back of this dress she was sold. It was revealing. The back was open to almost the waist. Yep, it was going home with her and later to Ren's house.

She sniffed the perfume again. It was also getting a new home, her bathroom counter. She was done. When she got back to her car and took the receipts out of the bag she choked at the amount of money she had spent. *If Ren dosen't make love to me sometime soon, I'm going to start a bon fire in his front yard and burn all this stuff.* Bellamy decided in her head. She knew it wasn't true but it sounded like a good plan in her head. She had worn

the dress out of the store and thrown her shirt and shorts in the store bag. She had put on a pair of white sandals to go shopping so that worked with the dress. She wanted to get comfortable in the dress before she went to Ren's house later. Bellamy was getting a little nervous about going to his house. She wondered what it looked like. Would it still look like a shrine to his late wife? Would it look like some kind of bachelor pad with mismatched furniture that had seen better days? She couldn't venture to guess. She hoped it would be like the Ren she was coming to know, refined. Oh sure, that wouldn't be apparent from seeing him slog to her house with mud caked on him or in a tatty shirt and jeans while they were up fishing. But there was this genteel feel she got when she was around him. She got a feeling his "momma had raised him right" as her parents used to comment on some of the boys she dated. Not many of the boys but a few. Bellamy didn't have the best track record with boys and it carried on into adulthood and men.

Chapter 10

Ren started up the long driveway to his house and could see a Sheriff's office 4x4 sitting in front of his house. As he drew nearer, there were other vehicles in the driveway as well that had been hidden behind a barrier of trees. Ren pulled up behind the closest 4x4 blocking it in his driveway. Of all people Roy stepped across the threshold of Ren's front door. Ren jumped out of his truck and slammed the door behind him. He had balled his hands up into tight fists and there was nothing he wanted to do more than beat the crap out of Roy. "What the hell are you doing here" He yelled at Roy as he crossed the hot pavement to his house.

"Search warrant, Mr. LaRue," Roy said handing Ren some paperwork.

"Mr. LaRue? Mr. LaRue? Now it is Mr. LaRue? What happened to Renny? Huh? You piece of shit!" Ren yelled in Roy's face standing a few inches from him. Detective Osborne and another deputy came towards them like wasps swarming to protect one of their own.

Roy stepped back a few steps. "Now Mr. LaRue," Roy placated. "Calm down, it is just routine. We have to check every avenue in a murder/arson." He was feigning professionalism and concern for Ren's feelings but it still made Ren want to kick him in the balls. "Now if you'll just wait out here it shouldn't be much longer until we are done."

"How the hell did you get in my house?" Ren yelled at Detective Osborne's back.

"We had to use a locksmith. You'll get the bill in the mail."

It took every ounce of reserve Ren had to walk away. In his head he was screaming at this man, at all of them. This was utter madness. It was a complete nightmare. He climbed back in his truck, started it for the air conditioning and tried to read the search warrant. He was so angry he couldn't. He would start to read it and his mind would go on a rampage. He would try again and again and again. Finally Ren gave up and threw the papers on the floor of his truck.

His phone rang and he saw it was Bellamy. "Ren, I'm sorry for calling you but I just got home and at the end of the road by your shop there are a bunch of YSO cars. What is going on? Are you okay?"

Ren swore again, under his breath. He really didn't want to offend or upset Bellamy. "Evidently they are serving a search warrant, like they are at my house right now." He tried to sound nonchalant but there was nothing nonchalant about it. He thought his head was going to shoot up into the sky like a rocket. He was livid.

Bellamy's voice rose a bit in octave. "What? What on earth for?"

"Well, if you believe what my friends say, the Sheriff's office thinks I have something to do with the fire and dead body. Oh wait, let me revise that, with a murder/arson. And our good buddy Deputy Roy Morse is spreading those suspicions around to anyone who will listen." Ren told her angrily.

"Again," Bellamy asked, "You are kidding me!"

"Listen, this has been a hell of a day already and I'm sure my house is going to be a disaster area by the time they get through trashing it, can I get a rain check on tonight?" Ren asked, afraid he wouldn't be the best of company for Bellamy tonight. "It might be time to put this relationship on hold. I'm afraid this is going to get much worse before it gets better and I don't want to get you mixed up in it. I don't want Deputy Dog here to get you in trouble with the Comm. Center."

"No, you can't have a rain check. And I am not agreeing to put *our* relationship on hold. I'm coming over. I'll be there shortly. I will help you clean up," she informed him.

Ren started to tell her no but before he could get it out, she had hung up. He looked at the time on his watch. It was still early.

Bellamy checked the time on her phone. It was only a little after three but she wasn't going to wait until six. She pulled her hair up on top of her head in a messy bun, did a cursory sniff of her arm pits, sprayed on a bit of her new perfume, studied herself in the mirror for a moment and put on some mascara and lip balm and was on her way. Jax was on her heels. He knew she was going someplace again and he didn't want to miss a car ride. Bellamy grabbed her purse and her Macy's bag with her bikini and started for the door. "You can't come Jax. You be a good boy and stay inside." She locked the doggy door so he couldn't get out while she was gone. Keys in hand she went out the door and locked it behind her. Once she had started her car and turned on the air conditioning, she made sure to turn on the alarm, security lights and cameras. If she came home after dark and she hoped she would, at least she would feel safe. She actually was hoping maybe it would be morning when she came home.

The drive to Ren's wasn't far but it took her a few minutes to figure out the route. Once she found the road to turn on, she realized where she was going. It was a private road that wound its way halfway up the hillside to one expansive home. She had always wondered who lived there. She had seen the various stages of the house as it was being built. She had driven by it several times on her way to an area she searched for arrow heads near Vantage. It was kind of a new version of a log lodge. It had been very visible when it was first being built, but now a portion of it was hidden by landscaping. One of her supervisory duties was known as MSAG. It involved mapping new streets and blocks for the upper valley. If a new house went in on a road, she had to make sure it was addressed correctly. She had to make sure new roads were added to the mapping system and the block numbers were accurate. That was the easy way to explain it but it took a great deal more time than one would think. At any rate, she had at one time added this property to the county map. She could have pulled it up now on the GIS data base and found out who lived there but she never thought of it when she was at work. If she did that with every house that caught her attention for one reason or another she would never get anything else done. She loved so many different kinds of architecture it was difficult for her to pick a favorite. But she thought this one was interesting. From what she had seen from the road it was rustic looking lodge with a modern edge. Now as she started up the road she knew who lived there.

She could see the Sheriff's office vehicles in the driveway. They must have every sworn deputy they employ out here today, between the house and Ren's shop, she thought. She pulled up next to Ren's truck. He was outside in the heat of the day, resting against the truck, smoking a cigarette as if he was angry at it. Roy was standing in front of him, gesturing with his hands about something. Ren turned, shaking his head and went to Bellamy's car and opened the door for her. She hesitated for a minute when she saw Ren's face. She had never seen him like this. He gave her his hand to help her out. She kept her eyes on Ren's and walked back towards his truck with him. Roy was still standing there. She took Ren's cigarette and took a drag. "What's going on guys?" She asked as though she had absolutely no idea what was going on between the men. Bellamy handed Ren's cigarette back to him. Ren looked at her with an expression of *what the hell are you doing Bellamy*. But he didn't stop her.

"I was asking Mr. LaRue if we could search his truck." Roy said. There was irritation grating his words.

"Oooh, Mr. LaRue, what did you say?" She turned to Ren. Her voice was light and whiney with a bit of sarcasm for good measure. She kind of sounded like the French whore she had played in her first college play, Jean Giraudoux's, "The Madwoman of Chaillot". There actually weren't any whores in the play, the director created them because he had too many people to cast and not enough roles. So he created her a one line role. She just stood on one side of the stage in fishnet stockings and short shorts smoking a cigarette. She had to learn how to smoke. She didn't know how. Sadly she took the role seriously. She had learned to smoke and never stopped.

"Get a warrant." Ren said. He had almost told Roy to go ahead and search the truck then remembered Bellamy's gun was in the jock box. He decided to change his tone.

"Oh let him search it Renny." She cajoled. "If you make him get a warrant he can have your truck impounded at your expense and make everyone stand around here for another hour or two until they find a judge dumb enough to believe this crap." Ren looked at her with his eyes narrowing at her placating tone.

"Hey, Roy, before you search it though, you should know my .9mm is in his glove box," Bellamy informed him offhandedly.

"What did you say?" Roy asked her to repeat what she had told him.

"My gun is in his glove compartment. Or at least it should be. Last night when we heard that guy shoot at Jax, I got my gun out and took it to Ren's truck while we were looking for the guy. He ended up putting it in his glove compartment and I completely forgot about it, until now, that is."

"You forgot you left it in his jockey box?" Roy asked her to clarify.

Bellamy looked at Ren coyly, "Um, yeah, after we stopped looking and figured the guy was long gone we were just sitting there waiting for you guys to show up. Things were kind of ahh, you know heating up. I had to do something with my gun so we just put it in his glove compartment. And you know, we, well, that gun was certainly not the one I was interested in." She felt herself blush. She didn't talk like that. Just the innuendo embarrassed her. She glanced again at Ren. He was smirking like the hound dog he was supposed to be looking down at the ground. When Bellamy looked up at Roy his mouth had gone slack. He was at a loss for words. Bellamy knew she had got his goat, so to speak. Inwardly she was laughing her ass off until she realized his body cam had been on and captured her entire act. She shivered then. That just became available for public disclosure. Shit that could be on the six o'clock news! So much for Ren and Bellamy keeping their new affair from becoming department fodder and she was sure it would be. She had no doubt Roy would make sure her immediate supervisor, Karen, got a copy of it, unofficially of course.

Bellamy groped around inside her purse and retrieved her wallet. "Here's my permit. Signed, sealed and approved by the good Sheriff Hastings." She said sternly and thrust the permit into Roy's hand. Her tone had taken on a sweet voice again. "So, Renny if that is what you were worried about, don't be honey. Let him search it so we can get on with our evening. There are other things I'd rather be doing." *Shut up Bellamy!* She was talking and she couldn't shut up!

Ren stepped aside and opened his arm to allow Roy entry into his vehicle. Roy was still gloved up from the house search. He immediately reached into the jockey box and seized Bellamy's .9mm. He took a plastic evidence bag out of a pouch on his waist and put the gun in it. He started to put the permit in the bag as well. Bellamy snatched the permit out of his hand. "The gun you can bag and tag but not my permit. It was not taken from the vehicle therefore you can not and will not seize it, unless of course you want to explain to the prosecutor your illegal seizure. You have WACIC/NCIC in your car, run me any time. It will be in there." Bellamy told him her voice as condescending as Roy's has been. "And I want a receipt for my gun." Bellamy added. She did not move her stance of arms crossed over her chest until Roy called a crime scene technician to the truck and asked him to finish tagging the gun and issuing a receipt for Bellamy.

Roy then ordered the technician to search the truck for any evidence that was listed on the warrant. Bellamy took the paper from Ren's hand and started reading it. It was quite restrictive. It looked like the judge had narrowed the scope of what could be done with the vehicle. Some warrants were so inclusive that a tech could go ahead and tow the vehicle and take it apart piece by piece. She planned to watch every move to make sure they did not go beyond the instructions of the warrant. She took out her phone and began to record the search. She was attempting to be just as intimidating as they were trying to be with Ren. She knew how to play the game. It irritated her that she even had to play the game. It was ridiculous to think that Ren was somehow involved in all of this.

The warrant only gave permission to take anything out of the vehicle that could have caused the death of the victim. How her gun fit into that she wasn't sure. She thought the victim had been burned alive. It also stated that they could fingerprint the vehicle for any prints. They could look for blood stains, fibers and any other sign of a crime. The guy went over the truck, inside and out. He used a different type of spray to check for blood, it had a name that ended in blue. She had never heard of it before. In daylight the tech had to use that spray to search for anything resembling a blood stain. The tech checked under the seats, behind the seats, under the dash as far as he could reach without taking it apart, the jockey box and the console. He moved around the outside of the truck and checked the short bed of the truck. There was nothing. The only evidence Bellamy saw him take were fingerprints and a long blond hair which she was sure was hers.

When he finished and started tagging the prints, Bellamy stopped filming him. She turned to Ren who had been watching the tech and Bellamy filming him. "Just for shits and giggles," She told the tech.

Chapter 11

Ren chuckled for the first time that day. It felt good. He took Bellamy in a tight hug. He realized her back was bare. He kissed her softly then held her at arms length. That is when he finally took in her attire. She looked and smelled great, not that she didn't before but this was different. He slowly twirled her around and looked at the back of her dress. It was bare to her waist. He looked appreciatively at the gentle curve of her back. She was flawless. He turned her back around and whispered in her ear, "You are so beautiful." Bellamy shivered. It didn't matter to either of them that half the Sheriff's office was watching them. She took in Ren's appearance for the first time. Damn he was hot, Bellamy thought. He cleans up good!

It almost looked like they had discussed their outfits to make sure they were color coordinated. It made her think of being a teenager planning to go somewhere with her friends. She and her best friend, Lauren would spend hours on the phone discussing what they wanted to wear and making sure it went with what the other one was going to wear. And now standing here with Ren, Bellamy felt they looked like they should be going out to an expensive restaurant or posing for a photo for a magazine or something.

"And you sir are gorgeous and your cologne makes me want to follow you anywhere." Bellamy complimented. She buried her head against his neck for a moment, breathing in his scent mingled with his cologne. They stood together then and smoked another cigarette waiting for the deputies and crime scene people to retreat from his house. He was surprised to find they appeared only to have only taken some papers from his house. He shook his head, all that time and all those people and that is all they were taking. It was probably another fifteen minutes until everyone had cleared out and was trying to leave. Both Ren and Bellamy ignored their attempts to maneuver around their vehicles. When Roy came out to get in his 4x4 he had to ask them to move their cars so they could leave. "What's the magic word, Roy?" she asked as though she was trying to teach him some manners.

"Please," he said through clenched teeth, his face blustering red.

"Hey, don't forget to have your people lock up when they leave my shop." Ren instructed as he got in to his truck to move it. Ren knew he probably should go to his shop and watch to see what they were doing there but he didn't care. They could impound every piece of equipment he had in there. He didn't care. He was already sick and tired of this idiotic investigation and it had only been a few days.

Bellamy and Ren moved their vehicles so the convoy of Sheriff's office cars and vans could leave. Bellamy nodded and saluted each driver as they drove passed her. She was hurt that they didn't salute her back. She felt a little betrayed and angry that Roy was treating her this way. She wasn't hiding anything. She wasn't trying to mislead Roy in any way. And she felt like he was treating her like a criminal.

When they had all left, she and Ren moved their vehicles closer to the house. Ren came to her car and opened the door for her.

She climbed out and grabbed her purse and Macy's bag. As she stood for a minute facing west she knew where Mt. Rainier and Mt. Adams should be but she couldn't see them. The haze she had noticed when she was driving to Ren's house had completely obscured them and a wide, purple shelf cloud completely obscured the view of the Cascade Mountains. She hoped that cloud stayed to the west so they could have their swim. She was actually excited to show off the bikini she had purchased earlier. She wasn't going to hold her breath that it would get the reaction she was hoping for but she had given it her best effort.

Ren escorted Bellamy into the house. It was beautiful, save for the mess the crime scene people had left. And even that wasn't too bad until they discovered the fingerprint dust on everything. Ren was especially irritated because his maid had just been there and cleaned house, which included dusting all the furniture.

Ren's house was open and expansive. The floors were hardwood. They were old and worn but polished to a high sheen. They definitely weren't original to this house. They looked as though they had been reclaimed from a much older building. This house was only a few years old but the floors looked like they could be a hundred years old. The kind of house Ren lived in had only crossed her mind that morning and this was not what she had envisioned. She was having a hard time taking it all in. To the right of the door was a living room with floor to ceiling windows on two sides of the room, to the north and to the west.

From there she could see an infinity pool, glistening in the late afternoon sun. On the south side of the room was a fireplace made of large river rock very similar to hers. The mantel was a slab of wood that had been buffed and coated to a silky high gloss. To the east and straight ahead of her was a huge entertaining area with a sectional facing the incline of the hill behind the house. Large windows opened up to let in the view. To the east was a room with another bank of floor to ceiling windows that opened to sunrise. Ren ushered her through that area passed a wide staircase of honey colored wood that wound up to the second level of his house. Beyond the staircase was the kitchen. Bellamy almost slobbered. It was a dream kitchen. At least it was her dream kitchen. "Wow," softly escaped her lips.

There was a long bar topped with a dark gray stone that actually glittered. On the side nearest to her were four bar stools with dark gray woven backs. The kitchen itself was an exaggerated 'L' shape. The cupboards were a light washed gray and tan that made them look like drift wood. It looked like the pulls for the cupboards were collected rocks that had been shaped and polished. The drawer handles were antlers. The countertops were the same dark granite as the bar top. The kitchen had all the appliances a cook of any metal would swoon over. Everything had a brushed stainless steel finish. There was a double sink with the kind of faucet that had a detachable sprayer. The backsplash was iridescent glass tile. Under cupboard lights made the countertop and all the pretty appliances glisten. She wondered if Ren would just let her move in to his kitchen. She could be happy there.

Ren noticed her expression and smiled. She was running her fingers lightly over the bar top. "Ren this is beautiful. And the drawer pulls, wow" She said. "Did you make them" She asked and went over to examine them closer. Again she ran her fingers gently over one of the antlers and then one of the rock spheres. "These are so cool" She added not waiting for him to answer.

"Thanks. Yeah, I made the antler pulls. I like them better being something functional than putting a deer head on the wall like some kind of trophy. I'm not much of a designer or decorator. Actually you are the first woman to ever see it. I mean, besides the maid. How did I do?"

"Oh my gosh!" Bellamy gushed. "It is gorgeous. I was just wondering if I could move in to the kitchen, just your kitchen. I wouldn't step foot in any other part of the house. But the kitchen? Wow! I promise I won't be any trouble at all."

Ren laughed then, the day of craziness falling from his shoulders like dust from his boots. "I have my doubts that you wouldn't be any trouble Amie. You seem to grip trouble and take it for a ride."

She laughed then. She did kind of have a knack for showing up in some very odd situations.

"I didn't have a clue what you were doing out there. You were amazing. You rocked that whole thing and took Roy down a couple of notches." He closed his eyes and shook his head remembering her voice. "Your dress didn't hurt, either" he added. "None of them could take their eyes off of you."

Bellamy curtsied. "Thank you sir. And thank the wild child who lived in the drama department in college. I guess I picked up a few tricks of the trade." He looked at her curiously. "I couldn't decide if I wanted to be a straight cop or a pot smoking hippy actress." He laughed out loud then. "But I couldn't act worth crap, so you know I went the straight cop route. Only I wasn't really good at that either, so here I am dispatcher extraordinary. Not a bad way to go. I get to tell cops where to go." She was babbling. "I just don't trust Roy. I could see him sending that body cam video to Karen or Brian." Bellamy told him.

"He wouldn't do that would he? Or should I say he couldn't do that could he? Bellamy I don't want to get you into trouble at the center."

"I don't know. But if he does, oh well, I jumped in the middle of this with both feet. If I get in trouble, it is my fault. Not yours."

Her words sounded sincere but the expression on her face said otherwise.

She was nervous being here. She was becoming aware that she was totally out of her element in this house. It was beautiful. Not that her house wasn't. She loved her house. But this was in a class she wasn't a part of. She felt like a foreigner in a strange country.

"Now that we are alone, would you like something to drink?" Ren asked.

"Surprise me, as long as it isn't beer." Bellamy told him.

Ren took a split of champagne out of the fridge under the bar and a bottle of gin. He went over to the cupboard and took out a couple of tall glasses. He filled them with ice from the dispenser and grabbed a lemon from the fruit tray.

He brought them over to where she was sitting on a bar stool. He expertly rolled the lemon, cut it half and squeezed its juice into a large shaker. He added the split of champagne and a couple of shots of gin. He reached below the counter and took a glass container with sugar in it. He added a couple of tablespoons of sugar to the mix. He put a lid on the shaker and shook it like he was accompanying an orchestra playing the bossanova. When he was pleased with his mix he took the lid off and filled the two glasses. "A French 75 for your approval."

She took a sip. The bubbles from the champagne tickled her nose as it should. She wrinkled her nose. "Perfect" she sighed. This could be a very dangerous drink. It was extremely refreshing on a hot summer evening.

"What do you want for dinner?" Ren asked. "I know it is really early for dinner but I have to make sure you get home at a decent hour. You have to work tomorrow, don't you? Do you like sushi?" he suggested.

"Ugh, don't remind me." She groaned thinking about work in the morning. "But sushi sounds perfect for a hot night summer night."

They sat at the bar studying the menu on their phones for a popular sushi place in town. Ren called for a delivery while the two of them sat enjoying their drink.

"Why don't you let me clean up some of this fingerprint powder while you tell me about your day," Bellamy offered.

"You don't have to do that. I can have the maid come in and take care of that."

"It's up to you but I really don't mind." Bellamy told him softly.

Ren was still trying to wrap his head around the events of the day as he filled Bellamy in on everything that had happened. "I'm surprised I'm not being blamed for Donald's heart attack." Ren lamented after telling her all his excitement.

"See there's a bright lining to the day. You helped save a man's life. That's what you signed up for when you became a firefighter, right" Bellamy told him.

Ren didn't share her optimism. "I kept him alive to get him in the ambulance, beyond that I don't know how he is doing. I'm hoping Amy will call and update me."

He took a sip of his drink, "Amie, thank you for ignoring me and coming over anyway. I would have been sitting here being angry and paranoid. Or I'd be in jail for punching out Roy or that Defective." Ren said, his voice gravelly.

Bellamy laughed. "No, you wouldn't have punched him. You are a better man than that. You might have ended up in jail for my gun in your truck though."

"Good thing you showed up when you did and talked him out of that one," he added. "But I thought you were supposed to be honest and upright."

"I was, for the most part. What I told him was the truth, just not in the order it happened exactly or how it happened" Bellamy assured him. "I was just following the instructions from when I got hired," she started, " 'We are hiring you because you are an honest person, once you start working here, we will teach you how to lie' " She parroted her boss.

"What?" Ren asked perplexed by what she had just said.

"We do it all the time when we are talking to someone on the phone. They are upset and scared and want to know where the cop is. We kind of tell the truth. That the cop is getting there as quickly as he can. Truth. It shouldn't be much longer. Lie. I don't know. You just get an idea of what you can and can't tell them to make them feel better. It's a thin line. But like today. I didn't lie to him. I just didn't elaborate on the sequence of events," Bellamy explained, "Or like we tell them on the phone. It's okay, calm down everything will be ok when we know good and well things are not going to be ok. And cops do it all the time when they talk to a suspect but they are allowed to lie to get the truth."

"Say that again."

"Oh yeah, like they may not have squat on a suspect but their gut instinct tells them that the suspect is sitting right across from them but won't talk. They lie. They might tell them that his buddy ratted him out or that they have evidence that they really don't have. Sometimes they have to use deceit to get the truth."

Ren switched gears. "Why didn't you become a cop?"

"Because I am a klutz. I have no upper body strength. I can't run. You know those cartoons on TV when it shows a character running, his feet pin wheeling going a mile a minute but when they show the entire frame you see he is going nowhere or going in slow motion. He only thinks he is running fast. Like those football players that are 300 pounds and their stats say they can run the 40 in 4.8 seconds or something like that. I couldn't run it in 10 seconds. I am a pathetic athlete." She laughed. "I told you, actress or cop. Unfortunately I wasn't good at either one. But I have learned a few things from those experiences along the way."

"That's an understatement. You drive like a maniac."

Bellamy laughed. "Yeah about that, I talked the department into letting me take the EVOC (Emergency vehicle operation course) training class on my own time and my own dime and my own car. They wouldn't let me drive a department car. They didn't want to have to pay for it if I crashed it or the engine blew up. But it was kick ass. I loved every minute of it. Turns out I'm a daredevil in a car. Not on the open road but like the other night. Just that made the class worth it. But, just for a second there I thought I was going to end up in the canal. We had to have had an angel with us," Bellamy said seriously.

"I was praying. Praying you knew what you were doing," Ren added seriously.

"Me too," Bellamy admitted laughing at the memory.

They enjoyed their dinner sitting at the bar, talking and laughing. Ren's horrible day was lost in her eyes. He thought he could sit across from her every day and never get tired of seeing her face. It was a very nice face.

It seemed the evening was closing in on them. Ren looked at the digital readout on the stove. It was still early, just now six in the evening but it was rather dark. "Does it seem dark to you?"

He stood up and looked out one of the windows facing the south. He couldn't really see anything. He strolled down a hallway between the kitchen and the stairway. He came back in a few minutes. "It looks like a storm is rolling in. If we want to take a dip in the pool, we probably should do it now," Ren suggested, "And I really do want to take a dip. I want to see that bikini. If it is anything like that dress you may not be spending the night at your house."

Her face flushed. He smiled as though he was joking but his eyes said he was serious. "Where can I change?" Bellamy asked.

Down the hallway from where he had just come, there was a large powder room. "Is this okay?"

"It's fine."

The bathroom put hers to shame. This was a large bathroom with a walk-in shower. The toilet was in another room completely. She had seen bathrooms like this in high end hotels but never in a private home. She liked it. It was a pretty neat idea. Ren hadn't left out any of the fine details of the room. He had foaming hand wash as well as lotion on the bathroom counter. The sink was like none she had ever seen before. It was a copper vessel that sat on the vanity. How cool, she thought. Huge, fluffy towels were rolled and placed in a round basket under the sink just begging to be used. Bellamy pushed back the soft cotton shower curtain very slowly so the rings on the curtain rod didn't make any noise. She was enjoying a little bit of snooping. The shower was tiled in smooth river pebbles with a shower head was the about twelve inches across. Holy Hannah, this isn't a shower, it's a waterfall. It was a striking room. The cream colored walls seemed to play against the rocks. Cream was not her favorite color but it was in this room. It made it lush and expensive. That was an understatement. It was lush and expensive.

She finally got over the design of the room and disrobed in front of gigantic mirror that showed far more than she really wanted to see. She couldn't remember the last time she had worn a bikini, college maybe. She wasn't sure. She hoped it looked as good on her now as it did in the dressing room at the store. It looked great. Her body was the problem. Her legs were tanned below the knee but faded to a ghost white from the knees up. The rest of her was white too until it got to her arms. She had a farmers tan for heaven's sake. It was embarrassing. She cringed.

She opened the door and peeked out. Ren was standing in the kitchen in a pair of dark blue swim trunks leaning against the bar with his legs crossed in front of him. "You ready?" He asked.

"As ready as I will ever be."

"Come on. I have some beach towels for us."

She stepped out of the bathroom and into the hallway. Bellamy, usually fairly confident, felt very vulnerable at this moment until she saw Ren looking at her. His eyes were doing that up and down guy assessment. His approval of her bathing suit was evident. "Nice," he whispered drawing the word out. She smiled shyly then walked towards him.

He took her hand and led her through the house and out onto the patio. It was still very hot but storm clouds had obstructed the direct sun so it wasn't searing the house. The view was spectacular. Bellamy's searching eyes took in the pool, it creeped her out. The water looked like it should be tumbling over the side of the hill. She wasn't sure she liked this infinity pool. But once Ren took her hand again and led her down the steps and into the cool water it wasn't nearly as frightening. As if he could read her thoughts his eyes assured her she was safe.

Ren sensed her apprehension. "Here, come with me," he invited. She hesitated only a moment before she floated towards him and the edge of the pool. Her stomach flip flopped the closer they got to the edge. He had her take hold of the edge and look over the side. She wasn't sure she could, she was so afraid of heights. When she did, she laughed at herself. There was a two maybe three foot drop and a wide expanse of flat lawn that sprawled out about thirty feet to a four foot stone wall. "You aren't going to fall off a cliff. It just feels that way." Ren assured her.

That view put her at ease a bit. It was still a freaky optical illusion. She turned her attention to Ren who was floating her away from the side of the pool and out into the middle. They splashed and played with a ball like they were children. In the water it felt like she was a kid again. She had forgotten the weightlessness the water provided.

When they had tired of batting the ball back and forth, Ren tossed it up on the patio. He took Bellamy in his arms then and kissed her long and sweet. He embraced her. This was the first real feel of skin on skin. It took her breath away. She could feel her body reacting to his touch. She wrapped her legs around his waist and her arms around his neck. He walked her back to the edge of the pool next to the house. There was a sloped ramp there. He gently leaned her back, her head resting on the top of the ramp. Her hair had escaped her messy bun and was floating around her head like a halo. He pressed his weight against her and she thought she was going to faint not from his weight but because of the sheer thrill his body was eliciting in her. She began kissing him again. Bellamy wanted more of him. Her desire for this man took her by surprise. A few days ago she couldn't stand him and now she couldn't stand not having all of him. She wanted to consume him.

Ren's hands slowly explored her body. She shivered at his touch. She softly moved her fingers against the sides of his chest. A low moan escaped his mouth. He wanted to caress the breasts she had pushed hard against his chest but he was afraid if he did he would go further than he should. He didn't want to become so intimate with her that there was no going back, not until he was sure he wasn't putting her in some kind of peril with her job or reputation. He outlined the under side of her breasts, his fingers just barely bushing them through the material. Bellamy drew a ragged breath.

She could feel his desire against her pelvis. She wanted to touch him, caress him but she was respecting the boundaries he had set for them. "Stop," she heard her voice whisper hoarsely. She heard the word come out of her mouth although she was unsure why. No, that wasn't true. She was sure why she had said it but it really was a lie. She wanted to experience and enjoy every inch of him. Ren leaned on his elbows and looked at her breathlessly. "If you don't want me to go crazy or force myself on you against your will, we need to stop. I, uh, I have never wanted to make love to someone as much as I want to make love to you at this very moment."

Ren took a deep breath and exhaled. "You are right. It's not fair to do this, to either one of us. I want you more than you know Bellamy, I really do. But you are right, we need to stop."

As if to accentuate the point there was a loud clap of thunder that was closer than either one of them had expected. "Okay we heard you God! Might be time to get out of the water," Ren suggested. The thunder rolled over the top of them ushering them in to the safety of the house.

Ren wrapped her in a beach towel, tightly swaddling her like she was a baby ready for a nap. "Better go get dressed Bellamy, you are shivering."

It wasn't the abrupt change from heat to air conditioning against her wet skin. It was being stopped at the brink of finally having all of him. And now as quickly as it had erupted it was gone. It was like being on a bungee cord plunging head first towards the ground and being yanked back to relative safety and then the subsequent drops. It was terrifying and exhilarating at the same time. She tried to convince herself that like the bungee jump she would be on the safety of the ground shortly and able to stop screaming in her head.

Her wet feet squeaked against the polished wood floors as she traipsed back to the powder room to dry off and put her dress back on. She tried to towel dry her hair. It was futile. It was knotted and looked like a rats nest as her mother used to call it.

When she emerged from the bathroom she found Ren in the kitchen brewing coffee. "I can make you something else." He offered standing in front of his coffee maker.

"Coffee sounds great."

"Café or Decafe," He asked?

"Really? You have to ask me that? I'm a dispatcher. I was weaned into this career on coffee strained through a sock. Caffeinated please."

"A sock," Ren repeated, laughing, not sure he had heard her correctly.

She laughed. "Truth. The first place I worked had a big industrial sized coffee brewer in the kitchen. Every morning the janitor would come in and start coffee for the oncoming shift. One day he ran out of coffee filters so he used a sock from the laundry. Clean laundry," Bellamy clarified. "Everyone asked what he had done differently, telling him it was such an improvement from what he usually brewed. He didn't reveal his secret for a very long time, but yeah, for the entire time I was there, that is how he made it. And we drank the coffee he brewed from the morning of one day until the following morning. So by the night shift it was like tar but we still drank it all night long."

Another clap of thunder rocked the house. They both jumped and laughed at each other.

Coffee in hand Ren led the way back into the room with the fireplace. They curled up on the couch and watched the lightning as it streaked across the evening sky. Bellamy loved it and watched spellbound at the light show. She shivered again. Ren tugged a blanket off of the back of the couch and wrapped the warm fuzzy throw around her cool shoulders and pulled her closer against him using it as an excuse to hold her close. Bellamy smiled at him finding contentment in his embrace. He looked like a movie star from the 30's or 40's she decided. He just had that look. Ren had that special something that would give him the leading role as lover or a gangster. He could be convincing in either role. Or he could be a cowboy in a Western, 'shoot 'em up' movie. He seemed to be able to fit any of those roles. He just had that look that would have made him able to pull off any of those personalities.

The storm was moving slowly to the north and east as it sometimes did with the show captivating them for quite some time. Suddenly Ren sat up straight and looked to the west. He got up and went to get a pair of binoculars lying on a table by the west facing windows. Bellamy got up and followed his gaze. Just as he got the binoculars focused on the glow, somewhere in the house a Plectron set off tone after tone. It made her jump like the thunder had. Plectrons were a precursor of pagers then replaced with cell phones. It replayed the high low pitches that the Zetron set off notifying specific fire districts of a call. Ren turned for a moment as if to listen more closely to the tones. Firefighters could somehow figure out who the tones were for. Bellamy, even though she set them off on a daily basis couldn't tell one district's set of tones from another. They all sounded the same to her. The tones continued to go off much longer than it took to tone out one district. Then Bellamy saw what Ren was looking at. It looked like a brilliant white dancing light shooting up into the dark sky. It was surrounded by a red and orange glow somewhere in town. With the exception of the bright white light shooting up like a search light it looked small but from this distance the entire city looked small.

"Can you tell what it is?" Bellamy asked. Before he could even answer she heard Greg's voice come on the air, rambling off district units in rapid fire, with the sound of excited city units responding on another channel in the background over the top of his dispatch. It was a structure fire at Mid-Valley Hops. It was being dispatched as what dispatchers referred to as a "Ya'll come" fire. In fire speak it was a five alarm fire or what would have been if they had taken it one alarm at a time. This went from zero to five immediately. Almost every district in the upper county was being used to either respond with the city to fight the fire or to back fill the empty city fire stations and respond to other calls in the city. Each district had a list of what their duties were.

"You have got to be kidding me!" Ren said putting the binoculars down and turning away then turning back as though he wasn't sure what to do in that instant.

"Do you need to go, Ren?" Knowing he was a volunteer for one of the fire districts being dispatched as well a paid city B.C.

"No. No. I'm unavailable." He told her. It was a status he could choose for both the volunteer fire agency and the city.

At that moment her phone started ringing somewhere in the house. It was in her purse on the kitchen counter. She was surprised she could even hear it over Ren's scanner. The minute she picked it up she saw it was a call from work. She couldn't ignore it no matter how much she wanted to. Some employees did but in good conscience she couldn't. Hesitantly she answered.

"Bellamy?" One of the call takers asked. Bellamy answered with the affirmative. "Greg wanted me to call. We need you to come in and go out with the Mobile Command unit."

She wanted to whine but she knew it was useless. As one of the supervisors that was one of their duties. A supervisor was supposed to man the Command Unit. Only as a last resort was a regular dispatcher sent with the Command Unit. Since she had to work in the morning she would be the last supervisor on the list that they would call in to man the

Mobile Command Unit. "Where am I going?" Bellamy asked, resignation leaking out.

"The radio shop. Garrett will meet you there."

"I'll be on my way." Bellamy ended the phone call. She started back in to the fireplace room and met Ren at the staircase. "I have to go in Ren. I have to go to the scene. Do you have a pair of department sweats I could borrow? It would save me a trip home. I don't think this would be, um, you know appropriate to wear to the fire ground." Ren took her appearance in again. She looked lovely. He admitted if he saw her like this at a fire scene he would be useless trying to concentrate on the fire. He was sad she was going. Ren nodded and trotted up the stairs to what she assumed was his bedroom. A few minutes later he returned with a pair of neatly folded dark blue sweats. 'Thank you," she said and kissed him solidly on the lips. "Welcome to my life." She added as she walked away towards the bathroom. She quickly pulled the sweats on and realized she didn't have a bra. The dress she was wearing came with one built in. She doubted Ren had one of those lying around. She took the dress off and pulled the sweatshirt on. Luckily it was loose enough that it didn't cling to any parts of her. The sweat pants were looser still and longer. She rolled the hem up on each leg and hoped she wouldn't trip on them. Her fire boots and 'go' bag were in the back of her car. Bellamy wadded up her dress and swim suit and tossed them into the one Macy's bag she had brought with her. She picked up her beach towel and carried it out to the living room. "I didn't know where to put this." she said offering him the soggy towel.

Ren took it from her and tossed it over the stair rail. He followed her out to her car. He started to open the car door for her but she went to the hatch and opened it. She sat on the edge of the cargo bay and reached for her 'go' bag. She took out a pair of socks and pulled them on and proceeded to wrestle on her steel toed boots and lace them up. She grabbed her bag and purse and slammed the hatch. Ren followed her to the driver's side door and held it for her. "I wish I didn't have to go." she said. He gathered her to him and wrapped his arms around her. Ren kissed her softly and let her go. "Can you tell I'm not wearing a bra?" she asked as an after thought. "You can't tell from looking, just don't let any of your boyfriends on the fire ground hug you." Ren teased. "Oooh, I'll have to make a sign…free feels accepted here." She pointed to her breasts. "If I can't, they can't." Ren said protectively. He was only half joking. She grinned then and got in the car.

Chapter 12

Twenty minutes later Bellamy pulled in to the parking lot of the radio shop. The storm was still lighting the sky periodically as it moved away from the area. Even though Garrett was coming from much further away, up in the Nile Valley he was already there. The bay door was open. He was doing the once around of the Mobile Command Unit removing charging lines. Bellamy opened the side door of the 32 foot converted motor home and tossed her go bag with her purse inside. Garrett raised his head in acknowledgement of her presence. "Hey sexy," he greeted jokingly as he took in her baggy sweats.

"Yeah, yeah. I know. I wasn't expecting to get called in. I was at a friend's house, swimming. I didn't want to take the time to go home to change." Bellamy shouted over the sound of the motor home's engine.

He looked at her quizzically and she realized she had just let one of the cat's feet out of the bag by saying she was at a friend's house swimming and evidently wearing a pair of her 'friend's" sweats, a pair of sweats far too large for her. He was trying to go through a list of Comm. Center personnel who had a pool, above ground or in ground. When he couldn't place anyone on that list he quickly went to the city fire department. He ruled out the police department since the sweats were fire department issue. She quickly tried to stuff the cat's foot back in the bag but she could see Garrett was well aware of the rest of the cat in that bag. *Stupid, stupid*! She admonished herself. He knew she had been at a city firefighter's house, swimming in a city firefighter's swimming pool.

"You ready?" She asked trying to divert the conversation to the task at hand.

"Yeah," he answered. He went around to the driver's side of the vehicle and hoisted himself up inside. Bellamy climbed in to the passenger seat. Garrett hit the horn and turned on the overhead lights as they pulled out onto the apron of parking lot. He closed the overhead door after he made sure the exhaust hose had detached from the tail pipe. Garrett hit the siren and cars started pulling over to give him access to the road. Bellamy held on while they headed down the road. It wasn't like they were a patrol car in pursuit of a bad guy doing a hundred miles an hour. The normal speed limit on this street was 35 mph. They were traveling at a whopping 45 miles per hour. But when they were coming to a stop light at 45, with no real intention of stopping and passing cars to the left when turning right it could be a little un-nerving.

Bellamy had driven the Command vehicle before and knew in an emergency she could do it. She knew how to set it up but she had no desire to do so when Garrett was available. She had darn near taken out a light stanchion the last time she had driven it cutting a corner too short. This 32 foot converted motor home did not maneuver like her car and it wasn't made for four wheeling even if it was just over a sidewalk curb. It had made her pucker in places she shouldn't. She had also forgotten to put the telescoping camera down and driven all the way back to the radio shop with it up in the air. She was extremely lucky she hadn't ripped it off going under an overpass or snagged a low hanging power line.

They were at the fire scene in ten minutes. In normal traffic to cross town at this time of night it usually took at least twenty minutes. Garrett maneuvered the motor home to where he was told to stage.

In the staging area Bellamy took in all the different apparatus waiting for their assignments. For some units, sitting in the staging area was their assignment. In between two units that were staging in front of the Command unit she could see a turnout with the letters ATF emblazoned on the back of it. In front of the person in the turnout was a camera on a tripod, facing the fire. The ATF person also had a camera he was slowly panning the scene with. It wasn't unusual to see someone in turnouts filming the fire and the bystanders watching the fire. It was never out of the possibility that in an arson fire the arsonist was watching his handy work. She was just a little surprised it was an ATF agent. She was also surprised that an ATF agent was at the scene this early in the fire. She hadn't heard a request for ATF over the radio but she may have missed it on her drive to the radio shop since she didn't have a scanner in her car.

While Garrett was making sure all the bells and whistles were as they should be before he went to auxiliary power, Bellamy stared ahead at the fire. The white emanating from the center of the warehouse was almost too bright to stare at. It looked like a huge sparkler. Bellamy had never seen anything like it.

Once Garrett had parked the unit and turned it off, he hopped out and started setting up the Command vehicle. Bellamy got to work setting up the interior of the unit. She had to switch things out. The vehicle was shared with the SWAT team and evidently they had used it last. She pulled down the white board and cleaned off the board with doodles of building schematics and arrows drawn on the board. While she waited for Garrett to get the generator started so she could bring up the computers, Bellamy got a big pot of coffee ready to perk when the power came on. She used a one gallon bottle of water to fill it. She took disposable cups, creamer and sugar and the stir sticks out of the drawers and put them on the counter. She was sure Red Cross would be called to the scene because it was quite evident this would be an all night fire fight but she knew it would be an hour or so before they were called and arrived to set up a canteen.

She had been at enough large fires to know she was going to be here until morning. She was glad she had opted to wear sweats even though she was sweating now she knew it would be cooling down quickly and she would be scrounging through the closets to find a pair of turnouts she could put on over the sweats to stay warm.

She wasn't sure exactly how this was going to go, considering she was due in to work her regular shift at 0800 hours. She was wondering if she would have to go ahead and cover that twelve hour shift too or if another dispatcher would be called in to cover it.

Garrrett came in the back door next to her cubicle and started setting up the telescoping camera so if the command staff or anyone else needed to see something from above the camera would be ready. He turned on the radio and made sure it was working. He told her the generator was on and he switched the power over. Bellamy plugged in the coffee maker. She turned on the computers and set them to the screens she needed to take over the fire ground traffic. She signed on the air at the scene while Garrett finished opening the slide-outs. Once he was finished with that he made sure the other odds and ends were done. He zipped around like he had already drank the contents of the coffee pot but that was his normal speed.

As soon as Bellamy signed on the air all of the fire ground traffic was switched over for her to handle. It allowed Greg to handle the other routine radio traffic of his shift. It also gave the fire ground staff their own dedicated dispatcher to handle their specific needs and help with logistics. She heard Garrett open the front door of the unit talking to someone outside. He brought in a man in turnouts she didn't recognize but that wasn't unusual. She knew most of the city firefighters and some of the district people but not many. She was busy listening to some traffic and half listening to Garrett as he told the guy about the telescoping camera. When Bellamy had finished her radio traffic, she turned to look at the man Garrett was referring to as Jake. "Bellamy, this is Agent Jake Aarons from ATF. He's filming the fire for an investigation they are doing. If I'm not in here and he has some questions or needs you to reposition the camera for him would you take care of that for me," Garrett asked?

"Sure, nice to meet you Agent Aarons."

"You too Bellamy," he said. Peter had talked about Bellamy. He was right. She was very pretty.

"Hey, when I was up at my friend's house and we spotted this fire, it looked really weird, like there was a big search light shooting up into the sky. And when we pulled in it looked like a white sparkler in the fire. Do either of you know why, or could you ask someone?" Bellamy asked as both the agent and Garrett were getting cups of coffee. It was probably going to be pretty weak. It hadn't been perking for very long.

Agent Aarons' cocked his head in her direction. "Magnesium," he told her. "Good question though. Most people wouldn't have caught that anomaly."

"That's what it looks like?" Bellamy exclaimed with an ah-ha moment. "My guys taught me about magnesium when they got so excited over a garage fire. I couldn't figure out what the big deal was. There wasn't a car in the garage or anything. Then they told me about the magnesium in lawn mowers. Before that I had no idea." She said then turned back to her phone that was ringing. It was one of the B.C.'s on scene calling for a mechanic and radio tech to come to the scene for standby. She got caught up in her duties and had barely notice the two of them leave out the back door.

Bellamy's job was sporadic. Most of the communication was between the Incident Commander and the staff officers on the fire ground. But occasionally he would need something brought in, like fuel or heavy equipment and it was Bellamy who made those calls and updated the information on the call screen. Other than that Bellamy just listened to instructions and monitored the other channels. It was a pretty easy job until you heard the heart stopping word "Mayday" yelled over the air. That was why they wanted seasoned dispatchers in the Command unit. Those dispatchers didn't have to think about what they needed to do. They immediately went on automatic auto pilot at the speed of sound. They had to be able to react without choking, so the speak, because the adage of seconds saved, saved lives. They didn't have time to look up the procedure on a 'Mayday' and go down the checklist. That checklist was part of the gold thread that sewed the lives on everyone on the fire ground to her heart and skills.

Bellamy had only had a couple of 'Maydays" and one of them wasn't even hers. It was a police dispatcher and the dispatcher froze. She completely froze. She had turned to Bellamy sitting on the fire side of the center, the expression of a deer in the headlights on her face. Bellamy stared back at her for just a moment until she realized the dispatcher wasn't going to do anything. The other police dispatcher was on a break. Bellamy jumped in on the police frequency and took over the police dispatcher's call clearing channels and starting medical units into the area as well as fire to stage as she listened to the officer in trouble screaming for help over the air. Microphones were open on officers' portable radios running in to assist him. Bellamy turned on the damned channel marker that told other officers to stay off the air that may have been on a break or other call and not heard the 'Mayday'. It was supposed to tell them something emergent was happening and to shut up. Most of the time the channel marker worked to keep the air clear. Other times it didn't and Bellamy wanted to reach through the radio and bitch slap an officer who cleared a traffic stop or lunch break. The channel marker, a tone that went off every ten seconds or so, was annoying to say the least and it also covered radio traffic with it's prolong beep. It was probably only a second long but it still covered radio transmissions.

It was a nightmare in motion. The officer had opened the passenger side of a vehicle to talk to a driver, when the driver reached down as though he reaching for something under the seat. The officer dove towards the driver trying to grab his arm. The driver had not put the car in park and hit the gas, yanking the officer off of his feet and halfway out of the car, until the car door slammed against the officer, pinning him half in and half out of the car and dragging him for about fifty feet before the driver turned to take a curve in the road, knocking the officer the rest of the way out of the car and almost running over him in the process. The officer ended up being severely injured in the ordeal but so did the driver who ended in a gun battle with the responding officers and eventually was mortally wounded. It boiled down to closing the channels, turning on a channel marker, answering officers who were responding and sending medical and fire. It sounded easy but when an officer was screaming for help over the radio it stopped hearts and breathing. If a dispatcher couldn't go on auto pilot and do it without thinking lives could be lost. The police dispatcher who had been on a break had taken her portable radio with her and came racing into the Comm. Center and took over the call. Bellamy was so high on adrenaline that when it was over and she tried to work on her own calls it sounded like she had a hammer pounding on the keyboard. Her fingers wouldn't work right she was trembling so much they were spastic.

The other 'Mayday' was just as traumatic for Bellamy but the outcome was far different. She had been called in to assist with a large brush fire and had sat down at the console, been updated on the situation and gave the other dispatcher a much needed break taking over the call while he stepped out for some fresh air.

Bellamy was taking care of regular radio traffic from the fire ground when on a channel not assigned to the fire she heard a voice call a 'Mayday'. The voice was not frantic it came across the channel very soft and controlled. She immediately responded by asking the unit calling a 'Mayday' to identify themselves. Nothing. She checked her call screen to see if there was another call she hadn't been told about. She decided it had to be an apparatus assigned to the brush fire. She waited a few moments and asked again more urgently. Finally a male voice responded, "Selah Engine 12 calling a mayday". Bellamy acknowledged him and immediately selected a multi-broadcast button closing the air to all radio traffic, advising other agencies, turning on the channel marker, getting medical and trying to pull up the call that Selah Engine 12 was assigned to. She couldn't find the Engine assigned to any call on her screen. She was frantically searching to find out their exact location on the AVL mapping screen and there was nothing. Her heart was beating a hundred miles a minute. The other fire dispatcher came running back from his break, raising his portable in his hands in a gesture that said he had no idea what was going on either, when a sheepish voice came over the county channel that the 'Mayday' had been a mistake. "Selah 1, uh, we were on the wrong channel. We are drilling. Disregard the Mayday." Bellamy acknowledged him. She was so relieved that there wasn't a real 'Mayday' she wasn't even angry. She opened all the channels and did the procedure in reverse until all was back to normal. Then she started swearing and shaking uncontrollably. Her fingers were banging away on the computer keyboard because they wouldn't work. She needed a cigarette. She had only been there for a few minutes but had used a year's worth of adrenaline.

Bellamy shivered and said a quick prayer that there would be no 'Maydays' tonight. She had had enough excitement for the night just remembering the two 'Maydays' she had gone through in the past. That was enough. Unfortunately, those calls bubbled to the surface at the least desirable times.

Once Garrett had the Command Center up and running, his job was basically done. He could kick back, drink coffee and visit with fire crews coming and going until it was time to break down the unit and return to the station. Garret was the fleet maintenance officer for the city fire department and police department. He kept track of all the police patrol vehicles as well as all the fire apparatus. If something broke, he made sure it got fixed. He made sure they were serviced on time and the tires were rotated or replaced. If it had wheels he was in charge of keeping it running. That included vehicles on the fire ground. He even made sure everything was in working order on Engine One. It was the oldest motorized vehicle in the fleet. He had taken on the responsibility of the Command Center as well. And since he was the most familiar with it and drove it the most he had taken on the extra duty of responding in it any time it was needed. There were only rare occasions when he wasn't available to drive it.

Garrett was also a volunteer firefighter for the Nile Fire District. He did search and rescue, fire fighting, snow rescue, water rescue. Essentially he was a man of all trades and abilities where the fire department was concerned. Bellamy had gotten to know both Garret and his wife over the years. She enjoyed their company when they would come into the center sometimes and visit on their off duty time.

She was freezing. Garrett had turned on the air conditioning inadvertently. The sun had set several hours ago and the wind had picked up following the thunderstorm. It was cold both inside and out of the Command Unit. She found the switch and turned it off. On her way back to her little cubicle she rummaged through the closets for a cap to put on. Her hair was still wet and it was making her colder still. Stuffed in the back of one of the closets behind an old wooly-pully she found an old SWAT ball cap. She yanked it out, twisted her hair into knot and stuffed it under the cap. Just as she was doing so Roy opened the door and came inside wearing his turnout gear. He was a volunteer firefighter for Cowiche Fire District.

"Bellamy, what a vision of loveliness you are," he commented sarcastically. Had he said that to her a week ago, she would have laughed at the comment, tonight she didn't find him so amusing. "Quite a change from what you were wearing earlier," he added referring to the dress she was wearing at Ren's house.

"What do you need Roy?" Bellamy asked, her voice monotone.

He pulled off his gloves and tucked them in his utility belt and took a cup off the counter and filled it with coffee. He raised the cup to her, showing he had a reason for coming in to the Command Center.

Roy had just taken a seat at one of the tables when a few more fire officers wandered in to the center, grabbing coffee or one of the bottles of water that Garrett had put up on the table. They sat and stood around discussing the fire and planning the next phase of the fire to get it put out.

As much as Garrett loved listening to the fire updates from the crews coming off the fire ground, he needed to get outside and check the wind direction to make sure the exhaust hose for the generator was still pointing down wind.

Bellamy had no desire to be in the Command vehicle with Roy in there. She grabbed a portable out of the charger, turned it on and made sure she had it scanning for radio traffic. She reached in her purse, took a cigarette out of her pack with trembling fingers. Digging around she found a lighter. She opened the rear door of the Command unit and took a step outside. She face planted. Garrett hadn't made sure the steps were out. Bellamy had assumed they were down and hadn't looked. Trying to save the portable radio from damage as well as her cigarette and lighter she splayed across the asphalt lot in what felt like slow motion. She broke her fall with the heels of her hands first landing then skidding forward. A four letter 'f' bomb would have come out of her mouth had the right side of her head not suddenly connected soundly with the pavement. She wanted to cry but didn't want to show that weak, girly side of her to a bunch of firefighters. Before she could even try to right herself Garrett and two firefighters came running over to her. "Bellamy, are you okay?" A chorus of male voices asked. Why was that always the first question out of someone's mouth when they knew good and well the person they were addressing was *not* okay? Bellamy wondered. She had just tumbled two feet out of a motor home and gone splat on hot asphalt sprinkled with gravel. She was just peachy! She was trying so hard not to cry that she couldn't answer. She gulped. Her right side had taken the bulk of her weight and she wasn't sure if she could even move. She managed to roll over on her back and started to sit up on her butt but she couldn't. Parts of her just weren't working like they should.

"Fuck!" Her voice was shaking. In that instant she realized that when she started this career she didn't swear. She didn't swear at all. Darn or gosh wasn't even in her vocabulary. Now, however, she could hold her own in any swearing contest. "My ankle and elbow aren't working right," she said as tears began to slip down her cheeks.

"Stay still, I'll get the ambulance crew." A young firefighter she didn't recognize told her. The other firefighter cradled her head in his hands, protecting her neck. As he was telling her not to move she tried to find the knob on the portable to turn it to city main frequency to ask Greg to take over the fire ground radio traffic. She would be out of service for a few. Greg answered her, probably thinking she had to go to the bathroom or something. Bellamy was so embarrassed she couldn't even look Garrett in the face. It seemed they were making a much bigger deal out of this than was necessary. Blood was welling up from the road rash on the heels of her hands. Without asking Garrett took the portable out of her hand and turned it off.

"I know I had the steps out. I did. I came in that way when I checked the radios and again when Agent Aarons and I came out." Garrett told her. "Bellamy I am so sorry."

Before she could respond to him the two man ambulance crew came up to Bellamy and knelt down beside her. There was a flurry of questions as they assessed her injuries and put a neck brace on her. She thought she was more embarrassed than physically injured. She hurt like hell but didn't think there was any major damage. In true EMT/Paramedic training why pull the pant leg or sleeve up to see the injuries when cutting them off was more fun. They weren't even her sweats. She wasn't sure which one but one of them radioed in that they would be transporting one to the hospital. He gave a code number that she wasn't familiar with. Bellamy tried to refuse but the Paramedic told her if she could get up and get into the Command vehicle he wouldn't transport her. In very quick order, she realized she was going to be Shanghai-ed in an ambulance and transported to the hospital.

She looked down at her knee. It was just scraped. There was no blood but her right knee had already swollen significantly and started turning a very unnatural color of blue or purple. They hadn't taken off her boots but she could feel her ankle throbbing against the leather cuff. One of the paramedics started to cut the boot. "Don't even think about it!" Bellamy snarled. "Do you have any idea how much those stupid boots cost me? Unlace them and yank them off." She told him. He did as she instructed. She immediately regretted it when he took the right boot off. She let loose with a long string of swear words. Had her mother heard her Bellamy would have been tasting Dial soap for a week.

The light from the Command vehicle was obstructed then by Roy who had come to the back door and was lounging in the doorway holding his coffee and looking down at Bellamy.

"Can I call anyone for you Bellamy?" Roy offered sarcastically. She knew he was just waiting for her to ask for Ren and she wasn't going to give him the satisfaction especially with Garrett looking between them as though he knew Roy knew who Bellamy was seeing. It was going to drive him nuts.

"No. But thank you for your concern. You've done quite enough for one day." She hissed. She caught Garrett looking between them again trying to figure out why she sounded so hostile all of sudden.

"I'll call Greg and let him know what is going on and see if they need to bring out another dispatcher. Don't worry about anything. I've got it." Garrett assured her as he patted her shoulder. "I don't think you'll be working tomorrow so I'll let him know to call someone to cover. Don't think you'll be driving tonight either. I'll have the PD guys keep an eye on your car." The radio shop wasn't in the best neighborhood in the city but then again most of the neighborhoods fell into that category. 'If they let you go home tonight let us know. We'll have someone come get you." he told her.

A gurney showed up beside her and she was loaded onto it and covered with a light flannel blanket and belted in. She was rolled away from the fire scene and into the back of an ambulance. She was such a klutz. She wanted to blame Roy for distracting her but she couldn't. It was her own fault for not watching where she stepped. A couple of tears escaped the side of her eyes and ran into her ears. But it was his fault for adding insult to injury and smiling at her like a Cheshire cat. She was really beginning to hate this man. She didn't use the word lightly. She knew she was supposed to love everyone but the Good Book didn't say anything about having to like them and she certainly didn't like him at the moment. That made her sad. He had always seemed like such a good guy. He was a cop and volunteered his time with the fire department. He also volunteered to work the fireworks stand each year that raised money for the sports teams at Highland High School. He just seemed like an all around nice guy. He sure hadn't been acting like that this last week.

Her nose was running. She sniffed. "I'm going to start an IV Bellamy and I will give you something for pain."

"No, really, I'm ok." she told him.

The young paramedic sat next to her and started an IV anyway. "Just a little pinch," he told her after the fact. "The ER doc gets upset if we don't have an IV started by the time we get our patient to the hospital. He's already ordered some pain meds for you." Bellamy just nodded. She wasn't going to object.

Ren had watched the fire grow from the large windows. He knew that white sparkler in the center of the fire was either magnesium or jet fuel. Those were about the only fuels he could think of that would produce that brilliant white flame. He was sure there were probably other fuels that burned that way but he couldn't think of any that would be in a hop warehouse. And how jet fuel would get in there was a stretch.

He listened to the scanner in the background. When he heard Bellamy on the radio he knew she was on the scene. He could tell from the professional tone she used that she was in her element like he was when he was on the fire ground.

He paced back and forth as he listened to the radio traffic. He liked working the big fires like that. He wouldn't say he liked big fires because of the loss to the person or company that owed the facility. He hated that but he loved the excitement. That was the time when every second of their evolutions or drills transformed them from everyday firefighter to the highly trained firefighter prepared to take on anything. He missed that when he became a battalion chief. His responsibilities changed over night. He had become an administrator more than a firefighter. All of a sudden he became the conductor of a symphony. He was no longer one of the musicians, he was the one who had to finesse the composition the composer had intended, 'use the five inch, Engine 95 when you come in take the hydrant, Engine 93 you will be RIT (Rapid Intervention Team), Engine 91 when you come in, take side B set up the aerial'. Ren could hear it in his head and on the scanner. He really missed running the aerial. It was a rush to be standing in a small cage high above a fire and directing a stream of water on the fire. It was one of the few jobs on the fire ground that only one person performed. The rest of his crew was on the ground making sure he was safe up above.

He was lost in a memory of his job. Bellamy's voice came on the radio and requested that Greg take back the fire ground traffic. Her voice didn't sound right. Something was seriously wrong. When he heard the ambulance advise their dispatcher that they were transporting one to the hospital his heart stopped for a second then began to slam into his chest wall.

Ren didn't hesitate. He went into the kitchen and grabbed his keys, wallet and phone off the counter and was out the door and on his way to the hospital. He had to find out what happened to Bellamy. He couldn't stand the thought that she may have been injured on the fire ground or had become ill. His mind ran through a myriad of situations that may have gotten Bellamy injured. Was it bad sushi? He tried to go through all of the scenarios. He was at a loss. All he knew was he had to get to her and make sure she was alright. As he was driving towards the hospital he wasn't even sure it was Bellamy. He could be way off and in a dither over nothing. He might get to the hospital and find it was a firefighter who had been injured. It didn't matter to him he had to know who was hurt or sick.

He heard the incident commander call for the ARFF unit from the airport. That was the apparatus they used for any type of emergency with a flying vessel. It had the foam that was needed to extinguish an engine fire or jet fuel. Ren thought about that request for a moment. It made sense to him. The incident commander had to believe the fire was magnesium driven. ARFF was the only apparatus with enough foam needed to extinguish that kind of fire. And, he remembered it was fun to drive. If needed, just one person could operate the vehicle.

Not only could one person operate it but it had some really unusual features that other apparatus didn't. It had a feature that allowed it to get closer to the fire than most vehicles. It had the ability to spray a mist under the ARFF apparatus to protect it from spreading jet fuel and keep the unit cool. The foam could be sprayed without anyone getting out of the apparatus. It had a directional 'stang' or 'monitor' nozzle that the operator could maneuver to spray the foam where it was needed. He knew how essential it would be to fight this fire if it was being caused or fueled by magnesium. That kept his mind occupied until he pulled in to the hospital parking lot.

He hurried inside and walked up to the registration desk to find out if she was there and where. The reception started to balk at giving him the information but the security officer standing by the desk recognized Renny. The officer was like many of them employed here. He was a retired police officer. He strode up to the desk and interrupted the clerk. "It's ok. He's a Battalion Chief, tell me where she is and I'll take him back."

"Hey Jerry, how are you?" Renny asked.

"Good. Come on I'll take you back." He told Renny. Jerry ushered Renny back to the emergency room. Jerry knew Bellamy too and was surprised to see Renny coming in to check on her. He hadn't been aware they were an 'item'. He was going to have to check that out with some of his friends still working at the department. He had actually made a couple of moves on her himself. She rebuffed all of them. It couldn't be because she knew he was married. That hadn't mattered to the other ladies he dated.

By the time the ambulance pulled under the canopy of the hospital ER, she was already starting to feel the affects of the pain medication. "Oooh weee, you gave me the good stuff didn't you," she asked, her speech slurred. The paramedic smiled at her and patted her shoulder. *Why does everybody keep patting my shoulder?*

They wheeled her into the hospital and she squinted at the bright fluorescent lights overhead. A nurse in scrubs came and directed them to a room. The attendants helped move her from the gurney to a hospital bed that felt just as hard as the gurney. When the ambulance crew had left the nurse who was about Bellamy's age with beautiful dark skin and eyes stepped into the room again. She started taking Bellamy's vitals and asking her questions. Bellamy answered as best she could under the circumstances. Her head still throbbed. The nurse checked Bellamy's IV and told her to just lean back and rest. The doctor would be in soon.

Bellamy leaned back on the rigid pillow and closed her eyes. She was so tired. She wanted to get this dang neck brace off. She wanted to get out of this smelly turnout coat she was still wearing and go home and go to sleep. Then she remembered Jax. He had been locked in the house for hours. She felt like a horrible dog mom. He probably felt like he had been abandoned.

Her radar ears could hear the nurses talking across the hall at the nurses' station. Her nurse was giving the information to a male, who was speaking quietly asking her questions. In a few minutes she could hear the sound of footsteps as they stopped at the edge of her room. When the curtain was being pulled back she opened her eyes. A baby doctor stepped up to the side of her bed. "Hi, I'm Doctor Ellis. And you are?" He asked not looking at her but at the chart he held in his hand. His face was as clean shaven as a baby's butt. There was no way this guy could be a real doctor. She doubted he was even old enough to drive a car.

"Bellamy Boisseau," she answered.

"Looks like you took a pretty good fall Bellamy. How did that happen?" This teenage, round faced doctor asked her? He even had a zit on his chin Bellamy noticed.

She explained what had happened. When she had finished, the doctor asked, "Had you been drinking?"

"I was working. No I wasn't drinking. Seriously, did you just ask me that?" She asked incredulously. "I was at a fire scene. It was light inside the Command vehicle. It was very dark outside, even with the fire. I stepped outside. The steps that were usually pulled out at every fire scene weren't. I took a step and fell. Period. That's it. I told you. No, I wasn't drinking." She was pissed. How dare this little twerp ask her something that stupid!

She wanted to throat punch him but her hands were stinging from the road rash.

He finally looked at her. "I have to ask." He explained. "Any drugs?" His face was devoid of any emotion.

She shot him a look that should have scared the crap out of him had he taken the time to look her in the face. "No. Only the ones you ordered and they gave me in the ambulance."

He went about doing his doctorly duties. He put on a pair of gloves and stood over her legs, examining them from afar. He didn't touch them. He just looked at them from several different angles. He called out to a nurse and asked her to help Bellamy get the turnout coat off and pull up the sleeve of her sweatshirt so he could examine her arm. He looked at her elbow, again with just a cursory look. He didn't touch it. He asked if she could move it this way and that. When she couldn't he sighed, "Well, I think we should get some x-rays and see if anything is broken. But right now I can tell you that your elbow has been dislocated. We will have to rotate that back in place. Then I'll have the nurse come in and get you cleaned and treat your wounds." He informed her. She just shook her head at him as best she could with the collar on as he started to leave the room. He stopped momentarily and snapped the gloves off and tossed them in the trash. Bellamy was thinking what a waste of resources that was. He hadn't even touched her. But by golly he had to be prepared. Her drug addled mind wondered if he put on a condom when he jerked off.

The ambulance crew had left her purse on her lap. She dug through the contents as best she could. Her hands hurt her fingers too. What was she thinking, everything hurt. She finally got a hold of her phone. She figured out how to type in his number and placed the phone next to her ear with her left hand. Ren answered on the first ring. "Ma Amie I knew something happened to you."

All she heard was Ma Amie. He was calling her his love. She hesitated for a moment, replaying those words in her head then recovered quickly. "I'm so sorry to call you twice in one day but could you do me a favor?" She asked.

"Anything Amie." She heard him say over the phone but it sounded like there was also an echo in the hallway. She knew she had bumped her head pretty hard but was that making her hear echoes. She was about to ask him to go to her house and let Jax out when a hand moved back the curtain and Ren walked in to her room.

His eyes showed concern and compassion. He came to her bed, leaned over and gently kissed her lips. "I'm here," he whispered. Tears that she had kept at bay welled up and ran down her face. He took a tissue from the box on a small table next to her and tenderly dabbed at them. "It's ok," he consoled. Bellamy was in complete control of her emotions in an emergency until someone showed her any sympathy speaking to her in a soothing tone. Then she lost it. She became a blithering idiot. She was trying her best not to ugly cry. She couldn't do that to Ren. He couldn't see that. Not yet. This poor man wasn't ready for that. She wasn't ready for that. She felt far too vulnerable when she was with him. She wanted to be perfect for him and ugly crying was not perfect. It was a sign of weakness and she didn't want him to think she was weak and needed to be babied. Like her doctor, Bellamy thought.

As he was wiping her tear streaked face the curtain opened again and an x-ray technician came in to wheel her down to x-ray. He took Bellamy's purse off of her lap and handed it to Ren. "Would you go let Jax out? You don't even have to get out of your truck. You just have to drive up and hit that key fob. It will open his doggy door. Will you take my purse too?" She asked. He nodded.

"I'll be right back." Ren assured her.

When she was returned to her room, she closed her eyes again. Her head was pounding like a bass drum. The nurse came in, and started scrubbing the dirt out of her hands with a small scrub brush. She was trying to be gentle but it burned. Bellamy thought they hurt before but this was like some medical brush torture. She had Bellamy hold them just so on her lap as she put some kind of cream on them and wrapped each hand. Without very much small talk the nurse assessed Bellamy's knee gently cleaned it with another scrub bush. She irrigated and patted it dry with more sterile gauze. "I have to wait to scrub your elbow. The doctor wants to put it back in place before I do that."

Before the nurse could stand up kindergarten doc came in, again engrossed in the writing on the chart. He had a manilla envelope that he pulled x-rays from. He held them up to the light and examined one then took all of them to a light box. He flicked on the light and snapped the x-rays up to examine them. He studied each x-ray closely. "I don't see any breaks. You can see you have what looks like a crack on your elbow, possibly a break." He said, "Your ankle? Right now I can't tell. Sometimes it is very difficult to see a break right away. So we will have you follow-up in a few days. I do know it is badly sprained which can actually be more painful than a break" he paused, "We need to wrap it and put it in an air cast. I don't want you to put any weight on it for a few days. Once we get another set of x-rays in a few days we can see where we are going to go from there. Your knees and hands are just scraped and bruised. I am thinking you got a pretty good concussion when your head came in contact with the ground but I didn't see any bleeds. And we can take off the neck brace. Your neck is probably going to be stiff and sore for a few days but other than that it should heal fine." He gave the nurse an order to administer valium and he would be back in to put Bellamy's elbow back in place. Bellamy was not looking forward to that. But by the time the valium in the IV hit her blood stream she no longer cared, about anything. It only took a minute for the toddler doc to yank it back in place. She thought she heard herself yell but wasn't sure. Then he started babbling.

"Now I can't release you until you have someone who can drive you home and stay with you at least for tonight. If you can't we'll keep you here overnight just for observation."

At that exact moment, Ren walked around the curtain, like her knight on a white steed. She was sure she heard trumpets announcing his arrival. She giggled. "I'll be taking her home and I'll stay with her for as long as she wants me there." Ren told the doctor.

Ren sat in the room with Bellamy until she was ready to be released. His eyes rarely left her as he watched her being treated. When she was trussed up like a Thanksgiving turkey they finally got ready to release her. The nurse came in and repeated all the post treatment instructions. Bellamy didn't hear half of them. She was chomping at the bit and wanted to get outside and have a cigarette after all that is the whole reason she was here. She had wanted a cigarette, that and to get away from Deputy Morse.

They brought in crutches and adjusted them to her when she stood up. Knowing how very coorMorganted she was, she felt she was in more peril using crutches than not, but she was willing to do anything to escape the ER. It felt like trying to use chop sticks for the first time only on much grander scale. The doctor didn't want her putting any weight on her right leg. It was a noble plan but not realistic at least for Bellamy.

Bellamy had to shimmy herself up in the truck and pretty much lie down on the seat to maneuver her right leg in. To anyone watching it must have been quite a laugh. She would have laughed were it not for the pain. Thankfully they had given her another shot of pain meds in her IV before they finished bandaging and taping all her booboos. That and the valium had turned her into a big slippery eel with legs.

Ren went around to the driver's side and opened the door. He flipped the console up to make the seat into a bench, tipped the steering wheel up to its highest setting and put his hands under Bellamy's armpits to help ease her into the truck.

His hands were cold and tickled. She started giggling which caused her to go even limper. An image came into her head and she started full on laughing. Ren stopped for a second and looked at her a bit irritated that she had just gone limp and was lying there laughing. "You really are doing the dummy drag." She laughed, snorting. Then Ren started laughing. The dummy drag was part of the entrance exam for firefighters and ongoing routine training. The two of them were laying half in half out of the truck trying to gain their composure to finish getting Bellamy in the truck. When Ren was able to start pulling her into the truck the rest of the way, she suddenly shrieked, "Stop!" He did immediately. "My pants, I mean your pants. Would you pull them up?" They had gotten caught on something and slid down over her hips, just her bikini underwear covering the important parts. They started laughing again. Ren did his best to pull them up. When she was finally in the truck, half sitting, half reclining, Ren closed the door and came around to the driver's side. He climbed in and had to slide her head into his lap to put on his seat belt. Putting on Bellamy's seat belt was not an option. He wasn't even going to try. She was a limp wet wash cloth.

When he had started the truck he looked down at Bellamy. Her eyes were glassy from the pain medication. "I love you sooooo much," she swooned, slurring just a little. His heart leaped even though he knew it had to be the drugs working.

"I love you too," he assured her. His response was from the heart and not drug induced.

"I'm so glad we got that settled." She sighed. "Are you hungry?"

Ren chuckled again. Bellamy would be just fine. Her mind was still skipping like a needle on a record with a scratch. Her mind went from loving him to food instantly. She definitely was stoned. She snuggled up against his crotch, her head rubbing against his manhood every time she turned her face to look up at him. He gritted his teeth. It was a purely innocent move on her part but he couldn't help responding to her touch as a much different image came to his mind. If she snuggled much more his reaction would be more than evident.

Bellamy relaxed for the first time since she had fallen. She slipped in to a contented stupor. She felt safe resting against Ren. She was vaguely aware of him ordering food at a drive-thru. The rest of the trip home was a blur. Soft country music was painting pictures in her head. Her head really hurt.

"Amie," Ren said softly, "You need to wake up."

"I'm awake. I was just resting my eyes."

The drool spot on his jeans' zipper said differently. He had unlocked the door and taken the food, her purse and her hospital papers inside. Jax was dancing at his heels.

Now Ren was trying to get Bellamy out of the truck. It was like trying to pick up melting Jello. She was all over the place. He finally got her upright but she felt like she was going to slip out of his hands like a wiggling fish. He finally grabbed her and flipped her over his shoulder in a fireman's carry. That woke her up but then she flopped right back down again.

Ren deposited her as carefully as he could on the couch and went back out to retrieve her crutches and lock his truck doors. When he came back in Bellamy was stretched out on the couch exactly as he had left her. He roused her and finally woke her up enough to get some food and iced coffee down her.

She ate a few bites of her breakfast sandwich and drank her coffee. Bellamy finally got the cigarette she had been wanting since before she fell. She took a long drag, closed her eyes enjoying the moment then exhaled. It felt foreign trying to smoke with her left hand. Her right arm was tightly wrapped and adhered by something to her body. She sighed. Bellamy was now conscious enough to talk to Ren. "I am so sorry for doing this to you. I could have called one of my girlfriends but the only person I wanted was you."

"Bellamy, don't apologize. I was already there before you called, remember?" He prompted.

"How did you know I was at the hospital?" She asked, the spider webs clearing up a bit in her head.

"I was listening to the scanner. I heard you sign off the air. You didn't sound right. And as soon as I heard the ambulance taking someone to the hospital I knew it was you. I just got in my truck and started heading down there. By the time you called I was already there."

"Wow! You are good." Bellamy commented her head swimming. She wasn't sure if it was the ingestion of nicotine added to the other ingredients in her system or what but it was kind of trippy. It took her back to her college days. "Thank you," she said sincerely. Immediately after she said, "I have to pee." How she was able to switch gears like that Ren didn't know. She talked the way she drove, in short erratic movements that made him wish he had an 'oh shit' handle for her mind.

She struggled to her feet and got one of the crutches under her arm pit and hobbled down the short distance to her bathroom. Ren was right behind her to make sure she didn't fall. Jax was on their heels trying to figure out exactly what was happening. Jax followed her into the bathroom, his job, as he saw it. "Do you need my help?" Ren asked from the door.

"Nooooooo, I will figure it out." Bellamy assured him. It was going to be rather tricky but she managed to get it done. When she had finished she started to wash her hands and realized she could only wash her finger tips. She hobbled out of the bathroom and stood studying her options. "Can we go to bed now?" She asked Ren's permission.

"That sounds like a good idea, Amie."

He helped her into the bedroom and before he could find the light switch, she had flopped on the bed, half on, half off. She was unconscious. At least her cast was on the bed. He lifted her other leg onto the bed. There was a light quilt at the bottom of the bed. He was able to get it out from under her feet and fluffed it across her. Ren went around to the other side of the bed, shucked his clothes, down to his boxer briefs and climbed in to bed next to her. He didn't want to crowd her but as soon as his arm touched hers she moved closer to him. He fell asleep on his side, his arm protectively across her waist.

By the time the sun was up the pain meds had worn off and Bellamy's entire body was aching. She tried to sit up and moaned as the realization of the previous night caught up with her. Like being in a car accident it hurt worse the next day. She tried to get her bearings. Ren was not in bed with her. She thought he had been but couldn't remember.

She smelled coffee and was trying to find her crutches to get herself off the bed to go get some. Bellamy had one under her arm pit and was about to lift herself off the bed when Ren came around the corner, fresh from a shower. He had a towel wrapped around his waist. He was glistening wet. He smiled sheepishly and holding the towel a little tighter he tucked a small piece of tissue paper he had in his hand inside the edge of the towel around his waist. Luckily she had looked down to make sure her crutch was where she needed it to be to stand up. "I thought I'd be done before you woke up." He went to the other side of the bed and pulled on his jeans. Ren pushed the small piece of tissue into his pocket. It was a little damp now and he hoped the circle he had traced wouldn't run or fade. The eyeliner he used to make it said on the tube it wouldn't run. He hoped not. "Here, let me help you." Ren offered.

Bellamy scanned his body appreciatively. His body was so beautiful. She couldn't think of a better sight to wake up to in the morning. He leaned over toward her and helped lift her to her feet, or foot as it were. He smelled fresh and clean and she wanted nothing more than to hold him to her. Instead she teetered on her crutch. Ren was about to get the other crutch for her but she told him not to get it. She was better off without the other crutch. Trying to maneuver one was bad enough but trying to use two was just asking for an accident to happen. As soon as she was fully upright blood rushed from her head to her feet and the throbbing pain started in her head and moved its way down. She stopped in the doorway and weighed her options, bathroom or coffee. Bathroom was closer and more urgent in nature. She hobbled down the short hall and went in to the bathroom trying to figure out how to proceed from there. "I'm not sure exactly sure how to do this," she told Ren who was standing in the doorway with Jax.

"You don't remember how you did it last night?" Ren asked smiling at her impishly. He would be surprised if she remembered much of anything after she had fallen. He could probably tell her all kinds of stories about what she had done, even though she hadn't, and she would believe him. She was in enough pain it wouldn't be fair to add insult to her injury.

"No" She said staring at the toilet. It wasn't like her bathroom was handicapped accessible with grab bars and a raised toilet seat for easier access. Bellamy propped the crutch against the wall behind the toilet and turned to hold on to the bathroom counter with her left hand to steady herself. She tried to figure out how to hold on to something and pull the sweats and her panties down and realized Ren was still standing there watching her with his arms crossed. "Um, Jax can stay, we have an understanding. But you have to leave." She told Ren. He slid against the wall and backed away out of view.

Bellamy was finally able to get her panties down and slide onto the toilet seat with a rather loud clattering of toilet seat against the rim.

"So what is your understanding?" Ren asked from around the corner.

"What?" Bellamy asked.

"With Jax," Ren clarified.

"He can stay as long as he doesn't repeat what he sees or hears." Bellamy told him. Ren was far too close to the bathroom door. He would be able to hear her pee. She just didn't feel comfortable with that yet. "Could you move a little further down the hall? Like maybe the kitchen" She suggested. She could hear him chuckling as he moved further down the hall and into the bedroom. It was only a few feet more but if it made her happy he would do it. When she had finished, she managed to get up on her crutch again and went to the sink to wash her hands. Well, that's not happening, she thought looking down at her right hand flapping disembodied from the rest of her arm trussed firmly to her chest. All she had was her left hand.

As if reading her mind he told her he found her wet wipes and they were on the counter. "Thank you," she said.

Bellamy hobbled out of the bathroom and started down the hall, when he stepped out of the bedroom scaring the crap out of her. "Don't do that!" She admonished him.

"Sorry." He said sincerely. He followed Bellamy the rest of the way down the hallway and out into the living room. "Lie down on the couch and I'll bring you some coffee."

She was glad he offered. She didn't think she could make it all the way to the kitchen. He returned with a cup of coffee and a blueberry muffin slathered with butter. Bellamy gave him a questioning look. "I can read and follow directions on the box." He explained.

Bellamy smiled at him appreciatively. Pedro or whoever had called her really did peg him right. He was a good guy. He went back into the kitchen. She followed him with her eyes. She really did appreciate him, all of him. Not just his heart and mind but his backside and his front side. He came back with his muffin, coffee and a glass of water balanced between the two. He sat next to her, perched on the coffee table. He finished his muffin and lightly rubbed the remaining crumbs carefully onto the plate. When she had finished, he took Bellamy's plate. He handed her the prescription the hospital had sent home with her. "You need to take one to get ahead of the pain." *Too late*, Bellamy thought at the same instance.

She did as she was told and followed him with her eyes as he took the plates back into the kitchen. She could hear him rinsing them in the sink. He started running down his agenda for the day. He knew Jon was taking care of the hops but Ren wanted to make sure their other kiln was set up and ready to go. He knew the employees they had put in charge of that task probably had everything ready to go but he felt he needed to see it himself. There were just a lot of little duties he needed to attend to as well as the big one, checking in with his insurance company again. He needed to know where they were on his claim and what they had turned up in their investigation.

Bellamy listened to him as he came back in to the living room. "I won't be gone long Amie. Your phone is right there. Just call me if you need me. Jax has been fed and watered. Don't be out running around on me while I'm gone." Ren told her. "Unless you would rather go back in the bedroom, I can help you get back in there." He offered. "I just thought you would enjoy watching TV or something." He had put the remote within reach for her.

"Thank you. I'll be fine. I'll give one of my girl friends a call to see if she can stay with me so you don't have to baby sit me." She told him. She really didn't want to inconvenience him.

"You don't want me here?" He asked standing in front of her, his hands now planted on his hips.

"No. I mean yes but I just don't want to put you out. I don't want to take up your time having to take care of me when I know how much you have to take care of before harvest."

"Amie it is my pleasure. If something comes up and I can't be here, then by all means call one of them. But, I want to be here." Ren told her and kissed Bellamy tenderly, lingering there for a moment and regretting he had to leave at all.

"Thank you, Ren, I love my girlfriends and we would do anything for each other but you are just so much more pleasant to look at."

"So, I'm just your house boy toy?" He asked lightly. She started to object to explain herself when he added, "I can live with that." He told her as he walked away toward the back door swishing his hips, exaggerating every step. As he was walking out he said, "Je t'amie, Amie."

"Je t'amie." Her heart was jumping in her chest. She meant it. Did he? She really did love him but she had also fallen in love with him. Her heart was soaring. She just hoped that when she came back to earth her heart wouldn't land like she did last night. She didn't think her heart would just be bruised. It would be crushed.

How could this have possibly happened so quickly? Was it really possible to fall in love with someone so quickly? She had never felt more certain of loving someone than she did right now. It wasn't the drugs talking. It was him. It was his heart. Of course there was the physical attraction but that seemed to be the least of it. It was the sound of his breathing. It was the smile he flashed at her. It was the fire she saw in his eyes when he got irritated with her. It was the way she wanted to protect him, to cherish him like she did. What an odd word, Bellamy thought to describe how she felt about him. She fell asleep pondering the meaning of word 'cherish' and why it had come to mind.

Bellamy woke up at Jax pushing his nose against her arm, whining. Ren was just coming in the back door. Bellamy realized Jax hadn't barked or growled at him as though he too had accepted Ren as one of the pack. Bellamy sat up a little and wiped her eyes with the back of her fingers. Ren looked at her with compassion as he placed a paper grocery bag, his keys and phone on the kitchen counter.

"Are you ready for some lunch?" Ren asked. When he turned around to face her again she had turned white. Every ounce of sun that had touched her face this summer was gone.

Bellamy started squirming, thrashing around with her one good hand and leg trying to wiggle her way up off of the couch. Nausea had suddenly beset her and she was trying to get her bearings and her crutch to get up and to the bathroom. At once she realized that was not going to happen. Her mouth had started to water and her stomach tightening as though forcing its contents upwards. She frantically looked for something to throw up in. All that was in front of her was the large water glass Ren had brought to her so she could take her pain medication. She latched on to it with a death grip and held it to her mouth as she started to wretch.

Ren grabbed a dish towel from her drainer and ran toward her. She managed to get her vomit in the glass. He gave her the towel. She spit into it then wiped her mouth out. Ren quickly whisked the glass out of her sight and hurried back to her as she tried again to get up from the couch. "Let me help." He offered softly. She unsteadily got to her feet and hobbled with her crutch down the hall to the bathroom. Ren followed behind her like he was herding a calf. Once she was inside she pushed the door shut. Ren pushed it back open. "It stays open Bellamy. I won't look or whatever you are afraid I'm going to do but you can't close the door."

Tears were mixing with the sweat streaming down her face. She got her toothbrush, realizing she couldn't put toothpaste on it. She swiveled around with her butt against the counter and handed it to Ren. Without a word he unscrewed the cap of her toothpaste and put a bead of it on the head of her brush for her. Vigorously and clumsily she scrubbed her teeth, and gums and tongue. Standing behind and watching her in the mirror Ren was afraid she was going to brush the enamel off of her teeth. She spit and ran water down the drain. Bellamy took a cup off of the counter and filled it with water. She slurped it up and spit it out. Once she was finished she made Ren turn around. She managed to do her business and pull her, uh, Ren's sweats, up. Or what was left of them. She would have to buy him a new pair. She used a wipe and cleaned her fingers off. The moment she did, the nausea arose again. She leaned over as close as she could to the toilet and threw up again. It was pretty much purple water from the blue berry muffin. Ren was next to her in a second. He got a wash cloth from a shelf behind the toilet, rinsed it in cold water and wrung it out. Ren pulled her hair away from her face and held her forehead with the cold wash rag. "It's ok, Amie. I've got you." He assured her. When she felt she was done puking and she had gone through her mouth cleaning process Ren helped her back out to the couch. Once she was settled, he found a bucket and put it next to the couch…just in case. He brought her some Ginger Ale he had bought and some saltines she had in one of her cupboards. The color was still drained from her face as she took a sip of the Ginger Ale. Ren studied her eyes. Her pupils were still unequal as expected. The vomiting was also expected but he wanted to stay with her now and keep a closer eye on her should she get worse. After she was finally able to get a cracker down, he gave her another pain pill and sat dabbing her face with the cool cloth. Neither one of them spoke. It was just a time when it felt right not to talk.

He got a small hand towel with water and wrapped it loosely around the back of her neck. In about twenty minutes she had fallen back to sleep.

Ren got up and tossed the contents of the glass she had puked in down the toilet and proceeded to wash it in the hottest water he could get out of the faucet and what seemed like a half bottle of dish soap. He rinsed it and put it in the dish rack to dry. He really wanted to throw it away but he didn't. He did however throw the dish towel away. He would buy her another one but that one had to go. He put it in a separate garbage bag, tied it and took it out to the garbage receptacle at the back of her yard. His mind was stuck in the yuck mode.

Yes he was a seasoned firefighter. He had seen buckets of puke in his career, some of it had been his. But there was just something different about seeing it come out of someone you loved. He wanted all trace of it to disappear, but that wasn't happening.

He was still contemplating that when his phone rang. He hurried to answer it. It was the city fire chief calling. Ren answered hesitantly. Chief Anderson addressed Ren officially, "Battalion Chief LaRue, this is Chief Anderson. I need you to come in this afternoon so we can have a discussion." He told Ren. He was all business. His tone set Ren on edge.

"Chief, what is this about? I really can't come in to the office right now." Ren told him.

"B.C. LaRue, this is a direct order. You will be in my office in the next hour or you will be charged with insuborMorgantion for failing to follow my direct order."

"What?" Ren asked before the full impact of what Chief Anderson had ordered hit home. "I want to have legal representation present. I won't be able to arrange that in an hour. Set a time tomorrow and I will arrive as directed sir." Ren countered. He could feel the tension rising on the other end of the call.

"The EMS director and the City Manager will be here in an hour. I highly suggest, no, I am ordering you to be here too."

"With all due respect Chief you have no authority to do that. I have the right to legal representation to be present at all formal interviews if I so choose, and I do so choose." Ren told him. His heart was thundering in his chest. He didn't know what this was about for certain but just by the order he knew it wasn't good. He managed to keep his wits about him and demand his rights. He had never gone against a direct order.

"I have an important call that I have to take. I will call you back." Chief Anderson told him and ended the call before Ren could say anything more. Ren was sure there was no call he had to take but one he had to make. He was going to have to walk back his order and threat. He wanted to check with the EMS Director and the City Manager for some guidance.

Ren had risen into the category of Administration which meant he no longer had Union protection. Since he served at the pleasure of the EMS Director and City Manager they could pretty much decide they didn't liked the way he parted his hair and dismiss him. He wouldn't have much recourse. He pulled up the attorney that represented Jon and their hop business and called him. After identifying himself to the secretary, she immediately put him through to his attorney Jim Wright. The immediate transfer made it feel as though he had been waiting for Ren's call. He had been expecting Ren's call but not for the reason Ren thought. His attorney was concerned about the fire and dead body. He was concerned that he may be charged with Arson and 1st degree Murder and wanted to advise Ren not to make any statements to anyone unless he was present or he could get a defense attorney for him. Ren was gobsmacked. Arson and Murder? Surely he was joking, Ren thought. Jim assured him he wasn't. Ren went on to request him for some kind of meeting with the heads of the Fire Department. He told Ren to let him know when and where and he would be there or have another attorney there to represent him. Ren ended the call and stood simmering in the hot afternoon sun. He shook his head in disbelief.

Jim was their corporate attorney and dealt with all manner of their business but Murder and Arson were not his strong suit. He immediately got Gabriel Jackson on the phone. He was the best defense attorney in the area and he was a real pit bull when it came to matters like this. He explained the situation to Gabe. Gabriel had heard about the fire and dead body. He didn't know any more than that. Jim didn't know a great deal either only that he could assure Gabriel that Ren was innocent. He asked Gabe to take the case. Gabe was excited to do so. Take on the city? Bring it on. And it had more substance than defending a DUI suspect.

Before Ren could get any angrier, the phone rang in his hand. It was an unfamiliar number but he answered it anyway. It was Amy from Mid-Valley Hops. Her voice was subdued when she told him who it was calling. "Hi Amy. How are you holding up?" Ren asked trying to lower his anger level. She was no doubt completely devastated at the destruction of Mid-Valley Hops. That was her life for many years and now it was gone. Loosing the warehouse wouldn't really disrupt doing business. They had a huge new facility on the west side of town and her job would just be relocated but Ren was sure it must feel unreal to her.

"Ren, I'm doing ok, I guess, under the circumstances. I wanted to call and tell you Donald passed away last night." She stopped, her voice quivering.

"Oh no, I, uh, I don't know what to say. I am so sorry. If you need anything or I can do anything for his family, please let me know. Amy, I am almost afraid to ask but any news about Jason?" He asked. He was reeling. The hits just kept coming.

"No, Ren, nothing so far. Because of the circumstances the FBI has taken over the case, so that is good I guess." She told Ren.

They talked a little longer and ended the call. Before he could even digest that information his phone rang again and it was the Chief. His voice was even more controlled as he re-ordered Ren to appear at 9 am the following morning. Ren told him he would be there with legal representation. He called Jim Wright again. Jim informed him Gabriel Jackson would be representing him and gave Ren his reason for hiring him. He gave Ren his phone number and asked him to call Gabriel. He hung up the phone and stared at it trying to decide if he just wanted to turn it off. He didn't know how much more crap he could take in one day. He walked back up onto the porch, sat down in the rocking chair and smoked a cigarette. He finished his cigarette and called Gabriel.

He was waiting for Ren's call. Ren went through the basics of what had happened so far and Gabe asked a few more questions to fill in the blanks. He advised Ren he would meet him at the Chief's office at nine in the morning. Ren sighed. He slowly got up and went back in the house and found Bellamy waking up and trying to get her phone.

He hurried to her side and grabbed her ringing phone for her. He glanced and saw it was from work. His heart sank. He was hoping it was just her boss checking in to see how she was doing but he had a very uneasy feeling it wasn't. Was this going to be a blitz attack on her too?

Ren looked at Bellamy giving her a very worried expression. "I'm going to put it on speaker for a minute." Ren said. She was perplexed. As much as she could she shrugged her shoulders. She answered and heard her immediate supervisor, Karen on the other end. Bellamy rolled her eyes. She shouldn't have done that. Rolling her eyes made her head really hurt. She didn't trust Karen as far as she could throw her. And Bellamy wouldn't have been able to throw her far, she was short and stout and Bellamy thought by her usual or unusual attire that she might be conflicted about her age and identity. Bellamy could visualize her on the other side of the phone in her black leggings two sizes two small to fit her large derriere and cottage cheese thighs that tapered down to her skinny chicken legs. Karen was probably wearing a short stretchy top that didn't quite meet the demands of her ample chest. It was hard to tell at times where her breasts stopped and the next roll of fat started. On rare occasions she would wear a long billowing vest over the top which would at least cover some of the train wreck. The worst part about Karen was her hair. Bellamy knew she had no room to speak because her hair could be wild and untamed when she wasn't working but Karen's was worthy of its own animation. She had long straight hair. The top half of her hair was black then faded to a bizarre shade of orange that defied description. It resembled the color of rust on a tin can that had been out in the rain too long. Bellamy tried to get the image of her out of her head. Sometimes Karen would wear her hair twisted up in the back and held in place with a big claw clip. The bottom of her hair stuck out the top of the claw and flopped around as she moved. It looked like the red comb on the top of a rooster. Overall she looked like a tough old bird. When she strutted it made her look like she might be gender conflicted. She had earned several colorful nicknames.

Bellamy's favorite she couldn't say. There were just too many too choose from that fit her personality perfectly. But she was sure that term, 'Don't be a Karen' evolved from people who had known *this* Karen. She had very little respect for her before she was hired. That tiny bit of respect had dwindled down to a drop and that drop was drying up. The longer Bellamy worked for Karen the harder it was for her to be civil to her. Their conversations had shriveled up as well and as much as possible were carried out through e-mails.

Karen in her best concerned tone of voice asked how Bellamy was doing? Bellamy didn't know what she should say. She finally responded, "I'm a banged up but I'll be fine."

"I'm glad you are fine." Karen told her. *Dumb shit! Did you not hear what I just said? Bellamy yelled in her head. Remember all that crap you drilled into us about active listening. Oh that's right that doesn't apply to you. None of the rules do!* That internal scream hurt her head.

"Bellamy, I need you to come into the office tomorrow. If you could come in today it would be even better. It is quite important." Karen told her.

"You realize I am now officially on sick leave. I don't need to come in to the office. If you want to order me in, I'll assume that I need Union Representation or legal representation which will require some time to contact prior to talking to you."

She heard Karen sigh heavily. Just from that she knew Karen was irritated that Bellamy would talk back to her and not immediately acquiesce. It was like a stand off on the phone. Ren put his finger over his lips telling Bellamy not to say anything. She needed to wait her out. "Bellamy, I'm going to put you on hold for a minute." Karen said and she was gone. Bellamy didn't say anything but raised her left hand palm up in the air and shrugged in a 'what the hell is going on' movement. Ren shook his head and pressed the mute button on her phone.

"Don't go in. You make sure you have representation there before you talk to them."

"What is going on?"

"Bellamy, I am afraid you are in trouble because of me." He said.

"We will need you in Brian's office at nine in the morning" Karen told her.

"I won't be able to do that Karen. I am unable to walk without assistance, I can't drive because of the air boot and I am taking pain medication which impairs me. I will call when I am able to come in or maybe a zoom meeting would suffice." Bellamy suggested. She was taunting Karen and they both knew it.

"I will talk to Brian and see what we can come up. We need you to sign off on some things." Karen added. She took a sharp breath and Bellamy went in for a shark bite.

"Really? What kind of things would that be, Karen?" Bellamy attacked, unexpected and fast, much faster than she thought her muddled brain was capable of under the circumstances. She glanced away from the phone and saw Ren watching her closely. She didn't think she would have to courage to attack her without Ren sitting next to her.

She could hear Karen shuffling papers and taking in a breath and blowing it out slowly to keep her anger in check. "We have some L&I paperwork from your fall and some from the kiln fire." Karen told her.

"I'll have someone come pick up the L&I paperwork. But if you have another complaint about Deputy Chief LaRue and me being rude to him, look at all the other complaints from him and my response. Pick one of those responses and put it on this report. Go ahead and sign and date it today's date. I assume this call is being recorded. If it is anything else, get back to me with a time and date so I can arrange for representation. I've taken enough of your crap for one day. I'm not going to talk to you about anything without a witness or attorney." Bellamy challenged. Her head was throbbing with every word. She was pissed. No, she wasn't pissed she was irate at this, this, woman! She lightly bit her tongue from calling her what she really was. Karen was like a cute little piranha fish. She didn't seem like a threat. How could something that small be such a threat? But Bellamy knew better. The shark she was channeling was about to come in for the kill and in one bite snap this annoying little fish in two. Bellamy must have been listening to Shark Week on the television while she was sleeping. She felt like an apex predator.

"We will reach out to you shortly to set up an appointment." Karen advised her professionally and then quite unprofessionally disconnected the call.

"Witch," Bellamy snapped! Ren turned the phone toward him and made sure the call was ended.

Bellamy let out a yell that made Ren jump and set Jax into a barking frenzy. Neither one of them was expecting that. Her head was about to explode and the nausea was returning.

She started the in through the nose, out through the mouth breathing trying to push it away. It took a few seconds but it did start to help. She took a sip of the Ginger Ale that was now tepid. It was not Pendleton but it would have to do. When she had calmed down a bit she looked at Ren, and got in his face. "What is it with your fricken brother Jon? Geez, he's a pain in my ass!"

Ren was taken aback for a moment that she would lash out at him. But he tried to put a twist on his response. "You should have had to share a bedroom with him." Ren told her.

She chuckled then. "Poor guy," She soothed Ren.

"Bellamy, is that what you think that call was about, Jon?" Ren asked her.

"Nah, something else is going on. Who knows? Karen and Brian are like Hitler and his minion. They sound benign but they lull you into a feeling of complacency then chew you up and spit out your bones. They have come up with this mindset of manning to Comm. Center with a superior race of dispatchers that do everything by the book, never wavering from their policies and procedures. It isn't feasible because we aren't robots. We are human. So, they go after the old and weak." Bellamy grumbled. "I'm probably their target of the week, or month, or year" Bellamy continued. "I guess, better me than someone more vulnerable." She took another sip of Ginger Ale.

Ren gently placed her phone on the table and took her hand. "Amie, I think I've gotten you into some serious trouble. Just before you woke up, I had a call from the Chief ordering me in. They wanted me to come in within the hour. Not happening." He took a cigarette out of his pack that was tucked in the pocket of his shirt and lit it. "It has to do with the fire and dead body. They referred to it as Arson and First Degree Murder."

"Murder," Bellamy asked? She was shocked and angry. Then as she ran the information through her head, she could see that the Sheriff's office might be considering the dead body in the truck a homicide. She couldn't for the life of her figure out what that would have to do with her or Ren.

"I think that's what the Sheriff's office is pushing towards. And they have decided I am their primary suspect. The city and/or county are trying to cover their asses. They are already circling the wagons to make sure they don't get some bad press or sued by someone in the wings. Deep pockets you know."

"Ren, that's just stupid. So you think they think I had something to do with it too? I was working. I'm good at multi-tasking but even I couldn't pull off an Arson/Murder." Bellamy said her voice taking on an edge Ren hadn't heard before. 'I can't even start a fire in my fireplace and they think I might be capable of arson?"

"Honey, it is about me. Someone has told them about us. This is what I was afraid of and here it is. They are making you guilty by association." He lamented.

"So? So what? We are together. What does that have to do with the…" Her voice trailed off. She had stepped into one of those sage rat holes and was going down through the maze of possibilities that surrounded this incident. "So they think I'm an accessory after the fact?" She said not so much as a question as a statement. Then her mind hit the landmine. "Fricken' Roy," She shouted! "I know that jerk is behind this. I bet you dollars to donuts he leaked his body cam video to them. They think because I was there with you that I'm involved with this stupid fire and body." She said lowering her voice. "I didn't mean it like that Ren. I mean it is stupid that they would suspect either one of us."

"I know Amie" Ren said. "May I have some Pendleton?" He asked.

"Of course and you don't need to ask. The first time you are here, you are a guest. The next time you are here, you are family. In other words, if you want it get it yourself." She told him. One of her friends had come up with that saying and she had adopted that custom. She thought she should have it printed on a sign however she never had any visitors to warrant it.

Ren chuckled at that. He went into the kitchen and poured a bit over ice and took it back into the living room where Bellamy sat with a pensive expression. "Well this is a fine mess you've gotten us into Ollie." She tried to mimic Laurel and Hardy.

Ren's confused expression made her shake her head. He had no idea what she was talking about. She forgot he was young. He was older than she was by a good bit but still young enough to not get the reference. She had been raised on Black and White movies. She had hated them back then wishing she could be watching what her friends did in the evening but her parents didn't want her watching all those immoral programs, so she had been very restricted on what she was allowed to watch. Once her parents had passed, Bellamy found one of the DVD's they had and watched it. It was hilarious and a comforting memory of her parents. Her desire to experience more of the old movies grew on their own merit. Now she pretty much watched those only.

"I take it you have no idea who Laurel and Hardy are?"

He shrugged.

"Oh baby. You don't know what you are missing. I take it you've never watched any old movies either. No black and white?" Bellamy quizzed.

Ren scrunched his eyes as if to say they really didn't interest him. "Will you humor me just this once?"

Ren shrugged again.

"Okay. In the middle drawer under the TV there are a bunch of DVDs. Get 'It Happened One Night." He found it and popped it in the DVD player.

She hoped he would like the movie. It was basically about a socialite who wanted to escape her father's rule so she could marry a man her father didn't approve of. She jumped ship, literally and went on the run. A news paper man recognized her and through his cunning ways befriended her to get the story. When they spent a night in a motor-court cabin together, he hung a blanket on a rope between their two beds and called it the wall of Jericho to assure her that her virtue wouldn't be compromised. By the end of the movie the journalist and socialite had wed and gone back to the same motor court they had stayed in. There was the sound of a toy trumpet and the male saying the walls of Jericho were falling down.

Ren sat down next to her and took a drink from his glass.

Bellamy took his glass and started to take a drink. Ren tried to take it back but she insisted. "I just want a sip to cleanse my palate of this stuff," She told him.

Ren was surprised when he found himself laughing at some of the slap-stick humor in the movie. He did like it but he still wasn't convinced he would want a steady diet of black and white movies.

Bellamy was grinning. She looked adorable even in her disheveled state. She squirmed and winced. Ren looked at the clock on the fireplace mantel. "You probably should take another pain pill." He suggested. He got up and brought back a glass of iced water for her. She was squirming again. "What is wrong?" He asked at her obvious discomfort.

"This f-ing mummy wrap. My back itches. I feel groady. I just want a shower." She grumbled. "I love your sweats, that I totally ruined but I just want my own clothes on." She continued, "Would you please remove this stupid wrap?" Bellamy asked struggling to find the little clips she knew were securing it. She was almost in a panic trying to find them. It felt like trying to get a tight dress off and having it get caught on her head or arms and not being able to get it off.

Ren started examining the wrap and found the little metal claws holding the elastic wrap on her right shoulder. He pulled them loose and helped un-wrap her. When she was free she let out a sigh of relief. Her arm was still wrapped in an elastic bandage, holding it in an 'L' shape.

Bellamy scooted herself around Ren and got her crutch under her arm pit. He helped her stand up and she hobbled down the hallway towards her bedroom to find something to wear. "Uh, Ren, I hate to ask but could you open my drawers?" She asked. He considered her request and grinned at her.

He'd love to get into her drawers even though he knew that wasn't what she meant.

He did as asked. "I need a pair of panties." On the top of the underwear was a pair of the printed panties she had bought for, well, him to hopefully remove from her someday soon. They weren't for lounging around the house. "Not those," she said quickly. He pulled out a gray pair of high cut cotton panties that might as well have had a stop sign printed on them. "Yes. Those are fine."

The next drawer he pulled out had t-shirts in it. She picked one of those and from the bottom drawer a pair of yoga pants, not that she did yoga, she just liked the pants.

She went into the bathroom, Ren following her. He put her clothing on the counter as he tried to figure out just exactly how she thought she was going to take a shower.

She hadn't thought the shower idea through. That wasn't going to work, she realized. She looked at the big package of wet wipes on the counter. She could freshen up with those, she supposed although it wasn't what she had in mind. Ren could hear her grumbling through the partially closed door.

"Do you have another dish pan?" Ren asked from the doorway.

"Uh, yeah, under the kitchen sink," She told him as she struggled to figure out a way to take a shower.

"Let's go back to the couch." He loaded his arms with some large bath towels, wash cloths and a bar of soap from her shower. He carried them with her clothing to the living room. He placed them on the coffee table and went to the kitchen. She heard the water running for a few minutes. He came back carefully carrying a small dish pan of hot water.

"What are we doing here?" She asked nervous about her immediate future? As she asked he sat her up straight on the couch shaking out a towel and placing it behind her.

"We are taking a bath." Ren informed her.

"Oh, no, no, no, no, no," she balked.

"Oh, yes, we are," Ren argued. "Bellamy, would you trust me, please?" His eyes locked on hers. She could see he was serious. It was a test. Would she trust him to care for her in a personal and intimate way without compromising her modesty? Had he got this idea from the movie they had just watched? She nodded her head and took another bungee jump, trusting that the singular elastic cord attached to her heart was going to snatch her from certain death. The elastic in the waist band had never protected her from other dangerous adventures.

Carefully and tenderly Ren disrobed her, making sure she was covered with another towel and revealing nothing to him. As though she was a porcelain doll he gently washed her with the utmost respect. She relaxed then and leaned back against the towel and started to close her eyes. Instead she watched him. His touch which always excited her was unexpectedly reassuring and loving. His eyes were nurturing. She surrendered to his touch as he bathed her. When he had finished her bath, he patted her dry and helped her to dress.

Bellamy stroked the side of his face with her left hand. That was a defining moment for her. She loved him. There were no reservations or fears. She loved him. "I really love you Ren." She told him as she touched his face. She hadn't really meant to tell him that but it was a revelation that she didn't want to keep to herself.

Ren regarded her seriously. He was trying to judge her level of pain meds. She was stone cold sober. Her eyes seemed to be speaking as loudly as her words.

"I never in a million years would have thought that I would say those words to you. I never thought I would be saying it in just a few days after getting to know you. And I never thought I would say it to anyone and mean it the way I do right now. My heart is out there right now, in front of you. I hope one day you'll feel the same way about me. Even if you don't, I still needed to tell you." Bellamy's voice was shaky. She was trembling as her hand lingered against his cheek.

He took her hand and kissed her fingers. "Bellamy you are the most amazing woman I have ever met. I'm like you. I never saw this coming but I love you more than I ever could have imagined." He paused then.

"I sense a 'but' in there," Bellamy said nervously.

"Yeah, I suppose so. I love you, don't ever doubt that, but I am just afraid at the end of all this you are going to change your mind. Decide that this isn't worth the risk of losing your job and everything you have worked for."

"Ren, love is always a risk. You of all people should realize that. And I guess that is why I told you now. Because we don't know what tomorrow may bring. But today, this moment and from here on for as long as you want me, I will be here. I love you." Bellamy assured him.

"I know Amie. I just don't want you to get hurt."

"The only way you would hurt me is if you," Bellamy's phone started to ring and she didn't finish her sentence. Again it was her office and it stopped her mid sentence. She answered it on speaker phone and put it on her leg. "Bellamy, this is Brian. You are on a recorded line. I have with me Yakima Country Prosecutor Edward Parrish. Bellamy, you are being put on paid administrative leave at this time by direction on the County EMS Director and this office. You are also, so ordered, to have no contact with anyone from this office until further notice. You are also, so ordered, to have no further contact with Rene LaRue pending the outcome of the Murder/Arson involving yourself and B.C. LaRue. Papers of this order will be delivered to your residence within the next hour. Should you have any contact with the parties in the stated order it will be grounds for termination. This information will also be served on your Union Representative." Brian told her professionally and unemotionally. "Do you have any questions for me at this time?" Brian asked. Bellamy looked at Ren. He mouthed the word 'no' at her. Brian stated the time and ended the call. Bellamy sat there completely thunder struck.

Ren stood up and turned away from her abruptly and started walking away. "I knew this was a bad idea. I am so sorry Bellamy. I wish it would have worked out." Ren told her. He gathered his phone and car keys and walked out the back door, making sure it locked behind him.

In complete shock she stared at her back door. She heard his truck start up, back out of her driveway and drive slowly down the dirt road towards Larue Road. *Where is he going? Bellamy wondered.* This had to be a nightmare. There was no other word to describe it. This had to be brought on by her concussion. She didn't know. But this entire situation was un-real.

Ren was shaking as he walked out of Bellamy's house. His mind was vacillating between anger and pain. He was angry that the city, possibly driven by the Sheriff's office, was attacking him and Bellamy but mostly Bellamy. He didn't care about his reputation or career but Bellamy didn't deserve this. She had done nothing wrong. The only thing she was guilty of was being with him. And that was his fault. If he hadn't kissed her that first night none of this would have happened. If he hadn't insinuated himself into her fishing trip none of this would have happened. She was being singled out for just associating with him.

He didn't bother to call Gabriel Jackson. He walked in to his office unexpected and unannounced. He stood, tapping his foot on the floor as he waited for the receptionist to call him back to Gabriel Jackson's office. When Ren was ushered back he started talking even before Gabe could properly introduce himself and greet him.

He realized how big Gabriel was even though they were separated by his desk. He was built like a body builder or magazine model he couldn't decide which. The guy was dressed like he had stepped out of a Brooks Brother's ad. He admitted the guy looked intimidating. Ren was six foot tall and had a good physic but this guy seemed huge.

As soon as Ren had taken in his appearance he went on to explain the situation to him. When he had finished he leaned across the desk. "I want to retain you as counsel for her. Whatever she needs make sure you are there. I can't be. I have to distance myself from her." There was more he wanted to say but the words just rumbled around in his head like a stomach demanding food.

Gabriel assured him he would take care of Bellamy. He immediately called her number but it went to voice mail. He left her a message telling her he would be representing her and how to reach him.

Ren had planned to go home but instead he drove passed his road on the highway and took a road further to the east that took him up and over the ridge on Konnowac Pass towards the lower valley. As he started to descend the crest of the hill the valley stretched out for miles beyond him. It was bathed in varying shades of green, gold and brown. Had it not been for the Roza canal that fed this valley with water it would be a massive panorama of sage brush and bunch grass.

The land above his house had not been cultivated and not irrigated by the canal that was still in its untouched virgin state to the ground that had been farmed on the other side of the ridge. The road wound down the hillside, first through young vineyards that had seemingly sprung up overnight. It was the newest trend in the valley. The valley wines had begun to attract the attention of wine connoisseurs from around the world. They had already won some very prestigious awards. It was a growing lucrative business as the entrepreneurs maneuvered for their place in the industry. Further down the hill, orchards of peaches, apples, pears, plums and cherries stretched for miles down towards the river below.

Ren sighed. This hillside was at least ten degrees cooler than the other side where his hops grew. He was looking forward to harvest despite all the turmoil in his life. It would provide a distraction. He knew it wouldn't be able to distract him from Bellamy.

His gut was in a knot. Several times he thought he was having a heart attack his chest hurt so badly but he knew it was hurting because he had hurt Bellamy. He hadn't wanted to leave her there alone but he had no other option. The city could fire her if he stayed and it would be his fault. He knew he had to leave before someone from the city or county saw him there. He couldn't forgive himself if she got fired on his account. He didn't know if he could ever forgive himself for leaving her without a word. He was afraid she would never forgive him.

He had fallen so fast and hard for Bellamy that it scared him and now he was walking away. He was leaving the best thing that had ever happened to him. It had nothing to do with his feelings for Melanie. At the time she was the best thing in his life but she was gone and if she could see what he felt towards Bellamy she would be elated for him. She would be elated until now that was. He didn't know what Melanie would think about the mess he had gotten Bellamy into.

He seriously thought about turning in his papers. It wasn't like he needed the job. Even as he was considering it he knew it wouldn't change the city's position on Bellamy or him. The job had become a part of who he was but he knew he could live without it. He didn't think he could live without Bellamy.

Ren had reached the bottom of the pass and found he was just sitting at the stop sign. He was looking in both directions trying to decide which direction to go. He wasn't sure how long he had been sitting there when he heard a vehicle idling behind him. It was a John Deere tractor of some kind. He turned to the right and in about a half mile he turned to the left to cross the Yakima River and start for the far side of the valley.

Apple orchards stretched to the south before turning into truck farms. He passed a couple of fruit stands as he continued south. He passed alfalfa fields and began to see another stretch of grapes and orchards. He could already smell the ripening fruit. The smell was comforting. The heat of the day was bringing out the scent and wafting through his open truck window. He had sweat pouring down his face and dampening his t-shirt. He could have rolled up his window and turned on the air conditioning but he would have missed all the spectacular scents that were the heart and soul of this valley. This was considered the lower valley, compared to the upper valley where he lived. The two valleys were separated by the Yakima Ridge that he had come over on the pass.

He pulled up his t-shirt and swiped his face. He turned at a four way stop and started west passed a cemetery. Before he even saw the fields he could smell mint growing. The aroma was strong and heavy as he passed the sprawling dark green fields. He breathed in deeply. The overpowering scent cleansed his mind.

How was he going to get through this without Bellamy? She made him feel stronger. He was a strong person but she seemed to fortify him. He marveled at the way her eyes turned from blue to green when she was angry or crying. He had laughed more this past week than he had in years. She was goofy. She made all these corny movie references that he laughed at, even though he would have to ask her later where they came from. She made him smile the way she curled up next to him on the couch to snuggle with him as they watched television.

The way she felt against him as they danced together was magical. It was a feeling of wanting to keep holding her and protecting her against the evils in the world. She made him feel like he could take on any battle and win it to save her until now. Now he felt helpless. The only thing he thought he could do to protect her was to walk out of her life. That's what he was trying to do now but he wasn't sure she realized that. She had to know he would never leave her. After several miles he came to an area not in any kind of production, it was just barren grassland that was slowly turning in to oak and further up pine. He drove up as far as he could then turned around at the guard station, waving at the occupants. He had been on the Yakama Indian Reservation once he had crossed the river but now he had reached the restricted area of the reservation. If you were not an enrolled member of the tribe you could not venture any further.

Ren continued then to the south. He came to Fort Simcoe which was closed to the public at this time. It was closed most of the time. He wasn't exactly sure why. It was a beautiful complex of an early military outpost. It was erected in the 1800's during the Indian wars. The buildings were for the army's highest ranking officers. One of the original stockades was still standing. It was a somber place. Every time he had been there it seemed he and the other visitors spoke in whispers. There was a reverence that seemed to permeate the fort.

Ren turned then and started to the east. The hay fields turned in to wheat fields and slowly evolved in to corn. He continued until he was so tired of driving he needed to go home and go to sleep. He decided that was the only way he would escape this debacle even if it was for just a short time.

Bellamy continued to stare at the back door until darkness seeped into the room. It wasn't until Jax dropped his empty food dish next to the couch that Bellamy stopped staring through the darkness in the direction of the back door expecting Ren to walk through it at any moment. Where had he gone? When would he be back?

Bellamy found her crutch and stood up as carefully as she could. As she stepped, she pushed the dog dish forward toward the kitchen and his dog food. It made her concentrate. When she had finally managed to get the bowl next to the container she kept his food in she steadied herself against the counter. She scooped some food out and poured in over his dish in the dark. Most of it landed where it was supposed to from the sound of it. Bellamy slid her butt along the counter. When she got to the stove she reached up and turned on the light on the hood fan. She scooted down the counter a little farther and got a pitcher out of a cupboard and filled it with water and scooted with it back down the counter. She poured it in his water bowl. She was afraid if she tried to bend over to pour it she would end up landing on the floor.

She hobbled back to the living room and turned on the TV for some ambient light. It was on a news channel. Voices drifted in and out of her ears. It seemed to be a foreign language. It wasn't making any sense to her. Nothing was making any sense to her. She picked up her phone and dialed Ren's number. It was blocked. She tried it again. It didn't go through.

Bellamy was sick again and again, and again. When daylight came she was still on the couch staring at the back door. She no longer expected him to come through it. He was gone. She knew he wasn't coming back, ever. But she couldn't stop staring at the door or listening for his truck.

Bellamy dialed her best friend's number. Lauren answered almost immediately. Bellamy tried to say hello but nothing came out but a sob. "Are you at home Bellamy?" She asked frantically. Another sob escaped her lips. "I'll be there in a minute." She said. Good to her word, Lauren was at her back door a short time later. She pounded on it while Jax barked and whined. His friend was there, the one with the good treats. Bellamy hobbled to the back door and fumbled to turn the lock to let her in. When Bellamy was finally able to open the door and back away for Lauren to come in and Jax to go out, Lauren sucked in a sharp breath. "Bellamy! What in the hell happened?"

All Bellamy could do was sob. Her shoulders heaved and heaved and so did her stomach. She heaved in the garbage can in the kitchen. There was nothing left to throw up. Lauren tossed her keys, purse and some official looking papers she had found between the screen door and door frame on the kitchen counter. She quickly dampened a paper towel and wiped Bellamy's face. She filled a glass with water and helped Bellamy take a drink. Bellamy swished the water around in her mouth and spit it out in the sink.

She followed Bellamy in to the living room and helped her sit down on the couch. "Do you want some ice water, honey?" Lauren asked. Bellamy nodded. Lauren hurried to the kitchen, her heels clicking on the floor. She returned with a glass of ice water and put it in Bellamy's left hand.

Lauren sat silently with Bellamy as she sobbed uncontrollably. Some time later, Lauren went to the kitchen. Bellamy heard Lauren call her office and tell them she would not be coming in to work. It had never entered Bellamy's mind that for normal people it was a work day. To Bellamy it was her day off. Lauren returned to the living room, kicked off her heels and curled up on the couch next to Bellamy and protectively draped her arm around Bellamy's shoulder.

The first words that found their way out of Bellamy's mouth was, "He's gone." Tears continued to stream down her face but she took a tissue and blew her nose with gusto. It was not a dainty little blow. It was a bucket of snot that was begging to get out. She tried to take a deep breath but it wasn't happening yet. Even after the blow she couldn't breathe through her nose.

It was the opening Lauren had been waiting for. "Who is gone?" She asked quickly.

The question breached another dam of tears. Lauren patted her back. She got up and went in to the kitchen and returned with a wooden tray. It had two glasses of ice, a couple of cans of Pepsi and the Pendleton. There was also a bag of sunflower seeds she had brought with the Pepsi. Lauren was glad she had. It may even turn in to a two bag day. She opened the grocery bag to hold the discarded shells of the seeds.

Bellamy's sobs had begun to subside and she poured herself some Pepsi. She left out the Pendleton. Lauren poured herself a drink but added the whiskey. Lauren figured it had to be happy hour somewhere. She was hoping it was catching and Bellamy would catch it. She was quite sure before this was over she was going to need it. She couldn't remember Bellamy ever being this upset. And the last time she could remember Bellamy being wrapped in that many elastic bandages was when she was a teenager and crashed her ten speed bike into a chain link fence, gravel and cement curb. Déjà vu, it looked like a rewind of those injuries. It was even the same side. While Bellamy gathered herself, Lauren asked if she could borrow a pair of shorts and shirt. It was way too uncomfortable to sit around in a tight skirt and blouse. Bellamy nodded and she went in to Bellamy's room to find something to wear.

It took hours but bit by bit Bellamy was able to tell Lauren the story of the last week. It hadn't even been a week. Lauren knew LaRue. She knew his whole family. It was a relatively tight community. Everybody knew everybody, or at least everyone knew who was doing who.

She had known Bellamy since they were in 3rd grade. She knew every guy Bellamy had ever been involved with. She revised that thought. She knew most of the guys. It had usually been Bellamy that had broken the guy's hearts. The few times she could remember Bellamy being dumped she had just had an easy come, easy go attitude. Bellamy never took any of them too seriously. Even into adulthood, Bellamy just played the field. The idea of settling down with one guy was just never seemed to be important to her. She was one of the last free spirits in the world. Now Bellamy was inconsolable over a man she had only been with for less than a week. *She hadn't even had sex with him for heaven's sake. Was that even done these days? Lauren wondered.*

Lauren tried to understand what was going on with her friend. She was able to logically understand the other stuff, work, the fire and the physical injuries but Bellamy's heart was a mystery? Lauren was completely stumped. Bellamy didn't just fall in love. Lauren had only seen her somewhat serious about one guy and when that was over she just stopped dating altogether. She had male friends she hung out with but there was no emotional attachment and definitely no physical attachment. This situation with LaRue had Lauren stymied. The sadness she saw in Bellamy's eyes was raw. It was much worse than any pain she appeared to be having from her elbow or ankle. Lauren had always thought that the LaRue boys were just a bunch of goat ropers. She never thought of them as any great catch. They were ok to look at, she guessed but get this upset over? Not Bellamy. She really must have bumped her head hard because this wasn't the Bellamy she knew.

Lauren stayed with Bellamy until quite late. She made sure she had eaten some soup and re-hydrated. She left it up to Bellamy if she wanted to take a pain pill or not. Bellamy shook her head. Lauren cleaned up the kitchen and put things away. She made sure Jax had come back in the house and had plenty of food and water before she left. She assured Bellamy her phone would be on if she needed anything. Bellamy thanked her and watched her as she locked the door and left. Bellamy was exhausted. It had been over 24 hours since she had slept. She stared at the muted TV screen. Finally she turned on the sound just to hear something besides Jax snoring on the floor next to her. She didn't know when but at some time in the night she fell asleep.

Lauren got to the end of the dirt road and tried to decide which way she was going to turn. It didn't take her long to decide. The small amount of whiskey she had had much earlier in the day on an empty stomach gave her an extra boost of moxie. She knew exactly where she was going. She knew where Renny lived. She thought everybody did. She was very surprised that Bellamy hadn't known until she drove up there to have dinner with Renny. It seemed everyone in the East Valley area had an opinion on the house and the occupant, none of them the same.

Right now she had an opinion of him and she was going to let him know exactly what it was. She found Renny's red truck parked in front of the sprawling house when she pulled up. The wide covered walk to the front door was lit up but the interior appeared dark. She didn't care if he was asleep or not. Her friend wasn't asleep. He shouldn't be either. She hadn't bothered to put her high heels back on and she strode barefooted across the cement to his front door and pounded on it like she was trying to raise the dead. She kept pounding until Renny yanked the door open and she almost fell inside. "You piece of shit," She yelled at him! He took a step back. He wasn't sure what this lunatic was going to do.

He took a better look and recognized her. It was Lauren, what's-her-name. He hadn't seen her in a long time but he remembered who she was. She was Bellamy's friend. They had all gone to school together. He had already graduated by the time they had come into high school but he still knew who they were. They never seemed to be far apart. Where you saw one, you saw the other. And now she looked like a stick of dynamite about to explode. She was dancing around like a chicken on her skinny legs. She was dinky. Where Bellamy was tall and curvy, Lauren was diminutive.

Renny started to say something, to ask her what she was doing on his doorstep but he didn't get a chance. She screamed swear words at him for a full ten minutes. It didn't take him long to figure out why. She was there on Bellamy's behalf.

When she stopped to take a breath she looked at him, really looked at him. He looked just as bad as Bellamy did, if not worse. He looked haggard. He too was barefooted, wearing a pair of baggy shorts and a torn, stained t-shirt. He hadn't shaved in how long she didn't know. His fine hair was sticking out in all directions. His dark blue eyes had bags under them. Big bags. Suitcases. They were red as though he too may have been crying. Lauren was about to start yelling at him again but after taking him in she lowered her voice. "You hurt my friend Renny, you don't deserve her. She is way too good for you."

"I know." He choked. "She is. I made a mistake letting it go this far. I had to leave to protect her." He stepped back and closed the door and leaned against it. He buried his face in his hands and did his best to stop the emotions that were crushing him.

"You better fix it, Renny!" It was the last thing he heard Lauren yell through the door. It wasn't long until he heard Lauren's car as she turned it on and started making her way down the hill. He stood there listening to it until the sound had died away. He locked the door and went back upstairs to his bedroom. He fell on his bed and considered all of his options in this matter.

When he and his Gabe Jackson had gone in for the mandatory meeting this morning, or yesterday morning, whatever day it was he had been given the same walking orders that Bellamy had. He didn't say a word during the entire meeting. He just kept staring straight ahead while Jackson did all of the talking for him. He wasn't even aware of when the meeting was over. He probably would still be sitting there if it weren't for Gabriel prodding him to get up and leave.

Ren thought about turning in his papers again. He could take an early retirement and not have to put up with this kind of crap anymore. But as he ran over that option he realized again that would do nothing to help Bellamy. It would look like an admission of guilt on his part. He wouldn't give them the satisfaction of that. It felt like this had completely derailed her career. He knew he should have just walked back into the hop yard that morning, instead of having a drink with her. He knew it as surely as he was lying here. And yet he had done it anyway. He predicted it was going to be trouble.

Bellamy hadn't had a thing to do with any of this and they were threatening her livelihood. He hadn't had anything to do with it either and they were threatening his livelihood too. From the sounds of it they were also threatening his freedom. He had no idea how he was supposed to fight all of this craziness. His energy was quickly being depleted and all he wanted to do was drive up and carry Bellamy off into the sunset or sunrise, any sunset or sunrise. Run, far, far away. As wonderful as it sounded he knew it wasn't a realistic idea. He had to stay and fight.

Chapter 14

Bellamy awoke the following morning to her phone bleating. She didn't even bother to look at the number. She hit the button sending it directly to voice mail. She didn't want to talk to anyone today, anyone but Ren that was. Her heart hurt again and she fought back tears. She hobbled to the bathroom and back out to the kitchen to start a cup of coffee. Jax was dancing and whining by the door. "Just a minute, buddy," she said hobbling toward the door. She opened the doggy door for him. He shot out into the yard.

When Jax had come back in she locked his door again. She wanted to keep him close just in case there was still some nut job out there trying to hurt her dog. She had just locked the doggy door when she heard a vehicle pull into her driveway. She pulled up the cameras on her phone and saw it was a Sheriff's 4x4. It idled for a few minutes before the occupant turned it off and got out. It was Roy. Bellamy swore under her breath. She contemplated hobbling to her bedroom and getting her shotgun and just blowing his ass away but decided against it because she would have too hard a time explaining it.

She leaned against the back door. Roy knocked and it resonated in her chest. Jax went nuts. He was a very unhappy dog. Evidently he sensed Bellamy's feelings and was going to back her up even if no one else did. In a whisper she told him 'enough' and he stopped immediately and sat next to her protectively. "What do you want Roy?" She asked through the closed and double locked door. He had the balls to actually try turning the door knob. Her heart jumped to her throat. Nobody did that especially a cop. You didn't go up to somebody's house and try the door knob without being invited in. That was just wrong.

"I was in the area on a call and just thought I'd stop by and see how you were doing." *Lying bucket of crap! Bellamy thought.*

"Fine. But I am really not up for company."

"I do have a few more questions for you, Bellamy, regarding the fire."

"Just a minute, Roy, I'm not dressed."

She hobbled to the living room out of sight of any windows even though all the curtains were drawn. She dialed 911 and asked for the Sheriff's office. She recognized Jenny's voice immediately. "Jenny, this is Bellamy. Roy is at my door, he says he has some more questions for me. If that isn't true would you advise him to get off my property immediately?" Bellamy said her voice shaking.

"Don't hang up Bellamy. Stay on the line a minute." Jenny didn't know what was going on but she could see that Roy had turned off the AVL on his car, meaning his location wasn't showing up on the map. She stood up and went in to the Sheriff's office that sat just behind the dispatch area. There was a meeting going on in his office but Jenny could hear the fear in Bellamy's voice. "I'm sorry to interrupt but I have Bellamy Boisseau on the line. She says Roy is at her house to ask her some questions. He has turned off the AVL on his car. She wants him to leave. What do you want me to do?" Jenny asked.

Sheriff Hastings sitting, leaning his elbows on his desk, fingers shaping a steeple, deferred to the ATF agent that Jenny had led back to his office about a half an hour ago. "Advise him to leave, now." The agent told her. "Have him detail the office." Jenny looked to the Sheriff. He nodded his approval.

Jenny hustled back to her console. "452, clear your location immediately and detail the station." She told Roy. Bellamy could hear Jenny's voice loud and clear over Roy's portable radio echo her order. Jenny got back on the line with Bellamy. "He's been advised to leave and come to the station." Jenny told her. 'I'm going to stay on the line with you until you hear him leave."

"Thanks Jenny. I heard that."

When Bellamy heard his SUV back out of her driveway and start down the road, she told Jenny he had left.

"Take care sister" she told her and hung up the call.

"As I was telling you Sheriff, I don't have enough to determine whether Roy had any part of this yet but we'd like your cooperation in putting him on administrative leave until we get it all sorted out. I'd like a release for his patrol vehicle. I'll have a tow enroute to pick up the car and have it towed to our secure facility. We aren't ready to apply for a warrant on his home or personal vehicle yet. We think if he was involved he used his duty vehicle. Time wise he was just too quick to get to the warehouse fire if he were coming from his residence and way to close to the kiln fire if he was in the lower valley where he was supposed to be. If we can find anything probative in his patrol vehicle we can use it to secure the other warrants." Agent Ramirez advised him.

"I keep hearing chatter that he leaked the video of part of the search of Renny's vehicle. That seems to be what incited both the 911 center and city fire department to suspend both Renny and Bellamy. Is that true?" Peter asked the Sheriff.

Detective Osborne who was also sitting in on the meeting nervously looked at a file folder lying on his lap. Sheriff Hastings leaned back in his chair now and folded his arms across his chest. His posture didn't go unnoticed to Agent Ramirez. Sheriff Hastings was staring at Detective Osborne. He looked back to Agent Ramirez. "We don't know but we will be looking into that allegation."

"We will be looking into it too." Agent Ramirez told him sternly. It was stern enough to make the Sheriff and Detective Osborne to believe it was a statement that they didn't believe everything they were telling the agent.

The Sheriff assured Ramirez that Roy would be put on leave as soon as he came in to the office and be made available for an interview.

"We will be reaching out to you as we get all of our ducks in a row." Peter told the Sheriff.

Agent Ramirez stood up and adjusted his dark blue business suit to more comfortably accommodate his shoulder holster. He shook hands with the Sheriff and Detective Osborne and started towards the door to leave. He stopped at the counter, "Thank you Jenny for your help." He said flashing a brilliant smile. Jenny felt herself blush a little bit. He was by far the hottest looking guy she had seen in a long time. He made her a little weak in the knees. His hair was perfectly trimmed in the newest style, short on the sides, a little longer on the top. It was raised a bit and swooped to the side. She imagined herself running her fingers through his glossy black hair. Then again she would really enjoy disrobing him with more than just her eyes too but she doubted that was going to happen. He was several years her junior but she couldn't help fantasizing. He seemed to have all the right parts in all the right places. The ZZ Top song suggested she really was crazy about how this guy dressed. Every inch of him oozed good looks and style. And he smelled divine. He was the whole package.

Chapter 15

Agent Ramirez climbed in to his black Chevy Suburban with blacked out windows. It didn't have government plates. They were regular run of the mill Washington State license plates with fictitious information attached to the registration. ATF, Alcohol, Tobacco, Firearms and a butt load of other things had spent far too long setting up this undercover operation to have deputy doo-dah screw it up. And the closer they got to closing it up the more they realized he wasn't just a bumbling idiot. He might also be involved. As it was Peter was concerned that people were starting to drop like flies around this investigation. The coroner's office promised the ATF they would have the DNA results on the dead guy in the pickup very soon. The state lab was always behind on DNA requests because each case had its own sense of urgency that put other cases further and further down the line. Agent Ramirez was hoping their case wasn't one being pushed further and further back on the list. Peter had his suspicions about who was in that vehicle. He was leaning towards Jason, from Mid-Valley Hops. All Peter knew for sure is that *he* wasn't the one in the truck although he had a feeling that whoever did this might have wanted him to keep the other guy in his truck company while it burned. It was just too convenient that Jason went missing a day before the corpse was found at Renny's kiln. His partner Agent Aarons theorized the same thing. It could be that Jason had overheard something at the office he shouldn't have or maybe he figured out that the amount of hop products they were selling didn't match the bottom line of the money showing on the books. Agent Aarons had worked with the FBI going through Mid-Valley Hops financials for the past ten years. There was no doubt they were making a lot more money than their tax records showed. Someone or multiple people in the business were walking away with millions of dollars. Initially they had thought it was being spread around but after their in-depth investigation they found no indication of that. Their initial belief that the company had been sharing their wealth with the largest growers was proving to be wrong. Agent Ramirez had already been put in place to follow one of the growers, Rene LaRue to see if he could get a feel for the possibility that some of the growers were skimming money too. Ramirez was sure that was not the case. LaRue kept a copy of company financials in his office that he referred to occasionally just for his own edification. When Renny was not at the ranch Agent Ramirez had ample time to go through the books too and forward copies to his office. Renny didn't lock anything up. If there was ever an example of transparency Renny's business was it.

LaRue Hops was one of the largest producers in the valley. If they were making more money than shown on their books, Agent Ramirez had easy access to the books to do some sleuthing. Renny kept copies of everything. He kept copies of copies it seemed to Peter but he had never been able to find anything that even suggested Renny or the company he owned with his brother Jon was involved in any wrongdoing. If they had another set of books they were keeping they weren't in Renny's possession. He was sure of that. Since Renny had given him access to everything in the office Agent Ramirez had made good use of it. He had torn that room apart, piece by piece as he had the chance and he couldn't find anything suspicious.

Agent Ramirez was the obvious plant for the field work. He had grown up doing stoop work in the agricultural fields throughout the west. His parents were first generation immigrants from Mexico and they wanted the American dream for their children. They had made it their utmost priority to make sure the children in the family learned English as they had. He and his siblings worked in the fields on the weekends with their parents but school was mandatory for them during the week through the school year. Sometimes he and his siblings would change schools two or three times a year following the crops but it was impressed on him that school was his way out of the fields. He took his parents' word for it.

He saw what other children had he didn't. He wanted the nice things they had. None of those kids had parents that worked in the fields. He wanted the friends they had. He fumbled his way through making friends finding that being an athlete was a perfect way to gain friends. He had a natural gift for athletics. Sometimes they were fast friends that he would only have for a while, who cared more about his physical prowess than who he really was but he enjoyed it while he had it.

Peter had continued to work the fields even after he graduated high school and went on to college on a scholarship for Agra-

Management. He received his bachelors at Stanford, with a minor in law enforcement administration. All of his siblings graduated high school and all attended college on scholarships as well. There was no way his parents would have been able to send one of their children to college let alone four children so it was a testament to his parent's persistence in pushing their children to excel in education that helped make college possible. Peter however was the one who took it one step further to get a Master's Degree in Agra-Management. His thesis had been on the history and future direction of the hop industry. Before the ink was dry on his Master's Degree he was being recruited by ATF. Looking back he had tried to figure out why they wanted to recruit him. He had never asked. He just thought at the time that it was because he was a Latino and had a Master's Degree, even though it was in Agra-Management and not in Law Enforcement. It had been a difficult decision for Peter. He had always pictured himself working in an administrative position somewhere in the agricultural business. But the opportunity to work for AFT was one he thought would really lead him out of agriculture and into an entirely different direction in life.

As soon as Deputy Morse pulled into the lot and parked a few spaces away from him Peter called the tow truck again and told him to come on in to the parking lot. He lined up the tow truck with Deputy Morse's SUV and had them load it on to the dolly. He didn't give the deputy a chance to take anything out of his vehicle. Whatever was in there at this moment would be processed for evidence.

He laughed to himself as he drove back towards his office. How foolish he had been. When this investigation started, he was immediately pulled in to take on the undercover position with LaRue Hops. He had all of the qualifications a grower could ask for. He was bi-lingual. He even had to laugh at that. He had to pretend to not be proficient at English. He had come close to slipping up a couple of times but managed to rein it in at the last minute. And in purely a twist of fate, he had taken a French class in high school and had fallen in love with the sounds it produced when spoken. The language of love, he had heard it called. He had hoped one day he would have a chance to whisper French in a girl's ear and make her immediately fall in love with him. That hadn't happened yet but he continued studying it. He laughed as he thought about it too. He studied it on his ear buds as he worked out in the fields on the weekends. He had become quite fluent. He never dreamed until he started his Master's Thesis on the hop industry the impact the French-Canadians had on the growing hop industry. Nor did he ever think he would be using it to translate conversations he overheard or how important it would become in this investigation.

Now here he was in his Armani suit and Beckett Simonon dress shoes. He really wasn't a snob, or a clothes horse. This suit was his only Armani. And sometimes, like today the suit was purely a power play. He wanted to be intimidating when he introduced himself and told the Sheriff's office that the ATF would be taking over their arson and homicide investigation. Agent Ramirez found that some jurisdictions got territorial when a federal agency came in and shut down their investigation. They didn't take kindly to it. He had tried the good old boy approach on other occasions but found that didn't bide well with most local jurisdictions when he was the one tasked with advising them ATF was taking over. Agent Aarons sometimes had good results using that approach but he hadn't. He didn't want to think it was because he was Hispanic but there were times it had felt that way. So if for some reason they were going to get all butt hurt over a federal agency stepping in, he figured he would just one up them. A good haircut and designer clothes tended to do the trick. He laughed again to himself when he had figured out that as much as men claimed they didn't notice fashion they did. They were very aware of the impact fashion had on people.

It was never more evident than in the hop industry. The big players in the business were much looser lipped in the presence of a Mexican field worker wearing a pair of baggy, faded jeans and a thin t-shirt showing under a flannel shirt with tears in it. If he swaggered in wearing this suit, the lips would close and he would be treated as a threat. He didn't swagger but just once he would like to try it to see how it felt to be a Latino John Wayne.

Peter's cell phone rang. He saw the number was the coroner's office. Peter answered the phone. Maybe they had the results of the DNA test and he would find out the identity of the corpse in the work truck the ATF had given him for his job at LaRues. Doctor Thana did. It was Jason Crone from Mid-Valley Hops. He wasn't missing anymore. How he ended up in Pedro's vehicle was still a mystery running circles in his mind, when he heard Dr. Thana continue. "But he didn't burn to death. He died of a gunshot wound to the back of the head. I can't really tell you what the weapon was other than a gun. There weren't any casings tagged as evidence from the scene but the fire department and Sheriff's office probably weren't looking for any. And the body has been so destroyed by fire that figuring out a caliber would just be speculation and not good speculation. I didn't find a slug in him." He paused for a moment.

"The other guy, Donald Jeffers, he died of a heart attack." Doctor Thana continued. That didn't surprise Peter. What surprised him was that someone had requested an autopsy on him. Peter shrugged his shoulders to himself as if to say what did that matter to his investigation. He waited then to see if the doctor had anything else to tell him and sure enough the man did. "The heart attack was brought on by a massive ingestion of methamphetamine. He was poisoned." Dr. Thana told him. "So it looks like you have two homicides in your corner. It was introduced into his body orally maybe in the lemonade he had been drinking."

"He was poisoned with meth?" Agent Ramirez asked. "Lemonade?"

"Meth," Dr. Thana confirmed.

"Meth? Isn't that rather unusual to use Meth as a poison? Are you sure he wasn't a user who accidentally overdosed?" Peter asked.

"No. This guy was as clean as they come. With the exception of high cholesterol and a heart that was getting close to the end of its expiration date, he was in pretty good shape. According to his family and medical records he was a tea toddler. Yeah, I'm sure it was intentional. That much methamphetamines and an older heart, he didn't have a chance."

"Wouldn't he have tasted it?"

"Maybe not, his office staff said he had been drinking lemonade. The tart of the lemonade could have masked it." Dr. Thana told him.

"Ok. Thank you doctor Thana for the information. That gives us a few more pieces to this ever expanding puzzle."

They ended the call and Agent Ramirez parked his vehicle in the secure lot and waited for the tow truck to arrive with Deputy Morse's SUV. He stood in the stifling heat waiting for the tow driver to unload the vehicle and finish filling out his information. He handed it to Agent Ramirez who entered his signature indicating the vehicle was now in his care. He handed all of the papers back to the driver and waited for get his copy of the documents. Then he went in to the cool interior of 'The Tower'. When he originally arrived in Yakima and was shown where the agency was housed, all four of the current employees, his boss, the administrative assistant, Agent Aarons and himself, he wondered why it was called 'The Tower'. He thought it odd that it didn't really have a name.

It was just a description of the building's size. After he got to their offices and looked out the window of his new office he understood. This city had grown out not up. There was only one other tall building in town, so this one got the upstanding moniker of 'The Tower'. He wandered if the other building was called 'The Other Tower'? He later learned the name of the other tower was the Larson Building.

When he walked in to the office, there was a buzz of activity. Most of the time when he came in it was quiet. With only three other people in the office most of the time there wasn't a lot of hubbub. But today everyone had a phone to their ear. Office doors were open and he could hear three distinctive conversations going on. He went in to his office after he had raised his chin up to each person in essence announcing his presence in the office.

First things first he thought. Stow the gun in his desk, turn on his computer, log on and go get some coffee.

The administrative assistant, Theresa was at the coffee pot when he walked up. She was a new agent waiting for an opening at Quantico to get her certification. "Aren't you a sight for sore eyes," she said rhetorically as she took him in. "I missed having you in the office Peter. I'm glad you are back".

"Thanks, I'm happy to be back, believe me." He told her honestly. He pointed out towards East Valley, indicating where he had been for the past year, "For this, I slaved to get a Master's Degree?" He was joking. He had enjoyed his undercover assignment.

"And for this, I got a Master's Degree." She swept her thin hand towards her open area office. She wasn't joking. Until she finished Quantico she had been assigned here. And now that she was so deeply involved in this case the boss had told her they wanted her to stay for the duration.

"You'll get there." Peter assured the young woman.

She looked around the office, "And leave all this? Be still my heart." She joked.

"You have to know how important you are in this investigation. You have been the glue that stuck all the pieces together and put them in some sort of order. That is no easy task and I have some more pieces to add to it. Well, I don't. The coroner does." Peter stopped there, "But you probably already have that information entered and collated." He glanced at her.

"Of course," she laughed, "Just finished" She held up her coffee cup to indicate that she was giving herself a well deserved break after completing that chore. "Peter, I do have a question though," she stopped him and leaned in close. She hadn't wanted to ask Special Agent Thompson. She was afraid he would laugh at her. "Why is this investigation so important? I mean it isn't like there are hundreds of hop warehouses in the United States. And as far as I can see the last commercial hop warehouse that caught fire was, like, five years ago. I don't get it." Theresa observed

Peter started to open his mouth to answer her but shut it again. He moved his head this way and then the other. Then he looked Theresa in the eyes, "You know, I have no idea, maybe because of the embezzlement, or maybe because it has international implications. I am not sure." He responded. He took a sip of his coffee and considered her question further. "But that's a good question." Peter shrugged his shoulders then and started into his office. "Or maybe it is important because some Senator likes beer."

Senior Agent Thompson came out of his office and strode up to the coffee pot to refill his cup. "Peter, it's good to have you in the office today. Let's get Agent Aarons and all sit down in the conference room to go over this case and decide where we are and where we want to go from here."

Peter went to get his files and Theresa locked the outer door and put up the little plastic sign in the window that said they would be back in the office in an hour, although it was a pretty good guess they wouldn't have any drop in traffic in the next hour. Not a lot of people just dropped by their local ATF office just to visit.

There were two murder books on the round conference table as well as two arson books.

There were also two white boards at either end of the room with diagrams of both buildings that had been burned. There were two cork boards on each side of the white boards. Those held photographs and push pins, pieces of string connecting this and that. To an outside onlooker they would appear to be something they had seen on a crime show but from the distance of the outer office they wouldn't be able to make out the information contained on them.

"So," Senior Agent Thompson began when Jake had pulled up a chair, "We have a lot of information to cover. But it is coming together quite neatly, I think. I want to get it tied up before anyone else gets a murder book." He said gently scratching the top of his bald head. Thompson was in his early 40's and built like a body builder. As Peter watched him he was amazed there were shirts that could accommodated the size of his biceps. They were immense. Peter was glad he had never had to grapple with him in P.T. This man could break him like a cracker. Peter himself was well built and toned but he had more of a swimmer's physic or a cyclist but Thompson looked like he ate cinder blocks for breakfast. He looked like he might turn green and shred his clothing when least expected.

"Sir, we have a new murder book. The coroner faxed the papers to me that Donald Jeffers had been poisoned. That's what caused his heart attack. He overdosed on meth. And since he is the major stake holder of Mid-Valley Hops it's a good bet his murder is somehow connected" Theresa told him.

"How does he know it wasn't an accidental overdose?" Thompson asked.

"From everything he had, Jeffers was a straight shooter. He was a teetotaler."

"Is there a police report covering it" Agent Thompson asked?

"I will check" Peter told him, making a note to follow up when Theresa spoke up and told them she had a copy of the report and had made additional copies for each of them.

They went through the financials that Jake had put together with the forensic accountants. "When we followed the money trail, Mark Jeffers appears to be the only recipient of the money. He's got it stashed in accounts from here to Switzerland. He's not the brightest or biggest embezzler we have ever gone after. Interpol is working on freezing all the accounts but as you know, anything international takes time and lots and lots of paperwork. We are tying up the knot on his noose. He has to be involved in the arson of Mid-Valley. He has to be. I think we can tie him to Jason's disappearance and murder too. I'm trying to run down all the paper on that. Daniel Jeffers the youngest son appears to be clueless to any of this." Jake informed the group.

Peter jumped in. "Mark has to be involved with the kiln fire at LaRue's farm. He, or should I say, Mid-Valley Hops is the only one who stands to make money if LaRue Brother's can't fulfill their contracts. And after Jon and Rene predicted they will have an outstanding crop this year and be able to deliver well above the amount to fill their contract, Mid-Valley would be losing money if they had to pay for the overages. That would cut into their bottom line. The warehouse that burned was still full, and I do mean full of product they hadn't sold. With an expected glut in this years harvest the price of hops is going to drop dramatically and they are going to lose even more money trying to move their product, because you realize, that the contracts they have with national and international companies are set at market prices from the previous harvest. So those companies are going to get a huge price break. Mid-Valley Hops probably thought burning down the warehouse would be the best option. Not just the building burned all of their excess products just sitting there burned too. And the insurance company was set to pay out on the building, equipment and the product in the warehouse. They stood to make a bundle of money, as long as Mark didn't ear mark it for himself," Peter said.

"The Arson Investigator from NAIC would probably have taken a cursory look and blamed it on spontaneous combustion. But we had already called them because of possible insurance fraud. The building and products value was highly inflated to raise the amount of insurance they had on it. So I think they were expecting something like this might happen." Agent Aarons added.

The rest of the small group stared at Peter. They had all got stuck on the words spontaneous combustion. Thompson thought that was an urban legend. Spontaneous combustion of hops seemed like a stretch. Peter could tell from their expressions they were having a difficult time accepting that as the cause of the fire. "I know, but look at how it works. I'm not saying it was spontaneous combustion. I'm saying they could have a case that it looks that way." Peter told them.

Thompson rubbed his shaved head, "Aarons you went in there with the local fire crew to do a pre-fire plan for each one of the hop warehouses in town. What made you suspect this one was going to burn like the informant said it would?"

Aarons flipped the edges of his papers making a motor sound. "He was right on the money, so to speak. When we did the pre-fire on that warehouse we were shocked. There was absolutely no fire alarm system. It was equipped with a sprinkler system but a fire would have to be ripping before they ever got set off. Even though all of the other warehouses have moved to an ozone based extract process because it isn't flammable this warehouse still used Hexane, which is extremely flammable. If there was even a small amount of moisture in a bale that had heated up, when those bales were opened up they would combust and if it happened near the Hexane, the entire production line would burst into flames. The bales are opened next to the Hexane. One of the bales must have had too much moisture. When it opened and hit the air it burst into flames, then hit the Hexane and the fire took off. That's what we saw the other night. The point of origin was right at the end of the conveyor belt where they opened the bales." He paused and took a drink of his now cold cup of coffee. "But," Aarons continued, "The fire was fueled by magnesium. That is why it burned so hot and white. The USDA is supposed to be checking for moisture to make sure the bales have less than a10% moisture content before coming to the warehouse from the kilns but checking every single bale from every single hop grower is impossible. They can only do random checks and monitor the moisture after they are in the warehouse."

"Hops in cold storage or already made into pellets and extract were non-issues but hops being made into hop extract using the

Hexane process were volatile if there was any moisture over 10 percent. That place, although not mandatory should have had at least a fire alarm system. The new warehouse Mid-Valley Hops has on the west side of town has a state of the art alarm and sprinkler system. My initial investigation of the fire scene was inconclusive. I mean that scenario of spontaneous combustion at the Hexane plant is a viable and logical reason for the fire that the insurance would most likely pay off with no question had we not been their wandering around doing our own investigation." Aarons said. "And had I not gone in with the fire crews and done pre-fires on those places, I would have been none the wiser and I would have sided with Mid-Valley Hops." Jake said.

"For the city boy here, explain to me this spontaneous combustion you two keep talking about. I mean, really? Is that possible?" Agent Thompson asked.

Peter and Jake exchanged looks trying to decide who would get to explain it. Jake deferred to Peter. "Hey you are the guy that wrote a Thesis on hops. You explain it."

Peter laughed. "It isn't far fetched. If you have ever mowed a lawn and piled the clippings up in a pile and left them to lay in the hot sun for a few days, you probably noticed what looked like steam coming off the pile. If you had reached your hand into the middle of that pile you would have burned your hand. Leave the pile long enough in the heat and it will burst into flames. The same thing happens with hops. If they aren't dried out enough, then are tightly baled in burlap the heat just builds up. When air hits it, spontaneous combustion occurs." Peter told them. "I mean that's the short story but if you want the chemical reactions of spontaneous combustion that will take a little longer to explain."

Thompson laughed, "Thanks, no, I get the idea."

Thompson looked between Jake and Peter. "What in the warehouse was made of magnesium?"

"Don't know," Aarons said. "There shouldn't have been anything. But it was magnesium. It's pretty clear if you watch the video I took at the fire scene. So is the explanation of how Bellamy Boisseau was injured." He looked at Peter then. "That cop you just had suspended, he retracted the back steps. Garrett, the guy who set up the Command unit had put them down. In fact you can see Garrett and me coming out of that door on the video and walking down the steps so we know they were down. But a moment later when the camera moved back around it caught Roy Morse putting them back up."

"You both have done an exemplary job on this and Peter, I'm sure you think that this past year has been a waste of time, working out in the field, literally, but I can assure you it wasn't. Not only were you able to get in close with one of the major growers that we suspected might be involved in this enterprise but you were able to eliminate him, well, he and his brother out of the equation. It helped us focus on the real suspects. And I think we can start working on probable cause for the primary player, Mark Jeffers. Now the other partner Daniel Jeffers is probably in on this too but we are having a difficult time finding a money trail on him and he is separated from the warehouse that burned and up in the newer warehouse. That in itself seems strange to me that two of the major owners are in that old rat infested warehouse while Daniel is up in the new building. But anyway, we want to start looking into Deputy Roy Morse. He just makes my radar twitch even more now after that intentional act of sabotage that made Ms. Boisseau fall and get hurt. And Deputy Morse just keeps showing up where he shouldn't be. That isn't quite right. He is showing up where he is supposed to be but much quicker than he should. I can't put my finger on it but something is just not right there. Peter did you get any idea how the city fire department got a copy of his body cam video of the search warrant Deputy Morse served on Ren's truck? Did the Sheriff's office intentionally release it to them?"

Peter sat up a little straighter, "No, I covered that with the Sheriff. He assured me that they would never release those videos because it is an open, ongoing investigation. That brings up another issue though. While I was in the Sheriff's office earlier, their dispatch center got a call from Bellamy Boisseau the one that got hurt because Roy put the steps up on the Command unit."

"She's the fire dispatcher that lives on the private road that Renny's machine shop is on. She was working the night of the kiln fire." Again, they looked at Peter like he was talking gibberish. "Ok, she and Renny were kind of, um, enemies but that isn't exactly the right word but she really didn't like Renny. Anyway, according to an internal report Roy made, she and Renny had gotten together after the fire and are/were doing the dirty deed and she might compromise their investigation by using the criminal and departmental data base to get information or get rid of information that could implicate Renny in the crime/crimes. So she and Renny have both been suspended." Peter told them. Special Agent Thompson motioned for Peter to continue.

"Anyway, while I was at the S.O. Bellamy called to report Deputy Morse was at her house wanting to ask her some more questions about the fire. For some reason it didn't sound right to her so she called the Sheriff's office to verify it. Their dispatcher told the Sheriff that Deputy Morse had turned off his AVL so they couldn't see where he was. And he had not been sent to her house to follow-up. I don't think she is connected to this case at all. But I saw the video that the fire department and the Communications Center got. It was quite obvious she was putting on a little show for Deputy Morse when YSO was serving the warrant at the house. I think she was just doing it to give a little push back for them going after LaRue. But it certainly appears she got under the deputy's skin and he is just out to pay her back. Deputy Morse most definitely appears to be stalking her or trying to hurt her."

Thompson shook his head. "I hope they called him in."

"Oh yeah, they had already decided to put him on admin leave and to advise him not to have any contact with her or anyone else associated with this case" Peter told him.

"If we can go back to the deaths of Donald Jeffers and Jason, I don't know if this has anything to do with Roy, but the coroner's office called me with cause of death on Donald and Jason. Theresa has already put that in the murder book and you should have copies of both of them. So do we have any leads on Jason's murder? We are missing something on this one and on the kiln fire. Obviously I can't be positive but I just can't see Ren killing Jason or burning down his own kiln. He doesn't have anything to gain by it. He doesn't need a new kiln? They have a much newer and larger one at the opposite end of the valley. This was just his small one for drying specialty hops. It wasn't really that important. I think it was more sentimental than anything. Their grandfather built it. And why would he kill Jason? Jason is the money maker. He's Mid-Valley's best international sales person. And seriously, kill the guy then stash him in a truck in front of your own kiln. Renny is smarter than that. So is Jon. They have worked too hard to pull something that stupid."

"You kind of alluded to Roy. How would he be involved?" Thompson asked looking for any help he could get to tag this guy to a crime, any crime.

"I'm not sure. He makes me twitch, like he does you. He knows all the parties involved. I mean he was always hanging out at the Mom and Pop café, having coffee, listening to their conversations. He could ask questions and no one would think a thing about telling him their deepest darkest trade secrets, because if you can't trust a cop who can you trust? He would know how to stage an arson fire, so it would burn quick and hot. He is a volunteer firefighter. He very easily could have access to meth. I am just hoping our forensic unit finds something that might tie him to some of these crimes so we can get a warrant for his arrest." Peter said. "And money could definitely be his motivation. They don't make crap working for the Sheriff's office."

"Makes sense, I guess. But LaRue was the last one to see Donald before he had his heart attack. What's to say he didn't poison him?" Jake asked.

"He could have, I suppose, but the staff in the office said Donald Jeffers started acting sick before Ren came in. And Ren doesn't travel in drug circles. What would be his motive? Why bite the hand that feeds him." Peter told him.

"True."

"So who do you like for Jason and Donald?" Thompson asked.

Theresa raised her hand. They all stared at her like she was in 5th grade answering a hard math question.

Thompson rubbed his head and told her to go ahead. "Um, obviously I've entered all the reports but nothing else. But it seems to me that Mark is kind of the obvious suspect. We already have him for embezzlement. Getting rid of Donald would just be one less person he had to step on to take over the company if that was his goal and he knew if Donald found out he was embezzling from the company Donald would turn him in for it. And Jason, I'm not sure about that but maybe he figured out what Mark was doing and was going to go to Donald with the information. It just seems to me, of all the suspects Mark is the one with the motive. I can't see him doing it alone. He doesn't seem like the kind of guy that would want to get his hands dirty. I can believe he could poison Donald but not that he would know where to get meth. And set an arson fire, he doesn't really have the knowledge does he? So yeah, from what you guys are saying I think he probably would have hired someone like Roy to do his real dirty work." She said, her long bobbed hair falling across her face.

"What do you think about this, guys?" Thompson asked Peter and Jake.

"I think she is right." Jake said and Peter agreed.

"So exactly how do we get the evidence to prove it? What do we need to arrest them on it especially Morse? We have enough to bring Mark in on embezzlement. What else we can dig up? We need more than speculation to arrest Roy. And," Thompson added, "We don't have a murder weapon for Jason, or an original crime scene. Jason didn't just teleport himself there. Where did he come from? If he had a car, where is it? Think about it and see if we can find a scenario that might hint at where he was killed and how he ended up at the kiln."

After another hour of discussion they came up with their game plan. He went back up to his office and called the crime scene lab to have them go down and process the vehicle. They promised to start processing it before the end of day. It couldn't be soon enough, Peter thought.

There was a federal courthouse a stone's throw from the Tower but it didn't have enough room to support all the federal agency's working in Yakima so they branched out to the Tower.

Thompson called the U.S. Marshall's office that just happened to be on the floor below them. He set up a meeting with the boss and went down immediately to take that meeting. Thompson and Corban, the U.S. Marshall in charge of their office in Yakima sat in Corban's office putting together a team to keep tabs on Mark Jeffers. "We already have him on embezzlement. We could bring him in on that but I really think he is good for the murder of Jason Crone and Donald Jeffers. We are pretty sure he didn't do it alone. He probably set up at least one of the arsons. The other fire we just don't know. So do we really surveil him or do we just let him think we are by letting him see us?" Thompson asked Corban.

"Surveil him for real, see what we see. If he doesn't make any moves, we turn up the heat after a day or so." Corban suggested.

"Ok, then Roy? I know he's involved. I can feel it. But that's all I've got. Well that and causing two good people to be put on administrative leave because of some internal video he leaked. What should we do with him?"

"We definitely surveil him. If you feel like he is involved, yeah. You can't just bring him in and interview him. You know he'd lawyer up in a minute, guilty or not. He's not going to take the chance. He's got too much to lose any way he goes. If he is guilty he isn't going to talk for fear of going to jail. If he isn't guilty he won't take the chance of saying the wrong thing and incriminating himself. Yeah, we need to be really careful with him." Corban emphasized.

"I agree." Thompson told him.

They set up their teams, picked the shifts and their vehicles and got to work. They didn't have enough people to cover the two houses so they also recruited the state patrol to assist until additional ATF agents from Spokane and Seattle could come in to do surveillance. He figured that might take a day or two. That was the problem with having a small agency in a big case. They really needed another five or six agents to cover both houses.

Jake and Peter were going to take the first watch on Roy's house. Thompson was going to team up with Theresa for the second watch. The U.S. Marshall's teams would take the duty on Mark's house. And so it would go, until they had additional units to trade off. Probable cause, Thompson prayed as he left the Marshall's office, Please Lord, give us some probable cause.

Chapter 16

Renny showered and shaved and got dressed in real clothes for the first time in a week. He dressed in his best everyday outfit. A short sleeved western shirt that fit just right. He put on a pair of Wranglers and a pair of clean, polished cowboy boots. He checked his pockets. He had his wallet, his phone and his keys. Before he stepped out of the door he put on his white woven straw hat. He settled it on his head the way he had settled this battle in his mind.

He was ready. He didn't have any idea when he was going to do this and he definitely had no idea how it was going to turn out but he was going to take the chance. Take the chance of a lifetime with some pink champagne. He hoped it wouldn't go flat and would last a lifetime.

Ren got to the bottom of his driveway and turned right. He hit the gas and didn't stop until he got to Columbia Center Mall. He hadn't been there in a very long time but he imagined the store was still where it used to be. He had already called Mr. Benz who had become a trusted jeweler for him, designing jewelry for Melanie as well as for his mother. He had always treated Ren fairly and made every piece of jewelry a piece of art. He parked and stepped out into the heat. It sucked the breath out of him. It had to be twenty degrees hotter than when he left his house. He was probably exaggerating that but it was really hot, especially walking across the asphalt parking lot. He could feel the heat through his boots and socks. He had a new appreciation for the turnout boots. They were made to withstand this kind of heat.

Once inside he looked at the kiosk showing where all the stores were. He was glad to see it was still where he thought it was in the Mall. Things changed so quickly these days he was afraid they may have moved even though he had just talked to the owner last night. He made his way down the wide corridor to the corner the store occupied. He knew exactly what he wanted and if they didn't have it, Mr. Benz assured him he would design it the way Ren had described it.

Ren walked in and the cool air from their air conditioning washed over him as he walked around the various counters looking for what he wanted. Hands clasped behind his back he slowly made his way to the case he was looking for. He carefully studied the rings displayed so beautifully. A lovely young lady came up to the counter to see if she could assist him.

"Yes, you may. You should be expecting me. I'm Rene LaRue."

"Oh yes, Mr. LaRue. I was told what you were looking for and I put together a tray of possible rings you might be interested in," she told him, "Let me get it for you." She turned and went in the back of the store and returned with several black trays. She put them down in front of him. He pulled up one of the tall chairs and sat down to examine what she had placed in front of him. He immediately saw what he was looking for.

"I'd like to see that one. May I have a jewelers loop?" He asked. She reached down behind the counter and found a loop with a bright light on it.

Ren positioned the loop up to his eye and flicked the little lever to turn on the light. He gingerly took the two carat diamond from the white velvet with a pair of tweezers. It was a beautiful two carat round brilliant cut champagne diamond that had a slight pink blush. He held his breath as he studied it for any fractures or flaws. It was perfect. It was exactly what he was looking for. "That's the one." He told the young woman.

"You don't want to look at any of the other stones?" She asked.

"No, that's the one." He told her again. She nodded and placed the diamond carefully in a clear cushioned blister container. She told him all the specifics of the stone, the total carat weight, the cut, the clarity and the color. The young woman went on to explain that that particular diamond was from the Argyle mines in Australia. It was the main source of colored diamonds and they had stopped mining it years ago. It was considered an old mine stone, which of course demanded more money. A lot more money, Ren would discover. But it was worth it if Bellamy would accept it.

"Now let's look at the settings. Rose gold, you told Mr. Benz?"

"Yes." He agreed.

She took another tray from under the diamond tray that held a selection of custom made rose gold settings. Once the setting from this tray was sold, there would not be another one exactly like it produced. Ren studied the tray for what he had in mind.

He reached for an antique looking filigree halo design with pink diamonds that would surround the champagne diamond. The dainty pink diamonds floated down the shanks.

He smiled appreciatively. "Yes, that's the one." Ren was imagining how it would look with the diamond in it. It would look perfect on her finger if she accepted it. The young woman took another two carat diamond from the other tray and held it with tweezers over where it would fit in the setting. Ren nodded his approval.

He went on to the bands. He wanted an eternity band with bevel set pink diamonds. He wanted the band to sit smoothly against her skin without prongs. After looking at a few he found the one he wanted. "That one," he said then continued, "I don't know the ring size but hopefully you can get it from this." Ren opened his wallet and took out a piece of tissue paper he had pressed between a photograph insert.

The young woman looked at him curiously. "She had a ring lying on the bathroom counter. I didn't have a lot of options since I didn't want her to know what I was doing. I used her eye liner to trace the inside of the ring." Ren told her.

"Very ingenious," She complimented. "I'll make sure I get the right size. We can have it back for you in a week. Will that work?" She asked.

Ren nodded and waited for her to put the items in a display box and then into a plastic bag with the piece of tissue in it.

"Is there anything else I can do for you?"

"No, that will do it if you will just ring it up for me." He said.

Thirty some odd thousand dollars later he walked out of the store with a smile on his face for the first time since he had walked away from Bellamy. Now if only he could figure out an idea to see Bellamy without her taking one of her guns and shooting him. She had every right to shoot him but he hoped she would at least give him time to beg forgiveness and explain why he had walked out.

The ring was a small price to pay if she said yes someday and if she liked it. He wandered around in the air conditioned corridors until he found a toy store. Meandering down row after row of toys he found what he was looking for. He got two, just in case she wanted to make some noise one day too. They were two gold coated plastic horns. He was taking no chances. He hoped maybe since she liked that black and white movie she might want her walls of Jericho to come tumbling down too.

He thought he was done with his shopping but as he started back towards the exit he found himself window shopping. Suits, he thought. He hadn't bought a new suit since Melanie's funeral. Maybe it was time to update the black to something less morbid. He stepped inside and within an hour he was walking out with his wallet even lighter but a new suit being tailored to his measurements.

That was it. He had had his fill of shopping for one day. There was absolutely no buyer's remorse as he returned to his truck. It was still so hot he burned his hand trying to open his truck door. It wasn't all that far from

East Valley but it felt like he had descended into the depths of hell. Where were his turnouts and gloves when he needed them? He couldn't imagine why people wanted to live down here. The area had grown up around the Hanford Nuclear plant into a sprawling three city community along the Columbia River. To him there was nothing attractive about the area. It reminded him of putting a dress on a pig. No matter how pretty the dress, there was still a pig under it. No matter how much green space they tried to plant to hide it, it was still a desert. It made going home a good thing for the first time in over a week.

Chapter 17

After a week and a few days, Bellamy went back to the ER to have x-rays re-done. She hoped there would be good news and she could remove these bandages and start using her arm and foot again. She wanted a shower. She wanted to wash her hair. Lauren had helped her wash her hair in the kitchen sink but it just wasn't the same as doing it herself.

Bellamy had managed to bath herself using a wash cloth and her bathroom basin full of warm water. It just wasn't the same as taking a shower and it most certainly wasn't the same as Ren giving her a sponge bath. In her mind's eye she could see his face as he tenderly bathed her. A tear splattered on the magazine she was trying to flip through. It was rather difficult to turn pages with one hand.

Lauren noticed and took the magazine from her and handed her a tissue. Bellamy dabbed her eyes and wiped at her nose. Lauren tried to remember what her friend had looked like without swollen red eyes. No matter what time of day Lauren stopped by to check on Bellamy her eyes were swollen from tears that just wouldn't stop. Lauren wished there was a plumber for shutting off tears. She was surprised her friend wasn't dehydrated just from crying. And her nose! She sounded like she was in the middle of a nasty cold that would not go away. Lauren wondered if she could give her an allergy pill. Maybe that would dry her up.

She couldn't help worrying about her friend's mental health. With the city putting her on administrative leave then Renny walking out on her she wasn't sure how much more Bellamy could take. She had seen Bellamy at some of the worst times in her life when her parents passed away within a week of each other. Bellamy was broken then, losing both parents so close together. Bellamy said her mom passed away from a broken heart, when the love of her life had passed away. Her mom just couldn't live without him.

Bellamy sat in the waiting room watching as patients arrived and left. Finally doctor dooty head had a nurse come out to get her and take her back to a small conference room. In a few minutes he came in carrying a manilla envelope again. He flicked on the light box on the wall. Without actually even acknowledging Bellamy's presence he put the various new x-rays up on the light box and studied them. He himmed and hawed and after he looked at them he turned to face Lauren and Bellamy. "I can't see any broken bones and it looks like you are recovering on time. I think we will take off the wraps. I'm going to put you in a walking boot, so you can get rid of that crutch. Now, your elbow, let's leave the wrap on that for another week. But when you are just sitting around the house you can take it off and just let it lay naturally." He paused for a moment. "I think you'll be able to start moving normally within another week or two. Same with your ankle but if there is any swelling at all you need to dial your activity back a little, maybe put the boot back on. But other than that it looks like you are doing well. Now if you need anything at all or have any concerns you can give us a call here at the ER or contact your regular doctor. I'll have the nurse come in and take those bandages off and get you into a walking boot." With that he walked out. He didn't say good bye or good luck, or anything. He just walked out. Lauren and Bellamy exchanged looks and laughed.

It was the first time Lauren had seen Bellamy laugh in what seemed like, forever, even though it had just been a week or so. "Don't you just want to breast feed him?" Lauren asked incredulously. "Oh my Gawd! They just get younger and younger, and I just keep getting older and older."

The nurse hustled in a few minutes later. She exchanged looks with Bellamy and Lauren and said, "You don't have to say a thing. I know exactly what you are thinking. But you think that's bad you should have to work with him." They all started laughing then. The nurse was an ancient, maybe twenty five year old and even she was commenting on this guy's age.

Bellamy wanted to skip out of the ER but she couldn't. She was however, able to walk to the car. On the advice of the nurse Bellamy used her crutch, until she got her balance back. That was fine. She had no problem with that. She felt free. She could take a shower and wash her hair all by herself. By herself if she didn't count Jax. Doing anything in the bathroom without Jax was not going to happen. He had to be there to protect and observe.

The minute Lauren got her in the house and left, Bellamy hobbled to the bathroom, disrobed and turned on the water for a shower. She couldn't believe how wonderful it felt to get in the shower. She was very careful not to slip. That was the last thing she wanted to happen. She didn't want to become the poster child for a commercial advertising a product to call for help if a person fell in the shower.

Bellamy had one of those shower radios 'as seen on TV'. She turned it on to a hard rock channel. She didn't really like hard rock she just wanted something loud to drown out the silence. She cranked it up as loud as it would go. The sound seemed to bounce off the shower tiles. She needed the distraction, the louder the better. Bellamy lingered in the shower until her fingers were prunes.

When Bellamy finally emerged from the shower Jax was no longer in the bathroom and she could hear him somewhere in the house barking and growling. She figured he just didn't like her choice of music or how loud it was but he usually didn't bark and growl. It sounded like he was in the bedroom or something but it was hard to tell over the ear splitting volume of the radio. She wrapped a big towel around her and tried to towel dry her hair with another towel. She still only had one hand but it was better than nothing. When she had done all she could do, she flipped her long blond hair up and over so she could start combing it out. She kept yelling "Enough" at Jax to get him to shut up but he continued the racket. The mirror on the medicine cabinet was still fogged up from her shower. She wiped off the mist and let out a scream. There behind her was Roy. He was just outside the bathroom. She screamed bloody murder. *Poor choice of words, she thought in a mille second.*

She leaned back against the counter. She was in shock. She had no idea what was going on. She screamed again. No one could hear her out here in the middle of nowhere over the radio blaring. Bellamy still screamed at the top of her lungs. She was about to yell for Jax to "get him" but didn't get the chance.

Roy yelled at her to shut up. She refused to shut up and reached behind her with her one good hand and started throwing stuff off the counter at him. All she could see were his eyes as they bored into her. They were black, blacker than night. She shuddered. She didn't even notice the huge knife in his hand at first. All of these thoughts were going through her head in bits and pieces of the seconds ticking by. She reached behind her and felt around for her hair spray. Aqua Net, probably the oldest hair spray brand on the market, but if you needed extra hold in your hair this was the go to hair spray. After all these years there was still a market for it. And she was glad she was part of that market. She whipped it around and aimed it right at Roy's eyes. She pressed the button and let it fly. He had started his jab but it went wild when the spray hit his eyes. She knew he had gone through pepper spray training so he knew how to fight through that but he had met his match with

Aqua Net. When the spray stopped flowing she threw the can at him. If she had had two good hands she would have lit the spray with the lighter on the counter and torched him. It was another mille second thought that raced through her mind. It seemed everything was happening in slow motion. It didn't feel real.

While he was still trying to wipe the goo out of his eyes she grabbed her crutch. Aiming for his balls with her crutch she knocked him backward out of the door. It was then she saw two men wearing vests at the end of the hallway aiming their guns at Roy or at her she wasn't sure. Bellamy had no idea what was going on but dropped her crutch and put her good hand in the air still holding her other arm protectively against her chest.

One armed man covered the other. The fairer complected of the two took Roy down to the ground and sat straddled over him and cuffed him. He looked up at Bellamy and smiled slightly, then yelled over the music, "Could you turn it down please" It took Bellamy a minute to react. Finally deciding it was safe to move she hobbled to the shower and turned the radio off. The sudden silence was deafening until she could hear Jax whining. She looked down and her towel had slipped and she was trying to gather it back around her. Jax continued to whine. It wasn't his "I'm going to eat you" whine. It was his "I'm locked in this room and I want to be with my friend" whine.

"Jax" She shouted!

The Hispanic man in the vest holstered his gun and went to the bedroom door and opened it without hesitation. "Hey Jax," he greeted in Spanish. Jax danced around the man like he was Jax's long lost friend. The guy reached down and scratched the fur around his collar. Jax turned his attention to the men on the floor. He sniffed them briefly and apparently satisfied they were not a threat, trotted around them to Bellamy. His whole rear end was wiggling from side to side as he whined at her to pet him.

All at once the realization that she almost died hit her and she slumped against the counter. "Can I sit down?" She asked but didn't wait for an answer as she flopped her backside on the toilet creating a loud clatter.

"You are okay now Bellamy. We got this." A familiar voice told her. "You want me to take him out to the car?" He asked the fairer complected man, hoisting Roy to his feet.

"I'll take him to the car. You've got some explaining to do." He told the Hispanic man with a Mexican flare to the word explaining.

"Bellamy, I'll wait out here for you if you would like to put some clothes on." The darker complected man suggested. He didn't think Ren would appreciate him appreciating Bellamy this way.

She tightly closed her eyes for a moment realizing with the exception of the bath towel she was naked. "Uh, yeah. How do you know my name?" She returned. The man had closed the door to give her some privacy and he didn't answer her.

Pulling on her clothes as quickly as she could her mind was racing around a track of pre-recorded voices. It came to a screeching stop and rewound, replayed, rewound and replayed. She stood up and put her crutch under her arm and opened the door. There stood this very handsome Hispanic man in a vest smiling at her. "Pedro?" She asked, searching his face for a trace of recognition. "Pedro?" Bellamy asked again. Without a second of hesitation, she wrapped her one good arm around his neck and hugged him tightly sobbing into his shoulder. Her crutch clattered to the floor. He gave her a light man hug. After a moment he gently moved her back and helped her get her crutch and reposition it.

"Come on, let's go sit down." He suggested in perfect, eloquent English. He steadied her as she made her way into the kitchen and they sat down at the kitchen table.

"My name is actually Peter. Peter Ramirez. I'm an ATF agent. I've been working under cover for about the past year as Pedro." He told her.

Bellamy stared at him in complete shock. He could have told her he was Donald Duck and she wouldn't have cared. It was Pedro and he wasn't dead. He was talking but she didn't hear him. Her mind had shorted out for a few minutes.

"Bellamy, you are going to have to trust me on this. You must not say a word about this until I let you know when you can. We almost have this tied up. It shouldn't take more than another week or so if you can just be patient. We want to make sure we have a solid case before we start wrangling weasels." He told her smiling a brilliant white smile she had never seen before. "And Roy just got us one step closer. I am so sorry he almost hurt you but he won't get another chance." Peter assured her.

Bellamy was nodding in understanding even though she wasn't sure at all what he was talking about. Peter was rambling off names she had never heard of before.

"We will clear up everything with the city for both you and Renny but until then, go take a nice vacation somewhere. The city will be paying for this one. And I will give you a call and let you know when you are free to talk about this ordeal and we will fill you in with the rest of the information." Peter suggested. "I'm going to have Jake come back in and take your statement Bellamy, on what just happened in here and then if you think you'll be ok, we will get out of here and let you get back to your life. We can give someone a call for you if you'd like someone to come be with you. I'd call Renny for you but he doesn't know about any of this and we really don't want him to know any of it right now." Bellamy nodded slightly. He had left her. He wasn't answering her calls and she had stopped calling. He had made it abundantly clear he didn't want to be involved with her.

"Uh, that's ok. I'll call my friend Lauren after you guys leave." She told Pedro/Peter.

Peter stood up to leave. Bellamy took his hand lightly to stop him. "Thank you for saving me today." All he did was nod.

"I promise I'll be in touch with you as soon as I can. You take care. You are safe now. But if you need anything, here's my card. My personal number is on the back. Call any time if you need me." He repeated. Now all she could do was nod. "Au revoir" Peter told her as he closed the door behind him.

It was him who called her in the middle of the night and asked her to take care of his hound dog. She hadn't even thought about that until he said good bye. She had been so happy to have lived through that lunatic Roy and to find out that Pedro/ Peter was still alive she hadn't even thought about the phone call. But yes, that was him.

She did start crying then. *I did take care of your hound dog, Peter, Bellamy sobbed, but he ran away from me and he won't come back. What am I supposed to do without him? She lamented inside.*

She had buried her face in her arm on the table and was crying, gasping for air, like a little kid. "Here," she heard a man say. She jumped then not even aware anyone had come in the house. It was the other Agent. He handed her a tissue from the box by her recliner. "Can I get you a glass of water?" He asked. She shook her head and tried to stop sobbing.

"I am really sorry. I hate it when I cry." Bellamy told the young man standing next to the table looking down at her. She inhaled and exhaled deeply, "Please, sit down," she told him as she tried to regain her composure. "Can I get you something to drink?" She asked him now. She ran through her offerings. He accepted a can of soda.

She got up and brought him a can of soda from the fridge and handed it to him, then got a glass and filled it with ice and took it back to the table for him. He opened his can of soda and poured it over the ice slowly as though he hoped the time it took him to do that would give her a bit more time to settle herself. She sat down across from him at the table waiting for him to start questioning her.

"If I can, I want to tape your statement so I can make sure nothing gets left out when our administrative assistant transcribes it?"

"That's fine," Bellamy told him. When he had started the tape he asked Bellamy to just explain what happened in her house a little while ago. Bellamy told him what had happened. It didn't take long. Then she looked at Agent Aarons and asked, "Why did he do that?" She paused a minute. "He got so weird after the kiln fire. It was like he was a completely different guy. The Roy I've had coffee with and laughed with would never act the way he did. And then today, his eyes were black. I mean completely black. I have never seen anything like that and I hope I never do again. I can't remember ever being that afraid or angry." Bellamy told him. She was running off at the mouth. And she started trembling. She knew it was just the adrenaline leveling off and would eventually stop but right now she couldn't control it.

"Bellamy, I am not really sure what was going through his head today. I think, maybe, after he got suspended he blamed you." Jake told her.

"He got suspended?"

"The day you called dispatch to report he was at your door." Agent Aarons told her.

"Wow! Uh, I didn't mean for that to happen. I just wanted him to leave." She told him honestly.

"He was about to be suspended anyway but I think he thought you were responsible. It had nothing to do with you." Agent Aarons assured her. "But Bellamy, you said he acted different after the kiln fire, how so?"

She told him what she had observed. When she was finished he thanked her for the information, gave the date and time and turned off the recorder.

"Now you tell me something. How did you know Roy was here?" Bellamy asked.

Agent Aarons explained to her that they had been doing surveillance on him and had followed him here. As soon as he pulled into her driveway they got out of their car and followed him up to the house. They were afraid he might do something. And sure enough he had. They had been lucky to have been there to stop him.

When Agent Aarons had finished telling her as briefly as he could what had happened without giving her too much information on why they were tailing him he thanked her for the soda and took his glass and can to the kitchen sink for her. "Now do you want us to send someone out to stand by with you until you get your door fixed?" He asked her. She shook her head. "We have a tow truck on the way to get his car out of your driveway."

Bellamy thanked him then as he opened the door Jax came in to sit beside her. "Hey, Agent Aarons, could you do me a favor?"

He gave her a hesitant nod. "Ask Roy to drop his pants." The agent's head shot up a couple of inches. "See if he has bite marks on his ass. If he does, he was the one prowling around here that Jax bit. YSO has the report and a jeans pocket Jax brought back." Bellamy told him.

"Yes ma'am," he replied enthusiastically.

She dropped her head and shook it. "Agent Aarons, I have had a very trying couple of weeks. Work, Getting hurt, had my hound dog run away, a toddler for a doctor but this? Ma'am? Really? What an indignity. I am your age and you just called me ma'am. Do that again and I will bitch slap you. Got it?"

"Yes, Maa, Bellamy. Got it." He scurried out the door.

Agent Aarons got in the car. He looked behind him and saw the plexi-glass was open between the front and back seat. He slid it shut, then said to Peter in a hushed voice, "She just threatened to bitch slap me."

"What did you do?" Peter asked laughing.

"All I said was yes ma'am. She told me she had had a rough couple of weeks, work, getting hurt and something about her hound dog running away. But it was the ma'am that pissed her off. I was just trying to be respectful. I don't get it."

Peter laughed at him again. "Ask your wife when you get home. She will explain it to you." He stopped laughing as the rest of her words hit home. "She said her hound dog ran away?" Peter asked Jake.

"That mean something to you?" Jake asked. "Maybe that was why she was crying when I went in." Jake added.

"Crap." Peter said quietly.

They sat in silence then until the tow truck came to tow Roy's car. When it arrived they discussed it and decided to take it to their impound lot. They would check with Thompson and see if he wanted to get a warrant to search it too or see if Roy would sign a waiver for them to search it. It was possible there might be evidence in there. When they had signed off on the impound sheet they took Roy directly to the county jail.

They got him out of the car in the sally port and started processing him to be booked. When the corrections officer started searching him, Jake called him away from Roy for a moment and asked him to have Roy drop his drawers, so he could check for bite marks. The corrections officer looked at Agent Aarons and smiled as though he couldn't wait to do as requested. Roy's right buttock was bruised and he had puncture marks oozing pus. My, my, my, Jax really had taken a big bite out of crime and the evidence was right there on Roy's butt cheek. They took several pictures and after consulting with the medic on duty were assured they would treat his wounds here at the jail and start him on some antibiotics.

Lauren arrived as the door company was packing up there equipment to leave. She parked her car next to Bellamy's car and walked up to Bellamy who was still standing by a brand new back door complete with doggy door. "Um, something you want to tell me about?" Lauren asked.

Bellamy shook her head slightly and motioned Lauren into the house. "Just another day in paradise," Bellamy said over her shoulder. When Lauren had kicked off her high heels and settled onto the couch with a drink, Bellamy began to explain the rest of her day after Lauren had returned her from the hospital.

Lauren was speechless. She didn't even know what to say to Bellamy. She was trying to absorb what Bellamy had told her. Finally she asked, "So why were they following Roy anyway?"

"I don't really know. I think it had something to do with the hop industry but Pedro couldn't really go into it." Bellamy told her. His name was out of her mouth before she could stop it.

"Peter, you mean." Lauren corrected.

"Pedro. Oh, wait. I didn't tell you that part. Pedro isn't dead. The guy in the truck wasn't Pedro." Bellamy explained to Lauren. "But you are sworn to secrecy."

"That's great. I'm sure Renny will be relieved to know that," Lauren commented.

"Uh, he doesn't know yet. ATF is still working on their case. I don't think they will tell him until after they make their case and an arrest. I wouldn't have known if Roy hadn't tried to hack me up." Bellamy told Lauren.

"I still don't think I'm driving on the same freeway you are. You are on some kind of roundabout. I'm not following you." Lauren told her friend.

"Oh, sorry, I guess I'm still a little rattled," Bellamy took a breath. "The ATF agent, Peter? He's actually Pedro. Other way around, Pedro is actually Peter. Peter was undercover as Pedro. Oh, but Lauren, Peter is hot! I mean, really, really hot."

"Pedro hot? Nah. Pedro was ok. But by no means hot." She had seen Pedro out in the fields sometimes when she stopped by

Bellamy's house. He was just kind of frumpy, average looking at best.

"From undercover to wanting him under your covers. I'm telling you Lauren, he is hot."

"Okay, whatever."

"I think he is single."

"Then you hit on him." Lauren tossed back lightly. She caught Bellamy's expression and immediately regretted her words. 'I am so sorry, honey. I didn't mean that."

Bellamy tried to shake it off but the words were stabbing at her heart. She missed Ren so much. He was the only one she wanted right now. She wanted him to hold her again and tell her she was safe and how much he loved her. But she knew that wasn't going to happen. He had walked out and was gone. She still wasn't sure what she had done to deserve it.

"Um, hey, if I promise not to cry all weekend would you want to go to the beach, my treat? I just need to get out of here for a while. Breathe in some nice salt air. Let Jax go run and play in the waves, chase some seagulls."

Lauren thought about it for a minute. "I think I can get some time off. I'll see if I can get a hold of my boss at home tonight. I'll let you know. When would you like to leave?"

"That's up to you, since, well, you are the one who has to drive." Bellamy told her holding up her walking boot.

"Right. Well then, I'll go put a few things in a bag and call you if I can get the time off." Lauren told her.

Chapter 18

By the time Peter and Jake had returned to their office and completed reports and filled out more paperwork to drop off at the jail, the sun was setting in the west. They were hoping that since their detail on Roy was done that maybe the marshals and or one of the additional agents they had brought in would take at least one more day of shifts on Mark Jeffers so Jake and Peter could take a day off but that was not going to happen. Their boss had made sure of that.

While Thompson and Theresa were on their stakeout, Thompson conference called Jake and Peter before they secured for the night. "You think Roy will turn on Jeffers if he is involved?" He asked.

Jake looked at Peter. "We don't think so. If he is involved, which we are certain he is, he is just going to lawyer up. He didn't say two words to us on the drive in or while we were in booking. He just went mute."

"You don't think he would talk in an interview?"

"Nah," Peter told him. "Boss, he knows how interviews work, even with an attorney. And he knows if we have enough evidence to charge him with one or all of those crimes, he's going to spend eternity in prison. He's been an officer long enough to know what is going to happen to him in there. He knows talking isn't going to help him." Peter told him.

Thompson said, "Once we have the evidence and start charging him, I think he might be willing to talk just to barter for where he ends up doing time for the rest of his life. If he thinks it might get him out of general population, or his attorney can convince Roy that is the way to go, I think we have a shot at getting him to talk. He won't be arraigned on the Assault charge until Monday. We also put him on a 72 hour investigative hold so we know he can't bail on it. That's going to give him some time to really think about what his life is going to be like if he ends up in prison. I think that will be the deciding factor in this. Let him chew on it for a day or two. Peter, you and I are going to sit down, come up with our strategy for an interview. Then you and I will take a shot at him. Get some rest and I'll sit down with the two of you in the morning before I secure for the night."

Jake and Peter looked at each other wearily. "I guess that means no day off." Jake told him.

"Guess not."

They parted ways in the parking garage and headed to their own individual SUV's. Both men headed west but Peter stopped at a drive-thru that was open late and picked up his idea of comfort food. It was Mexican fast food and he knew he would have to do some heavy workouts to fight the calories he would consume late this evening on his couch. Such was the life of a single federal agent.

Peter was exhausted. The day, as some were, had held some unexpected twists. Neither one of them had guessed that Roy would go after Bellamy like he did. He said a quick thank you to St. Michael for keeping her safe. Then he thought about Bellamy telling Jake that her hound dog had run away. Somehow he couldn't believe that Renny would walk away from Bellamy. He had seen the way Renny looked at her sometimes when they were working together and Renny had seen her in her yard. Even when he had poked fun at Renny for the way he looked at Bellamy, he knew Renny wished she would look at him the way he looked at her. He knew even then that Renny loved her, probably long before Renny knew it himself.

Peter muted his television and picked up his personal cell phone. He dialed Renny's number. Renny answered but there was hesitation in his voice. When Peter looked at the time on the television he realized how late it was and of course Renny would probably be wondering who was calling him at this late hour.

"Ami," Peter began in French, "Please just listen to me. I can't tell you much but there is something very important you need to know."

Before Peter had a chance to go on, Renny cut in quickly, "I don't know who you are but you are not my friend. Let's get that straight right now. And I doubt there is anything you could say that I need to hear."

"You need to know that Bellamy is safe. She is scared but she is safe. Renny, she loves you. She trusted you. Why did you walk out on her? She needs you now more than ever," Peter continued in French.

Renny's anger and pain burned in him. "I am trying to protect her you ass hole," He yelled at this jerk. Who was this talking to him like that in French no less? Then the guy's words sank in, "What do you mean she is safe?" Renny yelled at the phone panic setting in as the thought of something else may have happened to her.

"You aren't giving her enough credit Renny. She loves you and would do anything for you, even giving up her job to be with you. Don't you get that?"

"I do get that. If I didn't I wouldn't have bought a ring I don't even know if she will ever accept. So don't try to tell me I'm not trying to protect her, Pedro." He shouted into the phone without even a moment of hesitation. Pedro! Bellamy was right. "This is

Pedro isn't it?" Renny asked? But the phone had gone dead and Pedro or whoever was on the other end of the line was gone.

Talk about not showing your hand, you dope. Renny admonished himself. He had just told a complete stranger about protecting Bellamy and the ring he had bought. It was quite evident that neither he nor Bellamy should ever play poker.

Peter smiled to himself when he had hung up. *A ring? Holy crap, Renny really does love Bellamy. I knew he loved her but a ring, wow. Now that is what I call having faith in a woman. I wonder if she has a sister? Maybe that little Chicklet that shows up at Bellamy's house all the time. The one with legs that go up to, well they are long.*

Now Ren couldn't sleep thanks to the idiot that had just called him. He got up and wandered down stairs for a cup of coffee. The eastern sky was already getting light at this time of the year. The moon was waning and still low on the horizon, and one of the planets, he didn't know which one was bright above the moon. He wished Bellamy was here to share that with him. He just wanted to feel her touch him. His mind replayed every moment they had spent together, her face, the softness of her lips, the mindless conversations they had. He missed her so much it was tearing him apart. Would she ever forgive him? Would she ever be in his life again? He really doubted it.

He needed to pull himself together. He had a ranch he needed to get back to. He was suspended from the fire department. He had all the time he needed to get back to hops. He needed to get someone to run it if and when he went back to work at the city. Harvest was right around the corner and he should be focusing his time on that. Renny got dressed and filled a travel cup with strong coffee, mustered his resolve and started down towards the shop.

The sun was just stretching above the horizon and glowing gold as it slowly pushed above the hills. It was a sure sign it was going to be hot again. That was good for his crop but miserable for the people living in the valley.

Renny was holding his breath as he started down the dirt road to his shop. It was very early so he hoped Bellamy would still be sleeping and not notice his truck as it passed her house. There was no chance of speeding by the house. It was a dirt road. He had to take it slow, unlike Bellamy, he remembered. She drove like one of the dirt devils that tore through the valley lifting dust and debris into the sky then disappearing without a trace. She was gone from his life and he couldn't blame her if she never wanted to see him again.

Before Renny even got to the edge of her property Jax was at the road, barking and dancing as Renny's truck slowly went by her yard. Her sprinklers were on and Jax was getting soaked running back and forth along the road. When Renny was abreast of her driveway, he saw her friend was there and they were packing stuff into the back of Bellamy's car. Bellamy looked up to see who was going by so early in the morning, even though she knew. Jax knew who it was too and he stopped at the edge of the driveway and stared after his truck wondering why his friend hadn't stopped to visit him. She glanced at Ren quickly then looked away as though she hadn't noticed him.

Lauren stood up straight when he drove passed. Her dark eyes, even though he really couldn't see them, seemed to dare him to pull into the driveway. Her ire had gone from zero to sixty in a nanosecond. She didn't know what she would do to him but she would do something, maybe throw a rock at his truck. Something, she would do something. Even though she wanted to believe he didn't want to hurt Bellamy, he had.

When Bellamy thought her eyes had met his even though it was just for a moment it felt like a bolt of lightning had struck her. She lost her breath and her heart went into flight mode. When the connection between them had been broken he continued on down the road and Bellamy tried to control her emotions. She had to expect him to go back and forth on this road. It was their shared road. It was the only access he had to his shop. She decided she needed to accept that and move on. But she couldn't. Not right now. She felt like a dog abandoned on the side of the road, wondering why her owner had left her. Bellamy wanted to run after his truck. She wanted him to stop and tell her it was an accident, that he would never abandon her. Why had he left her the way he did? His lie of wanting to protect her fell flat. If someone wants to protect you, they stay by your side and fight your fight with you. They don't just walk out.

Bellamy went back into the house and got the rest of the items for the beach. It always amazed her how much stuff she took to the beach for just a few days. It seemed half of the essential stuff she took never made it out of the car when she got to the beach. But she didn't want to take the chance that she might need something and not have it.

Lauren had picked up Bellamy's phone to put it in her purse. "Bellamy, did you see you have a voice mail on here from a few days ago that you haven't listened to?"

"Oh, yeah, I'm sure it is just a spam call. I didn't recognize the number."

"Aren't you at least going to look at it? It might be important."

"You listen to it if you want. I'm just going to delete it when I remember." Bellamy said as she filled a cup with coffee to take with them, even though they would be making frequent stops the first of which would be an espresso stand. After that would be their pee breaks. It seemed on road trips that they could never coorMorgante their pee breaks, Jax included.

"Hello Bellamy," a male voice came over the phone. "My name Gabriel Jackson and I am an attorney here in Yakima. I have been retained for you, should you need an attorney to resolve the issue you are having with the city. If you should need me or have any questions, please give me a call at 509-000-5555. This will all work out for you. But again, you can give me a call at any time. Have a good day."

Bellamy looked at Lauren. "Okayyyy. What is that all about? Who retained this guy? I certainly didn't."

"I wish I could say it was me but I don't have the bucks to retain that attorney." Lauren admitted. She didn't know many people who did have the money or the need to have an attorney on retainer, maybe a business or a mobster or someone with big bucks. "Renny, maybe" Lauren suggested.

"No. That's crazy. He wouldn't do that. I'm going to call that guy and ask him?"

Bellamy said and started to dial the number. As she hit send it dawned on her that literally it was just dawn. He wouldn't be there. She continued with the call and left a voicemail anyway.

They finished loading up Bellamy's car and got Jax settled in the back seat. He was excited to be going somewhere, anywhere as long as he was with his human. And now, thanks to Renny they were going to smell wet dog all the way to the beach.

Chapter 19

As Jax paced in the back seat, Roy was pacing in his cell. He had asked for a phone call and was waiting for one of the guards to come and take him to a phone in the visiting area.

He hadn't slept. It was impossible to sleep in this place, with doors clanking and people talking and walking by his cell all night. The correction officers were treating him like a common criminal. They acted as though they had never met him before. It was a nightmare.

When the officer came to take him to the visitation room he handcuffed Roy before he opened the door to his cell. Roy looked at him with a pained look on his face. This couldn't be happening. He had known this officer for years and he was handcuffing him to walk 100 feet to the visitation area. He couldn't believe it.

In the visitation room the officer sat Roy on a chair with a pay phone in front of him. "Whoever you call has to accept the call, it is considered a long distance collect call." The officer told Roy. Roy knew he should be calling his wife to explain what had happened but he wasn't sure what was going through his head at the time or what he would say to his wife.

Roy thought he should call an attorney? A defense attorney? He didn't know any except for the ones who had come in to interviews with suspects he had arrested and needed to interview. *Wouldn't that be fun? Roy thought.* He would have to call a piece of crap defense attorney to help get him out of this mess.

He called Mark Jeffers. Mark had gotten him into this mess he needed to get him out. The phone rang for a long time and he was afraid he wouldn't answer. Eventually a groggy voice answered the call and an automated voice advised him he had a call from inmate, Roy said his name, at Yakima County Corrections Center, will you accept the charges? There was a long pause before he accepted the call against his better judgment. Maybe he was just touching base and didn't have his cell phone, Mark thought.

"Why are you calling me?" Mark asked in a voice just above a whisper. He didn't want his wife to wake up. He slipped out of bed and walked out the sliding glass doors of the bedroom on to the deck.

Thompson caught a flicker of movement on the upper deck. It was barely light enough to make out someone talking on a phone. He quickly lifted the parabolic microphone and pulled the headphones up he had hanging around his neck. He could only hear one side of the conversation but he was hoping it might be something good.

"Who else am I supposed to call?" Roy asked.

"Anyone else, an attorney?"

"You got me into this. You find an attorney for me. And it better be a good one. You had better get me out or I'm going to spill everything. I am not going to prison for you." Roy said in a loud whisper. "And if you do, you better hope you don't share a cell with me."

"What do you want me to do? You got paid for your services. Figure it out." He told Roy angrily. He almost hung up on Roy but something kept him on the line.

"You figure it out. I'm telling you, if you don't get me out of here you won't be able to make another glass of lemonade using me." Roy hissed. Roy thought he was being clever trying to talk in code to Mark. Not his brightest move he decided too late. He was so sleep deprived and freaked out about his situation he had completely forgotten that the calls were all recorded, as were the numbers inmates called. If any investigator listened to it he would be fried. He felt sweat beading on his upper lip. He swore at himself. He had already said way too much.

The automated voice told them their time was up and the call was terminated. Roy tried to figure out what he was going to do now.

Roy waited for the corrections officer to come and take him back to his cell.

Mark wanted to throw his phone but didn't. He just knotted his fist around it in a death grip and shook it wildly in the air. He looked around and found a pack of cigarettes he kept on the deck for moments like this. His wife wouldn't let him smoke in the house. He lit it and walked to the edge of the deck and stood looking out over his yard. Across the road he noticed a car off to the side of the road somewhat obscured by the trees and brush. Mark thought he could see movement in the car. A flicker of paranoia entered his mind that someone might be watching him. His house was on a hillside overlooking a valley west of the city. It was secluded. His nearest neighbor was at least a mile away and hidden behind a wall of trees. Across the road was an unobstructed view of the valley below him. There were no houses below him. He had a territorial view that prevented anyone developing the land below him that would block his view of the valley or river meandering through it. There was no reason for a car to be parked there. At first he thought it was some kids making out. But the sun was starting to come up so it was far too late for kids to be out. It could be migrant workers without a place to live yet just camping out on the side of the road. It still unnerved him.

That stupid moron had called him. Roy called him from jail. He wandered if those calls were recorded. He cringed. He hoped not. Roy was stupid but he couldn't be that stupid to call him on a recorded line. He tried to remember if Roy had said anything that might implicate him in the murders or arsons? He was sure he could talk himself out of anything. If he was accused of the murders or arsons he could figure out how to keep himself out of it but he hoped he wouldn't have to do that.

Ren walked in to the shop. It was so hot inside he immediately started sweating even though it was still quite cool outside. The metal building had absorbed the heat from yesterday and it had not cooled off at all. Usually because of the way these metal buildings were constructed when it cooled off at night it generally cooled down inside too but this morning the heat was oppressive.

He went in to his office and turned on an air conditioning unit in the wall above his desk. Even though the fluorescent light was always on overhead, he turned on a lamp on his desk. Ren sat down in his old office chair and looked at the shop phone. The red light on the answering machine was blinking frantically. Ren hit the button to play back the messages. There was only one business related call the remainder of the calls were people checking in on him to see how he was doing. There was one from Pierre apologizing profusely about the day in the café and none of them believed what Roy had told them. The last one which was the most recent call was from the man that had called him earlier. He almost hit the delete button but he listened anyway.

"Renny, this is Agent Peter Ramirez, from ATF. I've taken care of your harvest crew. Everyone from last year will be back with the exception of Pedro. But Pedro is alive. And I'm sure if you need him to break in your new field man Pedro will step in but after that he will be out of the ranch business. I think Rico Sanchez would be great for this job. He did a great job last year and I think he would be a good fit. And if it is still available he and his wife would probably be very grateful to have the house Pedro used to live in."

"All of the crew is excited to be back. Give Rico a call, his number is 509-000-5454. Renny I promise everything will work out. I just ask that you not share my identity with anyone in the industry yet. We are still working on our investigation. I promise we are just about done but we have a few more weasels to catch. Once we snare those weasels I am sure things will get back to normal. I apologize for the way this investigation went sideways but hopefully we can straighten it out very soon. I will get back to you as soon as I can. But if you have any concerns give our office a call. The number is 509-000-2020," Peter told him. Bellamy was right. She knew it was Pedro.

Renny sat back in total disbelief. He wondered why, when he called earlier, he didn't tell him all of this then. Maybe he thought Renny had heard this message earlier. He wasn't sure. A huge weight had been lifted from his shoulders though knowing Pedro was alive and his crew would be back this year. But now he had more questions than he did answers. If Pedro was alive then who the hell was in that truck? And if Pedro was alive why hadn't he just come back and told him? Was

Pedro Peter? Or was Peter Pedro? Was Pedro in trouble? Had he been hiding out as a field man? He couldn't wait to hear the rest of the story, or the true story, like Mike Rowe always did on his Pod Casts. A thousand new questions went spiraling through his head. He was getting a head ache.

Renny was at a loss again. What in the world was going on? He didn't know but he knew it was time to get back to work on the ranch. He called Jon knowing he would be up and in his office by now. He told Jon, without telling him, that he had his crew back. He told Jon he was back too and going to try to get some stuff done around the ranch.

He made some coffee and started putting his office together after the Sheriff's office had torn it apart. When he thought it was late enough in the morning, he called Rico and he graciously accepted Renny's offer to become his field man. And Peter was right, he was enthusiastic. He told Renny he would be there in an hour to start working. Good to his word, Rico was in his office in 45 minutes, a huge grin on his face. Renny shook hands with his new field man and they got to work.

Thompson sat down with Peter and they put together a game plan to interrogate or interview Roy depending on whether you used the old term or the kinder, gentler term. It was pretty much the same thing. They put together an idea of what they wanted to accomplish and how they were going to approach Roy. When they were satisfied with the general direction they wanted to steer their interview if he didn't lawyer up on them before they had a chance. Even if he did they would still do the interview, just take a little different tack. As soon as they got all the results back from Roy's truck they would conduct the interview, unless of course it didn't come back before his 72 hour hold expired and he managed to post bail on the Assault charge. If, if, if, ugh! Peter felt that was the bulk of his job, if.

Jake and Peter got to work studying the arson reports. Peter was lucky the truck had gotten a flat tire after he got the propane tanks filled and into the kiln for safe keeping. He had Jake come and pick him up in his personal vehicle to take him to his apartment. If he hadn't he may have been in the truck with Jason with a bullet hole in his head and charred beyond recognition.

It was evident from the initial reports that the point of origin for the kiln fire was at the truck. The point of origin for the truck was the gas tank. That was pretty straight forward. They sat and listened to the one and only 911 call they got on the fire. Peter kept listening to it over and over again. Finally Jake got irritated and asked him what he was hearing that Jake wasn't.

"I swear that is Roy. I'd bet money on it. Do you have the phone records for Mark Jeffers, home and cell?"

"I thought you said it sounded like Roy."

'It sounds like Roy but we only have one number for a cell phone for Roy. But what if he has a burner phone he uses to call Jeffers, maybe even call in that 911 call."

Jake thumbed through the file on Jeffers until he found the cell phone that called Mark Jeffers' on a frequent basis. He took the print out of the 911 call with the caller's phone number that had called in the kiln fire. The number was the same one that called Mark Jeffers. Then Peter took a print out of the 911 calls reporting the Mid-Valley Warehouse fire. One of the first calls that came in to 911 was the same number that called Jeffers frequently. If they could find that phone and put it in Roy's possession, figuratively and literally, they would have a connection between the two men.

"How about outgoing calls?" Peter asked. He was starting to get excited. This could be instrumental in their case if there were calls between the two men. Mark Jeffers had made frequent calls to that phone number as well.

"Sure enough," Jake said. They high fived each other.

While they were congratulating each other, their office phone rang. Right now Jake and Peter were the only ones in the office. Theresa and Thompson were sleeping.

Jake picked up the line. It was the forensic lab. He put it on speaker phone so Peter could hear too. It was a good thing that

Jake had put it on speaker phone because after they got the news they were jumping around the room like two guys whose football team had just won the Super Bowl. They had Roy by the gonads. They couldn't contain themselves. After they finished the call they were hooting and hollering like no tomorrow as they waited for the reports to come across the secure fax line. The crime scene people had found blood in the back of Roy's duty SUV. It matched Jason's DNA. The crime scene techs had also found a wicking material a cotton polyester blend material that was consistent with a piece of unburned material found on the ground near the gas tank of Pedro's truck. The outer margins of the material were burned as though it had fallen off a longer piece of material that had been stuffed in the gas tank and blown far enough away that it hadn't burned completely in the fire.

They had also found traces of magnesium powder when they vacuumed the back of the SUV. It was the same metal compound used at the Mid-Valley Hop fire. All the responding fire crews were certain that magnesium had been used to fuel the fire. Every firefighter, from probie on up knew the flame of magnesium. It was a bright white flame that could actually burn retinas if someone looked at it long enough. They had all been trained on fires containing magnesium, a common component in many engines. It was what made garage fires so difficult to extinguish. Once magnesium starts to burn it produces its own fuel making it a fire without end. Water is completely ineffective on a fire fueled by magnesium and chemicals used to fight fires at an airport have to be deployed.

The crime scene techs said they could see that Roy had hosed out the seat in the back of his SUV and vacuumed the cargo area but not well enough to destroy all of the evidence. They were all glad he had not managed to remove all the evidence that linked him to the fires and homicide.

The technician also told the agents they had found a cheap cell phone tucked up in the webbing under the driver's side seat. They were sure it was the phone they needed. When the tech gave them the phone number assigned to it the two men could contain themselves no longer and started whooping and hollering like they had won the lottery. They both thanked the tech and told him they owed him big time.

Jake and Peter knew they should wait for Thompson to finish his much needed sleep but they were like kids on Christmas morning. They were up at the crack of dawn and creating any kind of havoc they could to wake up their parents so they could open their presents. In this instance though, they couldn't wait to call their boss so they could wrap these two jerks in legal charges and tie the bows of evidence against them. It was almost childish the way they finally sat down and stared at the phone, "You call him." Peter told Jake.

"No you call him." Jake returned.

"No really, you call him. He likes you best." Peter rallied.

"Okay," Jake bartered. "I'll call but we put it on speaker phone, and you talk to him."

Before Peter could object, Jake had hit speed dial and turned the speaker on.

Thompson was not pleased at having his slumber interrupted. Peter started out hesitantly at the sound of his disgruntled boss. He was stammering around so much Jake couldn't stand it and jumped in taking the lead. Before they finished the call both of them were talking at hyper-speed. Thompson groaned.

"Okay, okay. I'll be right in. Don't do anything until I get there. Call Theresa I want her in the office too." The phone line went to a dial tone before Peter and Jake could hang up.

The rest of the day and into the night was like enjoying a five course meal, ending with a scrumptious dessert that just topped the meal off right. Once they had arrested Mark on the embezzlement charges and the murder of his brother Donald the interviews began. The two stooges couldn't wait to blame the other for everything from arson, to murder to embezzlement. It was worth every moment of the past year of hard work. And Peter couldn't wait to tell Bellamy that when they brought Roy in and he resisted the invitation to sit down, he and Jake had helped him and he yelped like a puppy whose paw got stepped on. In this case it was Roy's backside and it was still evidently quite painful. Peter would have to get Jax a big bone to celebrate his victory.

Peter was surprised that either one of them would talk about the case. They would end up both being charged for everything they worked on together. They had worked in concert, they would be charged as such.

All of their speculation had been on the mark, or on Mark, as it were. Mark was the one who orchestrated the whole thing. It was a case of greed. He wanted the business and he wanted the money. That was it.

Jason had been a liability. He had overheard Mark talking to Roy one night before he left for Germany. They were trying to decide how to get rid of Donald and the warehouse so Mark could get the insurance money. He had tried to get out of the warehouse before one of them caught him but just as he was getting in his car to leave Roy had come out and saw Jason leave. They couldn't let him ruin their plan.

When he returned from Germany, Roy was at the airport to pick him up. Thompson was able to verify that from the security video at the air terminal. Unfortunately Roy refused to tell them where he had killed Jason.

He had to do something with Jason's body. He couldn't carry him around in his duty SVU all night. He had turned off his AVL and planned to just dump Jason in one of the hop yards when he passed Ren's kiln. Pedro's truck was sitting there and no one was around. Roy had parked his duty SUV in the shadow of the grown hops. He drug Jason out of his car and managed to get him into the truck and set it on fire. He got back to his SUV drove up over the small pass and into the lower valley, turned his AVL back on and waited for the fire call to go out. Like a hero, he responded to the scene to assist in any way he could.

He had also provided the methamphetamine for Mark to use. It was policy to check the seats in the SUV every time they booked someone. It was amazing how many arrestees stuffed drugs down between the seats. Some vehicles had solid back seats with no cushions but Roy's was one that still had the back and the separate seat. It was just a matter of patience until he found some meth and didn't turn it in.

Once Donald was out of the way Mark decided it was time for Roy to gain access to the warehouse and set it on fire. He parked on the side of the building through a door Mark had left open for him. Roy took a case of sparklers he had purchased from the fireworks stand. He had wired them all together in a tight bundle. That with a container of magnesium powder that anyone could purchase on line he placed it at the base of the conveyer belt that carried the hops down to the Hexane. One match was all that was needed to light the place up. He drove out to the airport and sat in a parking lot waiting for all the tones to go out. As soon as he heard their station dispatched on the fifth alarm he waited for his fire chief to respond. When he heard him Roy called him on the phone and said he was west of the fire and would respond in his duty vehicle. He arrived and donned his turnout gear and stood by for his fire unit to arrive on scene. He saw the opportunity to push the steps back in the Command unit knowing that the next person out of that door would most likely be Bellamy. It served her right for what her dog did to him. But she wouldn't leave well enough alone, wouldn't leave Renny alone. So in the classic, if he couldn't have her Renny couldn't either he decided to get rid of her too. What snapped in his brain that made Roy go after Bellamy they weren't sure but he wouldn't be a threat to her anymore.

They had their case tied up with pretty black tape ribbons and on the prosecutor's desk, Peter requested a few days off. He got a week. He felt he needed it.

He waited a day until after the story had hit the six o'clock news before he drove out to Renny's house. As Pedro he had never been there. Now as Peter he was making a house call. Renny answered the door in a pair of knee length athletic shorts, baggy t-shirt and bare feet. He stood in the doorway staring Peter up and down. "You are good at your job. I want to punch you because I thought you were dead, but I won't because I'm glad you are alive and because you are a federal agent and I'd probably get in trouble for that." Renny said. Instead he pulled Peter inside the house and gave him a man hug.

When the two of them had stopped slapping each other on the back, Renny lead him into the bar area. "What can I get you, man?"

"You have a beer?" Peter asked. They both laughed. It had been established early on in there employee/employer relationship that neither one of them liked beer. Peter occasionally imbibed but beer wasn't his first choice of alcoholic beverages. Renny took a bottle of Pendleton, his new favorite, out of the freezer section of his beverage freezer under the bar. Renny held it up for Peter's approval. Peter nodded his head.

The two of them sat across from each other and Peter started by telling him that if he hadn't been notified yet he had been reinstated. Bellamy had been too. Peter explained that the money Renny had paid in wages for Pedro had been put in an escrow account and would be returned to him. And finally he looked Renny square in the eyes and asked, "How are you doing?"

Renny shook his head, squaring his jaw, keeping Peter's concerned stare. "Not good. I lost the best thing that ever happened to me because of this mess." He wanted to be angry at Peter because he had been involved in it but he knew he couldn't. It wasn't Peter's fault. Renny knew it was his own fault. He thought he was protecting Bellamy by walking away from her, to separate himself from her in hopes it would keep her from being fired. He felt as though he had destroyed her and their relationship unintentionally.

"But without this mess you never would have got her. So what are you going to do about it?" Peter pressed.

"I'm not sure. I hope someday, maybe she will forgive me and I can give her the ring I just bought for her."

"Ring," Peter asked remembering Renny had told him about it when he was talking to him on the phone before he knew who Peter was. He was trying to figure out where that came from when Renny opened the freezer under the counter again and produced a plastic zip lock bag with a small ring box in it. Peter thought it was an ingenious hiding place for a ring. Renny held the box towards Peter and snapped it open. "Damn!" was all Peter could say.

"Yeah, um, I had it custom made. See the diamond is a candle-light or champagne diamond and the pink diamonds are, well, pink diamonds. We were talking about bubbles and she told me the only beverage with bubbles that she liked was pink Muscato wine because it reminded her of this old movie where both Cary Grant and Deborah Kerr ordered pink champagne cocktails. Anyway, I wanted to make her a permanent pink champagne cocktail."

"And you went from only talking to her at work to a ring in less than a month." Peter asked trying to wrap his head around that.

"I knew it the second day, when we went fishing." Renny told him.

Peter reached across the bar and put the back of his hand against Renny's forehead.

"Dude, are you ok? This isn't the same guy I knew a month ago. And you aren't even sure she will ever talk to you again." Peter said.

"If it takes the rest of my life, I will keep trying." Renny told resolutely.

"Do you have a plan?"

"I was invited to a fancy fund raiser at this big ranch. It's to raise money for a no kill shelter. It's a catered dinner and barn dance. I thought maybe, well I know she wouldn't go with me but I thought maybe I could just buy a couple of tables and give her and her friend Lauren anonymous invitations. If Lauren went Bellamy would go. That's the way they have been since high school or further back. Where one is the other will be close by."

"Is that her friend with the long legs?" Peter asked.

Renny laughed. "That's her."

"You get the tables. How can I get a hold of Lauren? Maybe she and I could get together and figure out a way to get Bellamy there." Peter suggested.

"You and Lauren, huh?" Renny laughed again. "Not that you might want to get yourself a free dinner and a chance with the gal with the long legs."

Peter laughed then, "No. No. Not at all. It's all for you Bro."

Renny relented. If it meant getting Bellamy back he'd pay for the entire shelter if he had to. It would be worth every penny.

Chapter 21

The last night Bellamy and Lauren had at the beach, they drove out onto the beach to watch the sunset and have a small picnic dinner and share a small bottle of frozen harvest wine. It was a desert wine that Lauren had discovered. They both loved it and the first time they had shared a bottle a few years before, they had drank it all in one setting. Beach time had become their time to be free and let go. They didn't usually drink but the beach was their time to splurge. Luckily the bottles that wine came in were small or they would have ended up very drunk. It was that good.

Their picnic consisted of sitting in the car eating. This wasn't one of those hot southern beaches. This was a Washington Coast beach, in July, in the evening. It was windy and cold and the last condiment they wanted in their dinner was sand. So they sat in the car with the wind rocking the car and the waves crashing in front of them.

Jax was in the back seat, blowing bubbles out of the side of his mouth as he watched his human and her friend, tear pieces of tender meat from a roasted chicken breast and stuff them in their mouths. Then they would tear pieces off of the long bread they had slathered with pepper cream cheese. He was not happy but he knew if he sat silently in the back seat they may notice that he was starving. It had been at least an hour since Bellamy had filled his bowl and his stomach. As much as he wanted to whine to get Bellamy's attention he didn't. He trusted she would remember him and give him a bite.

He was right, she handed him a big chunk of chicken followed with a piece of bread, minus the cream cheese. He gulped it down with one chomp and sat hoping he would get more but he didn't.

Bellamy and Lauren put the remains of their dinner back in the sack they had brought it in and set it on the floor in front of Bellamy's seat. Then the two of them pulled on their heavy winter coats over the top of their hoodies and got out of the car. Bellamy opened the door for Jax and he hopped down and went for the waves at a dead run. Bellamy and Lauren followed in bare feet scanning the sand in front of them for some treasure the ocean had tossed up during the high tide. They stepped gingerly into the waves that were washing the day away. The two of them stayed ankle deep in the cold water. Jax on the other hand was belly deep and Bellamy had to call him back a couple of times to make sure he didn't get washed out to sea.

The sunset was spectacular. The two of them oohed and ahhed at it. The colors of orange and gold flared up above the bank of clouds coming in from the west. Lauren looked at her friend and asked, "Bellamy, would you take him back? I mean after all of this?"

The question had come out of nowhere it seemed and took Bellamy by surprise. "Absolutely, yes," Bellamy answered without hesitation.

"Even if it meant losing your job," Lauren asked?

Bellamy turned to her then, sniffling from the cold, "There are other jobs. There isn't another Ren."

That surprised Lauren. She had never heard Bellamy so committed to anything or anyone before. Whatever spell this man had put on Bellamy appeared to be unbreakable. She wandered if he felt the same way about Bellamy?

Bellamy stood, staring out at the changing colors of the sky. It was breathtaking. She could imagine herself standing here with Ren, his hand tightly clasping hers. Her whole body ached to have Ren here with her. Even if they just stood silently by each other it would be heavenly. *Would I take him back? She had to be kidding. Of course I would take him back. I may have to beat the crap out him for leaving but yeah, I would take him back.*

Chapter 22

"Bellamy, you have to go with me. I can't go by myself. I don't know this guy. What if he's a real dork? I don't want to be by myself when I meet him for the first time." Lauren pleaded.

"Then why did you agree to go as his date? You don't even know this man. What if he doesn't even show?" Bellamy asked.

"Hey it's a free gourmet dinner and a dance. How bad can it be? Come on? Please?" Lauren whined. "It will do you good to get out and just be with people, any people. He actually bought a table for us and for anyone I wanted to bring. I want to bring you." Lauren continued.

Bellamy finally gave in to Lauren's pressure. It was only one night. She could do that much for Lauren after all she had done for her the previous month. She could hang out with her while she met a blind date. Lauren had given Bellamy the best story she and Peter could come up with. And it wasn't far from the truth. They had never met. He had only spoken to her over the phone. She feared when she got to the dance he would just be Pedro in clean clothes. He would still be frumpy looking. But it was still a good excuse to go out and mingle.

After Bellamy agreed to go it became the two teenaged girls comparing outfits for a big night out with boys. "It's semi-formal Bellamy. Do you have a little black dress?" Lauren asked.

Bellamy rolled her eyes. "No. I haven't needed a little black dress for a very long time. Probably since I started working at the center.

Every time I got sent to training and they had their stupid hospitality rooms or banquets, I'd take a powder. I hate those things. I don't know how to mingle. Can you just tell everyone at this dinner that I'm a deaf mute?" Bellamy asked.

"Oh come on. Show me what you have in your closet."

Lauren and Bellamy went in to her bedroom and the two of them went through her closet. After discarding every dress that Bellamy owned, Lauren looked at her and said, "Girl, we are going shopping in the morning." Lauren was disappointed in the clothing choices Bellamy had in her closet even though she reminded herself that most of the time Bellamy wore a uniform. Lauren on the other hand worked in an office and had to wear dresses or a pant suits. Dressing for drinks was no big deal for her.

When Lauren had returned to work from the beach there had been a message for her on her desk to call the ATF and ask for Peter Ramirez. When she called, he had answered and asked her to wait a moment until he could close his office door. He had given Lauren the direct number to his office forgoing Theresa answering the office phone and transferring the call to him.

Peter introduced himself and after the pleasantries he explained the reason he called. He had felt somewhat responsible for what had happened between Ren and Bellamy. After getting to know them a bit throughout the past year and seen the transformation of their relationship after they thought Peter/Pedro had died and then Ren walking out and hurting Bellamy thinking he was protecting her, he wanted to see if he could help reunite them. "I mean you are Bellamy's friend, do you think she would want a chance to make up with Ren?"

Lauren almost laughed at the question. "I have no doubt in my mind that she would."

"I know Ren feels terrible for hurting her and he really is intent on getting her back. You should see this ring he had made for her. Holy crap!" Peter told her.

"A ring," Lauren asked thinking that maybe she had misheard him.

"Oh yeah. He told me if it took a lifetime he was going to try to win her back. He was so certain of it he had a ring made for her, an engagement ring." Peter told her.

"Wow! I knew he was smitten but I never would have guessed he would do something like that." Lauren told Peter.

"So, I was wondering if you might be willing to help with a plan Renny came up with to see her again and maybe have a chance to explain why he left," Peter asked.

"Count me in." Lauren told him without hesitating. If it meant reuniting them she was ready to help. If it in any way helped Bellamy smile again she was all for that too.

Peter went on to explain the fund raising dinner and dance. It was up to Lauren to get Bellamy to the dance. Peter told her what Ren had planned. Lauren was so excited she had to remind herself this was for Bellamy, not her.

On Saturday evening Lauren pulled in to Bellamy's driveway. She walked up the sidewalk to Bellamy's door, her high heels clicking on the concrete. She could still feel the extreme heat of the day through her strappy heels. She hoped it would be cooler in this barn they were going to than it was outside.

Bellamy was standing uneasily in her heels examining herself in the bathroom mirror. She had worn her hair down in big soft curls. She had pulled up some hair on top of her head and secured it with bobby pins with rhinestones on them. She pursed her lips on a tissue while she looked at herself in the mirror, making sure that her 12 hour lipstick was really stuck to her lips. Bellamy had spent the day painting her nails and toenails. It took her that long to get what she thought was the right color. The dress Lauren had talked her into was a peachy pink. It wasn't a color that Bellamy would have picked for herself but it worked. It was a form fitting strapless sheath dress that accentuated all of her curves. She just hoped she could sit down in it without busting a seam somewhere. At least she wouldn't get called out to a fire tonight she was on vacation. It wasn't a dress she would have chosen for herself and she hoped she would fit in with everyone else. The material had a shimmer to it that almost looked taupe. Her jewelry was a simple fake rose gold chain. Her shoes were a pair of taupe sandals with two inch heels. They were two inches taller than any other shoes she regularly wore. They could have been six inch heels as uncomfortable as they felt. Lauren had also insisted she get a small clutch purse that only had enough room for I.D., a little emergency cash, a lipstick, some tissue, her phone and keys. Even that was pushing it. She could barely close the clasp.

She met Lauren at the door. Lauren was wearing a navy blue sheath dress with tiny straps holding it in place. She had on a large tiered cubic zircon necklace and chandelier earrings. She was carrying a silver clutch purse and wearing silver high heels. She was beautiful, with her long brown hair straightened with every hair in place. She wondered if she had used Aqua Net to hold it in place. Bellamy had thrown her empty can away. She didn't want it as a reminder of that day, even though it may have saved her life. She would have to buy a new can without the memory attached to it.

Lauren held Bellamy at arms length then had her turn to get the full view of her in the dress. "Perfect," Lauren told her.

"So are you. I love that dress. The sandals really show off you legs." She told her friend. Her scrawny little friend from third grade had turned into a beautiful woman. To Bellamy it seemed she became more beautiful the older she got. "If this guy doesn't fall for you he's crazy."

"Yeah, right. He said he had a government job. You know what that means, right? He's probably a bush bunny out at the firing center. If he shows up in fatigues I am out of there, ok?" Lauren said.

"You haven't even told me his name." Bellamy said.

"Well, I don't know. He's been kind of mysterious. He said his name was Patrone, like the tequila. I mean, his pic didn't look bad on the dating site but you never know. He could be some bozo who used someone else's pic to get a date."

"So, why are we going again? You don't sound too thrilled about meeting this guy." Bellamy observed.

"Because it is a free dinner and dance and if he doesn't work out you know there will be other single men there. So who knows," Lauren told her. "And you are my ticket out if this meeting goes south."

"Great, I'm not your wing man I'm your excuse to leave." Bellamy said as they drove towards the barn.

"Exactly, isn't that what friends are for?" Lauren asked giggling.

Bellamy was just looking forward to going to this barn again. She had been there once as a wedding guest. It was such a gorgeous venue. The barn was huge. The lighting they used made the place look magical. There was a stage for a band and a large dance floor.

If the weather was good, they could open the doors that faced to the east. Outside there was also a dance area and a place to sit and watch the stars. A lighted walk way led down to an old wooden bridge that crossed a small stream.

There wouldn't be stars to gaze tonight. A haze again filled the sky. As the sun sank lower in the western sky it was being swallowed up by dark billowing clouds topped with what looked like big dollops of whipped cream. The very tops of the clouds had golden sprinkles. She didn't know how long they would be there but she was pretty sure there was a storm coming in. She had never paid much attention to the weather before going to work as a fire dispatcher then she became an amateur meteorologist. She learned what the different clouds were and what they indicated. She learned what the direction of the wind meant and kept track of wind speeds. But at the moment she was just enjoying the idea of a good thunder storm with no threat of being called in to work.

Bellamy was glad it was a still light when they pulled into the parking lot. It was a good hour or so before the sun set but with the clouds obstructing the sun it was already getting dark. Bellamy was glad she didn't have to traverse their parking lot in the dark. That was the worst part of going to the barn. The parking lot was gravel and had some good sized pot holes, in keeping with every street in Yakima. They were voted the number one worst city in the state for their streets as well as auto theft and gang shootings per capita. But it was the Palm Springs of Washington or so the sign said. The parking lot was packed. Lauren finally found a place to park at the far end of the parking lot.

The two of them tip-toed through the rocks like two teenagers sneaking out of the house to go to a kegger. They were giggling. Lauren paused with her arm hooked around Bellamy's elbow. "It's good to see you smile."

Bellamy smiled at her, listening to the country music coming from the band inside. "I'll cry later." She was afraid if they played a slow George Strait song she would lose it. When everything was going down the tubes George's songs always seemed to have the right words to let her know she wasn't the only one who had felt the way she did.

As soon as they stepped into the barn they were met with a waiter offering glasses of wine. Bellamy took a glass of something pink. It turned out to be Muscato. It wasn't sparkling but it was still sweet. Lauren took a glass of something white.

Most of the attendees were milling around, chatting. A few people were already sitting at their tables. She wasn't sure what to do, so she followed Lauren around like a puppy on a leash. Lauren stopped for a second as a handsome man in a very sharp cut suit strode up to her. "Lauren?" Bellamy heard a man ask in a very familiar voice. She quickly turned and there was Peter.

"Peter?" Bellamy said, "I'm so glad you are here. One more person I know."

He acknowledged Bellamy and gently touched her arm before turning to face Lauren again. "I'm Patrone. Actually, my name is Peter Ramirez."

Bellamy was watching Lauren's reaction. She thought Lauren's legs were going to buckle. She so much wanted to say, I told you he was hot. But she didn't. She would tell her later. Bellamy would tell her later unless she had to take a taxi home. They began chatting quietly and Peter took Lauren's elbow and led her through the growing throng of people. She felt like she had officially become the third wheel in this party. That hadn't crossed her mind. Bellamy figured Lauren would take one look at her blind date and head for the door after dinner. She didn't count on the blind date being Peter. She followed them to their table and took a seat. Luckily for Bellamy a lady that worked in records at the police department was seated at their table too. At least she would have someone to talk to during dinner because it was quite apparent that Peter and Lauren wouldn't be talking to her. They were absorbed in each other.

Their table was situated near the front of the barn, near the dance floor. There was a good view of the band. It made Bellamy a bit uneasy to have the majority of the people at tables behind her. She thought it was probably rude to turn around and peer through the crowd looking for familiar faces.

Course after course of food came to their table along with bottles of wine, white, red and rose. Bellamy was glad they also had a pitcher of water on the table. If she drank more than one glass of wine, her face and neck turned bright red. It didn't matter if it was white, rose or red. One glass was her limit otherwise she would look like a Chinese lantern.

It was dark when the dessert was served. Trays of temptation filled the tables. Bellamy was full but the cheesecake was so tempting she couldn't resist. She would eat it later she told herself, while everyone else was dancing. She had no desire to dance tonight. This night the barn felt empty even though it was packed with people. All Bellamy could think about was Ren and how much she missed the way his arms felt around her. She could almost feel him holding her in his arms and dancing her around in the living room. She missed his laugh and even that pissy voice that he used on the radio. She missed the way his eyes squinted when he smiled and deep lines etched the edges. She missed the feel of his lips against hers. She could feel tears starting to well up in her eyes and a lump growing in her throat. She took a drink of ice water hoping it would stop.

As soon as the band started playing some rock tunes, Lauren and Peter were up and out on the dance floor. They looked good together. Watching them it looked like they too had compared fashion options for the night. They looked like they had stepped off of a slick magazine cover. They were both exceptionally good looking people.

About halfway through the second set of music she found she had been sitting alone the whole time nursing a glass of lukewarm wine. When Lauren and Peter finally returned to the table, Bellamy asked Lauren if she could take her home. Lauren balked at the idea before she answered. Peter tried to convince her to stay. Finally he asked her to wait until the band took a break and they would both take her home. Peter excused himself and started toward the side of the stage. It was in the direction of the men's room.

Lauren started gushing. She excitedly told Bellamy this and that, and she had been right. He was hot. She was talking about how smart he was when he walked back to the table. He had just sat down when "Turn Around" by the Vogues started to play. Her mom used the play that record over and over again when she was little. She smiled to herself and looked across at Lauren. She was about to ask her if she remembered the song when she noticed both she and Peter were looking up over her shoulder at something behind her. Curious, she turned to see what they were looking at. Ren was walking towards the table, his eyes connecting with Bellamy's. As he got a few feet from their table he held out his hand to Bellamy. "Dance with me," he asked. Bellamy's heart was in her throat and she couldn't catch her breath. She put her hand in his and he helped her to her feet. She was glad he had because she wasn't sure she could stand let alone walk.

He led her out onto the dance floor and his other arm went around her back and embraced her. Had he not, she would have collapsed. She was shaking, not a feminine little tremble but a full on shake. She thought he could hear her teeth chattering. But as he held her closer she began to relax into his arms. Oddly she felt like she was melting into him becoming a part of him. She rested her head against his chest, listening to his heart. It was racing. His chin rested against her head.

The song ended but Ren continued to hold her until the band started playing the next song. It was another slow song by George Straight about a man always being in love with a woman even though he wasn't perfect. Bellamy wasn't sure she would be able to dance with Ren without falling apart. She had missed him so desperately and now he was holding her and not letting her go. When he did let go would he leave again?

She was on the verge of tears when Ren whispered in her ear. "Bellamy, I am so sorry I hurt you. It was my fault you got suspended and I just thought if I stayed away from you and didn't talk to you until this was all over it would help. I should have stayed. We should have fought this together. I am broken without you Bellamy. I love you so very much. Please, can you forgive me?" Ren asked, his voice breaking.

Bellamy felt hot tears running out of her closed eyes. "Never leave me again, Ren. I couldn't take it. I love you too much." She choked.

"Never," he promised.

She could think of nothing more that she wanted than to be in his arms on the dance floor living in this moment. Bellamy floated along with him to the song. All of the words struck her heart like chords on a guitar. She felt like she was in a dream, like one of the prints hanging on her bedroom wall. She felt herself shudder as his hand brushed against her lower back. Oh, his touch. Bellamy had missed that touch. She felt her body moving with his as she looked up into those beautiful blue eyes. They momentarily closed. It seemed to Bellamy that he had missed her touch too. She placed her head on his shoulder breathing in his scent mingled with his cologne. It was so much more intoxicating than the wine. Her chin kept bumping against something sharp in the upper inside pocket of his suit. She thought it was his cigarettes. She didn't care what it was as long as he came with it.

She dropped her hands as the song ended but Ren held her there. She looked around and no one else was on the dance floor. The room had become eerily quiet except for the roll of thunder as a storm came closer. She stepped back away from him a few steps to go back to her table but Ren took her hand and held her still. She was confused. What was he doing, waiting for another song to start playing?

Ren reached in his inside pocket and drew out a black ring box. Every girl in the world knew what a ring box looked like. He opened the box as he dropped to one knee, his blue eyes glistening in the soft light of the room. "Will you share the rest of your life with me?" Ren asked.

Bellamy saw the box open but she hadn't seen the ring. All she saw was Ren looking up at her. Her heart hurt she loved this man so much. She took his face in her hands then and lifted him up towards her. "Will you stay with me for the rest of your life and never leave?" She asked Ren? He nodded and whispered, "Yes." She kissed him like she had never kissed him before. She wanted this man to smile at her every morning across his coffee cup and to kiss her every night before his arm wrapped around her to sleep.

"Yes," she whispered in his ear. He stood her back a bit and took the ring and slid it on her ring finger.

That is when she saw the ring. Her jaw went slack and she looked from the ring to Ren. "This champagne will never go flat." He told her. It fit like Cinderella's slipper. People started clapping and she heard a collective "Ahhh". Bellamy felt herself blushing but it was okay. Ren was touching her back, leading her back toward his table.

"I have one more thing for you," Ren said as he reached down for something beside his chair. It was a gold plastic party trumpet. He whispered in her ear. "The walls of Jericho are coming down. Can we go home now?"

"Please. And Ren, tonight you are mine. All night," Bellamy told him. She blew the horn loudly.

Ren picked her up then and hoisted her over his shoulder in a fireman's carry. She continued to blow the horn as he carried her out to his pickup.

La fin

Made in the USA
Columbia, SC
11 March 2024